P9-DNQ-888

Mr. Mercedes

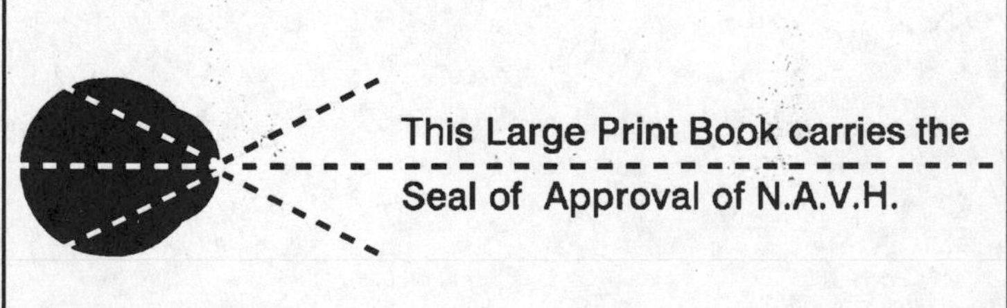
This Large Print Book carries the
Seal of Approval of N.A.V.H.

Mr. Mercedes

Stephen King

THORNDIKE PRESS
A part of Gale, Cengage Learning

Farmington Hills, Mich • San Francisco • New York • Waterville, Maine
Meriden, Conn • Mason, Ohio • Chicago

Thorndike Press, a part of Gale, Cengage Learning.

Thorndike Press® Large Print Basic.
The text of this Large Print edition is unabridged.
Other aspects of the book may vary from the original edition.
Set in 16 pt. Plantin.

LIBRARY OF CONGRESS CATALOGING-IN-PUBLICATION DATA

King, Stephen, 1947-
Mr. Mercedes / Stephen King.
pages cm — (Thorndike press large print basic)
ISBN 978-1-4104-6900-7 (hardcover) — ISBN 1-4104-6900-X (hardcover)
1. Mercedes automobiles—Fiction. 2. Serial murderers—Fiction. 3. Large type books. I. Title.
PS3561.I483M7 2014b
813'.54—dc23 2014015302

Published in 2014 by arrangement with Scribner, a division of Simon & Schuster, Inc.

Printed in the United States of America
1 2 3 4 5 6 7 18 17 16 15 14

Thinking of James M. Cain

They threw me off the hay truck about noon . . .

April 9–10, 2009

Augie Odenkirk had a 1997 Datsun that still ran well in spite of high mileage, but gas was expensive, especially for a man with no job, and City Center was on the far side of town, so he decided to take the last bus of the night. He got off at twenty past eleven with his pack on his back and his rolled-up sleeping bag under one arm. He thought he would be glad of the down-filled bag by three A.M. The night was misty and chill.

"Good luck, man," the driver said as he stepped down. "You ought to get something for just being the first one there."

Only he wasn't. When Augie reached the top of the wide, steep drive leading to the big auditorium, he saw a cluster of at least two dozen people already waiting outside the rank of doors, some standing, most sitting. Posts strung with yellow DO NOT CROSS tape had been set up, creating a complicated passage that doubled back on itself, mazelike.

Augie was familiar with these from movie theaters and the bank where he was currently overdrawn, and understood the purpose: to cram as many people as possible into as small a space as possible.

As he approached the end of what would soon be a conga-line of job applicants, Augie was both amazed and dismayed to see that the woman at the end of the line had a sleeping baby in a Papoose carrier. The baby's cheeks were flushed with the cold; each exhale came with a faint rattle.

The woman heard Augie's slightly out-of-breath approach, and turned. She was young and pretty enough, even with the dark circles under her eyes. At her feet was a small quilted carry-case. Augie supposed it was a baby support system.

"Hi," she said. "Welcome to the Early Birds Club."

"Hopefully we'll catch a worm." He debated, thought what the hell, and stuck out his hand. "August Odenkirk. Augie. I was recently downsized. That's the twenty-first-century way of saying I got canned."

She shook with him. She had a good grip, firm and not a bit timid. "I'm Janice Cray, and my little bundle of joy is Patti. I guess I got downsized, too. I was a housekeeper for a nice family in Sugar Heights. He, um, owns a car dealership."

Augie winced.

Janice nodded. "I know. He said he was sorry to let me go, but they had to tighten their belts."

"A lot of that going around," Augie said, thinking: *You could find no one to babysit? No one at all?*

"I had to bring her." He supposed Janice Cray didn't have to be much of a mind reader to know what he was thinking. "There's no one else. Literally no one. The girl down the street couldn't stay all night even if I could pay her, and I just can't. If I don't get a job, I don't know what we'll do."

"Your parents couldn't take her?" Augie asked.

"They live in Vermont. If I had half a brain, I'd take Patti and go there. It's pretty. Only they've got their own problems. Dad says their house is underwater. Not literally, they're not in the river or anything, it's something financial."

Augie nodded. There was a lot of that going around, too.

A few cars were coming up the steep rise from Marlborough Street, where Augie had gotten off the bus. They turned left, into the vast empty plain of parking lot that would no doubt be full by daylight tomorrow . . . still hours before the First Annual City Job Fair opened its doors. None of the cars looked new. Their drivers parked, and from most of them three or four job-seekers emerged, heading toward the doors of the auditorium. Augie was no longer at the end of the line. It had almost reached the first switchback.

"If I can get a job, I can get a sitter," she said. "But for tonight, me and Patti just gotta suck it up."

The baby gave a croupy cough Augie didn't care for, stirred in the Papoose, and then settled again. At least the kid was bundled up; there were even tiny mittens on her hands.

Kids survive worse, Augie told himself uneasily. He thought of the Dust Bowl, and the Great Depression. Well, this one was great enough for him. Two years ago, everything had been fine. He hadn't exactly been living large in the 'hood, but he *had* been making ends meet, with a little left over at the end of most months. Now everything had turned to shit. They had done something to the money. He didn't understand it; he'd been an office drone in the shipping department of Great Lakes Transport, and what he knew about was invoices and using a computer to route stuff by ship, train, and air.

"People will see me with a baby and think I'm irresponsible," Janice Cray fretted. "I know it, I see it on their faces already, I saw it on yours. But what else could I do? Even if the girl down the street could stay all night, it would have cost eighty-four dollars. *Eighty-four!* I've got next month's rent put aside, and after that, I'm skint." She smiled, and in the light of the parking lot's high arc-sodiums, Augie saw tears beading her eyelashes. "I'm babbling."

"No need to apologize, if that's what you're doing." The line had turned the first corner now, and had arrived back at where Augie was standing. And the girl was right. He saw lots of people staring at the sleeping kid in the Papoose.

"Oh, that's it, all right. I'm a single unmarried mother with no job. I want to apologize to everyone, for everything." She turned and looked at the banner posted above the rank of doors. 1000 **JOBS GUARENTEED!** it read. And below that: *"We Stand With the People of Our City!"* — **MAYOR RALPH KINSLER.**

"Sometimes I want to apologize for Columbine, and 9/11, and Barry Bonds taking steroids." She uttered a semi-hysterical giggle. "Sometimes I even want to apologize for the space shuttle exploding, and when that happened I was still learning to walk."

"Don't worry," Augie told her. "You'll be okay." It was just one of those things that you said.

"I wish it wasn't so damp, that's all. I've got her bundled up in case it was really cold, but this damp . . ." She shook her head. "We'll make it, though, won't we, Patti?" She gave Augie a hopeless little smile. "It just better not rain."

■ ■ ■ ■

It didn't, but the dampness increased until they could see fine droplets suspended in the light thrown by the arc-sodiums. At some point Augie realized that Janice Cray was asleep on her feet. She was hipshot and slump-shouldered, with her hair hanging in dank wings around her face and her chin nearly on her breastbone. He looked at his watch and saw it was quarter to three.

Ten minutes later, Patti Cray awoke and started to cry. Her mother (her *baby mama,* Augie thought) gave a jerk, voiced a horselike snort, raised her head, and tried to pull the infant out of the Papoose. At first the kid wouldn't come; her legs were stuck. Augie pitched in, holding the sides of the sling. As Patti emerged, now wailing, he could see drops of water sparkling all over her tiny pink jacket and matching hat.

"She's hungry," Janice said. "I can give her the breast, but she's also wet. I can feel it right through her pants. God, I can't change her in this — look how foggy it's gotten!"

Augie wondered what comical deity had arranged for him to be the one in line behind her. He also wondered how in hell this woman was going to get through the rest of her life — *all* of it, not just the next eighteen years or so when she would be responsible for the kid. To come out on a night like this, with nothing but a bag of diapers! To be that goddam desperate!

He had put his sleeping bag down next to Patti's diaper bag. Now he squatted, pulled the ties, unrolled it, and unzipped it. "Slide in there. Get warm and get *her* warm. Then I'll hand in whatever doodads you need."

She gazed at him, holding the squirming, crying baby. "Are you married, Augie?"

"Divorced."

"Children?"

He shook his head.

"Why are you being so kind to us?"

"Because we're here," he said, and shrugged.

She looked at him a moment longer, deciding, then handed him the baby. Augie held her out at arms' length, fascinated by the red, furious face, the bead of snot on the tiny upturned nose, the bicycling legs in the flannel onesie. Janice squirmed into the sleeping bag, then lifted her hands. "Give her to me, please."

Augie did, and the woman burrowed deeper into the bag. Beside them, where the line had doubled back on itself for the first time, two young men were staring.

"Mind your business, guys," Augie said, and they looked away.

"Would you give me a diaper?" Janice said. "I should change her before I feed her."

He dropped one knee to the wet pavement and unzipped the quilted bag. He was momentarily surprised to find cloth diapers instead of Pampers, then understood. The cloth ones could be used over and over. Maybe the woman wasn't entirely hopeless.

"I see a bottle of Baby Magic, too. Do you want that?"

From inside the sleeping bag, where now only a tuft of her brownish hair showed: "Yes, please."

He passed in the diaper and the lotion. The sleeping bag began to wiggle and bounce. At first the crying intensified. From one of the switchbacks farther down, lost in the thickening fog, someone said: "Can't you shut that kid up?" Another voice added: "Someone ought to call Social Services."

Augie waited, watching the sleeping bag. At last it stopped moving around and a hand emerged, holding a diaper. "Would you put it in the bag? There's a plastic sack for the dirty ones." She looked out at him like a mole from its hole. "Don't worry, it's not pooey, just wet."

Augie took the diaper, put it in the plastic bag (COSTCO printed on the side), then zipped the diaper bag closed. The crying from inside the sleeping bag (*so many bags,* he thought) continued for another minute or so, then abruptly cut out as Patti began to nurse in the City Center parking lot. From above the ranked doors that wouldn't open for another six hours, the banner gave a single lackadaisical flap. **1000 JOBS GUAREN-TEED!**

Sure, Augie thought. *Also, you can't catch AIDS if you load up on vitamin C.*

Twenty minutes passed. More cars came up the hill from Marlborough Street. More people joined the line. Augie estimated there already had to be four hundred people waiting. At that rate, there would be two thousand by the time the doors opened at nine, and that was a conservative estimate.

If someone offers me fry-cook at McDonald's, will I take it?

Probably.

What about a greeter at Walmart?

Oh, mos def. Big smile and *how're you today?* Augie thought he could wallop a greeter job right out of the park.

I'm a people person, he thought. And laughed.

From the bag: "What's funny?"

"Nothing," he said. "Cuddle that kid."

"I am." A smile in her voice.

At three-thirty he knelt, lifted the flap of the sleeping bag, and peered inside. Janice Cray was curled up, fast asleep, with the baby at her breast. This made him think of *The Grapes of Wrath.* What was the name of the girl who had been in it? The one who ended up nursing the man? A flower name, he thought. Lily? No. Pansy? Absolutely not. He thought of cupping his hands around his mouth, raising his voice, and asking the crowd, *WHO HERE HAS READ* THE GRAPES OF WRATH?

As he was standing up again (and smiling at this absurdity), the name came to him. Rose. That had been the name of the *Grapes of Wrath* girl. But not just Rose; Rose of *Sharon.* It sounded biblical, but he couldn't say so with any certainty; he had never been a Bible reader.

He looked down at the sleeping bag, in which he had expected to spend the small hours of the night, and thought of Janice Cray saying she wanted to apologize for Columbine, and 9/11, and Barry Bonds. Probably she would cop to global warming as well. Maybe when this was over and they had secured jobs — or not; not was probably just as likely — he would treat her to breakfast. Not a date, nothing like that, just some scrambled eggs and bacon. After that they would never see each other again.

More people came. They reached the end of the posted switchbacks with the self-important DO NOT CROSS tape. Once that was used up, the line began to stretch into the parking lot. What surprised Augie — and made him uneasy — was how *silent* they

were. As if they all knew this mission was a failure, and they were only waiting to get the official word.

The banner gave another lackadaisical flap.

The fog continued to thicken.

Shortly before five A.M., Augie roused from his own half-doze, stamped his feet to wake them up, and realized an unpleasant iron light had crept into the air. It was the furthest thing in the world from the rosy-fingered dawn of poetry and old Technicolor movies; this was an anti-dawn, damp and as pale as the cheek of a day-old corpse.

He could see the City Center auditorium slowly revealing itself in all its nineteen-seventies tacky architectural glory. He could see the two dozen switchbacks of patiently waiting people and then the tailback of the line disappearing into the fog. Now there was a little conversation, and when a janitor clad in gray fatigues passed through the lobby on the other side of the doors, a small satiric cheer went up.

"Life is discovered on other planets!" shouted one of the young men who had been staring at Janice Cray — this was Keith Frias, whose left arm would shortly be torn from his body.

There was mild laughter at this sally, and people began to talk. The night was over. The seeping light wasn't particularly encouraging,

but it was marginally better than the long small hours just past.

Augie knelt beside his sleeping bag again and cocked an ear. The small, regular snores he heard made him smile. Maybe his worry about her had been for nothing. He guessed there were people who went through life surviving — perhaps even thriving — on the kindness of strangers. The young woman currently snoozing in his sleeping bag with her baby might be one of them.

It came to him that he and Janice Cray could present themselves at the various application tables as a couple. If they did that, the baby's presence might not seem an indicator of irresponsibility but rather of joint dedication. He couldn't say for sure, much of human nature was a mystery to him, but he thought it was possible. He decided he'd try the idea out on Janice when she woke up. See what she thought. They couldn't claim marriage; she wasn't wearing a wedding ring and he'd taken his off for good three years before, but they could claim to be . . . what was it people said now? Partners.

Cars continued to come up the steep incline from Marlborough Street at steady tick-tock intervals. There would soon be pedestrians as well, fresh off the first bus of the morning. Augie was pretty sure they started running at six. Because of the thick fog, the arriving cars were just headlights with vague shadow-

shapes lurking behind the windshields. A few of the drivers saw the huge crowd already waiting and turned around, discouraged, but most kept on, heading for the few remaining parking spaces, their taillights dwindling.

Then Augie noticed a car-shape that neither turned around nor continued on toward the far reaches of the parking lot. Its unusually bright headlights were flanked by yellow fog-lamps.

HD headers, Augie thought. *That's a Mercedes-Benz. What's a Benz doing at a job fair?*

He supposed it might be Mayor Kinsler, here to make a speech to the Early Birds Club. To congratulate them on their gumption, their good old American git-up-and-git. If so, Augie thought, arriving in his Mercedes — even if it was an old one — was in bad taste.

An elderly fellow in line ahead of Augie (Wayne Welland, now in the last moments of his earthly existence) said: "Is that a Benz? It looks like a Benz."

Augie started to say of course it was, you couldn't mistake a Mercedes's HD headlamps, and then the driver of the car directly behind the vague shape laid on his horn — a long, impatient blast. The HD lights flashed brighter than ever, cutting brilliant white cones through the suspended droplets of the fog, and the car leaped forward as if the impatient horn had goosed it.

"Hey!" Wayne Welland said, surprised. It was his final word.

The car accelerated directly at the place where the crowd of job-seekers was most tightly packed, and hemmed in by the DO NOT CROSS tapes. Some of them tried to run, but only the ones at the rear of the crowd were able to break free. Those closer to the doors — the true Early Birds — had no chance. They struck the posts and knocked them over, they got tangled in the tapes, they rebounded off each other. The crowd swayed back and forth in a series of agitated waves. Those who were older and smaller fell down and were trampled underfoot.

Augie was shoved hard to the left, stumbled, recovered, and was pushed forward. A flying elbow struck his cheekbone just below his right eye and that side of his vision filled with bright Fourth of July sparkles. From the other eye he could see the Mercedes not just emerging from the fog but seeming to *create* itself from it. A big gray sedan, maybe an SL500, the kind with twelve cylinders, and right now all twelve were screaming.

Augie was driven to his knees beside the sleeping bag, and kicked repeatedly as he struggled to get back up: in the arm, in the shoulder, in the neck. People were screaming. He heard a woman cry, *"Look out, look out, he's not stopping!"*

He saw Janice Cray pop her head out of the sleeping bag, eyes blinking in bewilderment. Once more he was reminded of a shy mole peering from its hole. A lady mole with a bad case of bed head.

He scrambled forward on his hands and knees and lay down on the bag and the woman and baby inside, as if by doing this he could successfully shield them from a two-ton piece of German engineering. He heard people yelling, the sound of them almost lost beneath the approaching roar of the big sedan's motor. Someone fetched him a terrific wallop on the back of his head, but he barely felt it.

There was time to think: *I was going to buy Rose of Sharon breakfast.*

There was time to think: *Maybe he'll veer off.*

That seemed to be their best chance, probably their only chance. He started to raise his head to see if it was happening, and a huge black tire ate up his vision. He felt the woman's hand grip his forearm. He had time to hope the baby was still sleeping. Then time ran out.

Det.-Ret.

1

Hodges walks out of the kitchen with a can of beer in his hand, sits down in the La-Z-Boy, and puts the can down on the little table to his left, next to the gun. It's a .38 Smith & Wesson M&P revolver, M&P standing for Military and Police. He pats it absently, the way you'd pat an old dog, then picks up the remote control and turns on Channel Seven. He's a little late, and the studio audience is already applauding.

He's thinking of a fad, brief and baleful, that inhabited the city in the late eighties. Or maybe the word he really wants is *infected,* because it had been like a transient fever. The city's three papers had written editorials about it all one summer. Now two of those papers are gone and the third is on life support.

The host comes striding onstage in a sharp suit, waving to the audience. Hodges has watched this show almost every weekday since his retirement from the police force, and he thinks this man is too bright to be doing this job, one that's a little like scuba diving in a sewer without a wetsuit. He thinks the host is the sort of man who sometimes commits suicide and afterward all his friends and close relatives say they never had a clue anything was wrong; they talk about how cheerful he was the last time they saw him.

At this thought, Hodges gives the revolver another absent pat. It is the Victory model. An oldie but a goodie. His own gun, when he was active, was a Glock .40. He bought it — officers in this city are expected to buy their service weapons — and now it's in the safe in his bedroom. Safe in the safe. He unloaded it and put it in there after the retirement ceremony and hasn't looked at it since. No interest. He likes the .38, though. He has a sentimental attachment to it, but there's something beyond that. A revolver never jams.

Here is the first guest, a young woman in a short blue dress. Her face is a trifle on the vacant side but she's got a knockout bod. Somewhere inside that dress, Hodges knows, there will be the sort of tattoo now referred to as a tramp-stamp. Maybe two or three. The men in the audience whistle and stomp their feet. The women in the audience applaud more gently. Some roll their eyes. This is the kind of woman you don't like to catch your husband staring at.

The woman is pissed right from go. She

tells the host that her boyfriend has had a baby with another woman and he goes over to see them all the time. She still loves him, she says, but she hates that —

The next couple of words are bleeped out, but Hodges can lip-read *fucking whore.* The audience cheers. Hodges takes a sip of his beer. He knows what comes next. This show has all the predictability of a soap opera on Friday afternoon.

The host lets her run on for a bit and then introduces . . . THE OTHER WOMAN! She also has a knockout bod and several yards of big blond hair. There's a tramp-stamp on one ankle. She approaches the other woman and says, "I understand how you feel, but I love him, too."

She's got more on her mind, but that's as far as she gets before Knockout Bod One goes into action. Someone offstage rings a bell, as if this were the start of a prizefight. Hodges supposes it is, since all the guests on this show must be compensated; why else would they do it? The two women punch and claw for a few seconds, and then the two beefcakes with SECURITY printed on their tee-shirts, who have been watching from the background, separate them.

They shout at each other for awhile, a full and fair exchange of views (much of it bleeped out), as the host watches benignly, and this time it's Knockout Bod Two who initiates the fight, swinging a big roundhouse slap that rocks Knockout Bod One's head back. The bell rings again. They fall to the stage, their dresses rucking up, clawing and punching and slapping. The audience goes bugshit. The security beefcakes separate them and the host gets between them, talking in a voice that is soothing on top, inciteful beneath. The two women declare the depth of their love, spitting it into each other's faces. The host says they'll be right back and then a C-list actress is selling a diet pill.

Hodges takes another sip of his beer and knows he won't even finish half the can. It's funny, because when he was on the cops, he was damned near an alcoholic. When the drinking broke up his marriage, he assumed he *was* an alcoholic. He summoned all his willpower and reined it in, promising himself he would drink just as much as he goddam wanted once he had his forty in — a pretty amazing number, when fifty percent of city cops retired after twenty-five and seventy percent after thirty. Only now that he has his forty, alcohol no longer interests him much. He forced himself to get drunk a few times, just to see if he could still do it, and he could, but being drunk turned out to be no better than being sober. Actually it was a little worse.

The show returns. The host says he has another guest, and Hodges knows who that will be. The audience does, too. They yap their anticipation. Hodges picks up his father's gun, looks into the barrel, and puts it back down on the DirecTV guide.

The man over whom Knockout Bod One and Knockout Bod Two are in such strenuous conflict emerges from stage right. You knew what he was going to look like even before he comes strutting out and yup, he's the guy: a gas station attendant or a Target warehouse carton-shuffler or maybe the fella who detailed your car (badly) at the Mr. Speedy. He's skinny and pale, with black hair clumping over his forehead. He's wearing chinos and a crazy green and yellow tie that has a chokehold on his throat just below his prominent Adam's apple. The pointy toes of suede boots poke out beneath his pants. You knew that the women had tramp-stamps and you know this man is hung like a horse and shoots sperm more powerful than a locomotive and faster than a speeding bullet; a virginal maid who sits on a toilet seat after this guy jerked off will get up pregnant. Probably with twins. On his face is the half-smart grin of a cool dude in a loose mood. Dream job: lifetime disability. Soon the bell will ring and the women will go at each other again. Later, after they have heard enough of his smack, they will look at each other, nod slightly, and attack him together. This time the security personnel will wait a little longer, because this final battle is what the audience, both in the studio and at home, really wants to see: the hens going after the rooster.

That brief and baleful fad in the late eighties — the infection — was called "bum fighting." Some gutter genius or other got the idea, and when it turned a profit, three or four other entrepreneurs leaped in to refine the deal. What you did was pay a couple of bums thirty bucks each to go at each other at a set time and in a set place. The place Hodges remembered best was the service area behind a sleazy crab-farm of a strip club called Bam Ba Lam, over on the East Side. Once the fight card was set, you advertised (by word of mouth in those days, with widespread Internet use still over the horizon), and charged spectators twenty bucks a head. There had been better than two hundred at the one Hodges and Pete Huntley had busted, most of them making odds and fading each other like mad motherfuckers. There had been women, too, some in evening dress and loaded with jewelry, watching as those two wetbrain stewbums went at each other, flailing and kicking and falling down and getting up and yelling incoherencies. The crowd had been laughing and cheering and urging the combatants on.

This show is like that, only there are diet pills and insurance companies to fade the action, so Hodges supposes the contestants (that's what they are, although the host calls them "guests") walk away with a little more than thirty bucks and a bottle of Night Train. And there are no cops to break it up, because it's all as legal as lottery tickets.

When the show is over, the take-no-prisoners lady judge will show up, robed in her trademark brand of impatient righteousness, listening with barely suppressed rage to the small-shit petitioners who come before her. Next up is the fat family psychologist who makes his guests cry (he calls this "breaking through the wall of denial"), and invites them to leave if any of them dare question his methods. Hodges thinks the fat family psychologist might have learned those methods from old KGB training videos.

Hodges eats this diet of full-color shit every weekday afternoon, sitting in the La-Z-Boy with his father's gun — the one Dad carried as a beat cop — on the table beside him. He always picks it up a few times and looks into the barrel. Inspecting that round darkness. On a couple of occasions he has slid it between his lips, just to see what it feels like to have a loaded gun lying on your tongue and pointing at your palate. Getting used to it, he supposes.

If I could drink successfully, I could put this off, he thinks. I could put it off for at least a year. And if I could put it off for two, the urge might pass. I might get interested in gardening, or bird-watching, or even painting. Tim Quigley took up painting, down in Florida. In a retirement community that was loaded with old cops. By all accounts Quigley had really enjoyed it, and had even sold some of his work at the Venice Art Festival. Until his stroke, that was. After the stroke he'd spent eight or nine months in bed, paralyzed all down his right side. No more painting for Tim Quigley. Then off he went. Booya.

The fight bell is ringing, and sure enough, both women are going after the scrawny guy in the crazy tie, painted fingernails flashing, big hair flying. Hodges reaches for the gun again, but he has no more than touched it when he hears the clack of the front door slot and the flump of the mail hitting the hall floor.

Nothing of importance comes through the mail slot in these days of email and Facebook, but he gets up anyway. He'll look through it and leave his father's M&P .38 for another day.

2

When Hodges returns to his chair with his small bundle of mail, the fight-show host is saying goodbye and promising his TV Land audience that tomorrow there will be midgets. Whether of the physical or mental variety he does not specify.

Beside the La-Z-Boy there are two small plastic waste containers, one for returnable bottles and cans, the other for trash. Into the trash goes a circular from Walmart promising ROLLBACK PRICES; an offer for burial insurance addressed to OUR FAVORITE NEIGHBOR; an announcement that all DVDs are going to be fifty percent off for one week only at Discount Electronix; a postcard-sized plea for "your important vote" from a fellow running for a vacancy on the city council. There's a photograph of the candidate, and to Hodges he looks like Dr. Oberlin, the dentist who terrified him as a child. There's also a circular from Albertsons supermarket. This Hodges puts aside (covering up his father's gun for the time being) because it's loaded with coupons.

The last thing appears to be an actual letter — a fairly thick one, by the feel — in a business-sized envelope. It is addressed to `Det. K. William Hodges (Ret.)` at `63 Harper Road`. There is no return address. In the upper lefthand corner, where one usually goes, is his second smile-face of the day's mail delivery. Only this one's not the winking Walmart Rollback Smiley but rather the email emoticon of Smiley wearing dark glasses and showing his teeth.

This stirs a memory, and not a good one.

No, he thinks. No.

But he rips the letter open so fast and hard

the envelope tears and four typed pages spill out — not real typing, not *typewriter* typing, but a computer font that looks like it.

Dear Detective Hodges, the heading reads.

He reaches out without looking, knocks the Albertsons circular to the floor, finger-walks across the revolver without even noticing it, and seizes the TV remote. He hits the kill-switch, shutting up the take-no-prisoners lady judge in mid-scold, and turns his attention to the letter.

3

Dear Detective Hodges,

I hope you do not mind me using your title, even though you have been retired for 6 months. I feel that if incompetent judges, venal politicians, and stupid military commanders can keep their titles after retirement, the same should be true for one of the most decorated police officers in the city's history.

So Detective Hodges it shall be!

Sir (another title you deserve, for you are a true Knight of the Badge and Gun), I write for many reasons, but must begin by congratulating you on your years of service, 27 as a detective and 40 in all. I saw some of the Retirement Ceremony on TV (Public Access Channel 2, a resource overlooked by many), and happen to know there was a party at the Raintree Inn out by the airport the following night.

I bet that was the real Retirement Ceremony!

I have certainly never attended such a "bash," but I watch a lot of TV cop shows, and while I am sure many of them present a very fictional picture of "the policeman's lot," several have shown such retirement parties (NYPD Blue, Homicide, The Wire, etc., etc.), and I like to think they are ACCURATE portrayals of how the Knights of the Badge and Gun say "so-long" to one of their compatriots. I think they might be, because I have also read "retirement party scenes" in at least two Joseph Wambaugh books, and they are similar. He should know because he, like you, is a "Det. Ret."

I imagine balloons hanging from the ceiling, a lot of drinking, a lot of bawdy conversation, and plenty of reminiscing about the Old Days and the old cases. There is probably lots of loud and happy music, and possibly a stripper or two "shaking her tailfeathers." There are probably speeches that are a lot funnier and a lot truer than the ones at the "stuffed shirt ceremony."

How am I doing?

Not bad, Hodges thinks. Not bad at all.

According to my research, during your time as a detective, you broke literally hundreds of cases, many of them the kind the press (who Ted Williams called the Knights of the Keyboard) terms "high profile." You have caught Killers and Robbery Gangs and Arsonists and Rapists. In one article (published to coincide with your Retirement Ceremony), your longtime partner (Det. 1st

Grade Peter Huntley) described you as "a combination of by-the-book and intuitively brilliant."

A nice compliment!

If it is true, and I think it is, you will have figured out by now that I am one of those few you did not catch. I am, in fact, the man the press chose to call

a.) The Joker

b.) The Clown

or

c.) The Mercedes Killer.

I prefer the last!

I am sure you gave it "your best shot," but sadly (for you, not me), you failed. I imagine if there was ever a "perk" you wanted to catch, Detective Hodges, it was the man who deliberately drove into the Job Fair crowd at City Center last year, killing eight and wounding so many more. (I must say I exceeded my own wildest expectations.) Was I on your mind when they gave you that plaque at the Official Retirement Ceremony? Was I on your mind when your fellow Knights of the

Badge and Gun were telling stories about (just guessing here) criminals who were caught with their pants actually down or funny practical jokes that were played in the good old Squad Room?

I bet I was!

I have to tell you how much fun it was. (I'm being honest here.) When I "put the pedal to the metal" and drove poor Mrs. Olivia Trelawney's Mercedes at that crowd of people, I had the biggest "hard-on" of my life! And was my heart beating 200 a minute? "Hope to tell ya!"

Here was another Mr. Smiley in sunglasses.

I'll tell you something that's true "inside dope," and if you want to laugh, go ahead, because it is sort of funny (although I think it also shows just how careful I was). I was wearing a condom! A "rubber"! Because I was afraid of Spontaneous Ejaculation, and the DNA that might result! Well, that did not happen, but I have masturbated many times since while thinking of how they tried to run and couldn't (they were packed in like sardines), and how scared they all looked (that was so funny), and the way I jerked forward when the car "plowed" into them. So hard the seatbelt locked. Gosh it was exciting.

To tell the truth, I didn't know what might happen. I thought the chances were 50-50 that I would get caught. But I am "a cockeyed optimist," and I prepared for Success rather than Failure. The condom is "inside dope," but I bet your Forensics Department (I also watch CSI) was pretty darn disappointed when they didn't get any DNA from inside the clown mask. They must have said, "Damn! That crafty perk must have been wearing a hair net underneath!"

And so I was! I also washed it out with BLEACH!

I still relive the thuds that resulted from hitting them, and the crunching noises, and the way the car bounced on its springs when it went over the bodies. For power and control, give me a Mercedes 12-cylinder every time! When I saw in the paper that a baby was one of my victims, I was delighted!! To snuff out a life that young! Think of all she missed, eh? Patricia Cray, RIP! Got the mom, too! Strawberry jam in a sleeping bag! What a thrill, eh? I also enjoy thinking of the man who lost his arm and even more of the two who are paralyzed. The man only from the waist down, but Martine Stover is now your basic "head on a stick!" They didn't die but probably WISH they did! How about that, Detective Hodges?

Now you are probably thinking, "What kind of sick and twisted Pervo do we have here?" Can't really blame you, but we could argue about that! I think a great many people would enjoy doing what I did, and that is why they enjoy books and movies (and even TV shows these days) that feature Torture and Dismemberment, etc., etc., etc. The only difference is I really did it. Not because I'm mad, though (in either sense of the word). Just because I didn't know exactly what the experience would be like, only that it would be totally thrilling, with "memories to last a lifetime," as they say. Most people are fitted with Lead Boots when they are just little kids and have to wear them all their lives. These Lead Boots are called A CONSCIENCE. I have none, so I can soar high above the heads of the Normal Crowd. And if they had caught me? Well if it had been right there, if Mrs. Trelawney's Mercedes had stalled or something (small chance of that as it seemed very well maintained), I suppose the crowd might have torn me apart, I understood that possibility going in, and it added to the excitement. But I didn't think they really would, because most people are sheep and sheep don't eat meat. (I suppose I might have been beaten up a little, but I can take a beating.) Probably I would have been arrested and gone to trial, where I would have pleaded insanity. Maybe I even <u>am</u> insane (the idea has certainly crossed my mind), but it is a <u>peculiar</u> kind of insanity. Anyway, the coin came down heads and I got away.

The fog helped!

Now here is something else I saw, this time in a movie. (I don't remember the name.) There was a Serial Killer who was very clever and at first the cops (one was Bruce Willis, back when he still had some hair) couldn't catch him. So Bruce Willis said, "He'll do it again because he can't help himself and sooner or later he'll make a mistake and we will catch him."

Which they did!

That is not true in my case, Detective Hodges, because I have <u>absolutely no urge</u> to do it again. In my case, <u>once was enough</u>. I have my memories, and they are as clear as a bell. And of course, there was how frightened people were afterward, because they were sure I <u>would</u> do it again. Remember the public gatherings that were cancelled? That wasn't as much fun, but it was "tres amusant."

So you see, we are both "Ret."

Speaking of which, my one regret is that I couldn't attend your Retirement Party at the Raintree Inn and raise a toast to you, my good Sir Detective. You absolutely did give it your best shot. Detective Huntley too, of course, but if the papers and Internet reports of your respective careers are right, you were Major League and he was and always will be Triple A. I'm sure the case is still in the Active File, and that he takes those old reports out every now and then to study them, but he won't get anywhere. I think we both know that.

May I close on a Note of Concern?

In some of those TV shows (and also in one of the Wambaugh books, I think, but it might have been a James Patterson), the big party with the balloons and drinking and music is followed by a sad final scene. The Detective goes home and finds out that without his Gun and Badge, his life is pointless. Which I can understand. When you think of it, what is sadder than an Old Retired Knight? Anyway, the Detective finally shoots himself (with his Service Revolver). I looked it up on the Internet and discovered this type of thing isn't just fiction. It really happens!

Retired police have an <u>extremely high suicide rate</u>!!

In most cases, the cops who do this sad thing have no close family members who might see the Warning Signs. Many, like you, are divorced. Many have grown children living far away from home. I think of you all alone in your house on Harper Road, Detective Hodges, and <u>I grow concerned</u>. What kind of life do you have, now that the "thrill of the hunt" is behind you? Are you watching a lot of TV? Probably. Are you drinking more? Possibly. Do the hours go by more slowly because your life is now so empty? Are you suffering from insomnia? Gee, I hope not.

But I fear that might be the case!

You probably need a Hobby, so you'll have something to think about instead of "the one that got away" and how you will never catch me. It would be too bad if you started thinking your whole career had been a waste of time because the fellow who killed all those Innocent People "slipped through your fingers."

I wouldn't want you to start thinking about your gun.

But you <u>are</u> thinking of it, aren't you?

I would like to close with one final thought from "the one that got away." That thought is:

FUCK YOU, LOSER.

Just kidding!

Very truly yours,
THE MERCEDES KILLER

Below this was yet another smile-face. And below that:

PS! Sorry about Mrs. Trelawney, but when you turn this letter over to Det. Huntley, tell him not to bother looking at any photos I'm sure the police took at her funeral. I attended, but only in my imagination. (My imagination is very powerful.)

PPS: Want to get in touch with me? Give me your "feedback"? Try Under Debbie's Blue Umbrella. I even got you a username: "kermitfrog19." I might not reply, but "hey, you never know."

PPPS: Hope this letter has cheered you up!

4

Hodges sits where he is for two minutes, four minutes, six, eight. Completely still. He holds the letter in his hand, looking at the Andrew Wyeth print on the wall. At last he puts the pages on the table beside his chair and picks up the envelope. The postmark is right here in the city, which doesn't surprise him. His correspondent wants him to know he's close by. It's part of the taunt. As his correspondent would say, it's . . .

Part of the fun!

New chemicals and computer-assisted scanning processes can pick up excellent fingerprints from paper, but Hodges knows that if he turns this letter in to Forensics, they will find no prints on it but his. This guy is crazy, but his self-assessment — *one crafty perp* — is absolutely correct. Only he wrote *perk,* not *perp,* and he wrote it twice. Also . . .

Wait a minute, wait a minute.

What do you mean, *when you turn it in*?

Hodges gets up, goes to the window carrying the letter, and looks out on Harper Road. The Harrison girl putts by on her moped. She's really too young to have one of those things, no matter what the law allows, but at least she's wearing her helmet. The Mr. Tastey truck jangles by; in warm weather it works the city's East Side between school's out and dusk. A little black smart car trundles by. The graying hair of the woman behind the wheel is up in rollers. Or is it a woman? It could be a man wearing a wig and a dress. The rollers would be the perfect final touch, wouldn't they?

That's what he wants you to think.

But no. Not exactly.

Not *what.* It's *how* the self-styled Mercedes Killer (except he was right, it was really the papers and the TV news that styled him that) wants him to think.

It's the ice cream man!

No, it's the man dressed as a woman in the smart car!

Uh-uh, it's the guy driving the liquid

propane truck, or the meter-reader!

How did you spark paranoia like that? It helps to casually let drop that you know more than the ex-detective's address. You know he's divorced and at least imply that he has a kid or kids somewhere.

Looking out at the grass now, noticing that it needs cutting. If Jerome doesn't come around pretty soon, Hodges thinks, I'll have to call him.

Kid or kids? Don't kid *yourself.* He knows my ex is Corinne and we have one adult child, a daughter named Alison. He knows Allie's thirty and lives in San Francisco. He probably knows she's five-six and plays tennis. All that stuff is readily available on the Net. These days, *everything* is.

His next move should be to turn this letter over to Pete and Pete's new partner, Isabelle Jaynes. They inherited the Mercedes thing, along with a few other danglers, when Hodges pulled the pin. Some cases are like idle computers; they go to sleep. This letter will wake up the Mercedes case in a hurry.

He traces the progress of the letter in his mind.

From the mail slot to the hall floor. From the hall floor to the La-Z-Boy. From the La-Z-Boy to here by the window, where he can now observe the mail truck going back the way it came — Andy Fenster done for the day. From here to the kitchen, where the letter would go into a totally unnecessary Glad bag, the kind with the zip top, because old habits are strong habits. Next to Pete and Isabelle. From Pete to Forensics for a complete dilation and curettage, where the unnecessariness of the Glad bag would be conclusively proved by: no prints, no hairs, no DNA of any kind, paper available by the caseload at every Staples and Office Depot in the city, and — last but not least — standard laser printing. They may be able to tell what kind of computer was used to compose the letter (about this he can't be sure; he knows little about computers, and when he has trouble with his he turns to Jerome, who lives handily nearby), and if so, it would turn out to be a Mac or a PC. Big whoop.

From Forensics the letter would bounce back to Pete and Isabelle, who'd no doubt convene the sort of idiotic kop kolloquium you see on BBC crime shows like *Luther* and *Prime Suspect* (which his psychopathic correspondent probably loves). This kolloquium would be complete with whiteboard and photo enlargements of the letter, maybe even a laser pointer. Hodges watches some of those British crime shows, too, and believes Scotland Yard somehow missed the old saying about too many cooks spoiling the broth.

The kop kolloquium would accomplish only one thing, and Hodges believes it's what the psycho wants: with ten or a dozen detectives in attendance, the existence of the letter will inevitably leak to the press. The psycho is probably not telling the truth when he says he has no urge to repeat his crime, but of one thing Hodges is completely sure: he misses being in the news.

Dandelions are sprouting on the lawn. It is definitely time to call Jerome. Lawn aside, Hodges misses his face around the place. Cool kid.

Something else. Even if the psycho *is* telling the truth about feeling no urge to perpetrate another mass slaughter (unlikely, but not out of the question), he's still extremely interested in death. The letter's subtext could not be clearer. *Off yourself. You're thinking about it already, so take the next step. Which also happens to be the final step.*

Has he seen me playing with Dad's .38?

Seen me putting it in my mouth?

Hodges has to admit it's possible; he has never even thought of pulling the shades. Feeling stupidly safe in his living room when anybody could have a set of binocs. Or Jerome could have seen. Jerome bopping up the walk to ask about chores: what he is pleased to call *chos fo hos.*

Only if Jerome had seen him playing with that old revolver, he would have been scared to death. He would have said something.

Does Mr. Mercedes really masturbate when he thinks about running those people down?

In his years on the police force, Hodges has seen things he would never talk about with anyone who has not also seen them. Such toxic memories lead him to believe that his correspondent could be telling the truth about the masturbation, just as he is certainly telling the truth about having no conscience. Hodges has read there are wells in Iceland so deep you can drop a stone down them and never hear the splash. He thinks some human souls are like that. Things like bum fighting are only halfway down such wells.

He returns to his La-Z-Boy, opens the drawer in the table, and takes out his cell phone. He replaces it with the .38 and closes the drawer. He speed-dials the police department, but when the receptionist asks how she can direct his call, Hodges says: "Oh, damn. I just punched the wrong button on my phone. Sorry to have bothered you."

"No bother, sir," she says with a smile in her voice.

No calls, not yet. No action of any kind. He needs to think about this.

He really, really needs to think about this.

Hodges sits looking at his television, which is off on a weekday afternoon for the first time in months.

5

That evening he drives down to Newmarket Plaza and has a meal at the Thai restaurant. Mrs. Buramuk serves him personally. "Haven't seen you long time, Officer Hodges." It comes out *Offica Hutches.*

"Been cooking for myself since I retired."

"You let me cook. Much better."

When he tastes Mrs. Buramuk's Tom Yum Gang again, he realizes how sick he is of half-raw fried hamburgers and spaghetti with Newman's Own sauce. And the Sang Kaya Fug Tong makes him realize how tired he is of Pepperidge Farm coconut cake. If I never eat another slice of coconut cake, he thinks, I could live just as long and die just as happy. He drinks two cans of Singha with his meal, and it's the best beer he's had since the Raintree retirement party, which went almost exactly as Mr. Mercedes said; there was even a stripper "shaking her tailfeathers." Along with everything else.

Had Mr. Mercedes been lurking at the back of the room? As the cartoon possum was wont to say, "It's possible, Muskie, it's possible."

At home again, he sits in the La-Z-Boy and takes up the letter. He knows what the next step must be — if he's not going to turn it over to Pete Huntley, that is — but he also knows better than to try doing it after a couple of brewskis. So he puts the letter in the drawer on top of the .38 (he never did bother with the Glad bag) and gets another beer. The one from the fridge is just an Ivory Special, the local brand, but it tastes every bit as good as the Singha.

When it's gone, Hodges powers up his computer, opens Firefox, and types in *Under Debbie's Blue Umbrella.* The descriptor beneath isn't very descriptive: *A social site where interesting people exchange interesting views.* He thinks of going further, then shuts the computer down. Not that, either. Not tonight.

He has been going to bed late, because that means fewer hours spent tossing and turning, going over old cases and old mistakes, but tonight he turns in early and knows he'll sleep almost at once. It's a wonderful feeling.

His last thought before he goes under is of how Mr. Mercedes's poison-pen letter finished up. Mr. Mercedes wants him to commit suicide. Hodges wonders what he would think if he knew he had given this particular ex–Knight of the Badge and Gun a reason to live, instead. At least for awhile.

Then sleep takes him. He gets a full and restful six hours before his bladder wakes him. He gropes to the bathroom, pees himself empty, and goes back to bed, where he sleeps for another three hours. When he wakes, sunshine is slanting in the windows and the birds are twittering. He heads into the kitchen, where he cooks himself a full breakfast. As he's sliding a couple of hard-fried eggs onto a plate already loaded with bacon and toast, he stops, startled.

Someone is singing.

It's him.

6

Once his breakfast dishes are in the dishwasher, he goes into the study to tear the letter down. This is a thing he's done at least two dozen times before, but never on his own; as a detective he always had Pete Huntley to help him, and before Pete, two previous partners. Most of the letters were threatening communications from ex-husbands (and an ex-wife or two). Not much challenge in those. Some were extortion demands. Some were blackmail — really just another form of extortion. One was from a kidnapper demanding a paltry and unimaginative ransom. And three — four, counting the one from Mr. Mercedes — were from self-confessed murderers. Two of those were clearly fantasy. One might or might not have been from the serial killer they called Turnpike Joe.

What about this one? True or false? Real or fantasy?

Hodges opens his desk drawer, takes out a

yellow legal pad, tears off the week-old grocery list on the top. Then he plucks one of the Uni-Ball pens from the cup beside his computer. He considers the detail about the condom first. If the guy really was wearing one, he took it with him . . . but that makes sense, doesn't it? Condoms can hold fingerprints as well as jizz. Hodges considers other details: how the seatbelt locked when the guy plowed into the crowd, the way the Mercedes bounced when it went over the bodies. Stuff that wouldn't have been in any of the newspapers, but also stuff he could have made up. He even said . . .

Hodges scans the letter, and here it is: *My imagination is very powerful.*

But there were two details he could not have made up. Two details that had been withheld from the news media.

On his legal pad, below IS IT REAL?, Hodges writes: HAIRNET. BLEACH.

Mr. Mercedes had taken the net with him just as he had taken the condom (probably still hanging off his dick, assuming it had been there at all), but Gibson in Forensics had been positive there was one, because Mr. Mercedes had left the clown mask and there had been no hairs stuck to the rubber. About the swimming-pool smell of DNA-killing bleach there had been no doubt. He must have used a lot.

But it isn't just those things; it's everything.

The *assuredness.* There's nothing tentative here.

He hesitates, then prints: THIS IS THE GUY.

Hesitates again. Scribbles out GUY and prints BASTARD.

7

It's been awhile since he thought like a cop, and even longer since he did this kind of work — a special kind of forensics that doesn't require cameras, microscopes, or special chemicals — but once he buckles down to it, he warms up fast. He starts with a series of headings.

ONE-SENTENCE PARAGRAPHS.
CAPITALIZED PHRASES.
PHRASES IN QUOTATION MARKS.
FANCY PHRASES.
UNUSUAL WORDS.
EXCLAMATION POINTS.

Here he stops, tapping the pen against his lower lip and reading the letter through again from `Dear Detective Hodges` to `Hope this letter has cheered you up!` Then he adds two more headings on the sheet, which is now getting crowded.

USES BASEBALL METAPHOR, MAY BE

A FAN.
COMPUTER SAVVY (UNDER 50?).

He is far from sure about these last two. Sports metaphors have become common, especially among political pundits, and these days there are octogenarians on Facebook and Twitter. Hodges himself may be tapping only twelve percent of his Mac's potential (that's what Jerome claims), but that doesn't make him part of the majority. You had to start somewhere, though, and besides, the letter has a young feel.

He has always been talented at this sort of work, and a lot more than twelve percent of it is intuition.

He's listed nearly a dozen examples under UNUSUAL WORDS, and now circles two: *compatriots* and *Spontaneous Ejaculation.* Beside them he adds a name: *Wambaugh.* Mr. Mercedes is a shitbag, but a bright, book-reading shitbag. He has a large vocabulary and doesn't make spelling errors. Hodges can imagine Jerome Robinson saying, "Spellchecker, my man. I mean, *duh*?"

Sure, sure, these days anyone with a word processing program can spell like a champ, but Mr. Mercedes has written *Wambaugh,* not *Wombough,* or even *Wombow,* which is how it sounds. Just the fact that he's remembered to put in that silent *gh* suggests a fairly high level of intelligence. Mr. Mercedes's missive may not be high-class literature, but his writing is a lot better than the dialogue in shows like *NCIS* or *Bones.*

Homeschooled, public-schooled, or self-taught? Does it matter? Maybe not, but maybe it does.

Hodges doesn't think self-taught, no. The writing is too . . . what?

"Expansive," he says to the empty room, but it's more than that. "*Outward.* This guy writes outward. He learned with others. And wrote *for* others."

A shaky deduction, but it's supported by certain flourishes — those FANCY PHRASES. *Must begin by congratulating you,* he writes. *Literally hundreds of cases,* he writes. And — twice — *Was I on your mind.* Hodges logged As in his high school English classes, Bs in college, and he remembers what that sort of thing is called: incremental repetition. Does Mr. Mercedes imagine his letter being published in the newspaper, circulated on the Internet, quoted (with a certain reluctant respect) on *Channel Four News at Six*?

"Sure you do," Hodges says. "Once upon a time you read your themes in class. You liked it, too. Liked being in the spotlight. Didn't you? When I find you — *if* I find you — I'll find that you did as well in your English classes as I did." Probably better. Hodges can't remember ever using incremental repetition, unless it was by accident.

Only there are four public high schools in the city and God knows how many private ones. Not to mention prep schools, junior colleges, City College, and St. Jude's Catholic University. Plenty of haystacks for a poisoned needle to hide in. If he even went to school here at all, and not in Miami or Phoenix.

Plus, he's a sly dog. The letter is full of false fingerprints — the capitalized phrases like *Lead Boots* and *Note of Concern,* the phrases in quotation marks, the extravagant use of exclamation points, the punchy one-sentence paragraphs. If asked to provide a writing sample, Mr. Mercedes would include none of those stylistic devices. Hodges knows that as well as he knows his own unfortunate first name: Kermit, as in *kermitfrog19.*

But.

This asshole isn't quite as smart as he thinks. The letter almost certainly contains two *real* fingerprints, one smudged and one crystal clear.

The smudged print is his persistent use of numbers instead of the words for numbers: 27, not twenty-seven; 40 instead of forty. Det. 1st Grade instead of Det. First Grade. There are a few exceptions (he has written *one regret* instead of *1 regret*), but Hodges thinks they are the ones that prove the general rule. The numbers *might* only be more camouflage, he knows that, but the chances are good Mr. Mercedes is genuinely unaware of it.

If I could get him in IR4 and tell him to write *Forty thieves stole eighty wedding rings . . . ?*

Only K. William Hodges is never going to be in an interview room again, including IR4, which had been his favorite — his lucky IR, he always thought it. Unless he gets caught fooling with this shit, that is, and then he's apt to be on the wrong side of the metal table.

All right, then. *Pete* gets the guy in an IR. Pete or Isabelle or both of them. They get him to write *40 thieves stole 80 wedding rings.* What then?

Then they ask him to write *The cops caught the perp hiding in the alley.* Only they'd want to slur the *perp* part. Because, for all his writing skill, Mr. Mercedes thinks the word for a criminal doer is *perk.* Maybe he also thinks the word for a special privilege is a *perp,* as in *Traveling 1st class was one of the CEO's perps.*

Hodges wouldn't be surprised. Until college, he himself had thought that the fellow who threw the ball in a baseball game, the thing you poured water out of, and the framed objects you hung on the wall to decorate your apartment were all spelled the same. He had seen the word *picture* in all sorts of books, but his mind somehow refused to record it. His mother said *straighten that pitcher, Kerm, it's crooked,* his father sometimes gave him money for the *pitcher show,* and it had simply stuck in his head.

I'll know you when I find you, honeybunch, Hodges thinks. He prints the word and circles it again and again, hemming it in. You'll be the asshole who calls a perp a perk.

8

He takes a walk around the block to clear his head, saying hello to people he hasn't said hello to in a long time. Weeks, in some cases. Mrs. Melbourne is working in her garden, and when she sees him, she invites him in for a piece of her coffee cake.

"I've been worried about you," she says when they're settled in the kitchen. She has the bright, inquisitive gaze of a crow with its eye on a freshly squashed chipmunk.

"Getting used to retirement has been hard." He takes a sip of her coffee. It's lousy, but plenty hot.

"Some people never get used to it at all," she says, measuring him with those bright eyes. She wouldn't be too shabby in IR4, Hodges thinks. "Especially ones who had high-pressure jobs."

"I was a little at loose ends to start with, but I'm doing better now."

"I'm glad to hear it. Does that nice Negro

boy still work for you?"

"Jerome? Yes." Hodges smiles, wondering how Jerome would react if he knew someone in the neighborhood thinks of him as *that nice Negro boy.* Probably he would bare his teeth in a grin and exclaim, *I sho is!* Jerome and his chos fo hos. Already with his eye on Harvard. Princeton as a fallback.

"He's slacking off," she says. "Your lawn's gotten rather shaggy. More coffee?"

Hodges declines with a smile. Hot can only do so much for bad coffee.

9

Back home again. Legs tingling, head filled with fresh air, mouth tasting like newspaper in a birdcage, but brain buzzing with caffeine.

He logs on to the city newspaper site and calls up several stories about the slaughter at City Center. What he wants isn't in the first story, published under scare headlines on April eleventh of '09, or the much longer piece in the Sunday edition of April twelfth. It's in the Monday paper: a picture of the abandoned killcar's steering wheel. The indignant caption: HE THOUGHT IT WAS FUNNY. In the center of the wheel, pasted over the Mercedes emblem, is a yellow smile-face. The kind that wears sunglasses and shows its teeth.

There was a lot of police anger about that

photo, because the detectives in charge — Hodges and Huntley — had asked the news media to hold back the smile icon. The editor, Hodges remembers, had been fawningly apologetic. A missed communication, he said. Won't happen again. Promise. Scout's honor.

"Mistake, my ass," he remembers Pete fuming. "They had a picture that'd shoot a few steroids into their saggy-ass circulation, and they fucking used it."

Hodges enlarges the news photo until that grinning yellow face fills the computer screen. The mark of the beast, he thinks, twenty-first-century style.

This time the number he speed-dials isn't PD Reception but Pete's cell. His old partner picks up on the second ring. "Yo, you ole hossy-hoss. How's retirement treating you?" He sounds really pleased, and that makes Hodges smile. It also makes him feel guilty, yet the thought of backing off never crosses his mind.

"I'm good," he says, "but I miss your fat and hypertensive face."

"Sure you do. And we won in Iraq."

"Swear to God, Peter. How about we have lunch and catch up a little? You pick the place and I'll buy."

"Sounds good, but I already ate today. How about tomorrow?"

"My schedule is jammed, Obama was coming by for my advice on the budget, but I suppose I could rearrange a few things. Seeing's how it's you."

"Go fuck yourself, *Kermit.*"

"When you do it so much better?" The banter is an old tune with simple lyrics.

"How about DeMasio's? You always liked that place."

"DeMasio's is fine. Noon?"

"That works."

"And you're sure you've got time for an old whore like me?"

"Billy, you don't even need to ask. Want me to bring Isabelle?"

He doesn't, but says: "If you want."

Some of the old telepathy must still be working, because after a brief pause Pete says, "Maybe we'll make it a stag party this time."

"Whatever," Hodges says, relieved. "Looking forward."

"Me too. Good to hear your voice, Billy."

Hodges hangs up and looks at the teeth-bared smile-face some more. It fills his computer screen.

10

He sits in his La-Z-Boy that night, watching the eleven o'clock news. In his white pajamas he looks like an overweight ghost. His scalp gleams mellowly through his thinning hair. The big story is the Deepwater Horizon spill in the Gulf of Mexico where the oil is still

gushing. The newsreader says the bluefin tuna are endangered, and the Louisiana shellfish industry may be destroyed for a generation. In Iceland, a billowing volcano (with a name the newsreader mangles to something like *Eeja-fill-kull*) is still screwing up transatlantic air travel. In California, police are saying they may have finally gotten a break in the Grim Sleeper serial killer case. No names, but the suspect (the *perk,* Hodges thinks) is described as "a well-groomed and well-spoken African-American." Hodges thinks, Now if only someone would bag Turnpike Joe. Not to mention Osama bin Laden.

The weather comes on. Warm temperatures and sunny skies, the weather girl promises. Time to break out the bathing suits.

"I'd like to see you in a bathing suit, my dear," Hodges says, and uses the remote to turn off the TV.

He takes his father's .38 out of the drawer, unloads it as he walks into the bedroom, and puts it in the safe with his Glock. He has spent a lot of time during the last two or three months obsessing about the Victory .38, but tonight it hardly crosses his mind as he locks it away. He's thinking about Turnpike Joe, but not really; these days Joe is someone else's problem. Like the Grim Sleeper, that well-spoken African-American.

Is Mr. Mercedes also African-American?

It's technically possible — no one saw anything but the pullover clown mask, a long-sleeved shirt, and yellow gloves on the steering wheel — but Hodges thinks not. God knows there are plenty of black people capable of murder in this city, but there's the weapon to consider. The neighborhood where Mrs. Trelawney's mother lived is predominantly wealthy and predominantly white. A black man hanging around a parked Mercedes SL500 would have been noticed.

Well. Probably. People can be stunningly unobservant. But experience has led Hodges to believe rich people tend to be slightly more observant than the general run of Americans, especially when it comes to their expensive toys. He doesn't want to say they're *paranoid,* but . . .

The fuck they're not. Rich people can be generous, even the ones with bloodcurdling political views can be generous, but most believe in generosity on their own terms, and underneath (not so deep, either), they're always afraid someone is going to steal their presents and eat their birthday cake.

How about neat and well spoken, then?

Yes, Hodges decides. No hard evidence, but the letter suggests he is. Mr. Mercedes may dress in suits and work in an office, or he may dress in jeans and Carhartt shirts and balance tires in a garage, but he's no slob. He may not talk a lot — such creatures are care-

ful in all aspects of their lives, and that includes promiscuous blabbing — but when he does talk, he's probably direct and clear. If you were lost and needed directions, he'd give you good ones.

As he's brushing his teeth, Hodges thinks: DeMasio's. Pete wants to have lunch at DeMasio's.

That's okay for Pete, who still carries the badge and gun, and it seemed okay to Hodges when they were talking on the phone, because then Hodges had been *thinking* like a cop instead of a retiree who's thirty pounds overweight. It probably would be okay — broad daylight and all — but DeMasio's is on the edge of Lowtown, which is not a vacation community. A block west of the restaurant, beyond the turnpike spur overpass, the city turns into a wasteland of vacant lots and abandoned tenements. Drugs are sold openly on streetcorners, there's a burgeoning trade in illegal weaponry, and arson is the neighborhood sport. If you can call Lowtown a neighborhood, that is. The restaurant itself — a really terrific Italian joint — is safe, though. The owner is connected, and that makes it like Free Parking in Monopoly.

Hodges rinses his mouth, goes back into the bedroom, and — still thinking of DeMasio's — looks doubtfully at the closet where the safe is hidden behind the hanging pants, shirts, and the sportcoats he no longer wears (he's now too big for all but two of them).

Take the Glock? The Victory, maybe? The Victory's smaller.

No to both. His carry-concealed license is still in good standing, but he's not going strapped to a lunch with his old partner. It would make him self-conscious, and he's already self-conscious about the digging he plans to do. He goes to his dresser instead, lifts up a pile of underwear, and looks underneath. The Happy Slapper is still there, has been there since his retirement party.

The Slapper will do. Just a little insurance in a high-risk part of town.

Satisfied, he goes to bed and turns out the light. He puts his hands into the mystic cool pocket under the pillow and thinks of Turnpike Joe. Joe has been lucky so far, but eventually he'll be caught. Not just because he keeps hitting those highway rest areas but because he can't stop killing. He thinks of Mr. Mercedes writing, *That is not true in my case, because I have absolutely no urge to do it again.*

Telling the truth, or lying the way he was lying with his CAPITALIZED PHRASES and MANY EXCLAMATION POINTS and ONE-SENTENCE PARAGRAPHS?

Hodges thinks he's lying — perhaps to himself as well as to K. William Hodges, Det. Ret. — but right now, as Hodges lies here with sleep coming on, he doesn't care. What matters is the guy thinks he's safe. He's positively smug about it. He doesn't seem to realize the vulnerability he has exposed by writing a letter to the man who was, until his retirement, the lead detective on the City Center case.

You need to talk about it, don't you? Yes you do, honeybunch, don't lie to your old uncle Billy. And unless that Debbie's Blue Umbrella site is another red herring, like all those quotation marks, you've even opened a conduit into your life. You want to talk. You need to talk. And if you could goad me into something, that would just be the cherry on top of a sundae, wouldn't it?

In the dark, Hodges says: "I'm willing to listen. I've got plenty of time. I'm retired, after all."

Smiling, he falls asleep.

11

The following morning, Freddi Linklatter is sitting on the edge of the loading dock and smoking a Marlboro. Her Discount Electronix jacket is folded neatly beside her with her DE gimme cap placed on top of it. She's talking about some Jesus-jumper who gave her hassle. People are always giving her hassle, and she tells Brady all about it on break. She gives him chapter and verse, because Brady is a good listener.

"So he says to me, he goes, All homosexuals are going to hell, and this tract explains all about it. So I take it, right? There's a picture on the front of these two narrow-ass gay guys — in leisure suits, I swear to God — holding hands and staring into a cave filled with flames. Plus the devil! With a pitchfork! I am *not* shitting you. Still, I try to discuss it with him. I'm under the impression that he wants to have a dialogue. So I say, I go, You ought to get your face out of the Book of LaBitticus or whatever it is long enough to read a few scientific studies. Gays are *born* gay, I mean, hello? He goes, That is simply not true. Homosexuality is learned behavior and can be unlearned. So I can't believe it, right? I mean, you have *got* to be shitting me. But I don't say that. What I say is, Look at me, dude, take a real good look. Don't be shy, go top to bottom. What do you see? And before he can toss some more of his bullshit, I go, You see a *guy,* is what you see. Only God got distracted before he could slap a dick on me and went on to the next in line. So *then* he goes . . ."

Brady sticks with her — more or less — until Freddi gets to the Book of LaBitticus (she means Leviticus, but Brady doesn't care enough to correct her), and then mostly loses her, keeping track just enough to throw in the occasional *uh-huh.* He doesn't really mind the monologue. It's soothing, like the LCD

Soundsystem he sometimes listens to on his iPod when he goes to sleep. Freddi Linklatter is way tall for a girl, at six-two or -three she towers over Brady, and what she's saying is true: she looks like a girl about as much as Brady Hartsfield looks like Vin Diesel. She's togged out in straight-leg 501s, motorcycle skids, and a plain white tee that hangs dead straight, without even a touch of tits. Her dark blond hair is butched to a quarter inch. She wears no earrings and no makeup. She probably thinks Max Factor is a statement about what some guy did to some girl out behind old Dad's barn.

He says *yeah* and *uh-huh* and *right,* all the time wondering what the old cop made of his letter, and if the old cop will try to get in touch at the Blue Umbrella. He knows that sending the letter was a risk, but not a very big one. He made up a prose style that's completely different from his own. The chances of the old cop picking up anything useful from the letter are slim to nonexistent.

Debbie's Blue Umbrella is a slightly bigger risk, but if the old cop thinks he can trace him down that way, he's in for a big surprise. Debbie's servers are in Eastern Europe, and in Eastern Europe computer privacy is like cleanliness in America: next to godliness.

"So he goes, I swear this is true, he goes, There are plenty of young Christian women in our church who could show you how to fix yourself up, and if you grew your hair out, you'd look quite pretty. Do you believe it? So I tell him, With a little lipum-stickum, you'd look darn pretty yourself. Put on a leather jacket and a dog collar and you might luck into a hot date at the Corral. Get your first squirt on the Tower of Power. So that buzzes him bigtime and he goes, If you're going to get personal about this . . ."

Anyway, if the old cop wants to follow the computer trail, he'll have to turn the letter over to the cops in the technical section, and Brady doesn't think he'll do that. Not right away, at least. He's got to be bored sitting there with nothing but the TV for company. And the revolver, of course, the one he keeps beside him with his beer and magazines. Can't forget the revolver. Brady has never seen him actually stick it in his mouth, but several times he's seen him holding it. Shiny happy people don't hold guns in their laps that way.

"So I tell him, I go, Don't get mad. Somebody pushes back against your precious ideas, you guys always get mad. Have you noticed that about the Christers?"

He hasn't but says he has.

"Only this one listened. He actually did. And we ended up going down to Hosseni's Bakery and having coffee. Where, I know this is hard to believe, we actually did have something approaching a dialogue. I don't hold out much hope for the human race, but every now and then . . ."

Brady is pretty sure his letter will pep the old cop up, at least to start with. He didn't get all those citations for being stupid, and he'll see right through the veiled suggestion that he commit suicide the way Mrs. Trelawney did. *Veiled?* Not very. It's pretty much right out front. Brady believes the old cop will go all gung ho, at least for awhile. But when he fails to get anywhere, it will make the fall even more jarring. Then, assuming the old cop takes the Blue Umbrella bait, Brady can really go to work.

The old cop is thinking, *If I can get you talking, I can goad you.*

Only Brady is betting the old cop never read Nietzsche; Brady's betting the old cop is more of a John Grisham man. If he reads at all. *When you gaze into the abyss,* Nietzsche wrote, *the abyss also gazes into you.*

I am the abyss, old boy. Me.

The old cop is certainly a bigger challenge than poor guilt-ridden Olivia Trelawney . . . but getting to her was such a hot hit to the nervous system that Brady can't help wanting to try it again. In some ways prodding Sweet Livvy into high-siding it was a bigger thrill than cutting a bloody swath through that pack of job-hunting assholes at City Center. Because it took brains. It took dedication. It took planning. And a little bit of help from the cops didn't hurt, either. Did they guess their faulty deductions were partly to blame for Sweet Livvy's suicide? Probably not Huntley, such a possibility would never cross his plodder's mind. Ah, but Hodges. *He* might have his doubts. A few little mice nibbling at the wires back there in his smart-cop brain. Brady hopes so. If not, he may get a chance to tell him. On the Blue Umbrella.

Mostly, though, it was him. Brady Hartsfield. Credit where credit is due. City Center was a sledgehammer. On Olivia Trelawney, he used a scalpel.

"Are you listening to me?" Freddi asks.

He smiles. "Guess I drifted away there for a minute."

Never tell a lie when you can tell the truth. The truth isn't always the safest course, but mostly it is. He wonders idly what she'd say if he told her, *Freddi, I am the Mercedes Killer.* Or if he said, *Freddi, there are nine pounds of homemade plastic explosive in my basement closet.*

She is looking at him as if she can read these thoughts, and Brady has a moment of unease. Then she says, "It's working two jobs, pal. That'll wear you down."

"Yes, but I'd like to get back to college, and nobody's going to pay for it but me. Also there's my mother."

"The wino."

He smiles. "My mother is actually more of

a vodka-o."

"Invite me over," Freddi says grimly. "I'll drag her to a fucking AA meeting."

"Wouldn't work. You know what Dorothy Parker said, right? You can lead a whore to culture, but you can't make her think."

Freddi considers this for a moment, then throws back her head and voices a Marlboro-raspy laugh. "I don't know who Dorothy Parker is, but I'm gonna save that one." She sobers. "Seriously, why don't you just ask Frobisher for more hours? That other job of yours is strictly rinky-dink."

"I'll tell you why he doesn't ask Frobisher for more hours," Frobisher says, stepping out onto the loading platform. Anthony Frobisher is young and geekily bespectacled. In this he is like most of the Discount Electronix employees. Brady is also young, but better-looking than Tones Frobisher. Not that this makes him handsome. Which is okay. Brady is willing to settle for nondescript.

"Lay it on us," Freddi says, and mashes her cigarette out. Across the loading zone behind the big-box store, which anchors the south end of the Birch Hill Mall, are the employees' cars (mostly old beaters) and three VW Beetles painted bright green. These are always kept spotless, and late-spring sun twinkles on their windshields. On the sides, in blue, is COMPUTER PROBLEMS? CALL THE DISCOUNT ELECTRONIX

CYBER PATROL!

"Circuit City is gone and Best Buy is tottering," Frobisher says in a schoolteacherly voice. "Discount Electronix is *also* tottering, along with several other businesses that are on life support thanks to the computer revolution: newspapers, book publishers, record stores, and the United States Postal Service. Just to mention a few."

"Record stores?" Freddi asks, lighting another cigarette. "What are record stores?"

"That's a real gut-buster," Frobisher says. "I have a friend who claims dykes lack a sense of humor, but —"

"You have friends?" Freddi asks. "Wow. Who knew?"

"— but you obviously prove him wrong. You guys don't have more hours because the company is now surviving on computers alone. Mostly cheap ones made in China and the Philippines. The great majority of our customers no longer want the other shit we sell." Brady thinks only Tones Frobisher would say *the great majority.* "This is partly because of the technological revolution, but it's also because —"

Together, Freddi and Brady chant, "— *Barack Obama is the worst mistake this country ever made!*"

Frobisher regards them sourly for a moment, then says, "At least you listen. Brady, you're off at two, is that correct?"

"Yes. My other gig starts at three."

Frobisher wrinkles the overlarge schnozzola in the middle of his face to show what he thinks of Brady's other job. "Did I hear you say something about returning to school?"

Brady doesn't reply to this, because anything he says might be the wrong thing. Anthony "Tones" Frobisher must not know that Brady hates him. Fucking *loathes* him. Brady hates everybody, including his drunk mother, but it's like that old country song says: no one has to know right now.

"You're twenty-eight, Brady. Old enough so you no longer have to rely on shitty pool coverage to insure your automobile — which is good — but a little *too* old to be training for a career in electrical engineering. Or computer programming, for that matter."

"Don't be a turd," Freddi says. "Don't be a Tones Turd."

"If telling the truth makes a man a turd, then a turd I shall be."

"Yeah," Freddi says. "You'll go down in history. Tones the Truth-Telling Turd. Kids will learn about you in school."

"I don't mind a little truth," Brady says quietly.

"Good. You can don't-mind all the time you're cataloguing and stickering DVDs. Starting now."

Brady nods good-naturedly, stands up, and dusts the seat of his pants. The Discount

Electronix fifty-percent-off sale starts the following week; management in New Jersey has mandated that DE must be out of the digital-versatile-disc business by January of 2011. That once profitable line of merchandise has been strangled by Netflix and Redbox. Soon there will be nothing in the store but home computers (made in China and the Philippines) and flat-screen TVs, which in this deep recession few can afford to buy.

"You," Frobisher says, turning to Freddi, "have an out-call." He hands her a pink work invoice. "Old lady with a screen freeze. That's what she says it is, anyway."

"Yes, *mon capitan.* I live to serve." She stands up, salutes, and takes the call-sheet he holds out.

"Tuck your shirt in. Put on your cap so your customer doesn't have to be disgusted by that weird haircut. Don't drive too fast. Get another ticket and life as you know it on the Cyber Patrol is over. Also, pick up your fucking cigarette butts before you go."

He disappears inside before she can return his serve.

"DVD stickers for you, an old lady with a CPU probably full of graham cracker crumbs for me," Freddi says, jumping down and putting her hat on. She gives the bill a gangsta twist and starts across to the VWs without even glancing at her cigarette butts. She does pause long enough to look back at Brady, hands on her nonexistent boy hips. "This is *not* the life I pictured for myself when I was in the fifth grade."

"Me, either," Brady says quietly.

He watches her putt away, on a mission to rescue an old lady who's probably going crazy because she can't download her favorite mock-apple pie recipe. This time Brady wonders what Freddi would say if he told her what life was like for *him* when he was a kid. That was when he killed his brother. And his mother covered it up.

Why would she not?

After all, it had sort of been her idea.

12

As Brady is slapping yellow 50% OFF stickers on old Quentin Tarantino movies and Freddi is helping out elderly Mrs. Vera Willkins on the West Side (it's her keyboard that's full of crumbs, it turns out), Bill Hodges is turning off Lowbriar, the four-lane street that bisects the city and gives Lowtown its name, and in to the parking lot beside DeMasio's Italian Ristorante. He doesn't have to be Sherlock Holmes to know Pete got here first. Hodges parks next to a plain gray Chevrolet sedan with blackwall tires that just about scream city police and gets out of his old Toyota, a car that just about screams old retired fella. He touches the hood of the

Chevrolet. Warm. Pete has not beaten him by much.

He pauses for a moment, enjoying this almost-noon morning with its bright sunshine and sharp shadows, looking at the overpass a block down. It's been gang-tagged up the old wazoo, and although it's empty now (noon is breakfast time for the younger denizens of Lowtown), he knows that if he walked under there, he would smell the sour reek of cheap wine and whiskey. His feet would grate on the shards of broken bottles. In the gutters, more bottles. The little brown kind.

No longer his problem. Besides, the darkness beneath the overpass is empty, and Pete is waiting for him. Hodges goes in and is pleased when Elaine at the hostess stand smiles and greets him by name, although he hasn't been here for months. Maybe even a year. Of course Pete is in one of the booths, already raising a hand to him, and Pete might have refreshed her memory, as the lawyers say.

He raises his own hand in return, and by the time he gets to the booth, Pete is standing beside it, arms raised to envelop him in a bearhug. They thump each other on the back the requisite number of times and Pete tells him he's looking good.

"You know the three Ages of Man, don't you?" Hodges asks.

Pete shakes his head, grinning.

"Youth, middle age, and you look fuckin terrific."

Pete roars with laughter and asks if Hodges knows what the blond said when she opened the box of Cheerios. Hodges says he does not. Pete makes big amazed eyes and says, "Oh! Look at the cute little doughnut seeds!"

Hodges gives his own obligatory roar of laughter (although he does not think this a particularly witty example of Genus Blond), and with the amenities thus disposed of, they sit down. A waiter comes over — no waitresses in DeMasio's, only elderly men who wear spotless aprons tied up high on their narrow chicken chests — and Pete orders a pitcher of beer. Bud Lite, not Ivory Special. When it comes, Pete raises his glass.

"Here's to you, Billy, and life after work."

"Thanks."

They click and drink. Pete asks about Allie and Hodges asks about Pete's son and daughter. Their wives, both of the ex variety, are touched upon (as if to prove to each other — and themselves — that they are not afraid to talk about them) and then banished from the conversation. Food is ordered. By the time it comes, they have finished with Hodges's two grandchildren and have analyzed the chances of the Cleveland Indians, which happens to be the closest major league team. Pete has ravioli, Hodges spaghetti with garlic and oil, what he has always ordered here.

Halfway through these calorie bombs, Pete takes a folded piece of paper from his breast pocket and places it, with some ceremony, beside his plate.

"What's that?" Hodges asks.

"Proof that my detective skills are as keenly honed as ever. I don't see you since that horror show at Raintree Inn — my hangover lasted three days, by the way — and I talk to you, what, twice? Three times? Then, bang, you ask me to lunch. Am I surprised? No. Do I smell an ulterior motive? Yes. So let's see if I'm right."

Hodges gives a shrug. "I'm like the curious cat. You know what they say — satisfaction brought him back."

Pete Huntley is grinning broadly, and when Hodges reaches for the folded slip of paper, Pete puts a hand over it. "No-no-no-no. You have to say it. Don't be coy, *Kermit.*"

Hodges sighs and ticks four items off on his fingers. When he's done, Pete pushes the folded piece of paper across the table. Hodges opens it and reads:

1. Davis
2. Park Rapist
3. Pawnshops
4. Mercedes Killer

Hodges pretends to be discomfited. "You got me, Sheriff. Don't say a thing if you don't want to."

Pete grows serious. "Jesus, if you weren't interested in the cases that were hanging fire when you hung up your jock, I'd be disappointed. I've been . . . a little worried about you."

"I don't want to horn in or anything." Hodges is a trifle aghast at how smoothly this enormous whopper comes out.

"Your nose is growing, Pinocchio."

"No, seriously. All I want is an update."

"Happy to oblige. Let's start with Donald Davis. You know the script. He fucked up every business he tried his hand at, most recently Davis Classic Cars. Guy's so deep in debt he should change his name to Captain Nemo. Two or three pretty kitties on the side."

"It was three when I called it a day," Hodges says, going back to work on his pasta. It's not Donald Davis he's here about, or the City Park rapist, or the guy who's been knocking over pawnshops and liquor stores for the last four years; they are just camouflage. But he can't help being interested.

"Wife gets tired of the debt and the kitties. She's prepping the divorce papers when she disappears. Oldest story in the world. He reports her missing and declares bankruptcy on the same day. Does TV interviews and squirts a bucket of alligator tears. We know he killed her, but with no body . . ." He shrugs. "You were in on the meetings with Diana the Dope." He's talking about the city's district attorney.

"Still can't persuade her to charge him?"

"No corpus delicious, no charge. The cops in Modesto knew Scott Peterson was guilty as sin and still didn't charge him until they recovered the bodies of his wife and kid. You know that."

Hodges does. He and Pete discussed Scott and Laci Peterson a lot during their investigation of Sheila Davis's disappearance.

"But guess what? Blood's turned up in their summer cabin by the lake." Pete pauses for effect, then drops the other shoe. "It's hers."

Hodges leans forward, his food temporarily forgotten. "When was this?"

"Last month."

"And you didn't tell me?"

"I'm telling you now. Because you're asking now. The search out there is ongoing. The Victor County cops are in charge."

"Did anyone see him in the area prior to Sheila's disappearance?"

"Oh yeah. Two kids. Davis claimed he was mushroom hunting. Fucking Euell Gibbons, you know? When they find the body — if they find it — ole Donnie Davis can quit waiting for the seven years to be up so he can petition to have her declared dead and collect the insurance." Pete smiles widely. "Think of the time he'll save."

"What about the Park Rapist?"

"It's really just a matter of time. We know he's white, we know he's in his teens or twenties, and we know he just can't get enough of that well-maintained matronly pussy."

"You're putting out decoys, right? Because he likes the warm weather."

"We are, and we'll get him."

"It would be nice if you got him before he rapes another fifty-something on her way home from work."

"We're doing our best." Pete looks slightly annoyed, and when their waiter appears to ask if everything's all right, Pete waves the guy away.

"I know," Hodges says. Soothingly. "Pawnshop guy?"

Pete breaks into a broad grin. "Young Aaron Jefferson."

"Huh?"

"That's his actual name, although when he played football for City High, he called himself YA. You know, like YA Tittle. Although his girlfriend — also the mother of his three-year-old — tells us he calls the guy YA Titties. When I asked her if he was joking or serious, she said she didn't have any idea."

Here is another story Hodges knows, another so old it could have come from the Bible . . . and there's probably a version of it in there someplace. "Let me guess. He racks up a dozen jobs —"

"It's fourteen now. Waving that sawed-off around like Omar on *The Wire.*"

"— and keeps getting away with it because he has the luck of the devil. Then he cheats on baby mama. She gets pissed and rats him out."

Pete points a finger-gun at his old partner. "Hole in one. And the next time Young Aaron walks into a pawnshop or a check-cashing emporium with his bellygun, we'll know ahead of time, and it's angel, angel, down we go."

"Why wait?"

"DA again," Pete says. "You bring Diana the Dope a steak, she says cook it for me, and if it isn't medium-rare, I'll send it back."

"But you've got him."

"I'll bet you a new set of whitewalls that YA Titties is in County by the Fourth of July and in State by Christmas. Davis and the Park Rapist may take a little longer, but we'll get them. You want dessert?"

"No. Yes." To the waiter he says, "You still have that rum cake? The dark chocolate one?"

The waiter looks insulted. "Yes, sir. Always."

"I'll have a piece of that. And coffee. Pete?"

"I'll settle for the last of the beer." So saying, he pours it out of the pitcher. "You sure about that cake, Billy? You look like you've put on a few pounds since I saw you last."

It's true. Hodges eats heartily in retirement, but only for the last couple of days has food tasted good to him. "I'm thinking about Weight Watchers."

Pete nods. "Yeah? I'm thinking about the priesthood."

"Fuck you. What about the Mercedes Killer?"

"We're still canvassing the Trelawney neighborhood — in fact, that's where Isabelle is right now — but I'd be shocked if she or anyone else comes up with a live lead. Izzy's not knocking on any doors that haven't been knocked on half a dozen times before. The guy stole Trelawney's luxury sled, drove out of the fog, did his thing, drove back into the fog, dumped it, and . . . nothing. Never mind Monsewer YA Titties, it's the Mercedes guy who *really* had the luck of the devil. If he'd tried that stunt even an hour later, there would have been cops there. For crowd control."

"I know."

"Do you think *he* knew, Billy?"

Hodges tilts a hand back and forth to indicate it's hard to say. Maybe, if he and Mr. Mercedes should strike up a conversation on that Blue Umbrella website, he'll ask.

"The murdering prick could have lost control when he started hitting people and crashed, but he didn't. German engineering, best in the world, that's what Isabelle says. Someone could have jumped on the hood and blocked his vision, but no one did. One of the posts holding up the DO NOT CROSS tape could have bounced under the car and gotten hung up there, but that didn't happen, either. And someone could have seen him when he parked behind that warehouse and got out with his mask off, but no one did."

"It was five-twenty in the morning," Hodges points out, "and even at noon that area would have been almost as deserted."

"Because of the recession," Pete Huntley says moodily. "Yeah, yeah. Probably half the people who used to work in those warehouses were at City Center, waiting for the frigging job fair to start. Have some irony, it's good for your blood."

"So you've got nothing."

"Dead in the water."

Hodges's cake comes. It smells good and tastes better.

When the waiter's gone, Pete leans across the table. "My nightmare is that he'll do it again. That another fog will come rolling in off the lake and he'll do it again."

He says he won't, Hodges thinks, conveying another forkload of the delicious cake into his mouth. He says he has *absolutely no urge.* He says *once was enough.*

"That or something else," Hodges says.

"I got into a big fight with my daughter back in March," Pete says. "*Monster* fight. I didn't see her once in April. She skipped all her weekends."

"Yeah?"

"Uh-huh. She wanted to go see a cheerleading competition. Bring the Funk, I think it was called. Practically every school in the state was in it. You remember how crazy Candy always was about cheerleaders?"

"Yeah," Hodges says. He doesn't.

"Had a little pleated skirt when she was four or six or something, we couldn't get her out of it. Two of the moms said they'd take the girls. And I told Candy no. You know why?"

Sure he does.

"Because the competition was at City Center, that's why. In my mind's eye I could see about a thousand tweenyboppers and their moms milling around outside, waiting for the doors to open, dusk instead of dawn, but you know the fog comes in off the lake then, too. I could see that cocksucker running at them in another stolen Mercedes — or maybe a fucking Hummer this time — and the kids and the mommies just standing there, staring like deer in the headlights. So I said no. You should have heard her scream at me, Billy, but I still said no. She wouldn't talk to me for a month, and she still wouldn't be talking to me if Maureen hadn't taken her. I told Mo absolutely no way, don't you dare, and she said, That's why I divorced you, Pete, because I got tired of listening to *no way* and *don't you dare.* And of course nothing happened."

He drinks the rest of the beer, then leans forward again.

"I hope there are plenty of people with me when we catch him. If I nail him alone, I'm apt to kill him just for putting me on the outs with my daughter."

"Then why hope for plenty of people?"

Pete considers this, then smiles a slow smile. "You have a point there."

"Do you ever wonder about Mrs. Trelawney?" Hodges asks the question casually, but he has been thinking about Olivia Trelawney a lot since the anonymous letter dropped through the mail slot. Even before then. On several occasions during the gray time since his retirement, he has actually dreamed about her. That long face — the face of a woeful horse. The kind of face that says *nobody understands* and *the whole world is against me.* All that money and still unable to count the blessings of her life, beginning with freedom from the paycheck. It had been years since Mrs. T. had had to balance her accounts or monitor her answering machine for calls from bill collectors, but she could only count the curses, totting up a long account of bad haircuts and rude service people. Mrs. Olivia Trelawney with her shapeless boatneck dresses, said boats always listed either to starboard or to port. The watery eyes that always seemed on the verge of tears. No one had liked her, and that included Detective First Grade Kermit William Hodges. No one had been surprised when she killed herself, including that selfsame Detective Hodges. The deaths of eight people — not to mention the injuries of many more — was a lot to carry on your conscience.

"Wonder about her how?" Pete asks.

"If she was telling the truth after all. About the key."

Pete raises his eyebrows. "She thought she *was* telling it. You know that as well as I do. She talked herself into it so completely she could have passed a lie-detector test."

It's true, and Olivia Trelawney hadn't been a surprise to either of them. God knows they had seen others like her. Career criminals acted guilty even when they hadn't committed the crime or crimes they had been hauled in to discuss, because they knew damned well they were guilty of *something.* Solid citizens just couldn't believe it, and when one of them wound up being questioned prior to charging, Hodges knows, it was hardly ever because a gun was involved. No, it was usually a car. *I thought it was a dog I ran over,* they'd say, and no matter what they might have seen in the rearview mirror after the awful double thump, they'd believe it.

Just a dog.

"I wonder, though," Hodges says. Hoping

he seems thoughtful rather than pushy.

"Come on, Bill. You saw what I saw, and any time you need a refresher course, you can come down to the station and look at the photos."

"I suppose."

The opening bars of "Night on Bald Mountain" sound from the pocket of Pete's Men's Wearhouse sportcoat. He digs out his phone, looks at it, and says, "I gotta take this."

Hodges makes a be-my-guest gesture.

"Hello?" Pete listens. His eyes grow wide, and he stands up so fast his chair almost falls over. *"What?"*

Other diners stop eating and look around. Hodges watches with interest.

"Yeah . . . yeah! I'll be right there. What? Yeah, yeah, okay. Don't wait, just go."

He snaps the phone closed and sits down again. All his lights are suddenly on, and in that moment Hodges envies him bitterly.

"I should eat with you more often, Billy. You're my lucky charm, always were. We talk about it, and it happens."

"What?" Thinking, It's Mr. Mercedes. The thought that follows is both ridiculous and forlorn: He was supposed to be mine.

"That was Izzy. She just got a call from a State Police colonel out in Victory County. A game warden spotted some bones in an old gravel pit about an hour ago. The pit's less than two miles from Donnie Davis's summer place on the lake, and guess what? The bones appear to be wearing the remains of a dress."

He raises his hand over the table. Hodges high-fives it.

Pete returns the phone to its sagging pocket and brings out his wallet. Hodges shakes his head, not even kidding himself about what he feels: relief. *Enormous* relief. "No, this is my treat. You're meeting Isabelle out there, right?"

"Right."

"Then roll."

"Okay. Thanks for lunch."

"One other thing — hear anything about Turnpike Joe?"

"That's State," Pete says. "And the Feebles now. They're welcome to it. What I hear is they've got nothing. Just waiting for him to do it again and hoping to get lucky." He glances at his watch.

"Go, go."

Pete starts out, stops, returns to the table, and puts a big kiss on Hodges's forehead. "Great to see you, sweetheart."

"Get lost," Hodges tells him. "People will say we're in love."

Pete scrams with a big grin on his face, and Hodges thinks of what they sometimes used to call themselves: the Hounds of Heaven.

He wonders how sharp his own nose is these days.

13

The waiter returns to ask if there will be anything else. Hodges starts to say no, then orders another cup of coffee. He just wants to sit here awhile, savoring double happiness: it wasn't Mr. Mercedes and it *was* Donnie Davis, the sanctimonious cocksucker who killed his wife and then had his lawyer set up a reward fund for information leading to her whereabouts. Because, oh Jesus, he loved her so much and all he wanted was for her to come home so they could start over.

He also wants to think about Olivia Trelawney, and Olivia Trelawney's stolen Mercedes. That it *was* stolen no one doubts. But in spite of all her protests to the contrary, no one doubts that she enabled the thief.

Hodges remembers a case that Isabelle Jaynes, then freshly arrived from San Diego, told them about after they brought her up to speed on Mrs. Trelawney's inadvertent part in the City Center Massacre. In Isabelle's story it *was* a gun. She said she and her partner had been called to a home where a nine-year-old boy had shot and killed his four-year-old sister. They had been playing with an automatic pistol their father had left on his bureau.

"The father wasn't charged, but he'll carry that for the rest of his life," she said. "This will turn out to be the same kind of thing, wait and see."

That was a month before the Trelawney woman swallowed the pills, maybe less, and nobody on the Mercedes Killer case had given much of a shit. To them — and him — Mrs. T. had just been a self-pitying rich lady who refused to accept her part in what had happened.

The Mercedes SL was downtown when it was stolen, but Mrs. Trelawney, a widow who lost her wealthy husband to a heart attack, lived in Sugar Heights, a suburb as rich as its name where lots of gated drives led up to fourteen- and twenty-room McMansions. Hodges grew up in Atlanta, and whenever he drives through Sugar Heights he thinks of a ritzy Atlanta neighborhood called Buckhead.

Mrs. T.'s elderly mother, Elizabeth Wharton, lived in an apartment — a very nice one, with rooms as big as a political candidate's promises — in an upscale condo cluster on Lake Avenue. The crib had space enough for a live-in housekeeper, and a private nurse came three days a week. Mrs. Wharton had advanced scoliosis, and it was her Oxycontin that her daughter had filched from the apartment's medicine cabinet when she decided to step out.

Suicide proves guilt. He remembers Lieutenant Morrissey saying that, but Hodges himself has always had his doubts, and lately those doubts have been stronger than ever.

What he knows now is that guilt isn't the only reason people commit suicide.

Sometimes you can just get bored with afternoon TV.

14

Two motor patrol cops found the Mercedes an hour after the killings. It was behind one of the warehouses that cluttered the lakeshore.

The huge paved yard was filled with rusty container boxes that stood around like Easter Island monoliths. The gray Mercedes was parked carelessly askew between two of them. By the time Hodges and Huntley arrived, five police cars were parked in the yard, two drawn up nose-to-nose behind the car's back bumper, as if the cops expected the big gray sedan to start up by itself, like that old Plymouth in the horror movie, and make a run for it. The fog had thickened into a light rain. The patrol car roofracks lit the droplets in conflicting pulses of blue light.

Hodges and Huntley approached the cluster of motor patrolmen. Pete Huntley spoke with the two who had discovered the car while Hodges did a walk-around. The front end of the SL500 was only slightly crumpled — that famous German engineering — but the hood and the windshield were spattered with gore. A shirtsleeve, now stiffening with blood, was

snagged in the grille. This would later be traced to August Odenkirk, one of the victims. There was something else, too. Something that gleamed even in that morning's pale light. Hodges dropped to one knee for a closer look. He was still in that position when Huntley joined him.

"What the hell is that?" Pete asked.

"I think a wedding ring," Hodges said.

So it proved. The plain gold band belonged to Francine Reis, thirty-nine, of Squirrel Ridge Road, and was eventually returned to her family. She had to be buried with it on the third finger of her right hand, because the first three fingers of the left had been torn off. The ME guessed this was because she raised it in an instinctive warding-off gesture as the Mercedes came down on her. Two of those fingers were found at the scene of the crime shortly before noon on April tenth. The index finger was never found. Hodges thought that a seagull — one of the big boys that patrolled the lakeshore — might have seized it and carried it away. He preferred that idea to the grisly alternative: that an unhurt City Center survivor had taken it as a souvenir.

Hodges stood up and motioned one of the motor patrolmen over. "We've got to get a tarp over this before the rain washes away any —"

"Already on its way," the cop said, and

cocked a thumb at Pete. “First thing he told us.”

“Well aren’t *you* special,” Hodges said in a not-too-bad Church Lady voice, but his partner’s answering smile was as pale as the day. Pete was looking at the blunt, blood-spattered snout of the Mercedes, and at the ring caught in the chrome.

Another cop came over, notebook in hand, open to a page already curling with moisture. His name-tag ID’d him as F. SHAMMINGTON. “Car’s registered to a Mrs. Olivia Ann Trelawney, 729 Lilac Drive. That’s Sugar Heights.”

“Where most good Mercedeses go to sleep when their long day’s work is done,” Hodges said. “Find out if she’s at home, Officer Shammington. If she’s not, see if you can track her down. Can you do that?”

“Yes, sir, absolutely.”

“Just routine, right? A stolen-car inquiry.”

“You got it.”

Hodges turned to Pete. “Front of the cabin. Notice anything?”

“No airbag deployment. He disabled them. Speaks to premeditation.”

“Also speaks to him knowing how to do it. What do you make of the mask?”

Pete peered through the droplets of rain on the driver’s side window, not touching the glass. Lying on the leather driver’s seat was a rubber mask, the kind you pulled over your

head. Tufts of orange Bozo-ish hair stuck up above the temples like horns. The nose was a red rubber bulb. Without a head to stretch it, the red-lipped smile had become a sneer.

"Creepy as hell. You ever see that TV movie about the clown in the sewer?"

Hodges shook his head. Later — only weeks before his retirement — he bought a DVD copy of the film, and Pete was right. The mask-face was very close to the face of Pennywise, the clown in the movie.

The two of them walked around the car again, this time noting blood on the tires and rocker panels. A lot of it was going to wash off before the tarp and the techs arrived; it was still forty minutes shy of seven A.M.

"Officers!" Hodges called, and when they gathered: "Who's got a cell phone with a camera?"

They all did. Hodges directed them into a circle around what he was already thinking of as the deathcar — one word, deathcar, just like that — and they began snapping pictures.

Officer Shammington was standing a little apart, talking on his cell phone. Pete beckoned him over. "Do you have an age on the Trelawney woman?"

Shammington consulted his notebook. "DOB on her driver's license is February third, 1957. Which makes her . . . uh . . ."

"Fifty-two," Hodges said. He and Pete Huntley had been working together for a dozen years, and by now a lot of things didn't have to be spoken aloud. Olivia Trelawney was the right sex and age for the Park Rapist, but totally wrong for the role of spree killer. They knew there had been cases of people losing control of their vehicles and accidentally driving into groups of people — only five years ago, in this very city, a man in his eighties, borderline senile, had plowed his Buick Electra into a sidewalk café, killing one and injuring half a dozen others — but Olivia Trelawney didn't fit that profile, either. Too young.

Plus, there was the mask.

But . . .

But.

15

The bill comes on a silver tray. Hodges lays his plastic on top of it and sips his coffee while he waits for it to come back. He's comfortably full, and in the middle of the day that condition usually leaves him ready for a two-hour nap. Not this afternoon. This afternoon he has never felt more awake.

The *but* had been so apparent that neither of them had to say it out loud — not to the motor patrolmen (more arriving all the time, although the goddam tarp never got there until quarter past seven) and not to each other. The doors of the SL500 were locked and the ignition slot was empty. There was no sign of tampering that either detective could see, and later that day the head mechanic from the city's Mercedes dealership confirmed that.

"How hard would it be for someone to slim-jim a window?" Hodges had asked the mechanic. "Pop the lock that way?"

"All but impossible," the mechanic had said. "These Mercs are *built.* If someone did manage to do it, it would leave signs." He had tilted his cap back on his head. "What happened is plain and simple, Officers. She left the key in the ignition and ignored the reminder chime when she got out. Her mind was probably on something else. The thief saw the key and took the car. I mean, he *must* have had the key. How else could he lock the car when he left it?"

"You keep saying *she,*" Pete said. They hadn't mentioned the owner's name.

"Hey, come on." The mechanic smiling a little now. "This is Mrs. Trelawney's Mercedes. Olivia Trelawney. She bought it at our dealership and we service it every four months, like clockwork. We only service a few twelve-cylinders, and I know them all." And then, speaking nothing but the utter grisly truth: "This baby's a tank."

The killer drove the Benz in between the two container boxes, killed the engine, pulled off his mask, doused it with bleach, and exited the car (the gloves and hairnet probably tucked inside his jacket). Then a final fuck-you as he walked away into the fog: he locked the car with Olivia Ann Trelawney's smart key.

There was your *but.*

16

She warned us to be quiet because her mother was sleeping, Hodges remembers. Then she gave us coffee and cookies. Sitting in DeMasio's, he sips the last of his current cup while he waits for his credit card to be returned. He thinks about the living room in that whopper of a condo apartment, with its kick-ass view of the lake.

Along with coffee and cookies, she had given them the wide-eyed *of-course-I-didn't* look, the one that is the exclusive property of solid citizens who have never been in trouble with the police. Who can't imagine such a thing. She even said it out loud, when Pete asked if it was possible she had left her ignition key in her car when she parked it on Lake Avenue just a few doors down from her mother's building.

"Of course I didn't." The words had come through a cramped little smile that said *I find your idea silly and more than a bit insulting.*

The waiter returns at last. He puts down the little silver tray, and Hodges slips a ten and a five into his hand before he can straighten up. At DeMasio's the waiters split tips, a practice of which Hodges strongly disapproves. If that makes him old school, so be it.

"Thank you, sir, and *buon pomeriggio.*"

"Back atcha," Hodges says. He tucks away his receipt and his Amex, but doesn't rise immediately. There are some crumbs left on his dessert plate, and he uses his fork to snare them, just as he used to do with his mother's cakes when he was a little boy. To him those last few crumbs, sucked slowly onto the tongue from between the tines of the fork, always seemed like the sweetest part of the slice.

17

That crucial first interview, only hours after the crime. Coffee and cookies while the mangled bodies of the dead were still being identified. Somewhere relatives were weeping and rending their garments.

Mrs. Trelawney walking into the condo's front hall, where her handbag sat on an occasional table. She brought the bag back, rummaging, starting to frown, still rummaging, starting to be a little worried. Then smiling. "Here it is," she said, and handed it over.

The detectives looked at the smart key, Hodges thinking how ordinary it was for something that went with such an expensive car. It was basically a black plastic stick with a lump on the end of it. The lump was stamped with the Mercedes logo on one side. On the other were three buttons. One showed a padlock with its shackle down. On the button beside it, the padlock's shackle was up. The third button was labeled PANIC. Presumably if a mugger attacked you as you were unlocking your car, you could push that one and the car would start screaming for help.

"I can see why you had a little trouble locating it in your purse," Pete remarked in his best just-passing-the-time-of-day voice. "Most people put a fob on their keys. My wife has hers on a big plastic daisy." He smiled fondly as if Maureen were still his wife, and as if that perfectly turned-out fashion plate would ever have been caught dead hauling a plastic daisy out of her purse.

"How nice for her," Mrs. Trelawney said. "When may I have my car back?"

"That's not up to us, ma'am," Hodges said.

She sighed and straightened the boatneck top of her dress. It was the first of dozens of times they saw her do it. "I'll have to sell it, of course. I'd never be able to drive it after this. It's so upsetting. To think *my* car . . ." Now that she had her purse in hand, she prospected again and brought out a wad of pastel Kleenex. She dabbed at her eyes with them. "It's *very* upsetting."

"I'd like you to take us through it one more time," Pete said.

She rolled her eyes, which were red-rimmed and bloodshot. "Is that really necessary? I'm exhausted. I was up most of the night with my mother. She couldn't go to sleep until four. She's in such pain. I'd like a nap before Mrs. Greene comes in. She's the nurse."

Hodges thought, Your car was just used to kill eight people, and only eight if all the others live, and you want a nap. Later he would not be sure if that was when he started to dislike Mrs. Trelawney, but it probably was. When some people were in distress, you wanted to enfold them and say *there-there* as you patted them on the back. With others you wanted to slap them a hard one across the chops and tell them to man up. Or, in Mrs. T.'s case, to woman up.

"We'll be as quick as we can," Pete promised. He didn't tell her that this would be the first of many interviews. By the time they were done with her, she would hear herself telling her story in her sleep.

"Oh, very well, then. I arrived here at my mother's shortly after seven o'clock on Thursday evening . . ."

She visited at least four times a week, she said, but Thursdays were her night to stay over. She always stopped at B'hai, a very nice vegetarian restaurant located in Birch Hill Mall, and got their dinners, which she warmed up in the oven. ("Although Mother eats very little now, of course. Because of the pain.") She told them she always scheduled her Thursday trips so she arrived after seven, because that was when the all-night parking began, and most of the streetside spaces were empty. "I won't parallel park. I simply can't do it."

"What about the garage down the block?" Hodges asked.

She looked at him as though he were crazy. "It costs sixteen dollars to park there overnight. The streetside spaces are *free.*"

Pete was still holding the key, although he hadn't yet told Mrs. Trelawney they would be taking it with them. "You stopped at Birch Hill and ordered takeout for you and your mother at —" He consulted his notebook. "B'hai."

"No, I ordered ahead. From my house on Lilac Drive. They are always glad to hear from me. I am an old and valued customer. Last night it was kookoo sabzi for Mother — that's an herbal omelet with spinach and cilantro — and gheymeh for me. Gheymeh is a lovely stew with peas, potatoes, and mushrooms. Very easy on the stomach." She straightened her boatneck. "I've had terrible acid reflux ever since I was in my teens. One learns to live with it."

"I assume your order was —" Hodges began.

"And sholeh zard for dessert," she added. "That's rice pudding with cinnamon. And saffron." She flashed her strangely troubled smile. Like the compulsive straightening of her boatneck tops, the smile was a Trelawney-ism with which they would become very familiar. "It's the saffron that makes it special. Even Mother always eats the sholeh zard."

"Sounds tasty," Hodges said. "And your order, was it boxed and ready to go when you got there?"

"Yes."

"One box?"

"Oh no, three."

"In a bag?"

"No, just the boxes."

"Must have been quite a struggle, getting all that out of your car," Pete said. "Three boxes of takeout, your purse . . ."

"And the key," Hodges said. "Don't forget that, Pete."

"Also, you'd want to get it all upstairs as fast as possible," Pete said. "Cold food's no fun."

"I see where you're going with this," Mrs. Trelawney said, "and I assure you . . ." A slight pause. ". . . you *gentlemen* that you are barking up the wrong path. I put my key in my purse as soon as I turned off the engine, it's the first thing I always do. As for the boxes, they were tied together in a stack . . ."

She held her hands about eighteen inches apart to demonstrate. ". . . and that made them very easy to handle. I had my purse over my arm. Look." She crooked her arm, hung her purse on it, and marched around the big living room, holding a stack of invisible boxes from B'hai. "See?"

"Yes, ma'am," Hodges said. He thought he saw something else as well.

"As for hurrying — no. There was no need, since the dinners need to be heated up, anyway." She paused. "Not the sholeh zard, of course. No need to heat up rice pudding." She uttered a small laugh. Not a giggle, Hodges thought, but a titter. Given that her husband was dead, he supposed you could even call it a widder-titter. His dislike added another layer — almost thin enough to be invisible, but not quite. No, not quite.

"So let me review your actions once you got here to Lake Avenue," Hodges said. "Where you arrived at a little past seven."

"Yes. Five past, perhaps a little more."

"Uh-huh. You parked . . . what? Three or four doors down?"

"Four at most. All I need are two empty spaces, so I can pull in without backing. I hate to back. I always turn the wrong way."

"Yes, ma'am, my wife has exactly the same problem. You turned off the engine. You removed the key from the ignition and put it in your purse. You put your purse over your arm and picked up the boxes with the food in them —"

"The *stack* of boxes. Tied together with good stout string."

"The stack, right. Then what?"

She looked at him as though he were, of all the idiots in a generally idiotic world, the greatest. "Then I went to my mother's building. Mrs. Harris — the housekeeper, you know — buzzed me in. On Thursdays, she leaves as soon as I arrive. I took the elevator up to the nineteenth floor. Where you are now asking me questions instead of telling me when I can deal with my car. My *stolen* car."

Hodges made a mental note to ask the housekeeper if she had noticed Mrs. T.'s Mercedes when she left.

Pete asked, "At what point did you take your key from your purse again, Mrs. Trelawney?"

"Again? Why would I —"

He held the key up — Exhibit A. "To lock your car before you entered the building. You *did* lock it, didn't you?"

A brief uncertainty flashed in her eyes. They both saw it. Then it was gone. "Of course I did."

Hodges pinned her gaze. It shifted away, toward the lake view out the big picture window, and he caught it again. "Think carefully, Mrs. Trelawney. People are dead, and this is important. Do you specifically remember juggling those boxes of food so you could get your key out of your purse and push the LOCK button? And seeing the headlights flash an acknowledgement? They do that, you know."

"Of *course* I know." She bit at her lower lip, realized she was doing it, stopped.

"Do you remember that specifically?"

For a moment all expression left her face. Then that superior smile burst forth in all its irritating glory. "Wait. Now I remember. I put the key in my purse *after* I gathered up my boxes and got out. And after I pushed the button that locks the car."

"You're sure," Pete said.

"Yes." She was, and would remain so. They both knew that. The way a solid citizen who hit and ran would say, when he was finally tracked down, that of *course* it was a dog he'd hit.

Pete flipped his notebook closed and stood up. Hodges did likewise. Mrs. Trelawney looked more than eager to escort them to the door.

"One more question," Hodges said as they reached it.

She raised carefully plucked eyebrows. "Yes?"

"Where's your spare key? We ought to take that one, too."

There was no blank look this time, no cutting away of the eyes, no hesitation. She said,

"I have no spare key, and no need of one. I'm very careful of my things, Officer. I've owned my Gray Lady — that's what I call it — for five years, and the only key I've ever used is now in your partner's pocket."

18

The table where he and Pete ate their lunch has been cleared of everything but his half-finished glass of water, yet Hodges goes on sitting there, staring out the window at the parking lot and the overpass that marks the unofficial border of Lowtown, where Sugar Heights residents like the late Olivia Trelawney never venture. Why would they? To buy drugs? Hodges is sure there are druggies in the Heights, plenty of them, but when you live there, the dealers make housecalls.

Mrs. T. was lying. She *had* to lie. It was that or face the fact that a single moment of forgetfulness had led to horrific consequences.

Suppose, though — just for the sake of argument — that she was telling the truth.

Okay, let's suppose. But if we were wrong about her leaving her Mercedes unlocked with the key in the ignition, how were we wrong? And what *did* happen?

He sits looking out the window, remembering, unaware that some of the waiters have begun to look at him uneasily — the overweight retiree sitting slumped in his seat like a robot with dead batteries.

19

The *deathcar* had been transported to Police Impound on a carrier, still locked. Hodges and Huntley received this update when they got back to their own car. The head mechanic from Ross Mercedes had just arrived, and was pretty sure he could unlock the damn thing. Eventually.

"Tell him not to bother," Hodges said. "We've got her key."

There was a pause at the other end, and then Lieutenant Morrissey said, "You do? You're not saying *she* —"

"No, no, nothing like that. Is the mechanic standing by, Lieutenant?"

"He's in the yard, looking at the damage to the car. Damn near tears, is what I heard."

"He might want to save a drop or two for the dead people," Pete said. He was driving. The windshield wipers beat back and forth. The rain was coming harder. "Just sayin."

"Tell him to get in touch with the dealership and check something," Hodges said. "Then have him call me on my cell."

The traffic was snarled downtown, partly because of the rain, partly because Marlborough Street had been blocked off at City Center. They had made only four blocks when Hodges's cell rang. It was Howard McGrory, the mechanic.

"Did you have someone at the dealership check on what I was curious about?" Hodges asked him.

"No need," McGrory said. "I've worked at Ross since 1987. Must have seen a thousand Mercs go out the door since then, and I can tell you they all go out with two keys."

"Thanks," Hodges said. "We'll be there soon. Got some more questions for you."

"I'll be here. This is terrible. *Terrible.*"

Hodges ended the call and passed on what McGrory had said.

"Are you surprised?" Pete asked. Ahead was an orange DETOUR sign that would vector them around City Center . . . unless they wanted to light their blues, that was, and neither did. What they needed now was to talk.

"Nope," Hodges said. "It's standard operating procedure. Like the Brits say, an heir and a spare. They give you two keys when you buy your new car —"

"— and tell you to put one in a safe place, so you can lay hands on it if you lose the one you carry around. Some people, if they need the spare a year or two later, they've forgotten where they put it. Women who carry big purses — like that suitcase the Trelawney woman had — are apt to dump both keys into it and forget all about the extra one. If she's telling the truth about not putting it on a fob, she was probably using them interchangeably."

"Yeah," Hodges said. "She gets to her mother's, she's preoccupied with the thought of spending another night dealing with Mom's pain, she's juggling the boxes and her purse . . ."

"And left the key in the ignition. She doesn't want to admit it — not to us and not to herself — but that's what she did."

"Although the warning chime . . ." Hodges said doubtfully.

"Maybe a big noisy truck was going by as she was getting out and she didn't hear the chime. Or a police car, winding its siren. Or maybe she was just so deep in her own thoughts she ignored it."

It made sense then and even more later when McGrory told them the deathcar hadn't been jimmied to gain entry or hotwired to start. What troubled Hodges — the only thing that troubled him, really — was how much he *wanted* it to make sense. Neither of them had liked Mrs. Trelawney, she of the boatneck tops, perfectly plucked brows, and squeaky widder-titter. Mrs. Trelawney who hadn't asked for any news of the dead and injured, not so much as a single detail. She wasn't the doer — no way was she — but it would be good to stick her with some of the blame. Give her something to think about besides veggie dinners from B'hai.

"Don't complicate what's simple," his partner repeated. The traffic snarl had cleared and he put the pedal down. "She was given two keys. She claims she only had one. And now it's the truth. The bastard who killed those people probably threw the one she left in the ignition down a handy sewer when he walked away. The one she showed us was the spare."

That had to be the answer. When you heard hoofbeats, you didn't think zebras.

20

Someone is shaking him gently, the way you shake a heavy sleeper. And, Hodges realizes, he almost *has* been asleep. Or hypnotized by recollection.

It's Elaine, the DeMasio's hostess, and she's looking at him with concern. "Detective Hodges? Are you all right?"

"Fine. But it's just Mr. Hodges now, Elaine. I'm retired."

He sees concern in her eyes, and something more. Something worse. He's the only patron left in the restaurant. He observes the waiters clustered around the doorway to the kitchen, and suddenly sees himself as they and Elaine must be seeing him, an old fellow who's been sitting here long after his dining companion (and everyone else) has left. An old overweight fellow who sucked the last of his cake off his fork like a child sucking a lollipop and then just stared out the window.

They're wondering if I'm riding into the Kingdom of Dementia on the Alzheimer's Express, he thinks.

He smiles at Elaine — his number one, wide and charming. "Pete and I were talking about old cases. I was thinking about one. Kind of replaying it. Sorry. I'll clear out now."

But when he gets up he staggers and bumps the table, knocking over the half-empty water glass. Elaine grabs his shoulder to steady him, looking more concerned than ever.

"Detective . . . Mr. Hodges, are you okay to drive?"

"Sure," he says, too heartily. Pins and needles are doing wind-sprints from his ankles to his crotch and then back down to his ankles again. "Just had two glasses of beer. Pete drank the rest. My legs went to sleep, that's all."

"Oh. Are you better now?"

"Fine," he says, and his legs really are better. Thank God. He remembers reading somewhere that older men, especially older overweight men, should not sit too long. A blood clot can form behind the knee. You get up, the released clot does its own lethal wind-sprint up to the heart, and it's angel, angel, down we go.

She walks with him to the door. Hodges

finds himself thinking of the private nurse whose job it was to watch over Mrs. T.'s mother. What was her name? Harris? No, Harris was the housekeeper. The nurse was Greene. When Mrs. Wharton wanted to go into the living room, or visit the jakes, did Mrs. Greene escort her the way Elaine is escorting him now? Of course she did.

"Elaine, I'm fine," he says. "Really. Sober mind. Body in balance." He holds his arms out to demonstrate.

"All right," she says. "Come see us again, and next time don't wait so long."

"It's a promise."

He looks at his watch as he pushes out into the bright sunshine. Past two. He's missing his afternoon shows, and doesn't mind a bit. The lady judge and the Nazi psychologist can go fuck themselves. Or each other.

21

He walks slowly into the parking lot, where the only cars left, other than his, likely belong to the restaurant staff. He takes his keys out and jingles them on his palm. Unlike Mrs. T.'s, the key to his Toyota is on a ring. And yes, there's a fob — a rectangle of plastic with a picture of his daughter beneath. Allie at seventeen, smiling and wearing her City High lacrosse uni.

In the matter of the Mercedes key, Mrs.

Trelawney never recanted. Through all the interviews, she continued to insist she'd only ever had the one. Even after Pete Huntley showed her the invoice, with PRIMARY KEYS (2) on the list of items that went with her new car when she took possession back in 2004, she continued to insist. She said the invoice was mistaken. Hodges remembers the iron certainty in her voice.

Pete would say that she copped to it in the end. There was no need of a note; suicide is a confession by its very nature. Her wall of denial finally crumbled. Like when the guy who hit and ran finally gets it off his chest. *Yes, okay, it was a kid, not a dog. It was a kid and I was looking at my cell phone to see whose call I missed and I killed him.*

Hodges remembers how their subsequent interviews with Mrs. T. had produced a weird kind of amplifying effect. The more she denied, the more they disliked. Not just Hodges and Huntley but the whole squad. And the more they disliked, the more stridently she denied. Because she knew how they felt. Oh yes. She was self-involved, but not stu—

Hodges stops, one hand on the sun-warmed doorhandle of his car, the other shading his eyes. He's looking into the shadows beneath the turnpike overpass. It's almost mid-afternoon, and the denizens of Lowtown have begun to rise from their crypts. Four of them are in those shadows. Three big 'uns and one little 'un. The big 'uns appear to be pushing the little 'un around. The little 'un is wearing a pack, and as Hodges watches, one of the big 'uns rips it from his back. This provokes a burst of troll-like laughter.

Hodges strolls down the broken sidewalk to the overpass. He doesn't think about it and he doesn't hurry. He stuffs his hands in his sportcoat pockets. Cars and trucks drone by on the turnpike extension, projecting their shapes on the street below in a series of shadow-shutters. He hears one of the trolls asking the little kid how much money he's got.

"Ain't got none," the little kid says. "Lea me lone."

"Turn out your pockets and we see," Troll Two says.

The kid tries to run instead. Troll Three wraps his arms around the kid's skinny chest from behind. Troll One grabs at the kid's pockets and squeezes. "Yo, yo, I hear foldin money," he says, and the little kid's face squinches up in an effort not to cry.

"My brother finds out who you are, he bust a cap on y'asses," he says.

"That's a terrifyin idea," Troll One says. "Just about make me want to pee my —"

Then he sees Hodges, ambling into the shadows to join them with his belly leading the way. His hands deep in the pockets of his old shapeless houndstooth check, the one with the patches on the elbows, the one he can't bear to give up even though he knows it's shot to shit.

"Whatchoo want?" Troll Three asks. He's still hugging the kid from behind.

Hodges considers trying a John Wayne drawl, and decides not to. The only Wayne these scuzzbags would know is L'il. "I want you to leave the little man alone," he says. "Get out of here. Right now."

Troll One lets go of the little 'un's pockets. He is wearing a hoodie and the obligatory Yankees cap. He puts his hands on his slim hips and cocks his head to one side, looking amused. "Fuck off, fatty."

Hodges doesn't waste time. There are three of them, after all. He takes the Happy Slapper from his right coat pocket, liking its old comforting weight. The Slapper is an argyle sock. The foot part is filled with ball bearings. It's knotted at the ankle to make sure the steel balls stay in. He swings it at the side of Troll One's neck in a tight, flat arc, careful to steer clear of the Adam's apple; hit a guy there, you were apt to kill him, and then you were stuck in the bureaucracy.

There's a metallic *thwap.* Troll One lurches sideways, his look of amusement turning to pained surprise. He stumbles off the curb and falls into the street. He rolls onto his back, gagging, clutching his neck, staring up at the underside of the overpass.

Troll Three starts forward. "Fuckin —" he begins, and then Hodges lifts his leg (pins and needles all gone, thank God) and kicks him briskly in the crotch. He hears the seat of his trousers rip and thinks, Oh you fat fuck. Troll Three lets out a yowl of pain. Under here, with the cars and trucks passing overhead, the sound is strangely flat. He doubles over.

Hodges's left hand is still in his coat. He extends his index finger so it pokes out the pocket and points it at Troll Two. "Hey, fuck-face, no need to wait for the little man's big brother. I'll bust a cap on your ass myself. Three-on-one pisses me off."

"No, man, no!" Troll Two is tall, well built, maybe fifteen, but his terror regresses him to no more than twelve. "Please, man, we 'us just playin!"

"Then run, playboy," Hodges says. "Do it now."

Troll Two runs.

Troll One, meanwhile, has gotten on his knees. "You gonna regret this, fat ma—"

Hodges takes a step toward him, lifting the Slapper. Troll One sees it, gives a girly shriek, covers his neck.

"You better run, too," Hodges says, "or the fat man's going to tool up on your face. When your mama gets to the emergency room, she'll walk right past you." In that moment, with his adrenaline flowing and his blood pressure probably over two hundred, he absolutely means it.

Troll One gets up. Hodges makes a mock lunge at him, and Troll One jerks back most satisfyingly.

"Take your friend with you and pack some ice on his balls," Hodges says. "They're going to swell."

Troll One gets his arm around Troll Three, and they hobble toward the Lowtown side of the overpass. When Troll One considers himself safe, he turns back and says, "I see you again, fat man."

"Pray to God you don't, fuckwit," Hodges says.

He picks up the backpack and hands it to the kid, who's looking at him with wide mistrustful eyes. He might be ten. Hodges drops the Slapper back into his pocket. "Why aren't you in school, little man?"

"My mama sick. I goin to get her medicine."

This is a lie so audacious that Hodges has to grin. "No, you're not," he says. "You're skipping."

The kid says nothing. This is five-o, nobody else would step to it the way this guy did. Nobody else would have a loaded sock in his pocket, either. Safer to dummy up.

"You go skip someplace safer," Hodges says. "There's a playground on Eighth Avenue. Try there."

"They sellin the rock on that playground," the kid says.

"I know," Hodges says, almost kindly, "but you don't have to buy any." He could add You don't have to run any, either, but that would be naïve. Down in Lowtown, most of the shorties run it. You can bust a ten-year-old for possession, but try making it stick.

He starts back to the parking lot, on the safe side of the overpass. When he glances back, the kid is still standing there and looking at him. Pack dangling from one hand.

"Little man," Hodges says.

The kid looks at him, saying nothing.

Hodges lifts one hand and points at him. "I did something good for you just now. Before the sun goes down tonight, I want you to pass it on."

Now the kid's look is one of utter incomprehension, as if Hodges just lapsed into a foreign language, but that's all right. Sometimes it seeps through, especially with the young ones.

People would be surprised, Hodges thinks. They really would.

22

Brady Hartsfield changes into his other uniform — the white one — and checks his truck, quickly going through the inventory sheet the way Mr. Loeb likes. Everything is there. He pops his head in the office to say hi to Shirley Orton. Shirley is a fat pig, all too fond of the company product, but he wants to stay on her good side. Brady wants to stay on *everyone's* good side. Much safer that way. She has a crush on him, and that helps.

"Shirley, you pretty girly!" he cries, and she blushes all the way up to the hairline of her pimple-studded forehead. Little piggy, oink-oink-oink, Brady thinks. You're so fat your cunt probably turns inside out when you sit down.

"Hi, Brady. West Side again?"

"All week, darlin. You okay?"

"Fine." Blushing harder than ever.

"Good. Just wanted to say howdy."

Then he's off, obeying every speed limit even though it takes him forty fucking minutes to get into his territory driving that slow. But it has to be that way. Get caught speeding in a company truck after the schools let out for the day, you get canned. No recourse. But when he gets to the West Side — this is the good part — he's in Hodges's neighborhood, and with every reason to be there. Hide in plain sight, that's the old saying, and as far as Brady is concerned, it's a wise saying, indeed.

He turns off Spruce Street and cruises slowly down Harper Road, right past the old Det-Ret's house. Oh look here, he thinks.

The niggerkid is out front, stripped to the waist (so all the stay-at-home mommies can get a good look at his sweat-oiled sixpack, no doubt) and pushing a Lawn-Boy.

About time you got after that, Brady thinks. It was looking mighty shaggy. Not that the old Det-Ret probably took much notice. The old Det-Ret was too busy watching TV, eating Pop-Tarts, and playing with that gun he kept on the table beside his chair.

The niggerkid hears him coming even over the roar of the mower and turns to look. I know your name, niggerkid, Brady thinks. It's Jerome Robinson. I know almost everything about the old Det-Ret. I don't know if he's queer for you, but I wouldn't be surprised. It could be why he keeps you around.

From behind the wheel of his little Mr. Tastey truck, which is covered with happy kid decals and jingles with happy recorded bells, Brady waves. The niggerkid waves back and smiles. Sure he does.

Everybody likes the ice cream man.

Under Debbie's Blue Umbrella

1

Brady Hartsfield cruises the tangle of West Side streets until seven-thirty, when dusk starts to drain the blue from the late spring sky. His first wave of customers, between three and six P.M., consists of after-school kids wearing backpacks and waving crumpled dollar bills. Most don't even look at him. They're too busy blabbing to their buddies or talking into the cell phones they see not as accessories but as necessities every bit as vital as food and air. A few of them say thank you, but most don't bother. Brady doesn't mind. He doesn't want to be looked at and he doesn't want to be remembered. To these brats he's just the sugar-pusher in the white uniform, and that's the way he likes it.

From six to seven is dead time, while the little animals go in for their dinners. Maybe a few — the ones who say thank you — even talk to their parents. Most probably go right on poking the buttons of their phones while Mommy and Daddy yak to each other about their jobs or watch the evening news so they can find out all about the big world out there, where movers and shakers are actually doing shit.

During his last half hour, business picks up again. This time it's the parents as well as the kids who approach the jingling Mr. Tastey truck, buying ice cream treats they'll eat with their asses (mostly fat ones) snugged down in backyard lawnchairs. He almost pities them. They are people of little vision, as stupid as ants crawling around their hill. A mass killer is serving them ice cream, and they have no idea.

From time to time, Brady has wondered how hard it would be to poison a truckload of treats: the vanilla, the chocolate, the Berry Good, the Flavor of the Day, the Tastey Frosteys, the Brownie Delites, even the Freeze-Stix and Whistle Pops. He has gone so far as to research this on the Internet. He has done what Anthony "Tones" Frobisher, his boss at Discount Electronix, would probably call a "feasibility study," and concluded that, while it would be possible, it would also be stupid. It's not that he's averse to taking a risk; he got away with the Mercedes Massacre when the odds of being caught were better than those of getting away clean. But he doesn't want to be caught now. He's got work to do. His work this late spring and early summer is the fat ex-cop, K. William

Hodges.

He might cruise his West Side route with a truckload of poisoned ice cream after the ex-cop gets tired of playing with the gun he keeps beside his living room chair and actually uses it. But not until. The fat ex-cop bugs Brady Hartsfield. Bugs him bad. Hodges retired with full honors, they even threw him a *party,* and how was that right when he had failed to catch the most notorious criminal this city had ever seen?

2

On his last circuit of the day, he cruises by the house on Teaberry Lane where Jerome Robinson, Hodges's hired boy, lives with his mother, father, and kid sister. Jerome Robinson also bugs Brady. Robinson is good-looking, he works for the ex-cop, and he goes out every weekend with different girls. All of the girls are pretty. Some are even white. That's wrong. It's against nature.

"Hey!" Robinson cries. "Mr. Ice Cream Man! Wait up!"

He sprints lightly across his lawn with his dog, a big Irish setter, running at his heels. Behind them comes the kid sister, who is about nine.

"Get me a chocolate, Jerry!" she cries. *"Pleeeease?"*

He even has a white kid's name. Jerome.

Jerry. It's offensive. Why can't he be Traymore? Or Devon? Or Leroy? Why can't he be fucking Kunta Kinte?

Jerome's feet are sockless in his moccasins, his ankles still green from cutting the ex-cop's lawn. He's got a big smile on his undeniably handsome face, and when he flashes it at his weekend dates, Brady just bets those girls drop their pants and hold out their arms. Come on in, *Jerry.*

Brady himself has never been with a girl.

"How you doin, man?" Jerome asks.

Brady, who has left the wheel and now stands at the service window, grins. "I'm fine. It's almost quitting time, and that always makes me fine."

"You have any chocolate left? The Little Mermaid there wants some."

Brady gives him a thumbs-up, still grinning. It's pretty much the same grin he was wearing under the clown mask when he tore into the crowd of sad-sack job-seekers at City Center with the accelerator pedal pushed to the mat. "It's a big ten-four on the chocolate, my friend."

The little sister arrives, eyes sparkling, braids bouncing. "Don't you call me Little Mermaid, Jere, I hate that!"

She's nine or so, and also has a ridiculously white name: Barbara. Brady finds the idea of a black child named Barbara so surreal it's not even offensive. The only one in the family with a nigger name is the dog, standing on his hind legs with his paws planted on the side of the truck and his tail wagging.

"Down, Odell!" Jerome says, and the dog sits, panting and looking cheerful.

"What about you?" Brady asks Jerome. "Something for you?"

"A vanilla soft-serve, please."

Vanilla's what you'd like to be, Brady thinks, and gets them their orders.

He likes to keep an eye on Jerome, he likes to *know about* Jerome, because these days Jerome seems to be the only person who spends any time with the Det-Ret, and in the last two months Brady has observed them together enough to see that Hodges treats the kid as a friend as well as a part-time employee. Brady has never had friends himself, friends are dangerous, but he knows what they are: sops to the ego. Emotional safety nets. When you're feeling bad, who do you turn to? Your friends, of course, and your friends say stuff like *aw gee* and *cheer up* and *we're with you* and *let's go out for a drink.* Jerome is only seventeen, not yet old enough to go out with Hodges for a drink (unless it's soda), but he can always say *cheer up* and *I'm with you.* So he bears watching.

Mrs. Trelawney didn't have any friends. No husband, either. Just her old sick mommy. Which made her easy meat, especially after the cops started working her over. Why, they had done half of Brady's work for him. The rest he did for himself, pretty much right under the scrawny bitch's nose.

"Here you go," Brady says, handing Jerome ice cream treats he wishes were spiked with arsenic. Or maybe warfarin. Load them up with that and they'd bleed out from their eyes and ears and mouths. Not to mention their assholes. He imagines all the kids on the West Side dropping their packs and their precious cell phones while the blood poured from every orifice. What a disaster movie that would make!

Jerome gives him a ten, and along with his change, Brady hands back a dog biscuit. "For Odell," he says.

"Thanks, mister!" Barbara says, and licks her chocolate cone. "This is good!"

"Enjoy it, honey."

He drives the Mr. Tastey truck, and he frequently drives a Cyber Patrol VW on out-calls, but his real job this summer is Detective K. William Hodges (Ret.). And making sure Detective Hodges (Ret.) uses that gun.

Brady heads back toward Loeb's Ice Cream Factory to turn in his truck and change into his street clothes. He keeps to the speed limit the whole way.

Always safe, never sorry.

3

After leaving DeMasio's — with a side-trip to deal with the bullies hassling the little kid beneath the turnpike extension overpass — Hodges simply drives, piloting his Toyota through the city streets without any destination in mind. Or so he thinks until he realizes he is on Lilac Drive in the posh lakeside suburb of Sugar Heights. There he pulls over and parks across the street from a gated drive with a plaque reading 729 on one of the fieldstone posts.

The late Olivia Trelawney's house stands at the top of an asphalt drive almost as wide as the street it fronts. On the gate is a FOR SALE sign inviting Qualified Buyers to call MICHAEL ZAFRON REALTY & FINE HOMES. Hodges thinks that sign is apt to be there awhile, given the housing market in this Year of Our Lord, 2010. But somebody is keeping the grass cut, and given the size of the lawn, the somebody must be using a mower a lot bigger than Hodges's Lawn-Boy.

Who's paying for the upkeep? Got to be Mrs. T.'s estate. She had certainly been rolling in dough. He seems to recall that the probated figure was in the neighborhood of seven million dollars. For the first time since his retirement, when he turned the unsolved case of the City Center Massacre over to Pete Huntley and Isabelle Jaynes, Hodges wonders if Mrs. T.'s mother is still alive. He remembers the scoliosis that bent the poor old lady almost double, and left her in terrible pain . . . but scoliosis isn't necessarily fatal. Also, hadn't Olivia Trelawney had a sister living somewhere out west?

He fishes for the sister's name but can't come up with it. What he does remember is that Pete took to calling Mrs. Trelawney Mrs. Twitchy, because she couldn't stop adjusting her clothes, and brushing at tightly bunned hair that needed no brushing, and fiddling with the gold band of her Patek Philippe watch, turning it around and around on her bony wrist. Hodges disliked her; Pete had almost come to loathe her. Which made saddling her with some of the blame for the City Center atrocity rather satisfying. She had enabled the guy, after all; how could there be any doubt? She had been given two keys when she bought the Mercedes, but had been able to produce only one.

Then, shortly before Thanksgiving, the suicide.

Hodges remembers clearly what Pete said when they got the news: "If she meets those dead people on the other side — especially the Cray girl and her baby — she's going to have some serious questions to answer." For Pete it had been the final confirmation: somewhere in her mind, Mrs. T. had known all along that she had left her key in the ignition of the car she called her Gray Lady.

Hodges had believed it, too. The question is, does he still? Or has the poison-pen letter he got yesterday from the self-confessed Mercedes Killer changed his mind?

Maybe not, but that letter raises questions. Suppose Mr. Mercedes had written a similar missive to Mrs. Trelawney? Mrs. Trelawney with all those tics and insecurities just below a thin crust of defiance? Wasn't it possible? Mr. Mercedes certainly would have known about the anger and contempt with which the public had showered her in the wake of the killings; all he had to do was read the Letters to the Editor page of the local paper.

Is it possible —

But here his thoughts break off, because a car has pulled up behind him, so close it's almost touching his Toyota's bumper. There are no jackpot lights on the roof, but it's a late-model Crown Vic, powder blue. The man getting out from behind the wheel is burly and crewcut, his sportcoat no doubt covering a gun in a shoulder holster. If this were a city detective, Hodges knows, the gun would be a Glock .40, just like the one in his safe at home. But he's not a city detective. Hodges still knows them all.

He rolls down his window.

"Afternoon, sir," Crewcut says. "May I ask what you're doing here? Because you've been parked quite awhile."

Hodges glances at his watch and sees this is true. It's almost four-thirty. Given the rush-hour traffic downtown, he'll be lucky to get home in time to watch Scott Pelley on *CBS Evening News.* He used to watch NBC until he decided Brian Williams was a good-natured goof who's too fond of YouTube videos. Not the sort of newscaster he wants when it seems like the whole world is falling apa—

"Sir? Sincerely hoping for an answer here." Crewcut bends down. The side of his sport-coat gapes open. Not a Glock but a Ruger. Sort of a cowboy gun, in Hodges's opinion.

"And I," Hodges says, "am sincerely hoping you have the authority to ask."

His interlocutor's brow creases. "Beg pardon?"

"I think you're private security," Hodges says patiently, "but I want to see some ID. Then, you know what? I want to see your carry-concealed permit for the cannon you've got inside your coat. And it better be in your wallet and not in the glove compartment of your car, or you're in violation of section nineteen of the city firearms code, which, briefly stated, is this: 'If you carry concealed, you must also carry your *permit* to carry concealed.' So let's see your paperwork."

Crewcut's frown deepens. "Are you a cop?"

"Retired," Hodges says, "but that doesn't mean I've forgotten either my rights or your responsibilities. Let me see your ID and your carry permit, please. You don't have to hand them over —"

"You're damn right I don't."

"— but I want to see them. Then we can discuss my presence here on Lilac Drive."

Crewcut thinks it over, but only for a few seconds. Then he takes out his wallet and flips it open. In this city — as in most, Hodges thinks — security personnel treat retired cops as they would those on active duty, because retired cops have plenty of friends who *are* on active duty, and who can make life difficult if given a reason to do so. The guy turns out to be Radney Peeples, and his company card identifies him as an employee of Vigilant Guard Service. He also shows Hodges a permit to carry concealed, which is good until June of 2012.

"Radney, not Rodney," Hodges says. "Like Radney Foster, the country singer."

Foster's face breaks into a grin. "That's right."

"Mr. Peeples, my name is Bill Hodges, I ended my tour as a Detective First Class, and my last big case was the Mercedes Killer. I'm guessing that'll give you a pretty good idea of what I'm doing here."

"Mrs. Trelawney," Foster says, and steps back respectfully as Hodges opens his car door, gets out, and stretches. "Little trip down Memory Lane, Detective?"

"I'm just a mister these days." Hodges offers his hand. Peeples shakes it. "Otherwise, you're correct. I retired from the cops at about the same time Mrs. Trelawney retired from life in general."

"That was sad," Peeples said. "Do you know that kids egged her gate? Not just at Halloween, either. Three or four times. We caught one bunch, the others . . ." He shook his head. "Plus toilet paper."

"Yeah, they love that," Hodges says.

"And one night someone tagged the left-hand gatepost. We got it taken care of before she saw it, and I'm glad. You know what it said?"

Hodges shakes his head.

Peeples lowers his voice. "KILLER CUNT is what it said, in big drippy capital letters. Which was absolutely not fair. She goofed up, that's all. Is there any of us who haven't at one time or another?"

"Not me, that's for sure," Hodges says.

"Right. Bible says let him who is without sin cast the first stone."

That'll be the day, Hodges thinks, and asks (with honest curiosity), "Did you like her?"

Peeples's eyes shift up and to the left, an involuntary movement Hodges has seen in a great many interrogation rooms over the years. It means Peeples is either going to duck the question or outright lie.

It turns out to be a duck.

"Well," he says, "she treated us right at Christmas. She sometimes mixed up the names, but she knew who we all were, and we each got forty dollars and a bottle of whiskey. *Good* whiskey. Do you think we got that from her husband?" He snorts. "Ten bucks tucked inside a Hallmark card was what we got when that skinflint was still in the saddle."

"Who exactly does Vigilant work for?"

"It's called the Sugar Heights Association. You know, one of those neighborhood things. They fight over the zoning regulations when they don't like em and make sure everyone in the neighborhood keeps to a certain . . . uh, standard, I guess you'd say. There are lots of rules. Like you can put up white lights at Christmas but not colored ones. And they can't blink."

Hodges rolls his eyes. Peeples grins. They have gone from potential antagonists to colleagues — almost, anyway — and why? Because Hodges happened to recognize the guy's slightly off-center first name. You could call that luck, but there's always something that will get you on the same side as the person you want to question, *something,* and part of Hodges's success on the cops came from being able to recognize it, at least in most cases. It's a talent Pete Huntley never had, and Hodges is delighted to find his remains in good working order.

"I think she had a sister," he says. "Mrs. Trelawney, I mean. Never met her, though, and can't remember the name."

"Janelle Patterson," Peeples says promptly.

"You *have* met her, I take it."

"Yes indeed. She's good people. Bears a resemblance to Mrs. Trelawney, but younger and better-looking." His hands describe an hourglass shape in the air. "More filled out. Do you happen to know if there's been any progress on the Mercedes thing, Mr. Hodges?"

This isn't a question Hodges would ordinarily answer, but if you want to get information, you have to give information. And what he has is safe enough, because it isn't information at all. He uses the phrase Pete Huntley used at lunch a few hours ago. "Dead in the water."

Peeples nods as if this is no more than he expected. "Crime of impulse. No ties to any of the vics, no motive, just a goddam thrill-killing. Best chance of getting him is if he tries to do it again, don't you think?"

Mr. Mercedes says he won't, Hodges thinks, but this is information he absolutely *doesn't* want to give out, so he agrees. Collegial agreement is always good.

"Mrs. T. left a big estate," Hodges says, "and I'm not just talking about the house. I wonder if the sister inherited."

"Oh yeah," Peeples says. He pauses, then

says something Hodges himself will say to someone else in the not too distant future. "Can I trust your discretion?"

"Yes." When asked such a question, the simple answer is best. No qualifiers.

"The Patterson woman was living in Los Angeles when her sister . . . you know. The pills."

Hodges nods.

"Married, but no children. Not a happy marriage. When she found out she had inherited megabucks and a Sugar Heights estate, she divorced the husband like a shot and came east." Peeples jerks a thumb at the gate, the wide drive, and the big house. "Lived there for a couple of months while the will was going through probate. Got close with Mrs. Wilcox, down at 640. Mrs. Wilcox likes to talk, and sees me as a friend."

This might mean anything from coffee-buddies to afternoon sex.

"Miz Patterson took over visiting the mother, who lived in a condo building downtown. You know about the mother?"

"Elizabeth Wharton," Hodges says. "Wonder if she's still alive."

"I'm pretty sure she is."

"Because she had terrible scoliosis." Hodges takes a little hunched-over walk to demonstrate. If you want to get, you have to give.

"Is that so? Too bad. Anyway, Helen — Mrs. Wilcox — says that Miz Patterson visited as regular as clockwork, just like Mrs. Trelawney did. Until a month ago, that is. Then things must have got worse, because I believe the old lady's now in a nursing home in Warsaw County. Miz Patterson moved into the condo herself. And that's where she is now. I still see her every now and then, though. Last time was a week ago, when the real estate guy showed the house."

Hodges decides he's gotten everything he can reasonably expect from Radney Peeples. "Thanks for the update. I'm going to roll. Sorry we kind of got off on the wrong foot."

"Not at all," Peeples says, giving Hodges's offered hand two brisk pumps. "You handled it like a pro. Just remember, I never said anything. Janelle Patterson may be living downtown, but she's still part of the Association, and that makes her a client."

"You never said a word," Hodges says, getting back into his car. He hopes that Helen Wilcox's husband won't catch his wife and this beefcake in the sack together, if that is indeed going on; it would probably be the end of Vigilant Guard Service's arrangement with the residents of Sugar Heights. Peeples himself would immediately be terminated for cause. About that there is no doubt at all.

Probably she just trots out to his car with fresh-baked cookies, Hodges thinks as he drives away. You've been watching too much Nazi couples therapy on afternoon TV.

Not that Radney Peeples's love-life matters to him. What matters to Hodges as he heads back to his much humbler home on the West Side is that Janelle Patterson inherited her sister's estate, Janelle Patterson is living right here in town (at least for the time being), and Janelle Patterson must have done something with the late Olivia Trelawney's possessions. That would include her personal papers, and her personal papers might contain a letter — possibly more than one — from the freako who has reached out to Hodges. If such correspondence exists, he would like to see it.

Of course this is police business and K. William Hodges is no longer a policeman. By pursuing it he is skating well beyond the bounds of what is legal and he knows it — for one thing, he is withholding evidence — but he has no intention of stopping just yet. The cocky arrogance of the freako's letter has pissed him off. But, he admits, it's pissed him off in a good way. It's given him a sense of purpose, and after the last few months, that seems like a pretty terrific thing.

If I do happen to make a little progress, I'll turn the whole thing over to Pete.

He's not looking in the rearview mirror as this thought crosses his mind, but if he had been, he would have seen his eyes flick momentarily up and to the left.

4

Hodges parks his Toyota in the sheltering overhang to the left of his house that serves as his garage, and pauses to admire his freshly cut lawn before going to the door. There he finds a note sticking out of the mail slot. His first thought is Mr. Mercedes, but such a thing would be bold even for that guy.

It's from Jerome. His neat printing contrasts wildly with the bullshit jive of the message.

Dear Massa Hodges,

I has mowed yo grass and put de mower back in yo cah-pote. I hopes you didn't run over it, suh! If you has any mo chos for dis heah black boy, hit me on mah honker. I be happy to talk to you if I is not on de job wit one of my hos. As you know dey needs a lot of work and sometimes some tunin up on em, as dey can be uppity, especially dem high yallers! I is always heah fo you, suh!

Jerome

Hodges shakes his head wearily but can't help smiling. His hired kid gets straight As in advanced math, he can replace fallen gutters, he fixes Hodges's email when it goes blooey (as it frequently does, mostly due to his own mismanagement), he can do basic plumbing, he can speak French pretty well, and if you ask what he's reading, he's apt to bore you for half an hour with the blood symbolism of D. H. Lawrence. He doesn't want to be white, but being a gifted black male in an upper-middle-class family has presented him with what he calls "identity challenges." He says this in a joking way, but Hodges does not believe he's joking. Not really.

Jerome's college professor dad and CPA mom — both humor-challenged, in Hodges's opinion — would no doubt be aghast at this communication. They might even feel their son in need of psychological counseling. But they won't find out from Hodges.

"Jerome, Jerome, Jerome," he says, letting himself in. Jerome and his chos fo hos. Jerome who can't decide, at least not yet, on which Ivy League college he wants to attend; that any of the big boys will accept him is a foregone conclusion. He's the only person in the neighborhood whom Hodges thinks of as a friend, and really, the only one he needs. Hodges believes friendship is overrated, and in this way, if in no other, he is like Brady Hartsfield.

He has made it in time for most of the evening news, but decides against it. There is only so much Gulf oil-spill and Tea Party politics he can take. He turns on his computer instead, launches Firefox, and plugs **Under Debbie's Blue Umbrella** into the search field. There are only six results, a very small catch in the vast fishy sea of the Internet, and only one that matches the phrase exactly. Hodges clicks on it and a picture appears.

Under a sky filled with threatening clouds is a country hillside. Animated rain — a simple repeating loop, he judges — is pouring down in silvery streams. But the two people seated beneath a large blue umbrella, a young man and a young woman, are safe and dry. They are not kissing, but their heads are close together. They appear to be in deep conversation.

Below the picture, there's a brief description of the Blue Umbrella's raison d'être.

> Unlike sites such as Facebook and LinkedIn, Under Debbie's Blue Umbrella is a chat site where old friends can meet and new friends can get to know one another in TOTAL GUARENTEED ANONYMITY. No pictures, no porn, no 140-character Tweets, just GOOD OLD-FASHIONED CONVERSATION.

Below this is a button marked GET STARTED NOW! Hodges mouses his cursor onto it, then hesitates. About six months ago, Jerome had to delete his email address and give him a new one, because everyone in Hodges's address book had gotten a message saying he was stranded in New York, someone had stolen his wallet with all his credit cards inside, and he needed money to get home. Would the email recipient please send fifty dollars — more if he or she could afford it — to a Mail Boxes Etc. in Tribeca. "I'll pay you back as soon as I get this mess straightened out," the message concluded.

Hodges was deeply embarrassed because the begging request had gone out to his ex, his brother in Toledo, and better than four dozen cops he'd worked with over the years. Also his daughter. He had expected his phone — both landline and cell — to ring like crazy for the next forty-eight hours or so, but very few people called, and only Alison seemed actually concerned. This didn't surprise him. Allie, a Gloomy Gus by nature, has been expecting her father to lose his shit ever since he turned fifty-five.

Hodges had called on Jerome for help, and Jerome explained he had been a victim of phishing.

"Mostly the people who phish your address just want to sell Viagra or knockoff jewelry, but I've seen this kind before, too. It happened to my Environmental Studies teacher, and he ended up paying people back almost a thousand bucks. Of course, that was in the old days, before people wised up —"

"Old days meaning exactly when, Jerome?"

Jerome had shrugged. "Two, three years ago. It's a new world out there, Mr. Hodges. Just be grateful the phisherman didn't hit you with a virus that ate all your files and apps."

"I wouldn't lose much," Hodges had said. "Mostly I just surf the Web. Although I *would* miss the computer solitaire. It plays 'Happy Days Are Here Again' when I win."

Jerome had given him his patented I'm-too-polite-to-call-you-dumb look. "What about your tax returns? I helped you do em online last year. You want someone to see what you paid Uncle Sugar? Besides me, I mean?"

Hodges admitted he didn't.

In that strange (and somehow endearing) pedagogical voice the intelligent young always seem to employ when endeavoring to educate the clueless old, Jerome said, "Your computer isn't just a new kind of TV set. Get that out of your mind. Every time you turn it on, you're opening a window into your life. If someone wants to look, that is."

All this goes through his head as he looks at the blue umbrella and the endlessly falling rain. Other stuff goes through it, too, stuff from his cop-mind, which had been asleep but is now wide awake.

Maybe Mr. Mercedes wants to talk. On the other hand, maybe what he really wants is to look through that window Jerome was talking about.

Instead of clicking on GET STARTED NOW!, Hodges exits the site, grabs his phone, and punches one of the few numbers he has on speed-dial. Jerome's mother answers, and after some brief and pleasant chitchat, she hands off to young Mr. Chos Fo Hos himself.

Speaking in the most horrible Ebonics dialect he can manage, Hodges says: "Yo, my homie, you keepin dem bitches in line? Dey earnin? You representin?"

"Oh, hi, Mr. Hodges. Yes, everything's fine."

"You don't likes me talkin dis way on yo honkah, brah?"

"Uh . . ."

Jerome is honestly flummoxed, and Hodges takes pity on him. "The lawn looks terrific."

"Oh. Good. Thanks. Can I do anything else for you?"

"Maybe so. I was wondering if you could come by after school tomorrow. It's a computer thing."

"Sure. What's the problem this time?"

"I'd rather not discuss it on the phone," Hodges says, "but you might find it interesting. Four o'clock okay?"

"That works."

"Good. Do me a favor and leave Tyrone Feelgood *Dee*lite at home."

"Okay, Mr. Hodges, will do."

"When are you going to lighten up and call me Bill? Mr. Hodges makes me feel like your American History teacher."

"Maybe when I'm out of high school," Jerome says, very seriously.

"Just as long as you know you can make the jump any time you want."

Jerome laughs. The kid has got a great, full laugh. Hearing it always cheers Hodges up.

He sits at the computer desk in his little cubbyhole of an office, drumming his fingers, thinking. It occurs to him that he hardly ever uses this room during the evening. If he wakes at two A.M. and can't get back to sleep, yes. He'll come in and play solitaire for an hour or so before returning to bed. But he's usually in his La-Z-Boy between seven and midnight, watching old movies on AMC or TCM and stuffing his face with fats and sugars.

He grabs his phone again, dials Directory Assistance, and asks the robot on the other end if it has a number for Janelle Patterson. He's not hopeful; now that she is the Seven Million Dollar Woman, and newly divorced in the bargain, Mrs. Trelawney's sister has probably got an unlisted number.

But the robot coughs it up. Hodges is so surprised he has to fumble for a pencil and then punch 2 for a repeat. He drums his fingers some more, thinking how he wants to approach her. It will probably come to nothing, but it would be his next step if he were still on the cops. Since he's not, it will take a little extra finesse.

He is amused to discover how eagerly he welcomes this challenge.

5

Brady calls ahead to Sammy's Pizza on his way home and picks up a small pepperoni and mushroom pie. If he thought his mother would eat a couple of slices, he would have gotten a bigger one, but he knows better.

Maybe if it was pepperoni and Popov, he thinks. If they sold that, I'd have to skip the medium and go straight to a large.

There are tract houses on the city's North Side. They were built between Korea and Vietnam, which means they all look the same and they're all turning to shit. Most still have plastic toys on the crabgrassy lawns, although it's now full dark. Chez Hartsfield is at 49 Elm Street, where there are no elms and probably never were. It's just that all the streets in this area of the city — known, reasonably enough, as Northfield — are named for trees.

Brady parks behind Ma's rustbucket Honda, which needs a new exhaust system, new points, and new plugs. Not to mention an inspection sticker.

Let *her* take care of it, Brady thinks, but she won't. He will. He'll have to. The way he takes care of everything.

The way I took care of Frankie, he thinks. Back when the basement was just the basement instead of my control center.

Brady and Deborah Ann Hartsfield don't

talk about Frankie.

The door is locked. At least he's taught her that much, although God knows it hasn't been easy. She's the kind of person who thinks *okay* solves all of life's problems. Tell her *Put the half-and-half back in the fridge after you use it,* she says okay. Then you come home and there it sits on the counter, going sour. You say *Please do a wash so I can have a clean uni for the ice cream truck tomorrow,* she says okay. But when you poke your head into the laundry room, everything's still there in the basket.

The cackle of the TV greets him. Something about an immunity challenge, so it's *Survivor.* He has tried to tell her it's all fake, a set-up. She says yes, okay, she knows, but she still never misses it.

"I'm home, Ma!"

"Hi, honey!" Only a moderate slur, which is good for this hour of the evening. If I was her liver, Brady thinks, I'd jump out of her mouth some night while she's snoring and run the fuck away.

He nonetheless feels that little flicker of anticipation as he goes into the living room, the flicker he hates. She's sitting on the couch in the white silk robe he got her for Christmas, and he can see more white where it splits apart high up on her thighs. Her underwear. He refuses to think the word *pant-*

ies in connection with his mother, it's too sexy, but it's down there in his mind, just the same: a snake hiding in poison sumac. Also, he can see the small round shadows of her nipples. It's not right that such things should turn him on — she's pushing fifty, she's starting to flab out around the middle, she's his *mother,* for God's sake — but . . .

But.

"I brought pizza," he says, holding up the box and thinking, I already ate.

"I already ate," she says. Probably she did. A few lettuce leaves and a teensy tub of yogurt. It's how she keeps what's left of her figure.

"It's your favorite," he says, thinking, You enjoy it, honey.

"You enjoy it, sweetie," she says. She lifts her glass and takes a lady-like sip. Gulping comes later, after he's gone to bed and she thinks he's asleep. "Get yourself a Coke and come sit beside me." She pats the couch. Her robe opens a little more. White robe, white panties.

Underwear, he reminds himself. Underwear, that's all, she's my mother, she's Ma, and when it's your ma it's just underwear.

She sees him looking and smiles. She does not adjust the robe. "The survivors are on Fiji this year." She frowns. "I think it's Fiji. One of those islands, anyway. Come and watch with me."

"Nah, I guess I'll go downstairs and work for awhile."

"What project is this, honey?"

"A new kind of router." She wouldn't know a router from a grouter, so that's safe enough.

"One of these days you'll invent something that will make us rich," she says. "I know you will. Then, goodbye electronics store. And goodbye to that ice cream truck." She looks at him with wide eyes that are only a little watery from the vodka. He doesn't know how much she puts down in the course of an ordinary day, and counting empty bottles doesn't work because she ditches them somewhere, but he knows her capacity is staggering.

"Thanks," he says. Feeling flattered in spite of himself. Feeling other stuff, too. Very much in spite of himself.

"Come give your Ma a kiss, honeyboy."

He approaches the couch, careful not to look down the front of the gaping robe and trying to ignore that crawling sensation just below his belt buckle. She turns her face to one side, but when he bends to kiss her cheek, she turns back and presses her damp half-open mouth to his. He tastes booze and smells the perfume she always dabs behind her ears. She dabs it other places, as well.

She places a palm on the nape of his neck and ruffles his hair with the tips of her fingers, sending a shiver all the way down to the small of his back. She touches his upper lip with the tip of her tongue, just a flick, there and gone, then pulls back and gives him the wide-eyed starlet stare.

"My honeyboy," she breathes, like the heroine of some romantic chick-flick — the kind where the men wave swords and the women wear low-cut dresses with their cakes pushed up into shimmery globes.

He pulls away hastily. She smiles at him, then looks back at the TV, where good-looking young people in bathing suits are running along a beach. He opens the pizza box with hands that are shaking slightly, takes out a slice, and drops it in her salad bowl.

"Eat that," he says. "It'll sop up the booze. Some of it."

"Don't be mean to Mommy," she says, but with no rancor and certainly no hurt. She pulls her robe closed, doing it absently, already lost in the world of the survivors again, intent on discovering who will be voted off the island this week. "And don't forget about my car, Brady. It needs a sticker."

"It needs a lot more than that," he says, and goes into the kitchen. He grabs a Coke from the fridge, then opens the door to the basement. He stands there in the dark for a moment, then speaks a single word: "Control." Below him, the fluorescents (he installed them himself, just as he remodeled the basement himself) flash on.

At the foot of the stairs, he thinks of Frankie. He almost always does when he stands in the place where Frankie died. The only time he didn't think of Frankie was when he was preparing to make his run at City Center. During those weeks everything else left his mind, and what a relief that was.

Brady, Frankie said. His last word on Planet Earth. Gurgles and gasps didn't count.

He puts his pizza and his soda on the worktable in the middle of the room, then goes into the closet-sized bathroom and drops trou. He won't be able to eat, won't be able to work on his new project (which is certainly not a router), he won't be able to *think,* until he takes care of some urgent business.

In his letter to the fat ex-cop, he stated he was so sexually excited when he crashed into the job-seekers at City Center that he was wearing a condom. He further stated that he masturbates while reliving the event. If that were true, it would give a whole new meaning to the term autoerotic, but it isn't. He lied a lot in that letter, each lie calculated to wind Hodges up a little more, and his bogus sex-fantasies weren't the greatest of them.

He actually doesn't have much interest in girls, and girls sense it. It's probably why he gets along so well with Freddi Linklatter, his cyber-dyke colleague at Discount Electronix. For all Brady knows, she might think *he's* gay. But he's not gay, either. He's largely a mystery to himself — an occluded front — but one thing he knows for sure: he's not *asexual,* or not completely. He and his mother share a gothic rainbow of a secret, a thing not to be thought of unless it is absolutely necessary. When it does become necessary, it must be dealt with and put away again.

Ma, I see your panties, he thinks, and takes care of his business as fast as he can. There's Vaseline in the medicine cabinet, but he doesn't use it. He wants it to burn.

6

Back in his roomy basement workspace, Brady speaks another word. This one is *chaos.*

On the far side of the control room is a long shelf about three feet above the floor. Ranged along it are seven laptop computers with their darkened screens flipped up. There's also a chair on casters, so he can roll rapidly from one to another. When Brady speaks the magic word, all seven come to life. The number 20 appears on each screen, then 19, then 18. If he allows this countdown to reach zero, a suicide program will kick in, scrubbing his hard discs clean and overwriting them with gibberish.

"Darkness," he says, and the big countdown numbers disappear, replaced by desktop images that show scenes from *The Wild Bunch,* his favorite movie.

He tried *apocalypse* and *Armageddon,* much better start-up words in his opinion, full of ringing finality, but the word-recognition program has problems with them, and the last thing he wants is having to replace all his files because of a stupid glitch. Two-syllable words are safer. Not that there's much on six of the seven computers. Number Three is the only one with what the fat ex-cop would call "incriminating information," but he likes to look at that awesome array of computing power, all lit up as it is now. It makes the basement room feel like a real command center.

Brady considers himself a creator as well as a destroyer, but knows that so far he hasn't managed to create anything that will exactly set the world on fire, and he's haunted by the possibility that he never will. That he has, at best, a second-rate creative mind.

Take the Rolla, for instance. That had come to him in a flash of inspiration one night when he'd been vacuuming the living room (like using the washing machine, such a chore is usually beneath his mother). He had sketched a device that looked like a footstool on bearings, with a motor and a short hose attachment on the underside. With the addition of a simple computer program, Brady reckoned the device could be designed to move around a room, vacuuming as it went.

If it hit an obstacle — a chair, say, or a wall — it would turn on its own and start off in a new direction.

He had actually begun building a prototype when he saw a version of his Rolla trundling busily around the window display of an upscale appliance store downtown. The name was even similar; it was called a Roomba. Someone had beaten him to it, and that someone was probably making millions. It wasn't fair, but what is? Life is a crap carnival with shit prizes.

He has blue-boxed the TVs in the house, which means Brady and his ma are getting not just basic cable but all the premium channels (including a few exotic add-ins like Al Jazeera) for free, and there's not a damn thing Time Warner, Comcast, or XFINITY can do about it. He has hacked the DVD player so it will run not just American discs but those from every region of the world. It's easy — three or four quick steps with the remote, plus a six-digit recognition code. Great in theory, but does it get used? Not at 49 Elm Street, it doesn't. Ma won't watch anything that isn't spoon-fed to her by the four major networks, and Brady himself is mostly working one of his two jobs or down here in the control room, where he does his *actual* work.

The blue boxes are great, but they're also illegal. For all he knows, the DVD hacks are illegal, too. Not to mention his Redbox and

Netflix hacks. *All* his best ideas are illegal. Take Thing One and Thing Two.

Thing One had been on the passenger seat of Mrs. Trelawney's Mercedes when he left City Center on that foggy morning the previous April, with blood dripping from the bent grille and stippling the windshield. The idea came to him during the murky period three years ago, after he had decided to kill a whole bunch of people — what he then thought of as his *terrorist run* — but before he had decided just how, when, or where to do it. He had been full of ideas then, jittery, not sleeping much. In those days he always felt as though he had just swallowed a whole Thermos of black coffee laced with amphetamines.

Thing One was a modified TV remote with a microchip for a brain and a battery pack to boost its range . . . although the range was still pretty short. If you pointed it at a traffic light twenty or thirty yards away, you could change red to yellow with one tap, red to blinking yellow with two taps, and red to green with three.

Brady was delighted with it, and had used it several times (always while sitting parked in his old Subaru; the ice cream truck was far too conspicuous) at busy intersections. After several near misses, he had finally caused an actual accident. Just a fender-bender, but it had been fun to watch the two men arguing about whose fault it had been.

For awhile it had looked like they might actually come to blows.

Thing Two came shortly afterward, but it was Thing One that settled Brady on his target, because it radically upped the chances of a successful getaway. The distance between City Center and the abandoned warehouse he had picked as a dumping spot for Mrs. Trelawney's gray Mercedes was exactly 1.9 miles. There were eight traffic lights along the route he planned to take, and with his splendid gadget, he wouldn't have to worry about any of them. But on that morning — Jesus Christ, wouldn't you know it? — every one of those lights had been green. Brady understood the early hour had something to do with it, but it was still infuriating.

If I hadn't had it, he thinks as he goes to the closet at the far end of the basement, at least four of those lights would have been red. That's the way my life works.

Thing Two was the only one of his gadgets that turned out to be an actual moneymaker. Not big money, but as everyone knew, money isn't everything. Besides, without Thing Two there would have been no Mercedes. And with no Mercedes, no City Center Massacre.

Good old Thing Two.

A big Yale padlock hangs from the hasp of the closet door. Brady opens it with a key on his ring. The lights inside — more new fluorescents — are already on. The closet is small and made even smaller by the plain board shelves. On one of them are nine shoeboxes. Inside each box is a pound of homemade plastic explosive. Brady has tested some of this stuff at an abandoned gravel pit far out in the country, and it works just fine.

If I was over there in Afghanistan, he thinks, dressed in a head-rag and one of those funky bathrobes, I could have quite a career blowing up troop carriers.

On another shelf, in another shoebox, are five cell phones. They're the disposable kind the Lowtown drug dealers call burners. The phones, available at fine drugstores and convenience stores everywhere, are Brady's project for tonight. They have to be modified so that a single number will ring all of them, creating the proper spark needed to detonate the boom-clay in the shoeboxes at the same time. He hasn't actually decided to use the plastic, but part of him wants to. Yes indeed. He told the fat ex-cop he has no urge to replicate his masterpiece, but that was another lie. A lot depends on the fat ex-cop himself. If he does what Brady wants — as Mrs. Trelawney did what Brady wanted — he's sure the urge will go away, at least for awhile.

If not . . . well . . .

He grabs the box of phones, starts out of the closet, then pauses and looks back. On one of the other shelves is a quilted woodman's vest from L.L.Bean. If Brady were really going out in the woods, a Medium would suit him fine — he's slim — but this one is an XL. On the breast is a smile decal, the one wearing dark glasses and showing its teeth. The vest holds four more one-pound blocks of plastic explosive, two in the outside pockets, two in the slash pockets on the inside. The body of the vest bulges, because it's filled with ball bearings (just like the ones in Hodges's Happy Slapper). Brady slashed the lining to pour them in. It even crossed his mind to ask Ma to sew the slashes up, and that gave him a good laugh as he sealed them shut with duct tape.

My very own suicide vest, he thinks affectionately.

He won't use it . . . *probably* won't use it . . . but this idea also has a certain attraction. It would put an end to everything. No more Discount Electronix, no more Cyber Patrol calls to dig peanut butter or saltine crumbs out of some elderly idiot's CPU, no more ice cream truck. Also no more crawling snakes in the back of his mind. Or under his belt buckle.

He imagines doing it at a rock concert; he knows Springsteen is going to play Lakefront Arena this June. Or how about the Fourth of July parade down Lake Street, the city's main drag? Or maybe on opening day of the Summer Sidewalk Art Festival and Street Fair, which happens every year on the first Saturday in August. That would be good, except wouldn't he look funny, wearing a quilted vest on a hot August afternoon?

True, but such things can always be worked out by the creative mind, he thinks, spreading the disposable phones on his worktable and beginning to remove the SIM cards. Besides, the suicide vest is just a whatdoyoucallit, doomsday scenario. It will probably never be used. Nice to have it handy, though.

Before going upstairs, he sits down at his Number Three, goes online, and checks the Blue Umbrella. Nothing from the fat ex-cop.

Yet.

7

When Hodges uses the intercom outside Mrs. Wharton's Lake Avenue condo at ten the next morning, he's wearing a suit for only the second or third time since he retired. It feels good to be in a suit again, even though it's tight at the waist and under the arms. A man in a suit feels like a working man.

A woman's voice comes from the speaker. "Yes?"

"It's Bill Hodges, ma'am. We spoke last night?"

"So we did, and you're right on time. It's 19-C, Detective Hodges."

He starts to tell her that he's no longer a

detective, but the door is buzzing and so he doesn't bother. Besides, he told her he was retired when they talked on the phone.

Janelle Patterson is waiting for him at the door, just as her sister was on the day of the City Center Massacre, when Hodges and Pete Huntley came to interview her the first time. The resemblance between the two women is enough to give Hodges a powerful sense of déjà vu. But as he makes his way down the short hall from the elevator to the apartment doorway (trying to walk rather than lumber), he sees that the differences outweigh the similarities. Patterson has the same light blue eyes and high cheekbones, but where Olivia Trelawney's mouth was tight and pinched, the lips often white with a combination of strain and irritation, Janelle Patterson's seem, even in repose, ready to smile. Or to bestow a kiss. Her lips are shiny with wet-look gloss; they look good enough to eat. And no boatneck tops for this lady. She's wearing a snug turtleneck that cradles a pair of perfectly round breasts. They are not big, those breasts, but as Hodges's dear old father used to say, more than a handful is wasted. Is he looking at the work of good foundation garments or a post-divorce enhancement? Enhancement seems more likely to Hodges. Thanks to her sister, she can afford all the bodywork she wants.

She extends her hand and gives him a good

no-nonsense shake. "Thank you for coming." As if it had been at her request.

"Glad you could see me," he says, following her in.

That same kick-ass view of the lake smacks him in the face. He remembers it well, although they had only the one interview with Mrs. T. here; all the others were either at the big house in Sugar Heights or at the station. She had gone into hysterics during one of those station visits, he remembers. *Everybody is blaming me,* she said. The suicide had come not much later, only a matter of weeks.

"Would you like coffee, Detective? It's Jamaican. Very tasty, I think."

Hodges makes it a habit not to drink coffee in the middle of the morning, because doing so usually gives him savage acid reflux in spite of his Zantac. But he agrees.

He sits in one of the sling chairs by the wide living room window while he waits for her to come back from the kitchen. The day is warm and clear; on the lake, sailboats are zipping and curving like skaters. When she returns he stands up to take the silver tray she's carrying, but Janelle smiles, shakes her head no, and sets it on the low coffee table with a graceful dip of her knees. Almost a curtsey.

Hodges has considered every possible twist and turn their conversation might take, but his forethought turns out to be irrelevant. It is as if, after carefully planning a seduction, the object of his desire has met him at the door in a shortie nightgown and fuck-me shoes.

"I want to find out who drove my sister to suicide," she says as she pours their coffee into stout china mugs, "but I didn't know how I should proceed. Your call was like a message from God. After our conversation, I think you're the man for the job."

Hodges is too dumbfounded to speak.

She offers him a mug. "If you want cream, you'll have to pour it yourself. When it comes to additives, I take no responsibility."

"Black is fine."

She smiles. Her teeth are either perfect or perfectly capped. "A man after my own heart."

He sips, mostly to buy time, but the coffee is delicious. He clears his throat and says, "As I told you when we talked last night, Mrs. Patterson, I'm no longer a police detective. On November twentieth of last year, I became just another private citizen. We need to have that up front."

She regards him over the rim of her cup. Hodges wonders if the moist gloss on her lips leaves an imprint, or if lipstick technology has rendered that sort of thing obsolete. It's a crazy thing to be wondering, but she's a pretty lady. Also, he doesn't get out much these days.

"As far as I'm concerned," Janelle Patterson

says, "there are only two words that matter in what you just said. One is *private* and the other is *detective.* I want to know who meddled with her, who *toyed* with her until she killed herself, and nobody in the police department cares. They'd like to catch the man who used her car to kill those people, oh yes, but about my sister — may I be vulgar? — they don't give a shit."

Hodges may be retired, but he still has his loyalties. "That isn't necessarily true."

"I understand why you'd say that, Detective —"

"Mister, please. Just Mr. Hodges. Or Bill, if you like."

"Bill, then. And it *is* true. There's a connection between those murders and my sister's suicide, because the man who used the car is also the man who wrote the letter. And those other things. Those Blue Umbrella things."

Easy, Hodges cautions himself. Don't blow it.

"What letter are we talking about, Mrs. Patterson?"

"Janey. If you're Bill, I'm Janey. Wait here. I'll show you."

She gets up and leaves the room. Hodges's heart is beating hard — much harder than when he took on the trolls beneath the underpass — but he still appreciates that the view of Janey Patterson going away is as good as the one from the front.

Easy, boy, he tells himself again, and sips more coffee. Philip Marlowe you ain't. His mug is already half empty, and no acid. Not a trace of it. Miracle coffee, he thinks.

She comes back holding two pieces of paper by the corners and with an expression of distaste. "I found it when I was going through the papers in Ollie's desk. Her lawyer, Mr. Schron, was with me — she named him the executor of her will, so he had to be — but he was in the kitchen, getting himself a glass of water. He never saw this. I hid it." She says it matter-of-factly, with no shame or defiance. "I knew what it was right away. Because of *that.* The guy left one on the steering wheel of her car. I guess you could call it his calling-card."

She taps the sunglasses-wearing smile-face partway down the first page of the letter. Hodges has already noted it. He has also noted the letter's font, which he has identified from his own word processing program as American Typewriter.

"When did you find it?"

She thinks back, calculating the passage of time. "I came for the funeral, which was near the end of November. I discovered that I was Ollie's sole beneficiary when the will was read. That would have been the first week of December. I asked Mr. Schron if we could put off the inventory of Ollie's assets and possessions until January, because I had some business to take care of back in L.A. He agreed." She looks at Hodges, a level stare from blue eyes with a bright sparkle in them. "The business I had to take care of was divorcing my husband, who was — may I be vulgar again? — a philandering, coke-snorting asshole."

Hodges has no desire to go down this sidetrack. "You returned to Sugar Heights in January?"

"Yes."

"And found the letter then?"

"Yes."

"Have the police seen it?" He knows the answer, January was over four months ago, but the question has to be asked.

"No."

"Why not?"

"I already told you! Because I don't trust them!" That bright sparkle in her eyes overspills as she begins to cry.

8

She asks if he will excuse her. Hodges tells her of course. She disappears, presumably to get control of herself and repair her face. Hodges picks up the letter and reads it, taking small sips of coffee as he does so. The coffee really is delicious. Now, if he just had a cookie or two to go with it . . .

Dear Olivia Trelawney,

I hope you will read this letter all the way to the end before throwing it away or burning it up. I know I don't deserve your consideration, but I am begging for it just the same. You see, I am the man who stole your Mercedes and drove it into those people. Now I am burning like you might burn my letter, only with shame and remorse and sorrow.

Please, please, please give me a chance to explain! I can never have your forgiveness, that's another thing I know, and I don't expect it, but if I can only get you to understand, that would be enough. Will you give me that chance? Please? To the public I am a monster, to the TV news I am just another bloody story to sell commercials, to the police I am just another perk they want to catch and put in jail, but I am also a human being, just as you are. Here is my story.

I grew up in a physically and sexually abusive household. My stepfather was the first, and do you know what happened when my mother found out? She joined the fun! Have you stopped reading yet? I wouldn't blame you, it's disgusting, but I hope you have not, because I have to get this off my chest. I may not be "in the land of the living" much longer, you see, but I cannot end my life without someone knowing WHY I did what I did. Not that I understand it completely myself, but perhaps you, as an "outsider," will.

Here was Mr. Smiley-Face.

The sexual abuse went on until my stepfather died of a heart attack when I was 12. My mother said if I ever told, I would be blamed. She said if I showed the healed cigarette burns on my arms and legs and privates, she would tell people I did it myself. I was just a kid and I thought she was telling the truth. She also told me that if people did believe me, she would have to go to jail and I would be put in an orphan home (which was probably true).

I kept my mouth shut. Sometimes "the devil you know is better than the devil you don't!"

I never grew very much and I was very thin because I was too nervous to eat and when I did I often threw up (bulimia). Hence and because of this, I was bullied at school. I also developed a bunch of nervous tics, such as picking at my clothes and pulling at my hair (sometimes pulling it out in bunches). This caused me to be laughed at, not just by the other kids but by teachers too.

Janey Patterson has returned and is once again sitting opposite him, drinking her coffee, but for the moment Hodges barely notices her. He's thinking back to the four or five interviews he and Pete conducted with Mrs. T. He's remembering how she was always straightening the boatneck tops. Or tugging down her skirt. Or touching the corners of her pinched mouth, as if to remove a crumb of lipstick. Or winding a curl of hair around her finger and tugging at it. That too.

He goes back to the letter.

I was never a mean kid, Mrs.

Trelawney. I swear to you. I never tortured animals or beat up kids that were even smaller than I was. I was just a scurrying little mouse of a kid, trying to get through my childhood without being laughed at or humiliated, but at that I did not succeed.

I wanted to go to college, but I never did. You see, <u>I ended up taking care of the woman who abused me</u>! It's almost funny, isn't it? Ma had a stroke, possibly because of her drinking. Yes, she is also an alcoholic, or was when she could get to the store to buy her bottles. She can walk a little, but really not much. I have to help her to the toilet and clean her up after she "does her business." I work all day at a low-paying job (probably lucky to have a job at all in this economy, I know) and then come home and take care of her, because having a woman come in for a few hours on weekdays is all I can afford. It is a bad and stupid life. I have no friends and no possibility of advancement where I work. If Society is a bee-hive, then I am just another drone.

Finally I began to get angry. I wanted to make someone pay. I wanted to strike back at the world and make the world know I was alive. Can you understand that? Have you ever felt like that? Most likely not as you are wealthy and probably have the best friends money can buy.

Following this zinger, there's another of those sunglasses-wearing smile-faces, as if to say Just kidding.

One day it all got to be too much and I did what I did. I didn't plan ahead . . .

The fuck you didn't, Hodges thinks.

. . . and I thought the chances were at least 50-50 that I would get caught. I didn't care. And I SURE didn't know how it would haunt me afterward. I still relive the thuds that resulted from hitting them, and I still hear their screams. Then when I saw the news and found out <u>I had even killed a baby</u>, it really came home to me what a terrible thing I had done. I don't know how I live with myself.

Mrs. Trelawney, why oh why oh why did you leave your key in your ignition? If I had not seen that, walking one early morning because I could not sleep, none of this would have happened. If you hadn't left your key in your ignition, that little baby and her mother would still be alive. I am not blaming you, I'm sure your mind was full of your own problems and anxieties, but I wish things had turned out different and if you had remembered to take your key they would have. I would not be burning in this hell of guilt and remorse.

You are probably feeling guilt and remorse too, and I am sorry, especially because very soon you will find out how mean people can be. The TV news and the papers will talk about how your carelessness made my terrible act possible. Your friends will stop talking to you. The police will hound you. When you go to the supermarket, people will look at you and then whisper to each other. Some won't be content with just whispering and will "get in your face." I would not be surprised if there was vandalism to your home, so tell your security people (I'm sure you have them) to "watch out."

I don't suppose you would want to talk to me, would you? Oh, I don't mean face to face, but there is a safe place, safe for both of us, where we could talk using our computers. It's called Under Debbie's Blue Umbrella. I even got you a username if you should want to do this. The username is "otrelaw19."

I know what an ordinary person would do. An ordinary person would take this letter straight to the police, but let me ask a question. What have they done for you except hound you and cause you sleepless nights? Although here's a thought, if you want me dead, giving this letter to the police is the way to do it, as surely as putting a gun to my head and pulling the trigger, because I will kill myself.

Crazy as it may seem, you are <u>the only person keeping me alive</u>. Because you are the only one I can talk to. The only one who understands what it is like to be in Hell.

Now I will wait.

Mrs. Trelawney, I am so so so SORRY.

Hodges puts the letter down on the coffee table and says, "Holy shit."

Janey Patterson nods. "That was pretty much my reaction."

"He invited her to get in touch with him —"

Janey gives him an incredulous look. "*Invited* her? Try *blackmailed* her. 'Do it or I'll kill myself.' "

"According to you, she took him up on it. Have you seen any of their communications? Were there maybe printouts along with this letter?"

She shakes her head. "Ollie told my mother that she'd been chatting with what she called 'a very disturbed man' and trying to get him to seek help because he'd done a terrible thing. My mother was alarmed. She assumed

Ollie was talking with the very disturbed man face-to-face, like in the park or a coffee shop or something. You have to remember she's in her late eighties now. She knows about computers, but she's vague on their practical uses. Ollie explained about chat-rooms — or tried to — but I'm not sure how much Mom actually understood. What she remembers is that Ollie said she talked to the very disturbed man underneath a blue umbrella."

"Did your mother connect the man to the stolen Mercedes and the killings at City Center?"

"She never said anything that would make me believe so. Her short-term memory's gotten very foggy. If you ask her about the Japanese bombing Pearl Harbor, she can tell you exactly when she heard the news on the radio, and probably who the newscaster was. Ask her what she had for breakfast, or even where she is . . ." Janey shrugged. "She might be able to tell you, she might not."

"And where is she, exactly?"

"A place called Sunny Acres, about thirty miles from here." She laughs, a rueful sound with no joy in it. "Whenever I hear the name, I think of those old melodramas you see on Turner Classic Movies, where the heroine is declared insane and socked away in some awful drafty madhouse."

She turns to look out at the lake. Her face has taken on an expression Hodges finds interesting: a bit pensive and a bit defensive. The more he looks at her, the more he likes her looks. The fine lines around her eyes suggest that she's a woman who likes to laugh.

"I know who I'd be in one of those old movies," she says, still looking out at the boats playing on the water. "The conniving sister who inherits the care of an elderly parent along with a pile of money. The cruel sister who keeps the money but ships the Aged P off to a creepy mansion where the old people get Alpo for dinner and are left to lie in their own urine all night. But Sunny's not like that. It's actually very nice. Not cheap, either. And Mom asked to go."

"Yeah?"

"Yeah," she says, mocking him with a little wrinkle of her nose. "Do you happen to remember her nurse? Mrs. Greene. Althea Greene."

Hodges catches himself reaching into his jacket to consult a case notebook that's no longer there. But after a moment's thought he recalls the nurse without it. A tall and stately woman in white who seemed to glide rather than walk. With a mass of marcelled gray hair that made her look a bit like Elsa Lanchester in *The Bride of Frankenstein.* He and Pete had asked if she'd noticed Mrs. Trelawney's Mercedes parked at the curb when she left on that Thursday night. She had replied she was quite sure she had, which to the team of Hodges and Huntley meant she wasn't sure at all.

"Yeah, I remember her."

"She announced her retirement almost as soon as I moved back from Los Angeles. She said that at sixty-four she no longer felt able to deal competently with a patient suffering from such serious disabilities, and she stuck to her guns even after I offered to bring in a nurse's aide — two, if she wanted. I think she was appalled by the publicity that resulted from the City Center Massacre, but if it had been only that, she might have stayed."

"Your sister's suicide was the final straw?"

"I'm pretty sure it was. I won't say Althea and Ollie were bosom buddies or anything, but they got on, and they saw eye to eye about Mom's care. Now Sunny's the best thing for her, and Mom's relieved to be there. On her good days, at least. So am I. For one thing, they manage her pain better."

"If I were to go out and talk to her . . ."

"She might remember a few things, or she might not." She turns from the lake to look at him directly. "Will you take the job? I checked private detective rates online, and I'm prepared to do considerably better. Five thousand dollars a week, plus expenses. An eight-week minimum."

Forty thousand for eight weeks' work, Hodges marvels. Maybe he could be Philip Marlowe after all. He imagines himself in a ratty two-room office that gives on the third-floor hallway of a cheap office building. Hiring a va-voom receptionist with a name like Lola or Velma. A tough-talking blonde, of course. He'd wear a trenchcoat and a brown fedora on rainy days, the hat pulled down to one eyebrow.

Ridiculous. And not what attracts him. The attraction is not being in his La-Z-Boy, watching the lady judge and stuffing his face with snacks. He also likes being in his suit. But there's more. He left the PD with strings dangling. Pete has ID'd the pawnshop armed robber, and it looks like he and Isabelle Jaynes may soon be arresting Donald Davis, the mope who killed his wife and then went on TV, flashing his handsome smile. Good for Pete and Izzy, but neither Davis or the pawnshop shotgunner is the Big Casino.

Also, he thinks, Mr. Mercedes should have left me alone. And Mrs. T. He should have left her alone, too.

"Bill?" Janey's snapping her fingers like a stage hypnotist bringing a subject out of a trance. "Are you there, Bill?"

He returns his attention to her, a woman in her mid-forties who's not afraid to sit in bright sunlight. "If I say yes, you'll be hiring me as a security consultant."

She looks amused. "Like the men who work for Vigilant Guard Service out in the Heights?"

"No, not like them. They're bonded, for one thing. I'm not." I never had to be, he thinks. "I'd just be private security, like the kind of guys who work the downtown nightclubs. That's nothing you'd be able to claim as a deduction on your income tax, I'm afraid."

Amusement broadens into a smile, and she does the nose-wrinkling thing again. A fairly entrancing sight, in Hodges's opinion. "Don't care. In case you didn't know, I'm rolling in dough."

"What I'm trying for is full disclosure, Janey. I have no private detective's license, which won't stop me from asking questions, but how well I can operate without either a badge or a PI ticket remains to be seen. It's like asking a blind man to stroll around town without his guide dog."

"Surely there's a Police Department old boys' network?"

"There is, but if I tried to use it, I'd be putting both the old boys and myself in a bad position." That he has already done this by pumping Pete for information is a thing he won't share with her on such short acquaintance.

He lifts the letter Janey has showed him.

"For one thing, I'm guilty of withholding evidence if I agree to keep this between us." That he's already withholding a similar letter is another thing she doesn't need to know.

"Technically, at least. And withholding is a felony offense."

She looks dismayed. "Oh my God, I never thought of that."

"On the other hand, I doubt if there's much Forensics could do with it. A letter dropped into a mailbox on Marlborough Street or Lowbriar Avenue is just about the most anonymous thing in the world. Once upon a time — I remember it well — you could match up the typing in a letter to the machine that wrote it. If you could find the machine, that is. It was as good as a fingerprint."

"But this wasn't typed."

"Nope. Laser printer. Which means no hanging *A*s or crooked *T*s. So I wouldn't be withholding much."

Of course withholding is still withholding.

"I'm going to take the job, Janey, but five thousand a week is ridiculous. I'll take a check for two, if you want to write one. And bill you for expenses."

"That doesn't seem like anywhere near enough."

"If I get someplace, we can talk about a bonus." But he doesn't think he'll take one, even if he does manage to run Mr. Mercedes to ground. Not when he came here already determined to investigate the bastard, and to sweet-talk her into helping him.

"All right. Agreed. And thank you."

"Welcome. Now tell me about your relationship with Olivia. All I know is it was good enough for you to call her Ollie, and I could use more."

"That will take some time. Would you like another cup of coffee? And a cookie or two to go with it? I have lemon snaps."

Hodges says yes to both.

9

"Ollie."

Janey says this, then falls silent long enough for Hodges to sip some of his new cup of coffee and eat a cookie. Then she turns to the window and the sailboats again, crosses her legs, and speaks without looking at him.

"Have you ever loved someone without liking them?"

Hodges thinks of Corinne, and the stormy eighteen months that preceded the final split. "Yes."

"Then you'll understand. Ollie was my big sister, eight years older than I was. I loved her, but when she went off to college, I was the happiest girl in America. And when she dropped out three months later and came running back home, I felt like a tired girl who has to pick up a big sack of bricks again after being allowed to put it down for awhile. She wasn't mean to me, never called me names or pulled my pigtails or teased when I walked home from junior high holding hands with

Marky Sullivan, but when she was in the house, we were always at Condition Yellow. Do you know what I mean?"

Hodges isn't completely sure, but nods anyway.

"Food made her sick to her stomach. She got rashes when she was stressed out about anything — job interviews were the worst, although she finally did get a secretarial job. She had good skills and she was very pretty. Did you know that?"

Hodges makes a noncommittal noise. If he were to reply honestly, he might have said, I can believe it because I see it in you.

"One time she agreed to take me to a concert. It was U2, and I was mad to see them. Ollie liked them, too, but the night of the show she started vomiting. It was so bad that my parents ended up taking her to the ER and I had to stay home watching TV instead of pogoing and screaming for Bono. Ollie swore it was food poisoning, but we all ate the same meal, and no one else got sick. Stress is what it was. Pure stress. And you talk about hypochondria? With my sister, every headache was a brain tumor and every pimple was skin cancer. Once she got pinkeye and spent a week convinced she was going blind. Her periods were horroramas. She took to her bed until they were over."

"And still kept her job?"

Janey's reply is as dry as Death Valley. "Ollie's periods always used to last exactly forty-eight hours and they always came on the weekends. It was amazing."

"Oh." Hodges can think of nothing else to say.

Janey spins the letter around a few times on the coffee table with the tip of her finger, then raises those light blue eyes to Hodges. "He uses a phrase in here — something about having nervous tics. Did you notice that?"

"Yes." Hodges has noticed a great many things about this letter, mostly how it is in many ways a negative image of the one he received.

"My sister had her share, too. You may have noticed some of them."

Hodges pulls his tie first one way, then the other.

Janey grins. "Yes, that's one of them. There were many others. Patting light switches to make sure they were off. Unplugging the toaster after breakfast. She always said bread-and-butter before she went out somewhere, because supposedly if you did that, you'd remember anything you'd forgotten. I remember one day she had to drive me to school because I missed the bus. Mom and Dad had already gone to work. We got halfway there, then she became convinced the oven was on. We had to turn around and go back and check it. Nothing else would do. It was off, of course. I didn't make it to school until second period, and got hit with my first and only detention. I was furious. I was often furious with her, but I loved her, too. Mom, Dad, we all did. Like it was hardwired. But man, was she ever a sack of bricks."

"Too nervous to go out, but she not only married, she married money."

"Actually, she married a prematurely balding clerk in the investment company where she worked. Kent Trelawney. A nerd — I use the word affectionately, Kent was absolutely okay — with a love of video games. He started to invest in some of the companies that made them, and those investments paid off. My mother said he had the magic touch and my father said he was dumb lucky, but it was neither of those things. He knew the field, that's all, and what he didn't know he made it his business to learn. When they got married near the end of the seventies, they were only wealthy. Then Kent discovered Microsoft."

She throws her head back and belts out a hearty laugh, startling him.

"Sorry," she says. "Just thinking about the pure American irony of it. I was pretty, also well adjusted and gregarious. If I'd ever been in a beauty contest — which I call meatshows for men, if you want to know, and probably you don't — I would have won Miss Congeniality in a walk. Lots of girlfriends, lots of boyfriends, lots of phone calls, and lots of dates. I was in charge of freshman orientation during my senior year at Catholic High School, and did a great job, if I do say so myself. Soothed a lot of nerves. My sister was just as pretty, but she was the neurotic one. The obsessive-compulsive one. If she'd ever been in a beauty contest, she would have thrown up all over her bathing suit."

Janey laughs some more. Another tear trickles down her cheek as she does. She wipes it away with the heel of her hand.

"So here's the irony. Miss Congeniality got stuck with the coke-snorting dingbat and Miss Nervy caught the good guy, the money-making, never-cheat husband. Do you get it?"

"Yeah," Hodges says. "I do."

"Olivia Wharton and Kent Trelawney. A courtship with about as much chance of success as a six-months preemie. Kent kept asking her out and she kept saying no. Finally she agreed to have dinner with him — just to make him stop bothering her, she said — and when they got to the restaurant, she froze. Couldn't get out of the car. Shaking like a leaf. Some guys would have given up right there, but not Kent. He took her to McDonald's and got Value Meals at the drive-through window. They ate in the parking lot. I guess they did that a lot. She'd go to the movies with him, but always had to sit on the aisle. She said sitting on the inside made her short of breath."

"A lady with all the bells and whistles."

"My mother and father tried for years to get her to see a shrink. Where they failed, Kent succeeded. The shrink put her on pills, and she got better. She had one of her patented anxiety attacks on her wedding day — I was the one who held her veil while she vomited in the church bathroom — but she got through it." Janey smiles wistfully and adds, "She was a beautiful bride."

Hodges sits silently, fascinated by this glimpse of Olivia Trelawney before she became Our Lady of Boatneck Tops.

"After she married, we drifted apart. As sisters sometimes do. We saw each other half a dozen times a year until our father died, even less after that."

"Thanksgiving, Christmas, and the Fourth of July?"

"Pretty much. I could see some of her old shit coming back, and after Kent died — it was a heart attack — *all* of it came back. She lost a ton of weight. She went back to the awful clothes she wore in high school and when she was working in the office. Some of this I saw when I came back to visit her and Mom, some when we talked on Skype."

He nods his understanding. "I've got a friend who keeps trying to hook me up with that."

She regards him with a smile. "You're old school, aren't you? I mean *really.*" Her smile fades. “The last time I saw Ollie was May of last year, not long after the City Center thing.” Janey hesitates, then gives it its proper name. “The massacre. She was in terrible shape. She said the cops were hounding her. Was that true?”

“No, but she thought we were. It’s true we questioned her repeatedly, because she continued to insist she took her key and locked the Mercedes. That was a problem for us, because the car wasn’t broken into and it wasn’t hotwired. What we finally decided . . .” Hodges stops, thinking of the fat family psychologist who comes on every weekday at four. The one who specializes in breaking through the wall of denial.

“You finally decided what?”

“That she couldn’t bear to face the truth. Does that sound like the sister you grew up with?”

“Yes.” Janey points to the letter. “Do you suppose she finally told the truth to this guy? On Debbie’s Blue Umbrella? Do you think that’s why she took Mom’s pills?”

“There’s no way to be sure.” But Hodges thinks it’s likely.

“She quit her antidepressants.” Janey is looking out at the lake again. “She denied it when I asked her, but I knew. She never liked them, said they made her feel woolly-headed. She took them for Kent, and once Kent was dead she took them for our mother, but after

City Center . . ." She shakes her head, takes a deep breath. "Have I told you enough about her mental state, Bill? Because there's plenty more if you want it."

"I think I get the picture."

She shakes her head in dull wonder. "It's as if the guy knew her."

Hodges doesn't say what seems obvious to him, mostly because he has his own letter for comparison: he did. Somehow he did.

"You said she was obsessive-compulsive. To the point where she turned around and went back to check if the oven was on."

"Yes."

"Does it seem likely to you that a woman like that would have forgotten her key in the ignition?"

Janey doesn't answer for a long time. Then she says, "Actually, no."

It doesn't to Hodges, either. There's a first time for everything, of course, but . . . did he and Pete ever discuss that aspect of the matter? He's not sure, but thinks maybe they did. Only they hadn't known the depths of Mrs. T.'s mental problems, had they?

He asks, "Ever try going on this Blue Umbrella site yourself? Using the username he gave her?"

She stares at him, gobsmacked. "It never even crossed my mind, and if it had, I would have been too scared of what I might find. I guess that's why you're the detective and I'm the client. Will you try that?"

"I don't know what I'll try. I need to think about it, and I need to consult a guy who knows more about computers than I do."

"Make sure you note down his fee," she says.

Hodges says he will, thinking that at least Jerome Robinson will get some good out of this, no matter how the cards fall. And why shouldn't he? Eight people died at City Center and three more were permanently crippled, but Jerome still has to go to college. Hodges remembers an old saying: even on the darkest day, the sun shines on some dog's ass.

"What's next?"

Hodges takes the letter and stands up. "Next, I take this to the nearest UCopy. Then I return the original to you."

"No need of that. I'll scan it into the computer and print you one. Hand it over."

"Really? You can do that?"

Her eyes are still red from crying, but the glance she gives him is nonetheless merry. "It's a good thing you have a computer expert on call," she says. "I'll be right back. In the meantime, have another cookie."

Hodges has three.

10

When she returns with his copy of the letter, he folds it into his inner jacket pocket. "The original should go into a safe, if there's one here."

"There's one at the Sugar Heights house — will that do?"

It probably would, but Hodges doesn't care for the idea. Too many prospective buyers tromping in and out. Which is probably stupid, but there it is.

"Do you have a safe-deposit box?"

"No, but I could rent one. I use Bank of America, just two blocks over."

"I'd like that better," Hodges says, going to the door.

"Thank you for doing this," she says, and holds out both of her hands. As if he has asked her to dance. "You don't know what a relief it is."

He takes the offered hands, squeezes them lightly, then lets go, although he would have been happy to hold them longer.

"Two other things. First, your mother. How often do you visit her?"

"Every other day or so. Sometimes I take her food from the Iranian restaurant she and Ollie liked — the Sunny Acres kitchen staff is happy to warm it up — and sometimes I bring her a DVD or two. She likes the oldies, like with Fred Astaire and Ginger Rogers. I always bring her something, and she's always happy to see me. On her good days she *does* see me. On her bad ones, she's apt to call me Olivia. Or Charlotte. That's my aunt. I also have an uncle."

"The next time she has a good day, you ought to call me so I can go see her."

"All right. I'll go with you. What's the other thing?"

"This lawyer you mentioned. Schron. Did he strike you as competent?"

"Sharpest knife in the drawer, that was my impression."

"If I *do* find something out, maybe even put a name on the guy, we're going to need someone like that. We'll go see him, we'll turn over the letters —"

"Letters? I only found the one."

Hodges thinks Ah, shit, then regroups. "The letter and the copy, I mean."

"Oh, right."

"If I find the guy, it's the job of the police to arrest him and charge him. Schron's job is to make sure *we* don't get arrested for going off the reservation and investigating on our own."

"That would be criminal law, isn't it? I'm not sure he does that kind."

"Probably not, but if he's good, he'll know somebody who does. Someone who's just as good as he is. Are we agreed on that? We have to be. I'm willing to poke around, but if this turns into police business, we let the police take over."

"I'm fine with that," Janey says. Then she stands on tiptoe, puts her hands on the shoulders of his too-tight coat, and plants a kiss on his cheek. "I think you're a good guy, Bill. And the right guy for this."

He feels that kiss all the way down in the elevator. A lovely little warm spot. He's glad he took pains about shaving before leaving the house.

11

The silver rain falls without end, but the young couple — lovers? friends? — are safe and dry under the blue umbrella that belongs to someone, likely a fictional someone, named Debbie. This time Hodges notices that it's the boy who appears to be speaking, and the girl's eyes are slightly widened, as if in surprise. Maybe he's just proposed to her?

Jerome pops this romantic thought like a balloon. "Looks like a porn site, doesn't it?"

"Now what would a young pre–Ivy Leaguer like yourself know about porn sites?"

They are seated side by side in Hodges's study, looking at the Blue Umbrella start-up page. Odell, Jerome's Irish setter, is lying on his back behind them, rear legs splayed, tongue hanging from one side of his mouth, staring at the ceiling with a look of good-humored contemplation. Jerome brought him on a leash, but only because that's the law inside the city limits. Odell knows enough to stay out of the street and is about as harmless to passersby as a dog can be.

"I know what you know and what everybody with a computer knows," Jerome says. In his khaki slacks and button-down Ivy League shirt, his hair a close-cropped cap of curls, he looks to Hodges like a young Barack Obama, only taller. Jerome is six-five. And around him is the faint, pleasantly nostalgic aroma of Old Spice aftershave. "Porn sites are thicker than flies on roadkill. You surf the Net, you can't help bumping into them. And the ones with the innocent-sounding names are the ones most apt to be loaded."

"Loaded how?"

"With the kinds of images that can get you arrested."

"Kiddie porn, you mean."

"Or torture porn. Ninety-nine percent of the whips-and-chains stuff is faked. The other one percent . . ." Jerome shrugs.

"And you know this how?"

Jerome gives him a look — straight, frank, and open. Not an act, just the way he is, and what Hodges likes most about the kid. His mother and father are the same way. Even his little sis.

"Mr. Hodges, *everybody* knows. If they're under thirty, that is."

"Back in the day, people used to say don't trust anyone over thirty."

Jerome smiles. "I trust em, but when it comes to computers, an awful lot of em are clueless. They beat up their machines, then expect em to work. They open bareback email attachments. They go to websites like this, and all at once their computer goes HAL 9000 and starts downloading pictures of teenage escorts or terrorist videos that show people getting their heads chopped off."

It was on the tip of Hodge's tongue to ask who Hal 9000 is — it sounds like a gang-banger tag to him — but the thing about terrorist videos diverts him. "That actually happens?"

"It's been known to. And then . . ." Jerome makes a fist and raps his knuckles against the top of his head. "Knock-knock-knock, Homeland Security at your door." He unrolls his fist so he can point a finger at the couple under the blue umbrella. "On the other hand, this might be just what it claims to be, a chat site where shy people can be electronic penpals. You know, a lonelyhearts deal. Lots of people out there lookin for love, dude. Let's see."

He reaches for the mouse but Hodges grabs his wrist. Jerome looks at him inquiringly.

"Don't see on my computer," Hodges says. "See on yours."

"If you'd asked me to bring my laptop —"

"Do it tonight, that'll be fine. And if you happen to unleash a virus that swallows your cruncher whole, I'll stand you the price of a new one."

Jerome shoots him a look of condescending amusement. "Mr. Hodges, I've got the best virus detection and prevention program money can buy, and the second best backing it up. Any bug trying to creep into my machines gets swatted pronto."

"It might not be there to eat," Hodges says. He's thinking about Mrs. T.'s sister saying, *It's as if the guy knew her.* "It might be there to watch."

Jerome doesn't look worried; he looks excited. "How did you get onto this site, Mr. Hodges? Are you coming out of retirement? Are you, like, on the case?"

Hodges has never missed Pete Huntley so bitterly as he does at that moment: a tennis partner to volley with, only with theories and suppositions instead of fuzzy green balls. He has no doubt Jerome could fulfill that function, he has a good mind and a demonstrated talent for making all the right deductive leaps . . . but he's also a year from voting age, four from being able to buy a legal drink, and this could be dangerous.

"Just peek into the site for me," Hodges says. "But before you do, hunt around on the Net. See what you can find out about it. What I want to know most of all is —"

"If it has an actual history," Jerome cuts in, once more demonstrating that admirable deductive ability. "A whatdoyoucallit, back-story. You want to make sure it's not a straw man set up for you alone."

"You know," Hodges says, "you should quit doing chores for me and get a job with one of those computer-doctor companies. You could probably make a lot more dough. Which reminds me, you need to give me a price for this job."

Jerome is offended, but not by the offer of a fee. "Those companies are for geeks with bad social skills." He reaches behind him and scratches Odell's dark red fur. Odell thumps his tail appreciatively, although he would probably prefer a steak sandwich. "In fact there's one bunch that drives around in VW Beetles. You can't get much geekier than that. Discount Electronix . . . you know them?"

"Sure," Hodges says, thinking of the advertising circular he got along with his poison-pen letter.

"They must have liked the idea, because they have the same deal, only they call it the Cyber Patrol, and their VWs are green instead of black. Plus there are *mucho* independents. Look online, you can find two hundred right here in the city. I thinks I stick to chos, Massa Hodges."

Jerome clicks away from Under Debbie's Blue Umbrella and back to Hodges's screensaver, which happens to be a picture of Allie, back when she was five and still thought her old man was God.

"But since you're worried, I'll take precautions. I've got an old iMac in my closet with nothing on it but Atari Arcade and a few other moldy oldies. I'll use that one to check out the site."

"Good idea."

"Anything else I can do for you today?"

Hodges starts to say no, but Mrs. T.'s stolen Mercedes is still bugging him. There is something very wrong there. He felt it then and feels it more strongly now — so strongly he almost sees it. But *almost* never won a kewpie doll at the county fair. The wrongness is a ball he wants to hit, and have someone hit back to him.

"You could listen to a story," he says. In his mind he's already making up a piece of fiction that will touch on all the salient points. Who knows, maybe Jerome's fresh eye will spot something he himself has missed. Unlikely, but not impossible. "Would you be willing to do that?"

"Sure."

"Then clip Odell on his leash. We'll walk down to Big Licks. I've got my face fixed for a strawberry cone."

"Maybe we'll see the Mr. Tastey truck before we get there," Jerome says. "That guy's been in the neighborhood all week, and he's got some awesome goodies."

"So much the better," Hodges says, getting up. "Let's go."

12

They walk down the hill to the little shopping center at the intersection of Harper Road and Hanover Street with Odell padding between them on the slack leash. They can see the buildings of downtown two miles distant, City Center and the Midwest Culture and Arts Complex dominating the cluster of skyscrapers. The MAC is not one of I. M. Pei's finer creations, in Hodges's opinion. Not that his opinion has ever been solicited on the matter.

"So what's the story, morning glory?" Jerome asks.

"Well," Hodges says, "let's say there's this guy with a long-term lady friend who lives downtown. He himself lives in Parsonville." This is a municipality just beyond Sugar Heights, not as lux but far from shabby.

"Some of my friends call Parsonville Whiteyville," Jerome says. "I heard my father say it once, and my mother told him to shut up with the racist talk."

"Uh-huh." Jerome's friends, the black ones, probably call Sugar Heights Whiteyville, too, which makes Hodges think he's doing okay so far.

Odell has stopped to check out Mrs. Melbourne's flowers. Jerome pulls him away before he can leave a doggy memo there.

"So anyway," Hodges resumes, "the long-term lady friend has a condo apartment in the Branson Park area — Wieland Avenue, Branson Street, Lake Avenue, that part of town."

"Also nice."

"Yeah. He goes to see her three or four times a week. One or two nights a week he takes her to dinner or a movie and stays over. When he does that, he parks his car — a nice one, a Beemer — on the street, because it's a good area, well policed, plenty of those high-intensity arc-sodiums. Also, the parking's free from seven P.M. to eight A.M."

"I had a Beemer, I'd put it in one of the garages down there and never mind the free parking," Jerome says, and tugs the leash again. "Stop it, Odell, nice dogs don't eat out of the gutter."

Odell looks over his shoulder and rolls an eye as if to say You don't know what nice dogs do.

"Well, rich people have some funny ideas about economy," Hodges says, thinking of Mrs. T.'s explanation for doing the same thing.

"If you say so." They have almost reached the shopping center. On the way down the hill they've heard the jingling tune of the ice cream truck, once quite close, but it fades again as the Mr. Tastey guy heads for the housing developments north of Harper Road.

"So one Thursday night this guy goes to visit his lady as usual. He parks as usual — all kinds of empty spaces down there once the business day is over — and locks up his car as usual. He and his lady take a walk to a nearby restaurant, have a nice meal, then walk back. His car's right there, he sees it before they go in. He spends the night with his lady, and when he leaves the building in the morning —"

"His Beemer's gone bye-bye." They are now standing outside the ice cream shop. There's a bicycle rack nearby. Jerome fastens Odell's leash to it. The dog lies down and puts his muzzle on one paw.

"No," Hodges says, "it's there." He is thinking that this is a damned good variation on what actually happened. He almost believes it himself. "But it's facing the other way, because it's parked on the other side of the street."

Jerome raises his eyebrows.

"Yeah, I know. Weird, right? So the guy goes across to it. Car looks okay, it's locked up tight just the way he left it, it's just in a new place. So the first thing he does is check for his key, and yep, it's still in his pocket. So what the hell happened, Jerome?"

"I don't know, Mr. H. It's like a Sherlock

Holmes story, isn't it? A real three-pipe problem." There's a little smile on Jerome's face that Hodges can't quite parse and isn't sure he likes. It's a *knowing* smile.

Hodges digs his wallet out of his Levi's (the suit was good, but it's a relief to be back in jeans and an Indians pullover again). He selects a five and hands it to Jerome. "Go get our ice cream cones. I'll dog-sit Odell."

"You don't need to do that, he's fine."

"I'm sure he is, but standing in line will give you time to consider my little problem. Think of yourself as Sherlock, maybe that'll help."

"Okay." Tyrone Feelgood Delight pops out. "Only *you* is Sherlock! I is Doctah Watson!"

13

There's a pocket park on the far side of Hanover. They cross at the WALK light, grab a bench, and watch a bunch of shaggy-haired middle-school boys dare life and limb in the sunken concrete skateboarding area. Odell divides his time between watching the boys and the ice cream cones.

"You ever try that?" Hodges asks, nodding at the daredevils.

"No, suh!" Jerome gives him a wide-eyed stare. "I is *black.* I spends mah spare time shootin hoops and runnin on de cinder track at de high school. Us black fellas is mighty fast, as de whole worl' knows."

"Thought I told you to leave Tyrone at home." Hodges uses his finger to swop some ice cream off his cone and extends the dripping finger to Odell, who cleans it with alacrity.

"Sometimes dat boy jus' show up!" Jerome declares. Then Tyrone is gone, just like that. "There's no guy and no lady friend and no Beemer. You're talking about the Mercedes Killer."

So much for fiction. "Say I am."

"Are you investigating that on your own, Mr. Hodges?"

Hodges thinks this over, very carefully, then repeats himself. "Say I am."

"Does the Debbie's Blue Umbrella site have something to do with it?"

"Say it does."

A boy falls off his skateboard and stands up with road rash on both knees. One of his friends buzzes over, jeering. Road Rash Boy slides a hand across one oozing knee, flings a spray of red droplets at Jeering Boy, then rolls away, shouting "AIDS! AIDS!" Jeering Boy rolls after him, only now he's Laughing Boy.

"Barbarians," Jerome mutters. He bends to scratch Odell behind the ears, then straightens up. "If you want to talk about it —"

Embarrassed, Hodges says, "I don't think at this point —"

"I understand," Jerome says. "But I *did*

think about your problem while I was in line, and I've got a question."

"Yes?"

"Your make-believe Beemer guy, where was his spare key?"

Hodges sits very still, thinking how very quick this kid is. Then he sees a line of pink ice cream trickling down the side of his waffle cone and licks it off.

"Let's say he claims he never had one."

"Like the woman who owned the Mercedes did."

"Yes. Exactly like that."

"Remember me telling you how my mom got pissed at my dad for calling Parsonville Whiteyville?"

"Yeah."

"Want to hear about a time when my dad got pissed at my mom? The only time I ever heard him say, That's just like a woman?"

"If it bears on my little problem, shoot."

"Mom's got a Chevy Malibu. Candy-apple red. You've seen it in the driveway."

"Sure."

"He bought it new three years ago and gave it to her for her birthday, provoking massive squeals of delight."

Yes, Hodges thinks, Tyrone Feelgood has definitely taken a hike.

"She drives it for a year. No problems. Then it's time to re-register. Dad said he'd do it for her on his way home from work. He goes out to get the paperwork, then comes back in from the driveway holding up a key. He's not mad, but he's irritated. He tells her that if she leaves her spare key in the car, someone could find it and drive her car away. She asks where it was. He says in a plastic Ziploc bag along with her registration, her insurance card, and the owner's manual, which she had never opened. Still had the paper band around it that says thanks for buying your new car at Lake Chevrolet."

Another drip is trickling down Hodges's ice cream. This time he doesn't notice it even when it reaches his hand and pools there. "In the . . ."

"Glove compartment, yes. My dad said it was careless, and my mom said . . ." Jerome leans forward, his brown eyes fixed on Hodges's gray ones. "*She said she didn't even know it was there.* That's when he said it was just like a woman. Which didn't make her happy."

"Bet it didn't." In Hodges's brain, all sorts of gears are engaging.

"Dad says, Honey, all you have to do is forget once and leave your car unlocked. Some crack addict comes along, sees the buttons up, and decides to toss it in case there's anything worth stealing. He checks the glove compartment for money, sees the key in the plastic bag, and away he goes to find out who wants to buy a low-mileage Malibu for cash."

"What did your mother say to that?"

Jerome grins. "First thing, she turned it around. No one does that any better than my moms. She says, *You* bought the car and *you* brought it home. *You* should have told me. I'm eating my breakfast while they're having this little discussion and thought of saying, If you'd ever checked the owner's manual, Mom, maybe just to see what all those cute little lights on the dashboard signify, but I kept my mouth shut. My mom and dad don't get into it often, but when they do, a wise person steers clear. Even the Barbster knows that, and she's only nine."

It occurs to Hodges that when he and Corinne were married, this is something Alison also knew.

"The other thing she said was that she *never* forgets to lock her car. Which, so far as I know, is true. Anyway, that key is now hanging on one of the hooks in our kitchen. Safe, sound, and ready to go if the primary ever gets lost."

Hodges sits looking at the skateboarders but not seeing them. He's thinking that Jerome's mom had a point when she said her husband should have either presented her with the spare key or at least told her about it. You don't just assume people will do an inventory and find things by themselves. But Olivia Trelawney's case was different. She bought her own car, and should have known.

Only the salesman had probably overloaded her with info about her expensive new purchase; they had a way of doing that. When to change the oil, how to use the cruise control, how to use the GPS, don't forget to put your spare key in a safe place, here's how you plug in your cell phone, here's the number to call roadside assistance if you need it, click the headlight switch all the way to the left to engage the twilight function.

Hodges could remember buying his first new car and letting the guy's post-sales tutorial wash over him — uh-huh, yep, right, gotcha — just anxious to get his new purchase out on the road, to dig the rattle-free ride and inhale that incomparable new-car smell, which to the buyer is the aroma of money well spent. But Mrs. T. was obsessive-compulsive. He could believe she'd overlooked the spare key and left it in the glove compartment, but if she had taken her primary key that Thursday night, wouldn't she also have locked the car doors? She said she did, had maintained that to the very end, and really, think about it —

"Mr. Hodges?"

"With the new smart keys, it's a simple three-step process, isn't it?" he says. "Step one, turn off the engine. Step two, remove the key from the ignition. If your mind's on something else and you forget step two, there's a chime to remind you. Step three, close the door and push the button stamped with the padlock icon. Why would you forget that, with the key right there in your hand? Theft-Proofing for Dummies."

"True-dat, Mr. H., but some dummies forget, anyway."

Hodges is too lost in thought for reticence. "She was no dummy. Nervous and twitchy but not stupid. If she took her key, I almost have to believe she locked her car. And the car wasn't broken into. So even if she *did* leave the spare in her glove compartment, how did the guy get to it?"

"So it's a locked-car mystery instead of a locked room. Dis be a *fo'*-pipe problem!"

Hodges doesn't reply. He's going over it and over it. That the spare might have been in the glove compartment now seems obvious, but did either he or Pete ever raise the possibility? He's pretty sure they didn't. Because they thought like men? Or because they were pissed at Mrs. T.'s carelessness and wanted to blame her? And she *was* to blame, wasn't she?

Not if she really did lock her car, he thinks.

"Mr. Hodges, what does that Blue Umbrella website have to do with the Mercedes Killer?"

Hodges comes back out of his own head. He's been in deep, and it's a pretty long trudge. "I don't want to talk about that just now, Jerome."

"But maybe I can help!"

Has he ever seen Jerome this excited? Maybe once, when the debate team he captained his sophomore year won the citywide championship.

"Find out about that website and you will be helping," Hodges says.

"You don't want to tell me because I'm a kid. That's it, isn't it?"

It is part of the reason, but Hodges has no intention of saying so. And as it happens, there's something else.

"It's more complicated than that. I'm not a cop anymore, and investigating the City Center thing skates right up to the edge of what's legal. If I find anything out and don't tell my old partner, who's now the lead on the Mercedes Killer case, I'll be over the edge. You have a bright future ahead of you, including just about any college or university you decide to favor with your presence. What would I say to your mother and father if you got dragged into an investigation of my actions, maybe as an accomplice?"

Jerome sits quietly, digesting this. Then he gives the end of his cone to Odell, who accepts it eagerly. "I get it."

"Do you?"

"Yeah."

Jerome stands up and Hodges does the same. "Still friends?"

"Sure. But if you think I can help you,

promise me that you'll ask. You know what they say, two heads are better than one."

"That's a deal."

They start back up the hill. At first Odell walks between them as before, then starts to pull ahead because Hodges is slowing down. He's also losing his breath. "I've got to drop some weight," he tells Jerome. "You know what? I tore the seat out of a perfectly good pair of pants the other day."

"You could probably stand to lose ten," Jerome says diplomatically.

"Double that and you'd be a lot closer."

"Want to stop and rest a minute?"

"No." Hodges sounds childish even to himself. He means it about the weight, though; when he gets back to the house, every damn snack in the cupboards and the fridge is going into the trash. Then he thinks, Make it the garbage disposal. Too easy to weaken and fish stuff out of the trash.

"Jerome, it would be best if you kept my little investigation to yourself. Can I trust your discretion?"

Jerome replies without hesitation. "Absolutely. Mum's the word."

"Good."

A block ahead, the Mr. Tastey truck jingles its way across Harper Road and heads down Vinson Lane. Jerome tips a wave. Hodges can't see if the ice cream man waves back.

"*Now* we see him," Hodges said.

Jerome turns, gives him a grin. "Ice cream man's like a cop."

"Huh?"

"Never around when you need him."

14

Brady rolls along, obeying the speed limit (twenty miles per here on Vinson Lane), hardly hearing the jingle and clang of "Buffalo Gals" from the speakers above him. He's wearing a sweater beneath his white Mr. Tastey jacket, because the load behind him is cold.

Like my mind, he thinks. Only ice cream is *just* cold. My mind is also analytical. It's a machine. A Mac loaded with gigs to the googolplex.

He turns it to what he has just seen, the fat ex-cop walking up Harper Road Hill with Jerome Robinson and the Irish setter with the nigger name. Jerome gave him a wave and Brady gave it right back, because that's the way you blend in. Like listening to Freddi Linklatter's endless rants about how tough it was to be a gay woman in a straight world.

Kermit William "I wish I was young" Hodges and Jerome "I wish I was white" Robinson. What was the Odd Couple talking about? That's something Brady Hartsfield would like to know. Maybe he'll find out if the cop takes the bait and strikes up a conversation on Debbie's Blue Umbrella. It certainly worked with the rich bitch; once she started talking, nothing could stop her.

The Det-Ret and his darkie houseboy.

Also Odell. Don't forget Odell. Jerome and his little sister love that dog. It would really break them up if something happened to it. Probably nothing will, but maybe he'll research some more poisons on the Net when he gets home tonight.

Such thoughts are always flitting through Brady's mind; they are the bats in his belfry. This morning at DE, as he was inventorying another load of cheap-ass DVDs (why more are coming in at the same time they're trying to dump stock is a mystery that will never be solved), it occurred to him that he could use his suicide vest to assassinate the president, Mr. Barack "I wish I was white" Obama. Go out in a blaze of glory. Barack comes to this state often, because it's important to his reelection strategy. And when he comes to the state, he comes to this city. Has a rally. Talks about hope. Talks about change. Rah-rah-rah, blah-blah-blah. Brady was figuring out how to avoid metal detectors and random checks when Tones Frobisher buzzed him and told him he had a service call. By the time he was on the road in one of the green Cyber Patrol VWs, he was thinking about something else. Brad Pitt, to be exact. Fucking matinee idol.

Sometimes, though, his ideas stick.

A chubby little boy comes running down the sidewalk, waving money. Brady pulls over.

"I want chawww-klit!" the little boy brays. *"And I want it with springles!"*

You got it, you fatass little creep, Brady thinks, and smiles his widest, most charming smile. Fuck up your cholesterol all you want, I give you until forty, and who knows, maybe you'll survive the first heart attack. That won't stop you, though, nope. Not when the world is full of beer and Whoppers and chocolate ice cream.

"You got it, little buddy. One chocolate with sprinkles coming right up. How was school? Get any As?"

15

That night the TV never goes on at 63 Harper Road, not even for the *Evening News.* Nor does the computer. Hodges hauls out his trusty legal pad instead. Janelle Patterson called him old school. So he is, and he doesn't apologize for it. This is the way he has always worked, the way he's most comfortable.

Sitting in beautiful no-TV silence, he reads over the letter Mr. Mercedes sent him. Then he reads the one Mrs. T. got. Back and forth he goes for an hour or more, examining the letters line by line. Because Mrs. T.'s letter is a copy, he feels free to jot in the margins and circle certain words.

He finishes this part of his procedure by reading the letters aloud. He uses different voices, because Mr. Mercedes has adopted two different personae. The letter Hodges received is gloating and arrogant. *Ha-ha, you broken-down old fool,* it says. *You have nothing to live for and you know it, so why don't you just kill yourself?* The tone of Olivia Trelawney's letter is cringing and melancholy, full of remorse and tales of childhood abuse, but here also is the idea of suicide, this time couched in terms of sympathy: *I understand. I totally get it, because I feel the same.*

At last he puts the letters in a folder with MERCEDES KILLER printed on the tab. There's nothing else in it, which means it's mighty thin, but if he's still any good at his job, it will thicken with page after page of his own notes.

He sits for fifteen minutes, hands folded on his too-large middle like a meditating Buddha. Then he draws the pad to him and begins writing.

I think I was right about most of the stylistic red herrings. In Mrs. T.'s letter he doesn't use exclamation points, capitalized phrases, or many one-sentence paragraphs (the ones at the end are for dramatic effect). I was wrong about the quotation marks, he likes those. Also fond of underlining things. He may not be young after all, I could have been wrong about that . . .

But he thinks of Jerome, who has already forgotten more about computers and the Internet than Hodges himself will ever learn. And of Janey Patterson, who knew how to make a copy of her sister's letter by scanning, and who uses Skype. Janey Patterson, who's got to be almost twenty years younger than he is.

He picks up his pen again.

. . . but I don't think I am. Probably not a teenager (altho can't rule it out) but let's say in the range 20–35. He's smart. Good vocabulary, able to turn a phrase.

He goes through the letters yet again and jots down some of those turned phrases: *scurrying little mouse of a kid, strawberry jam in a sleeping bag, most people are sheep and sheep don't eat meat.*

Nothing that would make people forget Philip Roth, but Hodges thinks such lines show a degree of talent. He finds one more and prints it below the others: *What have they done for you except hound you and cause you sleepless nights?*

He taps the tip of his pen above this, creating a constellation of tiny dark blue dots. He thinks most people would write *give you sleepless nights* or *bring you sleepless nights,* but those weren't good enough for Mr. Mercedes, because he is a gardener planting seeds of doubt and paranoia. *They* are out to get you, Mrs. T., and *they* have a point, don't they? Because you *did* leave your key. The cops say so; I say so too, and I was there. How can we both be wrong?

He writes these ideas down, boxes them, then turns to a fresh sheet.

Best point of identification is still PERK for PERP, he uses it in both letters, but also note HYPHENS in the Trelawney letter. Bee-hive *instead of beehive.* Week-days *instead of weekdays. If I am able to ID this guy and get a writing sample, I can nail him.*

Such stylistic fingerprints wouldn't be enough to convince a jury, but Hodges himself? Absolutely.

He sits back again, head tilted, eyes fixed on nothing. He isn't aware of time passing; for Hodges, time, which has hung so heavy since his retirement, has been canceled. Then he lurches forward, office chair squalling an unheard protest, and writes in large capital letters: *HAS MR. MERCEDES BEEN WATCHING?*

Hodges feels all but positive he has been. That it's his MO.

He followed Mrs. Trelawney's vilification in the newspapers, he watched her two or three appearances on the TV news (curt and unflattering, those appearances drove her already low approval ratings into the basement). He may have done drive-bys on her house as well. Hodges should talk to Radney Peeples again and find out if Peeples or any other Vigilant employees noted certain cars cruising Mrs. Trelawney's Sugar Heights neighborhood in the weeks before she caught the bus. And someone sprayed KILLER CUNT on one of her gateposts. How long before her suicide was that? Maybe Mr. Mercedes did it himself. And of course, he could have gotten to know her better, *lots* better, if she took him up on his invitation to meet under the Blue Umbrella.

Then there's me, he thinks, and looks at the way his own letter ends: *I wouldn't want you to start thinking about your gun* followed by *But you* are *thinking of it, aren't you?* Is Mr. Mercedes talking about his theoretical service weapon, or has he seen the .38 Hodges sometimes plays with? No way of telling, but . . .

But I think he has. He knows where I live, you can look right into my living room from the street, and I think he's seen it.

The idea that he's been watched fills Hodges with excitement rather than dread or embarrassment. If he could match some vehicle the Vigilant people have noticed with a vehicle spending an inordinate amount of time on Harper Road —

That's when the telephone rings.

16

"Hi, Mr. H."

"S'up, Jerome?"

"I'm under the Umbrella."

Hodges puts his legal pad aside. The first four pages are now full of disjointed notes, the next three with a close-written case summary, just like in the old days. He rocks back in his chair.

"It didn't eat your computer, I take it?"

"Nope. No worms, no viruses. And I've already got four offers to talk with new friends. One's from Abilene, Texas. She says her name is Bernice, but I can call her Berni. With an *i.* She sounds cute as hell, and I won't say I'm not tempted, but she's probably a cross-dressing shoe salesman from Boston who lives with his mother. The Internet, dude — it's a wonderbox."

Hodges grins.

"First the background, which I partly got from poking around that selfsame Internet and mostly from a couple of Computer Science geeks at the university. You ready?"

Hodges grabs his legal pad again and turns to a fresh page. "Hit me." Which is exactly what he used to say to Pete Huntley when Pete came in with fresh information on a case.

"Okay, but first . . . do you know what the most precious Internet commodity is?"

"Nope." And, thinking of Janey Patterson:

"I'm old school."

Jerome laughs. "That you are, Mr. Hodges. It's part of your charm."

Dryly: "Thank you, Jerome."

"The most precious commodity is privacy, and that's what Debbie's Blue Umbrella and sites like it deliver. They make Facebook look like a partyline back in the nineteen-fifties. Hundreds of privacy sites have sprung up since 9/11. That's when the various first-world governments really started to get snoopy. The powers that be fear the Net, dude, and they're right to fear it. Anyway, most of these EP sites — stands for *extreme privacy* — operate out of Central Europe. They are to Internet chat what Switzerland is to bank accounts. You with me?"

"Yeah."

"The Blue Umbrella servers are in Olovo, a Bosnian ville that was mostly known for bullfights until 2005 or so. Encrypted servers. We're talking NASA quality, okay? Traceback's impossible, unless NSA or the Kang Sheng — that's the Chinese version of the NSA — have got some super-secret software nobody knows about."

And even if they do, Hodges thinks, they'd never put it to use in a case like the Mercedes Killer.

"Here's another feature, especially handy in the age of sexting scandals. Mr. H., have you ever found something on the Net — like a picture or an article in a newspaper — that you wanted to print, and you couldn't?"

"A few times, yeah. You hit print, and the Print Preview shows nothing but a blank page. It's annoying."

"Same thing on Debbie's Blue Umbrella." Jerome doesn't sound annoyed; he sounds admiring. "I had a little back-and-forth with my new friend Berni — you know, how's the weather there, what're your favorite groups, that kind of thing — and when I tried to print our conversation, I got a pair of lips with a finger across them and a message that says SHHH." Jerome spells this out, just to be sure Hodges gets it. "You *can* make a record of the conversation . . ."

You bet, Hodges thinks, looking fondly down at the jotted notes on his legal pad.

". . . but you'd have to take screen-shots or something, which is a pain in the ass. You see what I mean about the privacy, right? These guys are serious about it."

Hodges does see. He flips back to the first page of his legal pad and circles one of his earliest notes: COMPUTER SAVVY (UNDER 50?).

"When you click in, you get the usual choice — ENTER USERNAME or REGISTER NOW. Since I didn't have a username, I clicked REGISTER NOW and got one. If you want to talk with me under the Blue Umbrella, I'm tyrone40. Next, there's a questionnaire you fill out — age, sex, interests, things like that — and then you have to punch in your credit card number. It's thirty bucks a month. I did it because I have faith in your powers of reimbursement."

"Your faith will be rewarded, my son."

"The computer thinks it over for ninety seconds or so — the Blue Umbrella spins and the screen says SORTING. Then you get a list of people with interests similar to yours. You just bang on a few and pretty soon you're chatting up a storm."

"Could people use this to exchange porn? I know the descriptor says you can't, but —"

"You could use it to exchange *fantasies,* but no pix. Although I could see how weirdos — child abusers, crush freaks, that kind of thing — could use the Blue Umbrella to direct like-minded friends to sites where outlaw images *are* available."

Hodges starts to ask what crush freaks are, then decides he doesn't want to know.

"Mostly just innocent chat, then."

"Well . . ."

"Well what?"

"I can see how crazies might use it to exchange badass info. Like how to build bombs and stuff."

"Let's say I already have a username. What happens then?"

"Do you?" The excitement is back in Jerome's voice.

"Let's say I do."

"That would depend on whether you just made it up or if you got it from someone who wants to chat with you. Like he gave it to you on the phone or in an email."

Hodges grins. Jerome, a true child of his times, has never considered the possibility that information could be conveyed by such a nineteenth-century vehicle as a letter.

"Say you got it from someone else," Jerome goes on. "Like from the guy who stole that lady's car. Like maybe he wants to talk to you about what he did."

He waits. Hodges says nothing, but he is all admiration.

After a few seconds of silence, Jerome says, "Can't blame a guy for trying. Anyway, you go on and enter the username."

"When do I pay my thirty bucks?"

"You don't."

"Why not?"

"Because someone's already paid it for you." Jerome sounds sober now. Dead serious. "Probably don't need to tell you to be careful, but I will, anyway. Because if you already have a username, this guy's waiting for you."

17

Brady stops on his way home to get them supper (subs from Little Chef tonight), but his mother is gorked out on the couch. The TV is showing another of those reality things, a program that pimps a bunch of good-looking young women to a hunky bachelor who looks like he might have the IQ of a floor lamp. Brady sees Ma has already eaten — sort of. On the coffee table is a half-empty bottle of Smirnoff's and two cans of NutraSlim. High tea in hell, he thinks, but at least she's dressed: jeans and a City College sweatshirt.

On the off-chance, he unwraps her sandwich and wafts it back and forth beneath her nose, but she only snorts and turns her head away. He decides to eat that one himself and put the other one in his private fridge. When he comes back from the garage, the hunky bachelor is asking one of his potential fucktoys (a blonde, of course) if she likes to cook breakfast. The blonde's simpering reply: "Do you like something hot in the morning?"

Holding the plate with his sandwich on it, he regards his mother. He knows it's possible he'll come home some evening and find her dead. He could even help her along, just pick up one of the throw pillows and settle it over her face. It wouldn't be the first time murder was committed in this house. If he did that, would his life be better or worse?

His fear — unarticulated by his conscious mind but swimming around beneath — is that *nothing* would change.

He goes downstairs, voice-commanding the lights and computers. He sits in front of Number Three and goes on Debbie's Blue Umbrella, sure that by now the fat ex-cop will have taken the bait.

There's nothing.

He smacks his fist into his palm, feeling a dull throb at his temples that is the sure harbinger of a headache, a migraine that's apt to keep him awake half the night. Aspirin doesn't touch those headaches when they come. He calls them the Little Witches, only sometimes the Little Witches are big. He knows there are pills that are supposed to relieve headaches like that — he's researched them on the Net — but you can't get them without a prescription, and Brady is terrified of doctors. What if one of them discovered he was suffering from a brain tumor? A glioblastoma, which Wikipedia says is the worst? What if that's why he killed the people at the job fair?

Don't be stupid, a glio would have killed you months ago.

Okay, but suppose the doctor said his migraines were a sign of mental illness? Paranoid schizophrenia, something like that? Brady accepts that he *is* mentally ill, of course he is, normal people don't drive into crowds of people or consider taking out the President of the United States in a suicide attack. Normal people don't kill their little brothers. Normal men don't pause outside their mothers' doors, wondering if they're naked.

But abnormal men don't like other people to *know* they're abnormal.

He shuts off his computer and wanders aimlessly around his control room. He picks up Thing Two, then puts it down again. Even this isn't original, he's discovered; car thieves have been using gadgets like this for years. He hasn't dared to use it since the last time he used it on Mrs. Trelawney's Mercedes, but maybe it's time to bring good old Thing Two out of retirement — it's amazing what people leave in their cars. Using Thing Two is a little dangerous, but not very. Not if he's careful, and Brady can be very careful.

Fucking ex-cop, why hasn't he taken the bait?

Brady rubs his temples.

18

Hodges hasn't taken the bait because he understands the stakes: pot limit. If he writes the wrong message, he'll never hear from Mr. Mercedes again. On the other hand, if he does what he's sure Mr. Mercedes expects — coy and clumsy efforts to discover who the guy is — the conniving sonofabitch will run rings around him.

The question to be answered before he

starts is simple: who is going to be the fish in this relationship, and who is going to be the fisherman?

He has to write something, because the Blue Umbrella is all he has. He can call on none of his old police resources. The letters Mr. Mercedes wrote to Olivia Trelawney and Hodges himself are worthless without a suspect. Besides, a letter is just a letter, while computer chat is . . .

"A dialogue," he says.

Only he needs a lure. The tastiest lure imaginable. He can pretend he's suicidal, it wouldn't be hard, because until very recently he has been. He's sure that meditations on the attractiveness of death would keep Mr. Mercedes talking for awhile, but for how long before the guy realized he was being played? This is no hopped-up moke who believes the police really are going to give him a million dollars and a 747 that will fly him to El Salvador. Mr. Mercedes is a very intelligent person who happens to be crazy.

Hodges draws his legal pad onto his lap and turns to a fresh page. Halfway down he writes half a dozen words in large capitals:

I HAVE TO WIND HIM UP.

He puts a box around this, places the legal pad in the case file he has started, and closes the thickening folder. He sits a moment longer, looking at the screensaver photo of his daughter, who is no longer five and no longer thinks he's God.

"Good night, Allie."

He turns off his computer and goes to bed. He doesn't expect to sleep, but he does.

19

He wakes up at 2:19 A.M. by the bedside clock with the answer as bright in his mind as a neon bar sign. It's risky but right, the kind of thing you do without hesitation or you don't do at all. He goes into his office, a large pale ghost in boxer shorts. He powers up his computer. He goes to Debbie's Blue Umbrella and clicks GET STARTED NOW!

A new image appears. This time the young couple is on what looks like a magic carpet floating over an endless sea. The silver rain is falling, but they are safe and dry beneath the blue umbrella. There are two buttons below the carpet, REGISTER NOW on the left and ENTER PASSWORD on the right. Hodges clicks ENTER PASSWORD, and in the box that appears he types **kermitfrog19.** He hits return and a new screen appears. On it is this message:

merckill wants to chat with you!
Do you want to chat with merckill?
Y N

He puts the cursor on **Y** and clicks his mouse. A box for his message appears. Hodges types quickly, without hesitation.

20

Three miles away, at 49 Elm Street in Northfield, Brady Hartsfield can't sleep. His head thumps. He thinks: *Frankie.* My brother, who should have died when he choked on that apple slice. Life would have been so much simpler if things had happened that way.

He thinks of his mother, who sometimes forgets her nightgown and sleeps raw.

Most of all, he thinks of the fat ex-cop.

At last he gets up and leaves his bedroom, pausing for a moment outside his mother's door, listening to her snore. The most unerotic sound in the universe, he tells himself, but still he pauses. Then he goes downstairs, opens the basement door, and closes it behind him. He stands in the dark and says, "Control." But his voice is too hoarse and the dark remains. He clears his throat and tries again. "Control!"

The lights come on. *Chaos* lights up his computers and *darkness* stops the seven-screen countdown. He sits in front of his Number Three. Among the litter of icons is a small blue umbrella. He clicks on it, unaware that he's been holding his breath until he lets it out in a long harsh gasp.

kermitfrog19 wants to chat with you!
Do you want to chat with kermitfrog19?
Y N

Brady hits **Y** and leans forward. His eager expression remains for a moment before puzzlement seeps in. Then, as he reads the short message over and over, puzzlement becomes first anger and then naked fury.

Seen a lot of false confessions in my time, but this one's a dilly.
I'm retired but not stupid.
Withheld evidence proves you are not the Mercedes Killer.
Fuck off, asshole.

Brady feels an almost insurmountable urge to slam his fist through the screen but restrains it. He sits in his chair, trembling all over. His eyes are wide and unbelieving. A minute passes. Two. Three.

Pretty soon I'll get up, he thinks. Get up and go back to bed.

Only what good will that do? He won't be able to sleep.

"You fat fuck," he whispers, unaware that hot tears have begun to spill from his eyes. "You fat stupid useless fuck. It *was* me! It *was* me! *It was me!*"

Withheld evidence proves.

That is impossible.

He seizes on the necessity of hurting the fat ex-cop, and with the idea the ability to think returns. How should he do that? He considers the question for nearly half an hour, trying on and rejecting several scenarios. The answer, when it comes, is elegantly simple. The fat ex-cop's friend — his only friend, so far as Brady has been able to ascertain — is a nigger kid with a white name. And what does the nigger kid love? What does his whole family love? The Irish setter, of course. Odell.

Brady recalls his earlier fantasy about poisoning a few gallons of Mr. Tastey's finest, and starts laughing. He goes on the Internet and begins doing research.

My due diligence, he thinks, and smiles.

At some point he realizes his headache is gone.

Poison Bait

1

Brady Hartsfield doesn't need long to figure out how he's going to poison Jerome Robinson's canine pal, Odell. It helps that Brady is also Ralph Jones, a fictional fellow with just enough bona fides — plus a low-limit Visa card — to order things from places like Amazon and eBay. Most people don't realize how easy it is to whomp up an Internet-friendly false identity. You just have to pay the bills. If you don't, things can come unraveled in a hurry.

As Ralph Jones he orders a two-pound can of Gopher-Go and gives Ralphie's mail drop address, the Speedy Postal not far from Discount Electronix.

The active ingredient in Gopher-Go is strychnine. Brady looks up the symptoms of strychnine poisoning on the Net and is delighted to find that Odell will have a tough time of it. Twenty minutes or so after ingestion, muscle spasms start in the neck and head. They quickly spread to the rest of the body. The mouth stretches in a grin (at least in humans; Brady doesn't know about dogs). There may be vomiting, but by then too much of the poison has been absorbed and it's too late. Convulsions set in and get worse until the backbone turns into a hard and constant arch. Sometimes the spine actually snaps. When death comes — as a relief, Brady is sure — it's as a result of asphyxiation. The neural pathways tasked with running air to the lungs from the outside world just give up.

Brady can hardly wait.

At least it won't be a *long* wait, he tells himself as he shuts off his seven computers and climbs the stairs. The stuff should be waiting for him next week. The best way to get it into the dog, he thinks, would be in a ball of nice juicy hamburger. All dogs like hamburger, and Brady knows exactly how he's going to deliver Odell's treat.

Barbara Robinson, Jerome's little sister, has a friend named Hilda. The two girls like to visit Zoney's GoMart, the convenience store a couple of blocks from the Robinson house. They say it's because they like the grape Icees, but what they really like is hanging out with their other little friends. They sit on the low stone wall at the back of the store's four-car parking lot, half a dozen chickadees gossiping and giggling and trading treats. Brady has seen them often when he's driving the Mr. Tastey truck. He waves to them and they wave back.

Everybody likes the ice cream man.

Mrs. Robinson allows Barbara to make these trips once or twice a week (Zoney's isn't a drug hangout, a thing she has probably investigated for herself), but she has put conditions on her approval that Brady has had no trouble deducing. Barbara can never go alone; she always must be back in an hour; she and her friend must always take Odell. No dogs are allowed in the GoMart, so Barbara tethers him to the doorhandle of the outside restroom while she and Hilda go inside to get their grape-flavored ice.

That's when Brady — driving his personal car, a nondescript Subaru — will toss Odell the lethal burger-ball. The dog is big; he may last twenty-four hours. Brady hopes so. Grief has a transitive power which is nicely expressed by the axiom *shit rolls downhill.* The more pain Odell feels, the more pain the nigger girl and her big brother will feel. Jerome will pass his grief on to the fat ex-cop, aka Kermit William Hodges, and the fat ex-cop will understand the dog's death is *his* fault, payback for sending Brady that infuriating and disrespectful message. When Odell dies, the fat ex-cop will know —

Halfway up to the second floor, listening to his mother snoring, Brady stops, eyes wide with dawning realization.

The fat ex-cop will *know.*

And that's the trouble, isn't it? Because actions have consequences. It's the reason why Brady might *daydream* about poisoning a load of the ice cream he sells the kiddies, but wouldn't actually *do* such a thing. Not as long as he wants to keep flying under the radar, that is, and for now he does.

So far Hodges hasn't gone to his pals in the police department with the letter Brady sent. At first Brady believed it was because Hodges wanted to keep it between the two of them, maybe take a shot at tracking down the Mercedes Killer himself and getting a little post-retirement glory, but now he knows better. Why would the fucking Det-Ret want to track him down when he thinks Brady's nothing but a crank?

Brady can't understand how Hodges could come to that conclusion when he, Brady, knew about the bleach and the hairnet, details never released to the press, but somehow he has. If Brady poisons Odell, Hodges will call in his police pals. Starting with his old partner, Huntley.

Worse, it may give the man Brady hoped to goad into suicide a new reason to live, defeating the whole *purpose* of the artfully composed letter. That would be completely unfair. Pushing the Trelawney bitch over the edge had been the greatest thrill of his life, far greater (for reasons he doesn't understand, or care to) than killing all those people with her car, and he wanted to do it again. To get the chief investigator in the case to kill himself — what a triumph that would be!

Brady is standing halfway up the stairs, thinking hard.

The fat bastard still might do it, he tells himself. Killing the dog might be the final push he needs.

Only he doesn't really buy this, and his head gives a warning throb.

He feels a sudden urge to rush back down to the basement, go on the Blue Umbrella, and demand that the fat ex-cop tell him what bullshit "withheld evidence" he's talking about so he, Brady, can knock it down. But to do that would be a bad mistake. It would look needy, maybe even desperate.

Withheld evidence.

Fuck off, asshole.

But I did it! I risked my freedom, I risked my life, *and I did it! You can't take away the credit! It's not fair!*

His head throbs again.

You stupid cocksucker, he thinks. One way or the other, you're going to pay, but not until after the dog dies. Maybe your nigger friend will die, too. Maybe that whole nigger family will die. And after them, maybe a whole lot of other people. Enough to make what happened at City Center look like a picnic.

He goes up to his room and lies down on his bed in his underwear. His head is banging again, his arms are trembling (it's as if *he* has ingested strychnine). He'll lie here in agony until morning, unless —

He gets up and goes back down the hall. He stands outside his mother's open door for almost four minutes, then gives up and goes inside. He gets into bed with her and his headache begins to recede almost at once. Maybe it's the warmth. Maybe it's the smell of her — shampoo, body lotion, booze. Probably it's both.

She turns over. Her eyes are wide in the dark. "Oh, honeyboy. Are you having one of those nights?"

"Yes." He feels the warmth of tears in his eyes.

"Little Witch?"

"*Big* Witch this time."

"Want me to help you?" She already knows the answer; it's throbbing against her stomach. "You do so much for me," she says tenderly. "Let me do this for you."

He closes his eyes. The smell of the booze on her breath is very strong. He doesn't mind, although ordinarily he hates it. "Okay."

She takes care of him swiftly and expertly. It doesn't take long. It never does.

"There," she says. "Go to sleep now, honeyboy."

He does, almost at once.

When he wakes in the early morning light she's snoring again, a lock of hair spit-stuck to the corner of her mouth. He gets out of bed and goes back to his own room. His mind is clear. The strychnine-laced gopher poison is on its way. When it arrives, he'll poison the dog, and damn the consequences. *God* damn the consequences. As for those suburban niggers with the white-people names? They don't matter. The fat ex-cop goes next, after he's had a chance to fully experience Jerome Robinson's pain and Barbara Robinson's sorrow, and who cares if it's suicide? The important thing is that he *go.* And after that . . .

"Something big," he says as he pulls on a pair of jeans and a plain white tee. "A blaze of glory." Just what the blaze will be he doesn't know yet, but that's okay. He has time, and he needs to do something first. He needs to demolish Hodges's so-called "withheld evidence" and convince him that he, Brady, is indeed the Mercedes Killer, the monster Hodges failed to catch. He needs to rub it in until it hurts. He also needs it because if Hodges believes in this bogus "withheld evidence," the other cops — the *real* cops — must believe it, too. That is unacceptable. He needs . . .

"Credibility!" Brady exclaims to the empty kitchen. "I need credibility!"

He sets about making breakfast: bacon and eggs. The smell may waft upstairs to Ma and tempt her. If not, no big deal. He'll eat her share. He's pretty hungry.

2

This time it works, although when Deborah Ann appears, she's still belting her robe and barely awake. Her eyes are red-rimmed, her cheeks are pale, and her hair flies out every whichway. She no longer suffers hangovers, exactly, her brain and body have gotten too used to the booze for that, but she spends her mornings in a state of soft focus, watching game shows and popping Tums. Around two in the afternoon, when the world starts to sharpen up for her, she pours the day's first drink.

If she remembers what happened last night, she doesn't mention it. But then, she never does. Neither of them do.

We never talk about Frankie, either, Brady thinks. And if we did, what would we say? Gosh, too bad about that fall he took?

"Smells good," she says. "Some for me?"

"All you want. Coffee?"

"Please. Lots of sugar." She sits down at the table and stares at the television on the counter. It isn't on, but she stares at it anyway. For all Brady knows, maybe she thinks it *is* on.

"You're not wearing your uniform," she says — meaning the blue button-up shirt with

DISCOUNT ELECTRONIX on the pocket. He has three hanging in his closet. He irons them himself. Like vacuuming the floors and washing their clothes, ironing isn't in Ma's repertoire.

"Don't need to go in until ten," he says, and as if the words are a magic incantation, his phone wakes up and starts buzzing across the kitchen counter. He catches it just before it can fall off onto the floor.

"Don't answer it, honeyboy. Pretend we went out for breakfast."

It's tempting, but Brady is as incapable of letting a phone ring as he is of giving up his muddled and ever-changing plans for some grand act of destruction. He looks at the caller ID and isn't surprised to see TONES in the window. Anthony "Tones" Frobisher, the grand high panjandrum of Discount Electronix (Birch Hill Mall branch).

He picks up the phone and says, "It's my late day, Tones."

"I know, but I need you to make a service call. I really, really do." Tones can't *make* Brady take a call on his late day, hence the wheedling tone. "Plus it's Mrs. Rollins, and you know she tips."

Of course she does, she lives in Sugar Heights. The Cyber Patrol makes lots of service calls in Sugar Heights, and one of their customers — one of *Brady's* customers — was the late Olivia Trelawney. He was in her house twice on calls after he began conversing with her beneath Debbie's Blue Umbrella, and what a kick *that* was. Seeing how much weight she'd lost. Seeing how her hands had started to tremble. Also, having access to her computer had opened all sorts of possibilities.

"I don't know, Tones . . ." But of course he'll go, and not only because Mrs. Rollins tips. It's fun to go rolling past 729 Lilac Drive, thinking: *I'm* responsible for those closed gates. All I had to do to give her the final push was add one little program to her Mac.

Computers are wonderful.

"Listen, Brady, if you take this call, you don't have to work the store at all today, how's that? Just return the Beetle and then hang out wherever until it's time to fire up your stupid ice cream wagon."

"What about Freddi? Why don't you send her?" Flat-out teasing now. If Tones could have sent Freddi, she'd already be on her way.

"Called in sick. Says she got her period and it's killing her. Of course it's fucking bullshit. I know it, she knows it, and she knows I know it, but she'll put in a sexual harassment claim if I call her on it. She knows I know *that,* too."

Ma sees Brady smiling, and smiles back. She raises a hand, closes it, and turns it back and forth. *Twist his balls, honeyboy.* Brady's smile widens into a grin. Ma may be a drunk, she may only cook once or twice a week, she can be as annoying as shit, but sometimes she can read him like a book.

"All right," Brady says. "How about I take my own car?"

"You know I can't give you a mileage allowance for your personal vehicle," Tones says.

"Also, it's company policy," Brady says. "Right?"

"Well . . . yeah."

Schyn Ltd., DE's German parent company, believes the Cyber Patrol VWs are good advertising. Freddi Linklatter says that anyone who wants a guy driving a snot-green Beetle to fix his computer is insane, and on this point Brady agrees with her. Still, there must be a lot of insane people out there, because they never lack for service calls.

Although few tip as well as Paula Rollins.

"Okay," Brady says, "but you owe me one."

"Thanks, buddy."

Brady kills the connection without bothering to say You're not my buddy, and we both know it.

3

Paula Rollins is a full-figured blonde who lives in a sixteen-room faux Tudor mansion three blocks from the late Mrs. T.'s pile. She has all those rooms to herself. Brady doesn't know exactly what her deal is, but guesses she's some rich guy's second or third ex–trophy wife, and that she did very well for herself in the settlement. Maybe the guy was too entranced by her knockers to bother with the prenup. Brady doesn't care much, he only knows she has enough to tip well and she's never tried to slap the make on him. That's good. He has no interest in Mrs. Rollins's full figure.

She *does* grab his hand and just about pull him through the door, though.

"Oh . . . Brady! Thank God!"

She sounds like a woman being rescued from a desert island after three days without food or water, but he hears the little pause before she says his name and sees her eyes flick down to read it off his shirt, even though he's been here half a dozen times. (So has Freddi, for that matter; Paula Rollins is a serial computer abuser.) He doesn't mind that she doesn't remember him. Brady likes being forgettable.

"It just . . . I don't know what's *wrong*!"

As if the dimwitted twat ever does. Last time he was here, six weeks ago, it was a kernel panic, and she was convinced a computer virus had gobbled up all her files. Brady shooed her gently from the office and promised (not sounding too hopeful) to do what he could. Then he sat down, re-started the computer, and surfed for awhile before calling her in and telling her he had been able to fix the problem just in time. Another half hour, he said, and her files really *would* have been gone. She had tipped him eighty dollars. He and Ma had gone out to dinner that night, and split a not-bad bottle of champagne.

"Tell me what happened," Brady says, grave as a neurosurgeon.

"I didn't do *anything,*" she wails. She always wails. Many of his service call customers do. Not just the women, either. Nothing can unman a top-shelf executive more rapidly than the possibility that everything on his MacBook just went to data heaven.

She pulls him through the parlor (it's as long as an Amtrak dining car) and into her office.

"I cleaned up myself, I never let the housekeeper in here — washed the windows, vacuumed the floor — and when I sat down to do my email, the damn computer wouldn't even *turn on*!"

"Huh. Weird." Brady knows Mrs. Rollins has a spic maid to do the household chores, but apparently the maid isn't allowed in the office. Which is a good thing for her, because Brady has already spotted the problem, and if the maid had been responsible for it, she probably would have been fired.

"Can you fix it, Brady?" Thanks to the tears swimming in them, Mrs. Rollins's big blue eyes are bigger than ever. Brady suddenly flashes on Betty Boop in those old cartoons you can look at on YouTube, thinks *Poop-poop-pe-doop!,* and has to restrain a laugh.

"I'll sure try," he says gallantly.

"I have to run across the street to Helen Wilcox's," she says, "but I'll only be a few minutes. There's fresh coffee in the kitchen, if you want it."

So saying, she leaves him alone in her big expensive house, with fuck knows how many valuable pieces of jewelry scattered around upstairs. She's safe, though. Brady would never steal from a service client. He might be caught in the act. Even if he weren't, who would be the logical suspect? Duh. He didn't get away with mowing down those job-seeking idiots at City Center only to be arrested for stealing a pair of diamond earrings he wouldn't have any idea how to get rid of.

He waits until the back door shuts, then goes into the parlor to watch her accompany her world-class tits across the street. When she's out of sight, he goes back to the office, crawls under her desk, and plugs in her computer. She must have yanked the plug so she could vacuum, then forgot to jack it back in.

Her password screen comes on. Idly, just killing time, he types PAULA, and her desktop, loaded with all her files, appears. God, people are so dumb.

He goes on Debbie's Blue Umbrella to see if the fat ex-cop has posted anything new. He hasn't, but Brady decides on the spur of the moment to send the Det-Ret a message after all. Why not?

He learned in high school that thinking too long about writing doesn't work for him. Too many other ideas get into his head and start sliding all over each other. It's better to just fire away. That was how he wrote to Olivia Trelawney — white heat, baby — and it's also the way he wrote to Hodges, although he went over the message to the fat ex-cop a couple of times to make sure he was keeping his style consistent.

He writes in the same style now, only reminding himself to keep it short.

How did I know about the hairnet and bleach, Detective Hodges? THAT STUFF was withheld evidence because it was never in the paper or on TV. You say you are not stupid but IT SURE LOOKS THAT WAY TO ME. I think all that TV you watch has rotted your brain.

WHAT withheld evidence?

I DARE YOU TO ANSWER THIS.

Brady looks this over and makes one change: a hyphen in the middle of *hairnet.* He can't believe he'll ever become a person of interest, but he knows that if he ever does, they'll ask him to provide a writing sample. He almost wishes he could give them one. He wore a mask when he drove into the crowd, and he wears another when he writes as the Mercedes Killer.

He hits SEND, then pulls down Mrs. Rollins's Internet history. For a moment he stops, bemused, when he sees several entries for White Tie and Tails. He knows what that is from something Freddi Linklatter told him: a male escort service. Paula Rollins has a secret life, it seems.

But then, doesn't everybody?

It's no business of his. He deletes his visit to Under Debbie's Blue Umbrella, then opens his boxy service crate and takes out a bunch of random crap: utility discs, a modem (broken, but she won't know that), various thumb-drives, and a voltage regulator that has nothing whatsoever to do with computer repair but looks technological. He also takes out a Lee Child paperback that he reads until he hears his client come in the back door twenty minutes later.

When Mrs. Rollins pokes her head into the study, the paperback is out of sight and Brady is packing up the random shit. She favors him with an anxious smile. "Any luck?"

"At first it looked bad," Brady says, "but I tracked down your problem. The trimmer switch was bad and that shut down your danus circuit. In a case like that, the computer's programmed not to start up, because if it did, you might lose all your data." He looks at her gravely. "The darn thing might even catch fire. It's been known to happen."

"Oh . . . my . . . dear . . . *Jesus,*" she says, packing each word with drama and placing one hand high on her chest. "Are you sure it's okay?"

"Good as gold," he says. "Check it out."

He starts the computer and looks politely away while she types in her numbfuck password. She opens a couple of files, then turns to him, smiling. "Brady, you are a gift from God."

"My ma used to tell me the same thing until I got old enough to buy beer."

She laughs as if this were the funniest thing she has heard in her whole life. Brady laughs with her, because he has a sudden vision: kneeling on her shoulders and driving a butcher knife from her own kitchen deep into her screaming mouth.

He can almost feel the gristle giving way.

4

Hodges has been checking the Blue Umbrella site frequently, and he's reading the Mercedes Killer's follow-up message only minutes after Brady hit SEND.

Hodges is grinning, a big one that smooths his skin and makes him almost handsome.

Their relationship has been officially established: Hodges the fisherman, Mr. Mercedes the fish. But a *wily* fish, he reminds himself, one capable of making a sudden lunge and snapping the line. He will have to be played carefully, reeled toward the boat slowly. If Hodges is able to do that, if he's patient, sooner or later Mr. Mercedes will agree to a meeting. Hodges is sure of it.

Because if he can't nudge me into offing myself, that leaves just one alternative, and that's murder.

The smart thing for Mr. Mercedes to do would be to just walk away; if he does that, the road ends. But he won't. He's pissed, but that's only part of it, and the small part, at that. Hodges wonders if Mr. Mercedes knows just how crazy he is. And if he knows there's one nugget of hard information here.

I think all that TV you watch has rotted your brain.

Up to this morning, Hodges has only suspected that Mr. Mercedes has been watching his house; now he knows. Motherfucker has been on the street, and more than once.

He grabs his legal pad and starts jotting possible follow-up messages. It has to be good, because his fish feels the hook. The pain of it makes him angry even though he doesn't yet know what it is. He needs to be a lot angrier before he figures it out, and that means taking a risk. Hodges must jerk the line to seat the hook deeper, despite the risk the line may break. What . . . ?

He remembers something Pete Huntley said at lunch, just a remark in passing, and the answer comes to him. Hodges writes on his pad, then rewrites, then polishes. He reads the finished message over and decides it will do. It's short and mean. There's something you forgot, sucka. Something a false confessor couldn't know. Or a real confessor, for that matter . . . unless Mr. Mercedes checked out his rolling murder weapon from stem to stern before climbing in, and Hodges is betting the guy didn't.

If he's wrong, the line snaps and the fish swims away. But there's an old saying: no risk, no reward.

He wants to send the message right away, but knows it's a bad idea. Let the fish swim around in circles a little longer with that bad old hook in his mouth. The question is what to do in the meantime. TV never had less appeal for him.

He gets an idea — they're coming in bunches this morning — and pulls out the bottom drawer of his desk. Here is a box filled with the small flip-up pads he used to carry with him when he and Pete were doing street interviews. He never expected to need one of these again, but he takes one now and stows it in the back pocket of his chinos.

It fits just right.

5

Hodges walks halfway down Harper Road, then starts knocking on doors, just like in the old days. Crossing and re-crossing the street, missing no one, working his way back. It's a weekday, but a surprising number of people answer his knock or ring. Some are stay-at-home moms, but many are retirees like himself, fortunate enough to have paid for their homes before the bottom fell out of the economy, but in less than great shape otherwise. Not living day-to-day or even week-to-week, maybe, but having to balance out the cost of food against the cost of all those old-folks medicines as the end of the month nears.

His story is simple, because simple is always best. He says there have been break-ins a few blocks over — kids, probably — and he's checking to see if anyone in his own neighborhood has noticed any vehicles that seem out of place, and have shown up more than once. They'd probably be cruising even slower than the twenty-five-mile-an-hour speed limit, he says. He doesn't have to say any more; they all watch the cop shows and know what "casing the joint" means.

He shows them his ID, which has RE-

TIRED stamped in red across the name and vitals below his photo. He's careful to say that no, he hasn't been asked by the police to do this canvassing (the last thing in the world he wants is one of his neighbors calling the Murrow Building downtown to check up on him), it was his own idea. He lives in the neighborhood, too, after all, and has a personal stake in its security.

Mrs. Melbourne, the widow whose flowers so fascinated Odell, invites him in for coffee and cookies. Hodges takes her up on it because she seems lonely. It's his first real conversation with her, and he quickly realizes she's eccentric at best, downright bonkers at worst. Articulate, though. He has to give her that. She explains about the black SUVs she's observed ("With tinted windows you can't see through, just like on *24*"), and tells him about their special antennas. Whippers, she calls them, waving her hand back and forth to demonstrate.

"Uh-huh," Hodges says. "Let me make a note of that." He turns a page in his pad and jots *I have to get out of here* on the new one.

"That's a good idea," she says, bright-eyed. "I've just got to tell you how sorry I was when your wife left you, Detective Hodges. She did, didn't she?"

"We agreed to disagree," Hodges says with an amiability he doesn't feel.

"It's so nice to meet you in person and

know you're keeping an eye out. Have another cookie."

Hodges glances at his watch, snaps his pad closed, and gets up. "I'd love to, but I'd better roll. Got a noon appointment."

She scans his bulk and says, "Doctor?"

"Chiropractor."

She frowns, transforming her face into a walnut shell with eyes. "Think that over, Detective Hodges. Back-crackers are dangerous. There are people who have lain down on those tables and never walked again."

She sees him to the door. As he steps onto the porch, she says, "I'd check on that ice cream man, too. This spring it seems like he's *always* around. Do you suppose Loeb's Ice Cream checks out the people they hire to drive those little trucks? I hope so, because that one looks suspicious. He might be a peedaroast."

"I'm sure their drivers have references, but I'll look into it."

"Another good idea!" she exclaims.

Hodges wonders what he'd do if she produced a long hook, like in the old-time vaudeville shows, and tried to yank him back inside. A childhood memory comes to him: the witch in *Hansel and Gretel.*

"Also — I just thought of this — I've seen several vans lately. They *look* like delivery vans — they have business names on them — but anyone can make up a business name, don't you think?"

"It's always possible," Hodges says, descending the steps.

"You should call in to number seventeen, too." She points down the hill. "It's almost all the way down to Hanover Street. They have people who come late, and play loud music." She sways forward in the doorway, almost bowing. "It could be a dope den. One of those crack houses."

Hodges thanks her for the tip and trudges across the street. Black SUVs and the Mr. Tastey guy, he thinks. Plus the delivery vans filled with Al Qaeda terrorists.

Across the street he finds a stay-at-home dad, Alan Bowfinger by name. "Just don't confuse me with Goldfinger," he says, and invites Hodges to sit in one of the lawn chairs on the left side of his house, where there's shade. Hodges is happy to take him up on this.

Bowfinger tells him that he makes a living writing greeting cards. "I specialize in the slightly snarky ones. Like on the outside it'll say, 'Happy Birthday! Who's the fairest of them all?' And when you open it up, there's a piece of shiny foil with a crack running down the middle of it."

"Yeah? And what's the message?"

Bowfinger holds up his hands, as if framing it. " 'Not you, but we love you anyway.' "

"Kind of mean," Hodges ventures.

"True, but it ends with an expression of love. That's what sells the card. First the poke, then the hug. As to your purpose today, Mr. Hodges . . . or do I call you Detective?"

"Just Mister these days."

"I haven't seen anything but the usual traffic. No slow cruisers except people looking for addresses and the ice cream truck after school lets out." Bowfinger rolls his eyes. "Did you get an earful from Mrs. Melbourne?"

"Well . . ."

"She's a member of NICAP," Bowfinger says. "That stands for National Investigations Committee on Aerial Phenomena."

"Weather stuff? Tornadoes and cloud formations?"

"Flying saucers." Bowfinger raises his hands to the sky. "She thinks they walk among us."

Hodges says something that would never have passed his lips if he'd still been on active duty and conducting an official investigation. "She thinks Mr. Tastey might be a peedaroast."

Bowfinger laughs until tears squirt out of his eyes. "Oh God," he says. "That guy's been around for five or six years, driving his little truck and jingling his little bells. How many peeds do you think he's roasted in all that time?"

"Don't know," Hodges says, getting to his feet. "Dozens, probably." He holds out his hand and Bowfinger shakes it. Another thing Hodges is discovering about retirement: his neighbors have stories and personalities. Some of them are even interesting.

As he's putting his notepad away, a look of alarm comes over Bowfinger's face.

"What?" Hodges asks, at once on point.

Bowfinger points across the street and says, "You didn't eat any of her cookies, did you?"

"Yeah. Why?"

"I'd stay close to the toilet for a few hours, if I were you."

6

When he gets back to his house, his arches throbbing and his ankles singing high C, the light on his answering machine is blinking. It's Pete Huntley, and he sounds excited. "Call me," he says. "This is unbelievable. Unfucking-real."

Hodges is suddenly, irrationally sure that Pete and his pretty new partner Isabelle have nailed Mr. Mercedes after all. He feels a deep stab of jealousy, and — crazy but true — anger. He hits Pete on speed-dial, his heart hammering, but his call goes right to voicemail.

"Got your message," Hodges says. "Call back when you can."

He kills the phone, then sits still, drumming his fingers on the edge of his desk. He tells himself it doesn't matter who catches the psycho sonofabitch, but it does. For one thing, it's certainly going to mean that his correspondence with the perk (funny how that word gets in your head) will come out, and that may put him in some fairly warm soup. But it's not the important thing. The important thing is that without Mr. Mercedes, things will go back to what they were: afternoon TV and playing with his father's gun.

He takes out his yellow legal pad and begins transcribing notes on his neighborhood walk-around. After a minute or two of this, he tosses the pad back into the case-folder and slams it closed. If Pete and Izzy Jaynes have popped the guy, Mrs. Melbourne's vans and sinister black SUVs don't mean shit.

He thinks about going on Debbie's Blue Umbrella and sending **merckill** a message: *Did they catch you?*

Ridiculous, but weirdly attractive.

His phone rings and he snatches it up, but it's not Pete. It's Olivia Trelawney's sister.

"Oh," he says. "Hi, Mrs. Patterson. How you doing?"

"I'm fine," she says, "and it's Janey, remember? Me Janey, you Bill."

"Janey, right."

"You don't sound exactly thrilled to hear from me, Bill." Is she being the tiniest bit flirty? Wouldn't that be nice.

"No, no, I'm happy you called, but I don't have anything to report."

"I didn't expect you would. I called about Mom. The nurse at Sunny Acres who's most familiar with her case works the day shift in the McDonald Building, where my mother has her little suite of rooms. I asked her to call if Mom brightened up. She still does that."

"Yes, you told me."

"Well, the nurse called just a few minutes ago to tell me Mom's back, at least for the time being. She might be clear for a day or two, then it's into the clouds again. Do you still want to go see her?"

"I think so," Hodges says cautiously, "but it would have to be this afternoon. I'm waiting on a call."

"Is it about the man who took her car?" Janey's excited. As I should be, Hodges tells himself.

"That's what I need to find out. Can I call you back?"

"Absolutely. You have my cell number?"

"Yeah."

"Yeah," she says, gently mocking. It makes him smile, in spite of his nerves. "Call me as soon as you can."

"I will."

He breaks the connection, and the phone rings while it's still in his hand. This time it's Pete, and he's more excited than ever.

"Billy! I gotta go back, we've got him in an interview room — IR4, as a matter of fact, remember how you always used to say that was your lucky one? — but I had to call you. We got him, partner, we fucking got him!"

"Got who?" Hodges asks, keeping his voice steady. His heartbeat is steady now, too, but the beats are hard enough to feel in his temples: *whomp* and *whomp* and *whomp.*

"Fucking Davis!" Pete shouts. "Who else?"

Davis. Not Mr. Mercedes but Donnie Davis, the camera-friendly wife murderer. Bill Hodges closes his eyes in relief. It's the wrong emotion to feel, but he feels it nevertheless.

He says, "So the body that game warden found near his cabin turned out to be Sheila Davis's? You're sure?"

"Positive."

"Who'd you blow to get the DNA results so fast?" When Hodges was on the force, they were lucky to get DNA results within a calendar month of sample submission, and six weeks was the average.

"We don't need DNA! For the trial, sure, but —"

"What do you mean, you don't —"

"Shut up and listen, okay? He just walked in off the street and copped to it. No lawyer, no bullshit justifications. Listened to the Miranda and said he didn't want a lawyer, only wanted to get it off his chest."

"Jesus. As smooth as he was in all the

interviews we had with him? Are you sure he's not fucking with you? Playing some sort of long game?"

Thinking it's the kind of thing Mr. Mercedes would try to do if they nailed him. Not just a game but a *long* game. Isn't that why he tries to create alternate writing styles in his poison-pen letters?

"Billy, *it's not just his wife.* You remember those dollies he had on the side? Girls with big hair and inflated tits and names like Bobbi Sue?"

"Sure. What about them?"

"When this breaks, those young ladies are going to get on their knees and thank God they're still alive."

"I'm not following you."

"Turnpike Joe, Billy! Five women raped and killed at various Interstate rest stops between here and Pennsylvania, starting back in ninety-four and ending in oh-eight! Donnie Davis says it's him! *Davis is Turnpike Joe!* He's giving us times and places and descriptions. It all fits. This . . . it blows my mind!"

"Mine, too," Hodges says, and he absolutely means it. "Congratulations."

"Thanks, but I didn't do anything except show up this morning." Pete laughs wildly. "I feel like I won the Megabucks."

Hodges doesn't feel like that, but at least he hasn't *lost* the Megabucks. He still has a case to work.

"I gotta get back in there, Billy, before he changes his mind."

"Yeah, yeah, but Pete? Before you go?"

"What?"

"Get him a court-appointed."

"Ah, Billy —"

"I'm serious. Interrogate the shit out of him, but before you start, announce — for the record — that you're getting him lawyered up. You can wring him dry before anyone shows up at Murrow, but you have to get this right. Are you hearing me?"

"Yeah, okay. That's a good call. I'll have Izzy do it."

"Great. Now get back in there. Nail him down."

Pete actually crows. Hodges has read about people doing that, but hasn't ever heard it done — except by roosters — until now. "Turnpike Joe, Billy! *Fucking Turnpike Joe!* Do you believe it?"

He hangs up before his ex-partner can reply. Hodges sits where he is for almost five minutes, waiting until a belated case of the shakes subsides. Then he calls Janey Patterson.

"It wasn't about the man we're looking for?"

"Sorry, no. Another case."

"Oh. Too bad."

"Yeah. You'll still come with me to the nursing home?"

"You bet. I'll be waiting on the sidewalk."

Before leaving, he checks the Blue Umbrella site one last time. Nothing there, and he has no intention of sending his own carefully crafted message today. Tonight will be soon enough. Let the fish feel the hook awhile longer.

He leaves his house with no premonition that he won't be back.

7

Sunny Acres is ritzy. Elizabeth Wharton is not.

She's in a wheelchair, hunched over in a posture that reminds Hodges of Rodin's *Thinker.* Afternoon sunlight slants in through the window, turning her hair into a silver cloud so fine it's a halo. Outside the window, on a rolling and perfectly manicured lawn, a few golden oldies are playing a slow-motion game of croquet. Mrs. Wharton's croquet days are over. As are her days of standing up. When Hodges last saw her — with Pete Huntley beside him and Olivia Trelawney sitting next to her — she was bent. Now she's broken.

Janey, vibrant in tapered white slacks and a blue-and-white-striped sailor's shirt, kneels beside her, stroking one of Mrs. Wharton's badly twisted hands.

"How are you today, dear one?" she asks.

"You look better." If this is true, Hodges is horrified.

Mrs. Wharton peers at her daughter with faded blue eyes that express nothing, not even puzzlement. Hodges's heart sinks. He enjoyed the ride out here with Janey, enjoyed looking at her, enjoyed getting to know her even more, and that's good. It means the trip hasn't been entirely wasted.

Then a minor miracle occurs. The old lady's cataract-tinged eyes clear; the cracked lipstickless lips spread in a smile. "Hello, Janey." She can only raise her head a little, but her eyes flick to Hodges. Now they look cold. "Craig."

Thanks to their conversation on the ride out, Hodges knows who that is.

"This isn't Craig, lovey. This is a friend of mine. His name is Bill Hodges. You've met him before."

"No, I don't believe . . ." She trails off — frowning now — then says, "You're . . . one of the detectives?"

"Yes, ma'am." He doesn't even consider telling her he's retired. Best to keep things on a straight line while there are still a few circuits working in her head.

Her frown deepens, creating rivers of wrinkles. "You thought Livvy left her key in her car so that man could steal it. She told you and told you, but you never believed her."

Hodges copies Janey, taking a knee beside

the wheelchair. "Mrs. Wharton, I now think we might have been wrong about that."

"Of course you were." She shifts her gaze back to her remaining daughter, looking up at her from beneath the bony shelf of her brow. It's the only way she *can* look. "Where's Craig?"

"I divorced him last year, Mom."

She considers, then says, "Good riddance to bad rubbish."

"I couldn't agree more. Can Bill ask you a few questions?"

"I don't see why not, but I want some orange juice. And my pain pills."

"I'll go down to the nurses' suite and see if it's time," she says. "Bill, are you okay if I — ?"

He nods and flicks two fingers in a *go, go* gesture. As soon as she's out the door, Hodges gets to his feet, bypasses the visitor's chair, and sits on Elizabeth Wharton's bed with his hands clasped between his knees. He has his pad, but he's afraid taking notes might distract her. The two of them regard each other silently. Hodges is fascinated by the silver nimbus around the old lady's head. There are signs that one of the orderlies combed her hair that morning, but it's gone its own wild way in the hours since. Hodges is glad. The scoliosis has twisted her body into a thing of ugliness, but her hair is beautiful. Crazy and beautiful.

"I think," he says, "we treated your daughter badly, Mrs. Wharton."

Yes indeed. Even if Mrs. T. was an unwitting accomplice, and Hodges hasn't entirely dismissed the idea that she left her key in the ignition, he and Pete did a piss-poor job. It's easy — too easy — to either disbelieve or disregard someone you dislike. "We were blinded by certain preconceptions, and for that I'm sorry."

"Are you talking about Janey? Janey and Craig? He hit her, you know. She tried to get him to stop using that dope stuff he liked, and he hit her. She says only once, but I believe it was more." She lifts one slow hand and taps her nose with a pale finger. "A mother can tell."

"This isn't about Janey. I'm talking about Olivia."

"He made Livvy stop taking her pills. She said it was because she didn't want to be a dope addict like Craig, but it wasn't the same. She *needed* those pills."

"Are you talking about her antidepressants?"

"They were pills that made her able to go out." She pauses, considering. "There were other ones, too, that kept her from touching things over and over. She had strange ideas, my Livvy, but she was a good person, just the same. Underneath, she was a very good person."

Mrs. Wharton begins to cry.

There's a box of Kleenex on the nightstand. Hodges takes a few and holds them out to her, but when he sees how difficult it is for her to close her hand, he wipes her eyes for her.

"Thank you, sir. Is your name Hedges?"

"Hodges, ma'am."

"You were the nice one. The other one was very mean to Livvy. She said he was laughing at her. Laughing all the time. She said she could see it in his eyes."

Was that true? If so, he's ashamed of Pete. And ashamed of himself for not realizing.

"Who suggested she stop taking her pills? Do you remember?"

Janey has come back with the orange juice and a small paper cup that probably holds her mother's pain medication. Hodges glimpses her from the corner of his eye and uses the same two fingers to motion her away again. He doesn't want Mrs. Wharton's attention divided, or taking any pills that will further muddle her already muddled recollection.

Mrs. Wharton is silent. Then, just when Hodges is afraid she won't answer: "It was her pen-pal."

"Did she meet him under the Blue Umbrella? Debbie's Blue Umbrella?"

"She never met him. Not in person."

"What I mean —"

"The Blue Umbrella was make-believe." From beneath the white brows, her eyes are calling him a perfect idiot. "It was a thing in her computer. Frankie was her *computer* pen-pal."

He always feels a kind of electric shock in his midsection when fresh info drops. Frankie. Surely not the guy's real name, but names have power and aliases often have meaning. *Frankie.*

"He told her to stop taking her medicine?"

"Yes, he said it was hooking her. Where's Janey? I want my pills."

"She'll be back any minute, I'm sure."

Mrs. Wharton broods into her lap for a moment. "Frankie said he took all the same medicines, and that's why he did . . . what he did. He said he felt better after he stopped taking them. He said that after he stopped, he knew what he did was wrong. But it made him sad because he couldn't take it back. That's what he *said.* And that life wasn't worth living. I told Livvy she should stop talking to him. I said he was bad. That he was poison. And she said . . ."

The tears are coming again.

"She said she had to save him."

This time when Janey comes into the doorway, Hodges nods to her. Janey puts a pair of blue pills into her mother's pursed and seeking mouth, then gives her a drink of juice.

"Thank you, Livvy."

Hodges sees Janey wince, then smile. "You're welcome, dear." She turns to Hodges. "I think we should go, Bill. She's very tired."

He can see that, but is still reluctant to leave. There's a feeling you get when the interview isn't done. When there's at least one more apple hanging on the tree. "Mrs. Wharton, did Olivia say anything else about Frankie? Because you're right. He *is* bad. I'd like to find him so he can't hurt anyone else."

"Livvy never would have left her key in her car. *Never.*" Elizabeth Wharton sits hunched in her bar of sun, a human parenthesis in a fuzzy blue robe, unaware that she's topped with a gauze of silver light. The finger comes up again — admonitory. She says, "That dog we had never threw up on the rug again. Just that once."

Janey takes Hodges's hand and mouths, *Let's go.*

Habits die hard, and Hodges speaks the old formula as Janey bends down and kisses first her mother's cheek and then the corner of her dry mouth. "Thank you for your time, Mrs. Wharton. You've been very helpful."

As they reach the door, Mrs. Wharton speaks clearly. "She *still* wouldn't have committed suicide if not for the ghosts."

Hodges turns back. Beside him, Janey Patterson is wide-eyed.

"What ghosts, Mrs. Wharton?"

"One was the baby," she says. "The poor thing who was killed with all those others. Livvy heard that baby in the night, crying and crying. She said the baby's name was Patricia."

"In her house? Olivia heard this in her house?"

Elizabeth Wharton manages the smallest of nods, a mere dip of the chin. "And sometimes the mother. She said the mother would accuse her."

She looks up at them from her wheelchair hunch.

"She would scream, 'Why did you let him murder my baby?' *That's* why Livvy killed herself."

8

It's Friday afternoon and the suburban streets are feverish with kids released from school. There aren't many on Harper Road, but there are still some, and this gives Brady a perfect reason to cruise slowly past number sixty-three and peek in the window. Except he can't, because the drapes are drawn. And the overhang to the left of the house is empty except for the lawnmower. Instead of sitting in his house and watching TV, where he belongs, the Det-Ret is sporting about in his crappy old Toyota.

Sporting about where? It probably doesn't

matter, but Hodges's absence makes Brady vaguely uneasy.

Two little girls trot to the curb with money clutched in their hands. They have undoubtedly been taught, both at home and at school, to never approach strangers, especially strange *men,* but who could be less strange than good old Mr. Tastey?

He sells them a cone each, one chocolate and one vanilla. He joshes with them, asks how they got so pretty. They giggle. The truth is one's ugly and the other's worse. As he serves them and makes change, he thinks about the missing Corolla, wondering if this break in Hodges's afternoon routine has anything to do with him. Another message from Hodges on the Blue Umbrella might cast some light, give an idea of where the ex-cop's head is at.

Even if it doesn't, Brady wants to hear from him.

"You don't dare ignore me," he says as the bells tinkle and chime over his head.

He crosses Hanover Street, parks in the strip mall, kills the engine (the annoying chimes fall blessedly silent), and hauls his laptop out from under the seat. He keeps it in an insulated case because the truck is always so fucking cold. He boots it up and goes on Debbie's Blue Umbrella courtesy of the nearby coffee shop's Wi-Fi.

Nothing.

"You fucker," Brady whispers. "You don't *dare* ignore me, you fucker."

As he zips the laptop back into its case, he sees a couple of boys standing outside the comic book shop, talking and looking at him and grinning. Given his five years of experience, Brady estimates that they're sixth- or seventh-graders with a combined IQ of one-twenty and a long future of collecting unemployment checks. Or a short one in some desert country.

They approach, the goofier-looking of the pair in the lead. Smiling, Brady leans out his window. "Help you boys?"

"We want to know if you got Jerry Garcia in there," Goofy says.

"No," Brady says, smiling more widely than ever, "but if I did, I'd sure let him out."

They look so ridiculously disappointed, Brady almost laughs. Instead, he points down at Goofy's pants. "Your fly's unzipped," he says, and when Goofy looks down, Brady flicks a finger at the soft underside of his chin. A little harder than he intended — actually quite a lot — but what the hell.

"Gotcha," Brady says merrily.

Goofy smiles to show yes, he's been gotten, but there's a red weal just above his Adam's apple and surprised tears swim in his eyes.

Goofy and Not Quite So Goofy start away. Goofy looks back over his shoulder. His lower lip is pushed out and now he looks like a third-grader instead of just another preadolescent come-stain who'll be fucking up the halls of Beal Middle School come September.

"That really hurt," he says, with a kind of wonder.

Brady's mad at himself. A finger-flick hard enough to bring tears to the kid's eyes means he's telling the straight-up truth. It also means Goofy and Not Quite So Goofy will remember him. Brady can apologize, can even give them free cones to show his sincerity, but then they'll remember *that.* It's a small thing, but small things mount up and then maybe you have a big thing.

"Sorry," he says, and means it. "I was just kidding around, son."

Goofy gives him the finger, and Not Quite So Goofy adds his own middle digit to show solidarity. They go into the comics store, where — if Brady knows boys like these, and he does — they will be invited to either buy or leave after five minutes' browsing.

They'll remember him. Goofy might even tell his parents, and his parents might lodge a complaint with Loeb's. It's unlikely but not impossible, and whose fault was it that he'd given Goofy Boy's unprotected neck a snap hard enough to leave a mark, instead of just the gentle flick he'd intended? The ex-cop has knocked Brady off-balance. He's making him screw things up, and Brady doesn't like that.

He starts the ice cream truck's engine. The bells begin bonging a tune from the loudspeaker on the roof. Brady turns left on Hanover Street and resumes his daily round, selling cones and Happy Boys and Pola Bars, spreading sugar on the afternoon and obeying all speed limits.

9

Although there are plenty of parking spaces on Lake Avenue after seven P.M. — as Olivia Trelawney well knew — they are few and far between at five in the afternoon, when Hodges and Janey Patterson get back from Sunny Acres. Hodges spots one three or four buildings down, however, and although it's small (the car behind the empty spot has poached a little), he shoehorns the Toyota into it quickly and easily.

"I'm impressed," Janey says. "I could never have done that. I flunked my driver's test on parallel parking the first two times I went."

"You must have had a hardass."

She smiles. "The third time I wore a short skirt, and that did the trick."

Thinking about how much he'd like to see her in a short skirt — the shorter the better — Hodges says, "There's really no trick to it. If you back toward the curb at a forty-five-degree angle, you can't go wrong. Unless your car's too big, that is. A Toyota's perfect for city parking. Not like a —" He stops.

"Not like a Mercedes," she finishes. "Come up and have coffee, Bill. I'll even feed the meter."

"I'll feed it. In fact, I'll max it out. We've got a lot to talk about."

"You learned some stuff from my mom, didn't you? That's why you were so quiet all the way back."

"I did, and I'll fill you in, but that's not where the conversation starts." He's looking at her full in the face now, and it's an easy face to look into. Christ, he wishes he were fifteen years younger. Even ten. "I need to be straight with you. I think you're under the impression that I came looking for work, and that's not the case."

"No," she says. "I think you came because you feel guilty about what happened to my sister. I simply took advantage of you. I'm not sorry, either. You were good with my mother. Kind. Very . . . very gentle."

She's close, her eyes a darker blue in the afternoon light and very wide. Her lips open as if she has more to say, but he doesn't give her a chance. He kisses her before he can think about how stupid it is, how reckless, and is astounded when she kisses him back, even putting her right hand on the nape of his neck to make their contact a little firmer. It goes on for no more than five seconds, but it seems much longer to Hodges, who hasn't had a kiss like this one in quite awhile.

She pulls back, brushes a hand through his hair, and says, "I've wanted to do that all afternoon. Now let's go upstairs. I'll make coffee and you make your report."

But there's no report until much later, and no coffee at all.

10

He kisses her again in the elevator. This time her hands link behind his neck, and his travel down past the small of her back to the white pants, snug across her bottom. He is aware of his too-big stomach pressing against her trim one and thinks she must be revolted by it, but when the elevator opens, her cheeks are flushed, her eyes are bright, and she's showing small white teeth in a smile. She takes his hand and pulls him down the short hall between the elevator and the apartment door.

"Come on," she says. "Come on, we're going to do this, so come on, before one of us gets cold feet."

It won't be me, Hodges thinks. Every part of him is warm.

At first she can't open the door because the hand holding the key is shaking too badly. It makes her laugh. He closes his fingers over hers, and together they push the Schlage into the slot.

The apartment where he first met this

woman's sister and mother is shadowy, because the sun has traveled around to the other side of the building. The lake has darkened to a cobalt so deep it's almost purple. There are no sailboats, but he can see a freighter —

"Come on," she says again. "Come on, Bill, don't quit on me now."

Then they're in one of the bedrooms. He doesn't know if it's Janey's or the one Olivia used on her Thursday-night stays, and he doesn't care. The life of the last few months — the afternoon TV, the microwave dinners, his father's Smith & Wesson revolver — seems so distant that it might have belonged to a fictional character in a boring foreign movie.

She tries to pull the striped sailor shirt over her head and it gets caught on the clip in her hair. She gives a frustrated, muffled laugh. "Help me with this damn thing, would you please —"

He runs his hands up her smooth sides — she gives a tiny jump at his initial touch — and beneath the inside-out shirt. He stretches the fabric and lifts. Her head pops free. She's laughing in little out-of-breath gasps. Her bra is plain white cotton. He holds her by the waist and kisses between her breasts as she unbuckles his belt and pops the button on his slacks. He thinks, If I'd known this could happen at this stage of my life, I would have gotten back to the gym.

"Why —" he begins.

"Oh, shut up." She slides a hand down the front of him, pushing the zipper with her palm. His pants fall around his shoes in a jingle of change. "Save the talk for later." She grabs the hardness of him through his underpants and wiggles it like a gearshift, making him gasp. "That's a good start. Don't go limp on me, Bill, don't you dare."

They fall onto the bed, Hodges still in his boxer shorts, Janey in cotton panties as plain as her bra. He tries to roll her onto her back, but she resists.

"You're not getting on top of me," she says. "If you have a heart attack while we're screwing, you'll crush me."

"If I have a heart attack while we're screwing, I'll be the most disappointed man to ever leave this world."

"Stay still. Just stay still."

She hooks her thumbs into the sides of his boxers. He cups her hanging breasts as she does it.

"Now lift your legs. And keep busy. Use your thumbs a little, I like that."

He's able to obey both of these commands with no trouble; he's always been a multitasker.

A moment later she's looking down at him, a lock of her hair tumbled over one of her eyes. She sticks out her lower lip and blows it back. "Keep still. Let me do the work. And stay with me. I don't mean to be bossy, but I haven't had sex in two years, and the last I did have sucked. I want to enjoy this. I deserve it."

The clinging, slippery warmth of her encloses him in a warm hug, and he can't help raising his hips.

"Stay still, I said. Next time you can move all you want, but this is mine."

It's difficult, but he does as she says.

Her hair tumbles into her eyes again, and this time she can't use her lower lip to blow it back because she's gnawing at it in little bites he thinks she'll feel later. She spreads both hands and rubs them roughly through the graying hair on his chest, then down to the embarrassing swell of his gut.

"I need . . . to lose some weight," he gasps.

"You need to shut up," she says, then moves — just a little — and closes her eyes. "Oh God, that's deep. And nice. You can worry about your diet program later, okay?" She begins to move again, pauses once to readjust the angle, then settles into a rhythm.

"I don't know how long I can . . ."

"You better." Her eyes are still closed. "You just better hold out, Detective Hodges. Count prime numbers. Think of the books you liked when you were a kid. Spell *xylophone* backwards. Just stay with me. I won't need long."

He stays with her just long enough.

11

Sometimes when he's feeling upset, Brady Hartsfield retraces the route of his greatest triumph. It soothes him. On this Friday night he doesn't go home after turning in the ice cream truck and making the obligatory joke or two with Shirley Orton in the front office. He drives his clunker downtown instead, not liking the front-end shimmy or the too-loud blat of the engine. Soon he will have to balance off the cost of a new car (a new *used* car) against the cost of repairs. And his mother's Honda needs work even more desperately than his Subaru does. Not that she drives the Honda very often these days, and that's good, considering how much of her time she spends in the bag.

His trip down Memory Lane begins on Lake Avenue, just past the bright lights of downtown, where Mrs. Trelawney always parked her Mercedes on Thursday nights, and wends up Marlborough Street to City Center. Only this evening he gets no farther than the condo. He brakes so suddenly that the car behind almost rear-ends him. The driver hits his horn in a long, outraged blast, but Brady pays no attention. It might as well have been a foghorn on the other side of the lake.

The driver pulls around him, buzzing down his passenger-side window to yell *Asshole* at the top of his lungs. Brady pays no attention to that, either.

There must be thousands of Toyota Corollas in the city, and hundreds of *blue* Toyota Corollas, but how many blue Toyota Corollas with bumper stickers reading SUPPORT YOUR LOCAL POLICE? Brady is betting there's just one, and what the hell is the fat ex-cop doing in the old lady's condominium apartment? Why is he visiting Mrs. Trelawney's sister, who now lives there?

The answer seems obvious: Detective Hodges (Ret.) is hunting.

Brady is no longer interested in reliving last year's triumph. He pulls an illegal (and completely out-of-character) U-turn, now heading for the North Side. Heading for home with a single thought in his head, blinking on and off like a neon sign.

You bastard. You bastard. You bastard.

Things are not going the way they are supposed to. Things are slipping out of his control. It's not right.

Something needs to be done.

12

As the stars come out over the lake, Hodges and Janey Patterson sit in the kitchen nook, gobbling takeout Chinese and drinking oolong tea. Janey is wearing a fluffy white bathrobe. Hodges is in his boxers and tee-shirt. When he used the bathroom after making love (she was curled in the middle of the bed, dozing), he got on her scale and was delighted to see he's four pounds lighter than the last time he weighed himself. It's a start.

"Why me?" Hodges says now. "Don't get me wrong, I feel incredibly lucky — even blessed — but I'm sixty-two and overweight."

She sips tea. "Well, let's think about that, shall we? In one of the old detective movies Ollie and I used to watch on TV when we were kids, I'd be the greedy vixen, maybe a nightclub cigarette girl, who tries to charm the crusty and cynical private detective with her fair white body. Only I'm not the greedy type — nor do I have to be, considering the fact that I recently inherited several million dollars — and my fair white body has started to sag in several vital places. As you may have noticed."

He hasn't. What he has noticed is that she hasn't answered his question. So he waits.

"Not good enough?"

"Nope."

Janey rolls her eyes. "I wish I could think of a way to answer you that's gentler than 'Men are very stupid' or more elegant than 'I was horny and wanted to brush away the cobwebs.' I'm not coming up with much, so let's go with those. Plus, I was attracted to you. It's been thirty years since I was a dewy debutante and much too long since I got laid.

I'm forty-four, and that allows me to reach for what I want. I don't always get it, but I'm allowed to reach." He stares at her, honestly amazed. Forty-*four*?

She bursts into laughter. "You know what? That look's the nicest compliment I've had in a long, long time. And the most honest one. Just that stare. So I'm going to push it a little. How old did you think I was?"

"Maybe forty. At the outside. Which would make me a cradle-robber."

"Oh, bullshit. If you were the one with the money instead of me, everyone would take the younger-woman thing for granted. In that case, people would take it for granted if you were sleeping with a twenty-five-year-old." She pauses. "Although that *would* be cradle-robbing, in my humble opinion."

"Still —"

"You're old, but not *that* old, and you're on the heavyweight side, but not *that* heavy. Although you will be if you keep on the way you're going." She points her fork at him. "That's the kind of honesty a woman can only afford after she's slept with a man and still likes him well enough to eat dinner with him. I said I haven't had sex in two years. That's true, but do you know when I last had sex with a man I actually liked?"

He shakes his head.

"Try junior college. And he wasn't a man, he was a second-string tackle with a big red pimple on the end of his nose. He was very sweet, though. Clumsy and far too quick, but sweet. He actually cried on my shoulder afterward."

"So this wasn't just . . . I don't know . . ."

"A thank-you fuck? A mercy-fuck? Give me a little credit. And here's a promise." She leans forward, the robe gaping to show the shadowed valley between her breasts. "Lose twenty pounds and I'll risk you on top."

He can't help laughing.

"It was great, Bill. I have no regrets, and I have a thing for big guys. The tackle with the pimple on his nose went about two-forty. My ex was a beanpole, and I should have known no good could come of it the first time I saw him. Can we leave it at that?"

"Yeah."

"Yeah," she says, smiling, and stands up. "Come on in the living room. It's time for you to make your report."

13

He tells her everything except for his long afternoons watching bad TV and flirting with his father's old service revolver. She listens gravely, not interrupting, her eyes seldom leaving his face. When he's done, she gets a bottle of wine out of the fridge and pours them each a glass. They are big glasses, and he looks at his doubtfully.

"Don't know if I should, Janey. I'm driving."

"Not tonight you're not. You're staying here. Unless you've got a dog or a cat?"

Hodges shakes his head.

"Not even a parrot? In one of those old movies, you'd at least have a parrot in your office that would say rude things to prospective clients."

"Sure. And you'd be my receptionist. Lola instead of Janey."

"Or Velma."

He grins. There's a wavelength, and they're on it.

She leans forward, once again creating that enticing view. "Profile this guy for me."

"That was never my job. We had guys who specialized in that. One on the force and two on call from the psych department at the state university."

"Do it anyway. I Googled you, you know, and it looks to me like you were just about the best the police department had. Commendations up the wazoo."

"I got lucky a few times."

It comes out sounding falsely modest, but luck really is a big part of it. Luck, and being ready. Woody Allen was right: eighty percent of success is just showing up.

"Take a shot, okay? If you do a good job, maybe we'll revisit the bedroom." She wrinkles her nose at him. "Unless you're too old for twosies."

The way he feels right now, he might not be too old for threesies. There have been a lot of celibate nights, which gives him an account to draw on. Or so he hopes. Part of him — a large part — still can't believe this isn't an incredibly detailed dream.

He sips his wine, rolling it around in his mouth, giving himself time to think. The top of her robe is closed again, which helps him concentrate.

"Okay. He's probably young, that's the first thing. I'm guessing between twenty and thirty-five. That's partly because of his computer savvy, but not entirely. When an older guy murders a bunch of people, the ones he mostly goes after are family, co-workers, or both. Then he finishes by putting the gun to his own head. You look, you find a reason. A motive. Wife kicked him out, then got a restraining order. Boss downsized him, then humiliated him by having a couple of security guys stand by while he cleaned out his office. Loans overdue. Credit cards maxed out. House underwater. Car repo'd."

"But what about serial killers? Wasn't that guy in Kansas a middle-aged man?"

"Dennis Rader, yeah. And he was middle-aged when they bagged him, but only thirty or so when he started. Also, those were sex killings. Mr. Mercedes isn't a sex-killer, and he's not a serial killer in the traditional sense.

He started with a bunch, but since then he's settled on individuals — first your sister, now me. And he didn't come after either of us with a gun or a stolen car, did he?"

"Not yet, anyway," Janey says.

"Our guy is a hybrid, but he has certain things in common with younger men who kill. He's more like Lee Malvo — one of the Beltway Snipers — than Rader. Malvo and his partner planned to kill six white people a day. Just random killings. Whoever had the bad luck to walk into their gunsights went down. Sex and age didn't matter. They ended up getting ten, not a bad score for a couple of homicidal maniacs. The stated motive was racial, and with John Allen Muhammad — he was Malvo's partner, much older, a kind of father figure — that might have been true, or partially true. I think Malvo's motivation was a lot more complex, a whole stew of things he didn't understand himself. Look closely and you'd probably find sexual confusion and upbringing were major players. I think the same is true with our guy. He's young. He's bright. He's good at fitting in, so good that a lot of his associates don't realize he's basically a loner. When he's caught, they'll all say, 'I can't believe it was so-and-so, he was always so nice.' "

"Like Dexter Morgan on that TV show."

Hodges knows the one she's talking about and shakes his head emphatically. Not just because the show is fantasyland bullshit, either.

"Dexter knows why he's doing what he's doing. Our guy doesn't. He's almost certainly unmarried. He doesn't date. He may be impotent. There's a good chance he's still living at home. If so, it's probably with a single parent. If it's Father, the relationship is cold and distant — ships passing in the night. If it's Mother, there's a good chance Mr. Mercedes is her surrogate husband." He sees her start to speak and raises his hand. "That doesn't mean they're having a sexual relationship."

"Maybe not, but I'll tell you something, Bill. You don't have to sleep with a guy to be having a sexual relationship with him. Sometimes it's in the eye contact, or the clothes you wear when you know he's going to be around, or what you do with your hands — touching, patting, caressing, hugging. Sex has got to be in this somewhere. I mean, that letter he sent you . . . the stuff about wearing a condom while he did it . . ." She shivers in her white robe.

"Ninety percent of that letter is white noise, but sure, sex is in it somewhere. Always is. Also anger, aggression, loneliness, feelings of inadequacy . . . but it doesn't do to get lost in stuff like that. It's not profiling, it's analysis. Which was way above my pay-grade even when I had a pay-grade."

"Okay . . ."

"He's broken," Hodges says simply. "And evil. Like an apple that looks okay on the outside, but when you cut it open, it's black and full of worms."

"Evil," she says, almost sighing the word. Then, to herself rather than him: "Of course he is. He battened on my sister like a vampire."

"He could have some kind of job where he meets the public, because he's got a fair amount of surface charm. If so, it's probably a low-paying job. He never advances because he's unable to combine his above-average intelligence with long-term concentration. His actions suggest he's a creature of impulse and opportunity. The City Center killings are a perfect example. I think he had his eye on your sister's Mercedes, but I don't think he knew what he was actually going to do with it until just a few days before the job fair. Maybe only a few hours. I just wish I could figure out how he stole it."

He pauses, thinking that thanks to Jerome, he has a good idea about half of it: the spare key was very likely in the glove compartment all along.

"I think ideas for murder flip through this guy's head as fast as cards in a good dealer's fast shuffle. He's probably thought of blowing up airliners, setting fires, shooting up schoolbuses, poisoning the water system, maybe assassinating the governor or the president."

"Jesus, Bill!"

"Right now he's fixated on me, and that's good. It will make him easier to catch. It's good for another reason, too."

"Which is?"

"I'd rather keep him thinking small. Keep him thinking one-on-one. The longer he keeps doing that, the longer it will be before he decides to try putting on another horror show like the one at City Center, maybe on an even grander scale. You know what creeps me out? He's probably already got a list of potential targets."

"Didn't he say in his letter that he had no urge to do it again?"

He grins. It lights up his whole face. "Yeah, he did. And you know how you tell when guys like this are lying? Their lips are moving. Only in the case of Mr. Mercedes, he's writing letters."

"Or communicating with his targets on the Blue Umbrella site. Like he did with Ollie."

"Yeah."

"If we assume he succeeded with her because she was psychologically fragile . . . forgive me, Bill, but does he have reason to believe he can succeed with you for the same reason?"

He looks at his glass of wine and sees it's empty. He starts to pour himself another half a glass, thinks what that might do to his chances of a successful return engagement in the bedroom, and settles for a small puddle in the bottom instead.

"Bill?"

"Maybe," he says. "Since my retirement, I've been drifting. But I'm not as lost as your sister . . ." Not anymore, at least. ". . . and that's not the important thing. It's not the take-away from the letters, and from the Blue Umbrella communications."

"Then what is?"

"*He's been watching.* That's the take-away. It makes him vulnerable. Unfortunately, it also makes him dangerous to my known associates. I don't think he knows I've been talking to you —"

"Quite a bit more than talking," she says, giving her eyebrows a Groucho waggle.

"— but he knows Olivia had a sister, and we have to assume he knows you're in the city. You need to start being super-careful. Make sure your door is locked when you're here —"

"I always do."

"— and don't believe what you hear on the lobby intercom. Anyone can say he's from a package service and needs a signature. Visually identify all comers before you open your door. Be aware of your surroundings when you go out." He leans forward, the splash of wine untouched. He doesn't want it anymore.

"Big thing here, Janey. When you *are* out, keep an eye on traffic. Not just driving but when you're on foot. Do you know the term BOLO?"

"Cop-speak for *be on the lookout.*"

"That's it. When you're out, you're going to BOLO any vehicles that seem to keep reappearing in your immediate vicinity."

"Like that lady's black SUVs," she says, smiling. "Mrs. Whozewhatsit."

Mrs. Melbourne. Thinking of her tickles some obscure associational switch in the back of Hodges's mind, but it's gone before he can track it down, let alone scratch it.

Jerome's got to be on the lookout, too. If Mr. Mercedes is cruising Hodges's place, he'll have seen Jerome mowing the lawn, putting on the screens, cleaning out the gutters. Both Jerome and Janey are probably safe, but probably isn't good enough. Mr. Mercedes is a random bundle of homicide, and Hodges has set out on a course of deliberate provocation.

Janey reads his mind. "And yet you're . . . what did you call it? Winding him up."

"Yeah. And very shortly I'm going to steal some time on your computer and wind him up a little more. I had a message all worked out, but I'm thinking of adding something. My partner got a big solve today, and there's a way I can use that."

"What was it?"

There's no reason not to tell her; it will be in the papers tomorrow, Sunday at the latest. "Turnpike Joe."

"The one who kills women at rest stops?" And when he nods: "Does he fit your profile of Mr. Mercedes?"

"Not at all. But there's no reason for our guy to know that."

"What do you mean to do?"

Hodges tells her.

14

They don't have to wait for the morning paper; the news that Donald Davis, already under suspicion for the murder of his wife, has confessed to the Turnpike Joe killings leads the eleven P.M. news. Hodges and Janey watch it in bed. For Hodges, the return engagement has been strenuous but sublimely satisfactory. He's still out of breath, he's sweaty and in need of a shower, but it's been a long, long time since he felt this happy. This *complete.*

When the newscaster moves on to a puppy stuck in a drainpipe, Janey uses the remote to kill the TV. "Okay. It could work. But *God,* is it risky."

He shrugs. "With no police resources to call on, I see it as my best way forward." And it's fine with him, because it's the way he *wants* to go forward.

He thinks briefly of the makeshift but very effective weapon he keeps in his dresser drawer, the argyle sock filled with ball bearings. He imagines how satisfying it would be to use the Happy Slapper on the sonofabitch who ran one of the world's heaviest passenger sedans into a crowd of defenseless people. That probably won't happen, but it's possible. In this best (and worst) of all worlds, most things are.

"What did you make of what my mother said at the end? About Olivia hearing ghosts?"

"I need to think about that a little more," Hodges says, but he's already thought about it, and if he's right, he might have another path to Mr. Mercedes. Given his druthers, he wouldn't involve Jerome Robinson any more than he already has, but if he's going to follow up on old Mrs. Wharton's parting shot, he may have to. He knows half a dozen cops with Jerome's computer savvy and can't call on a single one of them.

Ghosts, he thinks. Ghosts in the machine.

He sits up and swings his feet out onto the floor. "If I'm still invited to stay over, what I need right now is a shower."

"You are." She leans over and sniffs at the side of his neck, her hand lightly clamped on his upper arm giving him a pleasurable shiver. "And you certainly do."

When he's showered and back in his boxers, he asks her to power up her computer.

Then, with her sitting beside him and looking on attentively, he slips under Debbie's Blue Umbrella and leaves a message for **merckill.** Fifteen minutes later, and with Janey Patterson nestled next to him, he sleeps . . . and never so well since childhood.

15

When Brady gets home after several hours of aimless cruising, it's late and there's a note on the back door: *Where you been, honeyboy? There's homemade lasagna in the oven.* He only has to look at the unsteady, downslanting script to know she was seriously loaded when she wrote it. He untacks the note and lets himself in.

Usually he checks on her first thing, but he smells smoke and hustles to the kitchen, where a blue haze hangs in the air. Thank God the smoke detector in here is dead (he keeps meaning to replace it and keeps forgetting, too many other fish to fry). Thanks are also due for the powerful stove fan, which has sucked up just enough smoke to keep the rest of the detectors from going off, although they soon will if he can't air the place out. The oven is set at three-fifty. He turns it off. He opens the windows over the sink, then the back door. There's a floor fan in the utility closet where they keep the cleaning supplies. He sets it up facing the runaway stove, and turns it on at the highest setting.

With that done he finally goes into the living room and checks on his mother. She's crashed out on the couch, wearing a housedress that's open up top and rucked to her thighs below, snoring so loudly and steadily she sounds like an idling chainsaw. He averts his eyes and goes back into the kitchen, muttering *fuck-fuck-fuck-fuck* under his breath.

He sits at the table with his head bent, his palms cupping his temples, and his fingers plunged deep into his hair. Why is it that when things go wrong, they have to *keep on* going wrong? He finds himself thinking of the Morton Salt motto: "When it rains it pours."

After five minutes of airing-out, he risks opening the oven. As he regards the black and smoking lump within, any faint hunger pangs he might have felt when he got home pass away. Washing will not clean that pan; an hour of scouring and a whole box of Brillo pads will not clean that pan; an industrial laser probably wouldn't clean that pan. That pan is a gone goose. It's only luck that he didn't get home to find the fucking fire department here and his mother offering them vodka collinses.

He shuts the oven — he doesn't want to look at that nuclear meltdown — and goes back to look at his mother instead. Even as his eyes are running up and down her bare legs, he's thinking, It would be better if she *did* die. Better for her and better for me.

He goes downstairs, using his voice commands to turn on the lights and his bank of computers. He goes to Number Three, centers the cursor on the Blue Umbrella icon . . . and hesitates. Not because he's afraid there won't be a message from the fat ex-cop but because he's afraid there will be. If so, it won't be anything he wants to read. Not the way things are going. His head is fucked up already, so why fuck it up more?

Except there might be an answer to what the cop was doing at the Lake Avenue condo. Has he been questioning Olivia Trelawney's sister? Probably. At sixty-two, he's surely not boffing her.

Brady clicks the mouse, and sure enough:

kermitfrog19 wants to chat with you!
Do you want to chat with kermitfrog19?
Y N

Brady settles the cursor on **N** and circles the curved back of his mouse with the pad of his index finger. Daring himself to push it and end this thing right here and right now. It's obvious he won't be able to nudge the fat ex-cop into suicide the way he did Mrs. Trelawney, so why not? Isn't that the smart thing?

But he has to know.

More importantly, the Det-Ret doesn't get to win.

He moves the cursor to **Y**, clicks, and the message — quite a long one this time — flashes onto the screen.

If it isn't my false-confessing friend again. I shouldn't even respond, guys like you are a dime a dozen, but as you point out, I'm retired and even talking to a nut is better than Dr. Phil and all those late-night infomercials. One more 30-minute OxiClean ad and I'll be as crazy as you are, HAHAHA. Also, I owe you thanks for introducing me to this site, which I otherwise would not have found. I have already made 3 new (and non-crazy) friends. One is a lady with a delightfully dirty mouth!!! So OK, my "friend," let me clue you in.

First, anyone who watches CSI could figure out that the Mercedes Killer was wearing a hairnet and used bleach on the clown mask. I mean, DUH.

Second, if you were really the guy who stole Mrs. Trelawney's Mercedes, you would have mentioned the valet key. That's something you couldn't have figured out from watching CSI. So, at the risk of repeating myself, DUH.

☺

Third (I hope you're taking notes), I got a call from my old partner today. He caught a bad guy, one who specializes in TRUE confessions. Check the news, my friend, and then guess what else this guy's going to confess to in the next week or so.

Have a nice night and BTW, why don't you go bother someone else with your fantasies?

Brady vaguely remembers some cartoon character — maybe it was Foghorn Leghorn, the big rooster with the southern accent — who would get so mad first his neck and then his head would turn into a thermometer with the temperature going up and up from BAKE to BROIL to NUKE. Brady can almost feel that happening to him as he reads this arrogant, insulting, infuriating post.

Valet key?

Valet key?

"What are you talking about?" he says, his voice somewhere between a whisper and a growl. "What the fuck are you *talking* about?"

He gets up and strides around in an unsteady circle on legs like stilts, yanking at his hair so hard his eyes water. His mother is forgotten. The blackened lasagna is forgotten. Everything is forgotten except for this hateful post.

He has even had the nerve to put in a

smiley-face!

A *smiley-face*!

Brady kicks his chair, hurting his toes and sending it rolling all the way across the room, where it bangs the wall. Then he turns and runs back to his Number Three computer, hunching over it like a vulture. His first impulse is to reply immediately, to call the fucking cop a liar, an idiot with fat-induced early-onset Alzheimer's, an anal ranger who sucks his nigger yardboy's cock. Then some semblance of rationality — fragile and wavering — reasserts itself. He retrieves his chair and goes to the city paper's website. He doesn't even have to click on BREAKING NEWS in order to see what Hodges has been raving about; it's right there on the front page of tomorrow's paper.

Brady follows local crime news assiduously, and knows both Donald Davis's name and his handsomely chiseled features. He knows the cops have been chasing Davis for the murder of his wife, and Brady has no doubt the man did it. Now the idiot has confessed, but not just to *her* murder. According to the newspaper story, Davis has also confessed to the rape-murders of five *more* women. In short, he's claiming to be Turnpike Joe.

At first Brady is unable to connect this with the fat ex-cop's hectoring message. Then it comes to him in a baleful burst of inspiration: while he's in a breast-baring mood,

Donnie Davis also means to confess to the City Center Massacre. May have done so already.

Brady whirls around like a dervish — once, twice, three times. His head is splitting. His pulse is thudding in his chest, his neck, his temples. He can even feel it in his gums and tongue.

Did Davis say something about a valet key? Is that what brought this on?

"There *was* no valet key," Brady says . . . only how can he be sure of that? What if there was? And *if* there was . . . if they hang this on Donald Davis and snatch away Brady Hartsfield's great triumph . . . after the *risks* he took . . .

He can no longer hold back. He sits down at his Number Three again and writes a message to **kermitfrog19**. Just a short one, but his hands are shaking so badly it takes him almost five minutes. He sends it as soon as he's done, without bothering to read it over.

YOU ARE FULL OF SHIT YOU ASSHOLE. OK the key wasn't in the ignition but it was no VALET KEY. It was a spare in the glove complartment and how I uynlocked the car IS FOR YOU TO FIGURE OUT FUCKFACE. Donald Davis did not do this crime. I repeat, DONALD DAVIUS DID NOT DO THIS CRIME. If you

tell people he did I will kill you altho it wouldn'tr be killing much as washed up as you are.

Signed,

The REAL Mercedes Killer

PS: Your mother was a whore, she took it up the ass & licked cum out of gutters.

Brady shuts off his computer and goes upstairs, leaving his mother to snore on the couch instead of helping her to bed. He takes three aspirin, adds a fourth, and then lies in his own bed, wide-eyed and shaking, until the first streaks of dawn come up in the east. At last he drops off for two hours, sleep that is thin and dream-haunted and unrestful.

16

Hodges is making scrambled eggs when Janey comes into the kitchen on Saturday morning in her white robe, her hair wet from the shower. With it combed back from her face, she looks younger than ever. He thinks again, Forty-*four*?

"I looked for bacon, but didn't see any. Of course it might still be there. My ex claims that the great majority of American men suffer from the disease of Refrigerator Blindness. I don't know if there's a help line for that."

She points at his midsection.

"Okay," he says. And then, because she seems to like it: "Yeah."

"And by the way, how's your cholesterol?"

He smiles and says, "Toast? It's whole grain. As you probably know, since you bought it."

"One slice. No butter, just a little jam. What are you going to do today?"

"Not sure yet." Although he's thinking he'd like to check in with Radney Peeples out in Sugar Heights if Radney's on duty and being Vigilant. And he needs to talk to Jerome about computers. Endless vistas there.

"Have you checked the Blue Umbrella?"

"Wanted to make you breakfast first. And me." It's true. He woke up actually wanting to feed his body rather than trying to plug some empty hole in his head. "Also, I don't know your password."

"It's Janey."

"My advice? Change it. Actually it's the advice of the kid who works for me."

"Jerome, right?"

"That's the one."

He has scrambled half a dozen eggs and they eat them all, split right down the middle. It has crossed his mind to ask if she had any regrets about last night, but decides the way she's going through her breakfast answers the question.

With the dishes in the sink, they go on her

computer and sit silently for nearly four minutes, reading and re-reading the latest message from **merckill**.

"Holy cow," she says at last. "You wanted to wind him up, and I'd say he's fully wound. Do you see all the mistakes?" She points out *complartment* and *uynlocked.* "Is that part of his — what did you call it? — stylistic masking?"

"I don't think so." Hodges is looking at *wouldn'tr* and smiling. He can't help smiling. The fish is feeling the hook, and it's sunk deep. It hurts. It *burns.* "I think that's the kind of typing you do when you're mad as hell. The last thing he expected was that he'd have a credibility problem. It's making him crazy."

"Er," she says.

"Huh?"

"Crazi*er.* Send him another message, Bill. Poke him harder. He deserves it."

"All right." He thinks, then types.

17

When he's dressed, she walks down the hall with him and treats him to a lingering kiss at the elevator.

"I still can't believe last night happened," he tells her.

"Oh, it did. And if you play your cards right, it might happen again." She searches his face with those blue eyes of hers. "But no promises or long-term commitments, okay? We take it as it comes. A day at a time."

"At my age, I take everything that way." The elevator doors open. He steps in.

"Stay in touch, cowboy."

"I will." The elevator doors start to close. He stops them with his hand. "And remember to BOLO, cowgirl."

She nods solemnly, but he doesn't miss the twinkle in her eye. "Janey will BOLO her ass off."

"Keep your cell phone handy, and it might be wise to program nine-one-one on your speed dial."

He drops his hand. She blows him a kiss. The doors roll shut before he can blow one back.

His car is where he left it, but the meter must have run out before the free parking kicked in, because there's a ticket stuck under the windshield wiper. He opens the glove compartment, stuffs the ticket inside, and fishes out his phone. He's good at giving Janey advice that he doesn't take himself — since he pulled the pin, he's always forgetting the damned Nokia, which is pretty prehistoric, as cell phones go. These days hardly anyone calls him anyway, but this morning he has three messages, all from Jerome. Numbers two and three — one at nine-forty last night, the other at ten-forty-five — are impatient inquiries about where he is and why he doesn't call. They are in Jerome's normal voice. The original message, left at six-thirty yesterday evening, begins in his exuberant Tyrone Feelgood Delight voice.

"Massah Hodges, where you at? Ah needs to *jaw* to y'all!" Then he becomes Jerome again. "I think I know how he did it. How he stole the car. Call me."

Hodges checks his watch and decides Jerome probably won't be up quite yet, not on Saturday morning. He decides to drive over there, with a stop at his house first to pick up his notes. He turns on the radio, gets Bob Seger singing "Old Time Rock and Roll," and bellows along: take those old records off the shelf.

18

Once upon a simpler time, before apps, iPads, Samsung Galaxies, and the world of blazing-fast 4G, weekends were the busiest days of the week at Discount Electronix. Now the kids who used to come in to buy CDs are downloading Vampire Weekend from iTunes, while their elders are surfing eBay or watching the TV shows they missed on Hulu.

This Saturday morning the Birch Hill Mall DE is a wasteland.

Tones is down front, trying to sell an old lady an HDTV that's already an antique.

Freddi Linklatter is out back, chain-smoking Marlboro Reds and probably rehearsing her latest gay rights rant. Brady is sitting at one of the computers in the back row, an ancient Vizio that he's rigged to leave no keystroke tracks, let alone a history. He's staring at Hodges's latest message. One eye, his left, has picked up a rapid, irregular tic.

> **Quit dumping on my mother, okay? ☺Not her fault you got caught in a bunch of stupid lies. Got a key out of the glove compartment, did you? That's pretty good, since Olivia Trelawney had both of them. The one missing was the valet key. She kept it in a small magnetic box under the rear bumper. The REAL Mercedes Killer must have scoped it.**
>
> **I think I'm done writing to you, dick-wad. Your Fun Quotient is currently hovering around zero, and I have it on good authority that Donald Davis is going to cop to the City Center killings. Which leaves you where? Just living your shitty little unexciting life, I guess. One other thing before I close this charming correspondence. You threatened to kill me. That's a felony offense, but guess what? I don't care. Buddy, you are just another chickenshit asshole. The Internet is full of them. Want to come to my house (I know you know where I live)**

and make that threat in person? No? I thought not. Let me close with two words so simple even a thud like you should be able to understand them.

Go away.

Brady's rage is so great he feels frozen in place. Yet he's also still burning. He thinks he will stay this way, hunched over the piece-of-shit Vizio ridiculously sale-priced at eighty-seven dollars and eighty-seven cents, until he either dies of frostbite or goes up in flames or somehow does both at the same time.

But when a shadow rises on the wall, Brady finds he can move after all. He clicks away from the fat ex-cop's message just before Freddi bends over to peer at the screen. "What you looking at, Brades? You moved awful fast to hide it, whatever it was."

"A *National Geographic* documentary. It's called *When Lesbians Attack.*"

"Your humor," she says, "might be exceeded by your sperm count, but I tend to doubt it."

Tones Frobisher joins them. "Got a service call over on Edgemont," he says. "Which one of you wants it?"

Freddi says, "Given a choice between a service call in Hillbilly Heaven and having a wild weasel stuck up my ass, I'd have to pick the weasel."

"I'll take it," Brady says. He's decided he has an errand to run. One that can't wait.

19

Jerome's little sis and a couple of her friends are jumping rope in the Robinson driveway when Hodges arrives. All of them are wearing sparkly tees with silkscreens of some boy band on them. He cuts across the lawn, his case-folder in one hand. Barbara comes over long enough to give him a high-five and a dap, then hurries back to grab her end of the rope. Jerome, dressed in shorts and a City College tee-shirt with the sleeves torn off, is sitting on the porch steps and drinking orange juice. Odell is by his side. He tells Hodges his folks are off Krogering, and he's got babysitting duty until they get back.

"Not that she really needs a sitter anymore. She's a lot hipper than our parents think."

Hodges sits down beside him. "You don't want to take that for granted. Trust me on this, Jerome."

"Meaning what, exactly?"

"Tell me what you came up with first."

Instead of answering, Jerome points to Hodges's car, parked at the curb so as not to interfere with the girls' game. "What year is that?"

"Oh-four. No show-stopper, but it gets good mileage. Want to buy it?"

"I'll pass. Did you lock it?"

"Yeah." Even though this is a good neighborhood and he's sitting right here looking at it. Force of habit.

"Give me your keys."

Hodges digs in his pocket and hands them over. Jerome examines the fob and nods. "PKE," he says. "Started to come into use during the nineteen-nineties, first as an accessory but pretty much standard equipment since the turn of the century. Do you know what it stands for?"

As lead detective on the City Center Massacre (and frequent interviewer of Olivia Trelawney), Hodges certainly does. "Passive keyless entry."

"Right." Jerome pushes one of the two buttons on the fob. At the curb, the parking lights of Hodges's Toyota flash briefly. "Now it's open." He pushes the other button. The lights flash again. "Now it's locked. And you've got the key." He puts it in Hodges's palm. "All safe and sound, right?"

"Based on this discussion, maybe not."

"I know some guys from the college who have a computer club. I'm not going to tell you their names, so don't ask."

"Wouldn't think of it."

"They're not bad guys, but they know all the bad tricks — hacking, cloning, infojacking, stuff like that. They tell me that PKE systems are pretty much a license to steal.

When you push the button to lock or unlock your car, the fob emits a low-frequency radio signal. A code. If you could hear it, it would sound like the boops and beeps you get when you speed-dial a fax number. With me?"

"So far, yeah."

In the driveway the girls chant Sally-in-the-alley while Barbara Robinson darts deftly in and out of the loop, her sturdy brown legs flashing and her pigtails bouncing.

"My guys tell me that it's easy to capture that code, if you have the right gadget. You can modify a garage door opener or a TV remote to do it, only with something like that, you have to be really close. Say within twenty yards. But you can also build one that's more powerful. All the components are available at your friendly neighborhood electronics store. Total cost, about a hundred bucks. Range up to a hundred yards. You watch for the driver to exit the target vehicle. When she pushes the button to lock her car, you push *your* button. Your gadget captures the signal and stores it. She walks away, and when she's gone, you push your button again. The car unlocks, and you're in."

Hodges looks at his key, then at Jerome. "This works?"

"Yes indeed. My friends say it's tougher now — the manufacturers have modified the system so that the signal changes every time you push the button — but not impossible.

Any system created by the mind of man can be hacked by the mind of man. You feel me?"

Hodges hardly hears him, let alone feels him. He's thinking about Mr. Mercedes before he *became* Mr. Mercedes. He might have purchased one of the gadgets Jerome has just told him about, but it's just as likely he built it himself. And was Mrs. Trelawney's Mercedes the first car he ever used it on? Unlikely.

I have to check on car robberies downtown, he thinks. Starting in . . . let's say 2007 and going right through until early spring of 2009.

He has a friend in records, Marlo Everett, who owes him one. Hodges is confident Marlo will run an unofficial check for him without a lot of questions. And if she comes up with a bunch of reports where the investigating officer concludes that "complainant may have forgotten to lock his vehicle," he'll know.

In his heart he knows already.

"Mr. Hodges?" Jerome is looking at him a little uncertainly.

"What is it, Jerome?"

"When you were working on the City Center case, didn't you check out this PKE thing with the cops who handle auto theft? I mean, they have to know about it. It's not new. My friends say it's even got a name: stealing the peek."

"We talked to the head mechanic from the

Mercedes dealership, and he told us a key was used," Hodges says. To his own ears, the reply sounds weak and defensive. Worse: incompetent. What the head mechanic did — what they all did — was *assume* a key had been used. One left in the ignition by a ditzy lady none of them liked.

Jerome offers a cynical smile that looks odd and out of place on his young face. "There's stuff that people who work at car dealerships don't talk about, Mr. Hodges. They don't lie, exactly, they just banish it from their minds. Like how airbag deployment can save your life but also drive your glasses into your eyes and blind you. The high rollover rate of some SUVs. Or how easy it is to steal a PKE signal. But the auto theft guys must be hip, right? I mean, they *must.*"

The dirty truth is Hodges doesn't know. He should, but he doesn't. He and Pete were in the field almost constantly, working double shifts and getting maybe five hours of sleep a night. The paperwork piled up. If there was a memo from auto theft, it will probably be in the case files somewhere. He doesn't dare ask his old partner about it, but realizes he may have to tell Pete everything soon. If he can't work it out for himself, that is.

In the meantime, Jerome needs to know everything. Because the guy Hodges is dicking with is crazy.

Barbara comes running up, sweaty and out

of breath. "Jay, can me n Hilda n Tonya watch *Regular Show*?"

"Go for it," Jerome says.

She throws her arms around him and presses her cheek to his. "Will you make us pancakes, my darling brother?"

"No."

She quits hugging and stands back. "You're *bad.* Also lazy."

"Why don't you go down to Zoney's and get some Eggos?"

"No money is why."

Jerome digs into his pocket and hands her a five. This earns him another hug.

"Am I still bad?"

"No, you're *good*! Best brother ever!"

"You can't go without your homegirls," Jerome says.

"And take Odell," Hodges says.

Barbara giggles. "We *always* take Odell."

Hodges watches the girls bop down the sidewalk in their matching tees (talking a mile a minute and trading Odell's leash back and forth), with a feeling of deep disquiet. He can hardly put the Robinson family in lockdown, but those three girls look so *little.*

"Jerome? If somebody tried to mess with them, would Odell — ?"

"Protect them?" Jerome is grave now. "With his life, Mr. H. With his life. What's on your mind?"

"Can I continue to count on your discretion?"

"Yassuh!"

"Okay, I'm going to put a lot on you. But in return, you have to promise to call me Bill from now on."

Jerome considers. "It'll take some getting used to, but okay."

Hodges tells him almost everything (he omits where he spent the night), occasionally referring to the notes on his legal pad. By the time he finishes, Barbara and her friends are returning from the GoMart, tossing a box of Eggos back and forth and laughing. They go inside to eat their mid-morning treat in front of the television.

Hodges and Jerome sit on the porch steps and talk about ghosts.

20

Edgemont Avenue looks like a war zone, but being south of Lowbriar, at least it's a mostly *white* war zone, populated by the descendants of the Kentucky and Tennessee hillfolk who migrated here to work in the factories after World War II. Now the factories are closed, and a large part of the population consists of drug addicts who switched to brown-tar heroin when Oxy got too expensive. Edgemont is lined with bars, pawnshops, and check-cashing joints, all of them shut up tight on this Saturday morning. The only two stores open for business are a Zoney's and the site of Brady's service call, Batool's Bakery.

Brady parks in front, where he can see anybody trying to break into his Cyber Patrol Beetle, and totes his case inside to the good smells. The greaseball behind the counter is arguing with a Visa-waving customer and pointing to a cardboard sign reading CASH ONLY TIL COMPUTER FIX.

Paki Boy's computer is suffering the dreaded screen freeze. While continuing to monitor his Beetle at thirty-second intervals, Brady plays the Screen Freeze Boogie, which consists of pushing *alt, ctrl,* and *del* at the same time. This brings up the machine's Task Manager, and Brady sees at once that the Explorer program is currently listed as nonresponsive.

"Bad?" Paki Boy asks anxiously. "Please tell me not bad."

On another day, Brady would string this out, not because guys like Batool tip — they don't — but to see him sweat a few extra drops of Crisco. Not today. This is just his excuse to get off the floor and go to the mall, and he wants to finish as soon as possible.

"Nah, gotcha covered, Mr. Batool," he says. He highlights END TASK and reboots Paki Boy's PC. A moment later the cash register function is back up, complete with all four credit card icons.

"You genius!" Batool cries. For one awful moment, Brady is afraid the perfume-smelling sonofabitch is going to hug him.

21

Brady leaves Hillbilly Heaven and drives north toward the airport. There's a Home Depot in the Birch Hill Mall where he could almost certainly get what he wants, but he makes the Skyway Shopping Complex his destination instead. What he's doing is risky, reckless, and unnecessary. He won't make matters worse by doing it in a store only one corridor over from DE. You don't shit where you eat.

Brady does his business at Skyway's Garden World and sees at once that he's made the right choice. The store is huge, and on this midday late-spring Saturday, it's crammed with shoppers. In the pesticide aisle, Brady adds two cans of Gopher-Go to a shopping cart already loaded with camouflage items: fertilizer, mulch, seeds, and a short-handled gardening claw. He knows it's madness to be buying poison in person when he's already ordered some which will come to his safe mail-drop in another few days, but he can't wait. Absolutely cannot. He probably won't be able to actually poison the nigger family's dog until Monday — and it might even be

Tuesday or Wednesday — but he has to be doing *something.* He needs to feel he's . . . how did Shakespeare put it? Taking arms against a sea of troubles.

He stands in line with his shopping cart, telling himself that if the checkout girl (another greaseball, the city is drowning in them) says anything about the Gopher-Go, even something completely innocuous like *This stuff really works,* he'll drop the whole thing. Too great a chance of being remembered and identified: *Oh yes, he was being the nervous young man with the garden claw and the gopher poison.*

He thinks, Maybe I should have worn sunglasses. It's not like I'd stand out, half the men in here are wearing them.

Too late now. He left his Ray-Bans back at Birch Hill, in his Subaru. All he can do is stand here in the checkout line and tell himself not to sweat. Which is like telling someone not to think of a blue polar bear.

I was noticing him because he was having the sweat, the greaseball checkout girl (a relative of Batool the Baker, for all Brady knows) will tell the police. Also because he was buying the gopher poison. The kind having the strychnine.

For a moment he almost flees, but now there are people behind him as well as ahead of him, and if he breaks from the line, won't people notice *that*? Won't they wonder —

A nudge from behind him. "You're up, buddy."

Out of options, Brady rolls his cart forward. The cans of Gopher-Go are a screaming yellow in the bottom of his shopping cart; to Brady they seem the very color of insanity, and that's just as it should be. Being here *is* insane.

Then a comforting thought comes to him, one that's as soothing as a cool hand on a fevered brow: Driving into those people at City Center was even more insane . . . but I got away with it, didn't I?

Yes, and he gets away with this. The greaseball runs his purchases under the scanner without so much as a glance at him. Nor does she look up when she asks him if it will be cash or credit.

Brady pays cash.

He's not *that* insane.

Back in the VW (he's parked it between two trucks, where its fluorescent green hardly shows at all), he sits behind the wheel, taking deep breaths until his heartbeat is steady again. He thinks about the immediate road ahead, and that calms him even more.

First, Odell. The mutt will die a miserable death, and the fat ex-cop will know it's his own fault, even if the Robinsons do not. (From a purely scientific standpoint, Brady will be interested to see if the Det-Ret owns up. He thinks Hodges won't.) Second, the man himself. Brady will give him a few days to marinate in his guilt, and who knows? He may opt for suicide after all. Probably not, though. So Brady will kill him, method yet to be determined. And third . . .

A grand gesture. Something that will be remembered for a hundred years. The question is, what might that grand gesture be?

Brady keys the ignition and tunes the Beetle's shitty radio to BAM-100, where every weekend is a rock-block weekend. He catches the end of a ZZ Top block and is about to punch the button for KISS-92 when his hand freezes. Instead of switching the station, he turns the volume up. Fate is speaking to him.

The deejay informs Brady that the hottest boy band in the country is coming to town for one gig only — that's right, 'Round Here will be playing the MAC next Thursday. "The show's already almost sold out, children, but the BAM-100 Good Guys are holding on to a dozen tickets, and we'll be giving em out in pairs starting on Monday, so listen for the cue to call in and —"

Brady switches the radio off. His eyes are distant, hazy, contemplative. The MAC is what people in the city call the Midwest Culture and Arts Complex. It takes up a whole city block and has a gigantic auditorium.

He thinks, What a way to go out. Oh my God, what a way that would be.

He wonders what exactly the capacity of the MAC's Mingo Auditorium might be. Three thousand? Maybe four? He'll go online tonight and check it out.

22

Hodges grabs lunch at a nearby deli (a salad instead of the loaded burger his stomach is rooting for) and goes home. His pleasant exertions of the previous night have caught up with him, and although he owes Janey a call — they have business at the late Mrs. Trelawney's Sugar Heights home, it seems — he decides that his next move in the investigation will be a short nap. He checks the answering machine in the living room, but the MESSAGE WAITING window shows zero. He peeks beneath Debbie's Blue Umbrella and finds nothing new from Mr. Mercedes. He lies down and sets his internal alarm for an hour. His last thought before closing his eyes is that he left his cell phone in the glove compartment of his Toyota again.

Ought to go get that, he thinks. I gave her both numbers, but she's new school instead of old school, and that's the one she'd call first if she needed me.

Then he's asleep.

It's the old school phone that wakes him,

and when he rolls over to grab it, he sees that his internal alarm, which never let him down during his years as a cop, has apparently decided it is also retired. He's slept for almost three hours.

"Hello?"

"Do you never check your messages, Bill?" Janey.

It crosses his mind to tell her the battery in his cell phone died, but lying is no way to start a relationship, even one of the day-at-a-time variety. And that's not the important thing. Her voice is blurry and hoarse, as if she's been shouting. Or crying.

He sits up. "What's wrong?"

"My mother had a stroke this morning. I'm at Warsaw County Memorial Hospital. That's the one closest to Sunny Acres."

He swings his feet out onto the floor. "Christ, Janey. How bad is it?"

"Bad. I've called my aunt Charlotte in Cincinnati and uncle Henry in Tampa. They're both coming. Aunt Charlotte will undoubtedly drag my cousin Holly along." She laughs, but the sound has no humor in it. "Of course they're coming — it's that old saying about following the money."

"Do you want *me* to come?"

"Of course, but I don't know how I'd explain you to them. I can't very well introduce you as the man I hopped into bed with almost as soon as I met him, and if I tell them

I hired you to investigate Ollie's death, it's apt to show up on one of Uncle Henry's kids' Facebook pages before midnight. When it comes to gossip, Uncle Henry's worse than Aunt Charlotte, but neither one of them is exactly a model of discretion. At least Holly's just weird." She takes a deep, watery breath. "*God,* I could sure use a friendly face right now. I haven't seen Charlotte and Henry in years, neither of them showed up at Ollie's funeral, and they sure haven't made any effort to keep up with *my* life."

Hodges thinks it over and says, "I'm a friend, that's all. I used to work for the Vigilant security company in Sugar Heights. You met me when you came back to inventory your sister's things and take care of the will with the lawyer. Chum."

"Schron." She takes a deep, watery breath. "That could work."

It will. When it comes to spinning stories, no one can do it with a straighter face than a cop. "I'm on my way."

"But . . . don't you have things to take care of in the city? To investigate?"

"Nothing that won't wait. It'll take me an hour to get there. With Saturday traffic, maybe even less."

"Thank you, Bill. With all my heart. If I'm not in the lobby —"

"I'll find you, I'm a trained detective." He's slipping into his shoes.

"I think if you're coming, you better bring a change of clothes. I've rented three rooms in the Holiday Inn down the street. I'll rent one for you as well. The advantages of having money. Not to mention an Amex Platinum Card."

"Janey, it's an easy drive back to the city."

"Sure, but she might die. If it happens today or tonight, I'm *really* going to need a friend. For the . . . you know, the . . ."

Tears catch her and she can't finish. Hodges doesn't need her to, because he knows what she means. For the arrangements.

Ten minutes later he's on the road, headed east toward Sunny Acres and Warsaw County Memorial. He expects to find Janey in the ICU waiting room, but she's outside, sitting on the bumper of a parked ambulance. She gets into his Toyota when he pulls up beside her, and one look at her drawn face and socketed eyes tells him everything he needs to know.

She holds together until he parks in the visitors' lot, then breaks down. Hodges takes her in his arms. She tells him that Elizabeth Wharton passed from the world at quarter past three, central daylight time.

About the same time I was putting on my shoes, Hodges thinks, and hugs her tighter.

23

Little League season is in full swing, and Brady spends that sunny Saturday afternoon at McGinnis Park, where a full slate of games is being played on three fields. The afternoon is warm and business is brisk. Lots of tweeny-bop girls have come to watch their little brothers do battle, and as they stand in line waiting for their ice cream, the only thing they seem to be talking about (the only thing Brady hears them talking about, anyway) is the upcoming 'Round Here concert at the MAC. It seems they are all going. Brady has decided that he will go, too. He just needs to dope out a way to get in wearing his special vest — the one loaded with the ball bearings and blocks of plastic explosive.

My final bow, he thinks. A headline for the ages.

The thought improves his mood. So does selling out his entire truckload of goodies — even the JuCee Stix are gone by four o'clock. Back at the ice cream factory, he hands the keys over to Shirley Orton (who never seems to leave) and asks if he can switch with Rudy Stanhope, who's down for the Sunday afternoon shift. Sundays — always assuming the weather cooperates — are busy days, with Loeb's three trucks working not just McGinnis but the city's other four large parks. He accompanies his request with the boyishly winning smile Shirley is a sucker for.

"In other words," Shirley says, "you want two afternoons off in a row."

"You got it." He explains that his mother wants to visit her brother, which means at least one overnight and possibly two. There is no brother, of course, and when it comes to trips, the only one his mother is interested in making these days is the scenic tour that takes her from the couch to the liquor cabinet and back to the couch.

"I'm sure Rudy will say okay. Don't you want to call him yourself?"

"If the request comes from you, it's a done deal."

The bitch giggles, which puts acres of flesh in rather disturbing motion. She makes the call while Brady's changing into his street clothes. Rudy is happy to give up his Sunday shift and take Brady's on Tuesday. This gives Brady two free afternoons to stake out Zoney's GoMart, and two should be enough. If the girl doesn't show up with the dog on either day, he'll call in sick on Wednesday. If he has to, but he doesn't think it will take that long.

After leaving Loeb's, Brady does a little Krogering of his own. He picks up half a dozen items they need — staples like eggs, milk, butter, and Cocoa Puffs — then swings by the meat counter and picks up a pound of hamburger. Ninety percent lean. Nothing but the best for Odell's last meal.

At home, he opens the garage and unloads everything he bought at Garden World, being careful to put the canisters of Gopher-Go on a high shelf. His mother rarely comes out here, but it doesn't do to take chances. There's a mini-fridge under the worktable; Brady got it at a yard sale for seven bucks, a total steal. It's where he keeps his soft drinks. He stows the package of hamburger behind the Cokes and Mountain Dews, then totes the rest of the groceries inside. What he finds in the kitchen is delightful: his mother shaking paprika over a tuna salad that actually looks tasty.

She catches his look and laughs. "I wanted to make up for the lasagna. I'm sorry about that, but I was just so *tired.*"

So drunk is what you were, he thinks, but at least she hasn't given up entirely.

She pouts her lips, freshly dressed in lipstick. "Give Mommy a kiss, honeyboy."

Honeyboy puts his arms around her and gives her a lingering kiss. Her lipstick tastes of something sweet. Then she slaps him briskly on the ass and tells him to go down and play with his computers until dinner's ready.

Brady leaves the cop a brief one-sentence message — **I'm going to fuck you up, Grampa**. Then he plays *Resident Evil* until his mother calls him to dinner. The tuna salad is great, and he has two helpings. She actually *can* cook when she wants, and he says nothing as she pours the first drink of the evening, an extra-big one to make up for the two or three smaller ones she denied herself that afternoon. By nine o'clock, she's snoring on the couch again.

Brady uses the opportunity to go online and learn all about the upcoming 'Round Here concert. He watches a YouTube video where a giggle of girls discusses which of the five boys is the hottest. The consensus is Cam, who sings lead on "Look Me in My Eyes," a piece of audio vomit Brady vaguely recalls hearing on the radio last year. He imagines those laughing faces torn apart by ball bearings, those identical Guess jeans in burning tatters.

Later, after he's helped his mother up to bed and he's sure she's totally conked, he gets the hamburger, puts it in a bowl, and mixes in two cups of Gopher-Go. If that isn't enough to kill Odell, he'll run the goddam mutt over with the ice cream truck.

This thought makes him snicker.

He puts the poisoned hamburger in a Baggie and stows it back in the mini-fridge, taking care to hide it behind the cans of soda again. He also takes care to wash both his hands and the mixing bowl in plenty of hot, soapy water.

That night, Brady sleeps well. There are no

headaches and no dreams about his dead brother.

24

Hodges and Janey are loaned a phone-friendly room down the hall from the hospital lobby, and there they split up the deathwork.

He's the one who gets in touch with the funeral home (Soames, the same one that handled Olivia Trelawney's exit rites) and makes sure the hospital is prepared to release the body when the hearse arrives. Janey, using her iPad with a casual efficiency Hodges envies, downloads an obituary form from the city paper. She fills it out quickly, speaking occasionally under her breath as she does so; once Hodges hears her murmur the phrase *in lieu of flowers.* When the obit's emailed back, she produces her mother's address book from her purse and begins making calls to the old lady's few remaining friends. She's warm with them, and calm, but also quick. Her voice wavers only once, while she's talking to Althea Greene, her mother's nurse and closest companion for almost ten years.

By six o'clock — roughly the same time Brady Hartsfield arrives home to find his mother putting the finishing touches on her tuna salad — most of the *t*'s have been crossed and the *i*'s dotted. At ten to seven, a white Cadillac hearse pulls into the hospital drive and rolls around back. The guys inside know where to go; they've been here plenty of times.

Janey looks at Hodges, her face pale, her mouth trembling. "I'm not sure I can —"

"I'll take care of it."

The transaction is like any other, really; he gives the mortician and his assistant a signed death certificate, they give him a receipt. He thinks, I could be buying a car. When he comes back to the hospital lobby, he spies Janey outside, once more sitting on the bumper of the ambulance. He sits down next to her and takes her hand. She squeezes his fingers hard. They watch the white hearse until it's out of sight. Then he leads her back to his car and they drive the two blocks to the Holiday Inn.

Henry Sirois, a fat man with a moist handshake, shows up at eight. Charlotte Gibney appears an hour later, herding an overloaded bellman ahead of her and complaining about the terrible service on her flight. And the crying babies, she says — you don't want to know. They don't, but she tells them anyway. She's as skinny as her brother is fat, and regards Hodges with a watery, suspicious eye. Lurking by Aunt Charlotte's side is her daughter Holly, a spinster roughly Janey's age but with none of Janey's looks. Holly Gibney never speaks above a mutter and seems to have a problem making eye contact.

"I want to see Betty," Aunt Charlotte announces after a brief dry embrace with her niece. It's as if she thinks Mrs. Wharton might be laid out in the motel lobby, lilies at her head and carnations at her feet.

Janey explains that the body has already been transported to Soames Funeral Home in the city, where Elizabeth Wharton's earthly remains will be cremated on Wednesday afternoon, after a viewing on Tuesday and a brief nondenominational service on Wednesday morning.

"Cremation is *barbaric,*" Uncle Henry announces. Everything these two say seems to be an announcement.

"It's what she wanted." Janey speaks quietly, politely, but Hodges observes the color rising in her cheeks.

He thinks there may be trouble, perhaps a demand to see a written document specifying cremation over burial, but they hold their peace. Perhaps they're remembering all those millions Janey inherited from her sister — money that is Janey's to share. Or not. Uncle Henry and Aunt Charlotte might even be considering all the visits they did not make to their elderly sister during her final suffering years. The visits Mrs. Wharton got during those years were made by Olivia, whom Aunt Charlotte does not mention by name, only calling her "the one with the problems." And of course it was Janey, still hurting from her abusive marriage and rancorous divorce, who was there at the end.

The five of them have a late dinner in the almost deserted Holiday Inn dining room. From the speakers overhead, Herb Alpert toots his horn. Aunt Charlotte has a salad and complains about the dressing, which she has specified should come on the side. "They can put it in a little pitcher, but bottled from the supermarket is still bottled from the supermarket," she announces.

Her muttering daughter orders something that sounds like *sneezebagel hellbun.* It turns out to be a cheeseburger, well done. Uncle Henry opts for fettuccini alfredo and sucks it down with the efficiency of a high-powered Rinse N Vac, fine droplets of perspiration appearing on his forehead as he approaches the finish line. He sops up the remains of the sauce with a chunk of buttered bread.

Hodges does most of the talking, recounting stories from his days with Vigilant Guard Service. The job is fictional, but the stories are mostly true, adapted from his years as a cop. He tells them about the burglar who got caught trying to squirm through a basement window and lost his pants in his efforts to wriggle free (this earns a small smile from Holly); the twelve-year-old boy who stood behind his bedroom door and cold-cocked a home invader with his baseball bat; the housekeeper who stole several pieces of her employer's jewelry only to have them drop out of her underwear while she served dinner. There are darker stories, many of them, that he keeps to himself.

Over dessert (which Hodges skips, Uncle Henry's unapologetic gluttony serving as a minatory power of example), Janey invites the new arrivals to stay at the house in Sugar Heights starting tomorrow, and the three of them toddle off to their prepaid rooms. Charlotte and Henry seem cheered by the prospect of inspecting at first hand just how the other half lives. As for Holly . . . who knows?

The newcomers' rooms are on the first floor. Janey and Hodges are on the third. As they reach the side-by-side doors, she asks if he will sleep with her.

"No sex," she says. "I never felt less sexy in my life. Basically, I just don't want to be alone."

That's okay with Hodges. He doubts if he would be capable of getting up to dickens, anyway. His stomach and leg muscles are still sore from last night . . . and, he reminds himself, last night she did almost all the work. Once they're beneath the coverlet, she snuggles up to him. He can hardly believe the warmth and firmness of her. The *thereness* of her. It's true he feels no desire at the moment, but he's glad the old lady had the courtesy to stroke out after he got his ashes hauled rather than before. Not very nice, but there it is. Corinne, his ex, used to say that men were born with a shitty-bone.

She pillows her head on his shoulder. "I'm so glad you came."

"Me too." It's the absolute truth.

"Do you think they know we're in bed together?"

Hodges considers. "Aunt Charlotte knows, but she'd know even if we weren't."

"And you can be sure of that because you're a trained —"

"Right. Go to sleep, Janey."

She does, but when he wakes up in the early hours of the morning, needing to use the toilet, she's sitting by the window, looking out at the parking lot and crying. He puts a hand on her shoulder.

She looks up. "I woke you. I'm sorry."

"Nah, this is my usual three A.M. pee-muster. Are you all right?"

"Yes. *Yeah.*" She smiles, then wipes at her eyes with her fisted hands, like a child. "Just hating on myself for shipping Mom off to Sunny Acres."

"But she wanted to go, you said."

"Yes. She did. It doesn't seem to change how I feel." Janey looks at him, eyes bleak and shining with tears. "Also hating on myself for letting Olivia do all the heavy lifting while I stayed in California."

"As a trained detective, I deduce you were trying to save your marriage."

She gives him a wan smile. "You're a good guy, Bill. Go on and use the bathroom."

When he comes back, she's curled up in bed again. He puts his arms around her and they sleep spoons the rest of the night.

25

Early on Sunday morning, before taking her shower, Janey shows him how to use her iPad. Hodges ducks beneath Debbie's Blue Umbrella and finds a new message from Mr. Mercedes. It's short and to the point: **I'm going to fuck you up, Grampa**.

"Yeah, but tell me how you *really* feel," he says, and surprises himself by laughing.

Janey comes out of the bathroom wrapped in a towel, steam billowing around her like a Hollywood special effect. She asks him what he's laughing about. Hodges shows her the message. She doesn't find it so funny.

"I hope you know what you're doing."

Hodges hopes so, too. Of one thing he's sure: when he gets back home, he'll take the Glock .40 he carried on the job out of his bedroom safe and start carrying it again. The Happy Slapper is no longer enough.

The phone next to the double bed warbles. Janey answers, converses briefly, hangs up. "That was Aunt Charlotte. She suggests the Fun Crew meet for breakfast in twenty minutes. I think she's anxious to get to Sugar

Heights and start checking the silverware."

"Okay."

"She also shared that the bed was *much* too hard and she had to take an allergy pill because of the foam pillows."

"Uh-huh. Janey, is Olivia's computer still at the Sugar Heights house?"

"Sure. In the room she used for her study."

"Can you lock that room so they can't get in there?"

She pauses in the act of hooking her bra, for a moment frozen in that pose, elbows back, a female archetype. "Hell with that, I'll just tell them to keep out. I am *not* going to be intimidated by that woman. And what about Holly? Can you understand anything she says?"

"I thought she ordered a sneezebagel for dinner," Hodges admits.

Janey collapses into the chair he awoke to find her crying in last night, only now she's laughing. "Sweetie, you're one bad detective. Which in this sense means good."

"Once the funeral stuff is over and they're gone —"

"Thursday at the latest," she says. "If they stay longer, I'll have to kill them."

"And no jury on earth would convict you. Once they're gone, I want to bring my friend Jerome in to look at that computer. I'd bring him in sooner, but —"

"They'd be all over him. And me."

Hodges, thinking of Aunt Charlotte's bright and inquisitive eyes, agrees.

"Won't the Blue Umbrella stuff be gone? I thought it disappeared every time you left the site."

"It's not Debbie's Blue Umbrella I'm interested in. It's the ghosts your sister heard in the night."

26

As they walk down to the elevator, he asks Janey something that's been troubling him ever since she called yesterday afternoon. "Do you think the questions about Olivia brought on your mother's stroke?"

She shrugs, looking unhappy. "There's no way to tell. She was very old — at least seven years older than Aunt Charlotte, I think — and the constant pain beat her up pretty badly." Then, reluctantly: "It could have played a part."

Hodges runs a hand through his hastily combed hair, mussing it again. "Ah, Jesus."

The elevator dings. They step in. She turns to him and grabs both of his hands. Her voice is swift and urgent. "I'll tell you something, though. If I had to do it over again, I still would. Mom had a long life. Ollie, on the other hand, deserved a few more years. She wasn't terribly happy, but she was doing okay until that bastard got to her. That . . . that *cuckoo* bird. Stealing her car and using it to kill eight people and hurt I don't know how many more wasn't enough for him, was it? Oh, no. He had to steal her *mind.*"

"So we push forward."

"Goddam right we do." Her hands tighten on his. "This is *ours,* Bill. Do you get that? This is *ours.*"

He wouldn't have stopped anyway, the bit is in his teeth, but the vehemence of her reply is good to hear.

The elevator doors open. Holly, Aunt Charlotte, and Uncle Henry are waiting in the lobby. Aunt Charlotte regards them with her inquisitive crow's eyes, probably prospecting for what Hodges's old partner used to call the freshly fucked look. She asks what took them so long, then, without waiting for an answer, tells them that the breakfast buffet looks very thin. If they were hoping for an omelet to order, they're out of luck.

Hodges thinks that Janey Patterson is in for several very long days.

27

Like the day before, Sunday is brilliant and summery. Like the day before, Brady sells out by four, at least two hours before dinnertime approaches and the parks begin emptying. He thinks about calling home and finding out what his mom wants for supper, then decides to grab takeout from Long John Silver's and surprise her. She loves the Langostino Lobster Bites.

As it turns out, Brady is the one surprised.

He comes into the house from the garage, and his greeting — *Hey, Mom, I'm home!* — dies on his lips. This time she's remembered to turn off the stove, but the smell of the meat she charred for her lunch hangs in the air. From the living room there comes a muffled drumming sound and a strange gurgling cry.

There's a skillet on one of the front burners. He peers into it and sees crumbles of burnt hamburger rising like small volcanic islands from a film of congealed grease. On the counter is a half-empty bottle of Stoli and a jar of mayonnaise, which is all she ever uses to dress her hamburgers.

The grease-spotted takeout bags drop from his hands. Brady doesn't even notice.

No, he thinks. It can't be.

It is, though. He throws open the kitchen refrigerator and there, on the top shelf, is the Baggie of poisoned meat. Only now half of it is gone.

He stares at it stupidly, thinking, She never checks the mini-fridge in the garage. *Never.* That's *mine.*

This is followed by another thought: How do you know what she checks when you're not here? For all you know she's been through all your drawers and looked under your mattress.

That gurgling cry comes again. Brady runs for the living room, kicking one of the Long John Silver's bags under the kitchen table and leaving the refrigerator door open. His mother is sitting bolt upright on the couch. She's in her blue silk lounging pajamas. The shirt is covered with a bib of blood-streaked vomit. Her belly protrudes, straining the buttons; it's the belly of a woman who is seven months pregnant. Her hair stands out from her parchment-pale face in a mad spray. Her nostrils are clotted with blood. Her eyes bulge. She's not seeing him, or so he thinks at first, but then she holds out her hands.

"Mom! *Mom!*"

His initial idea is to thump her on the back, but he looks at the mostly eaten hamburger on the coffee table next to the remains of what must have been a perfectly enormous screwdriver, and knows back-thumps will do no good. The stuff's not lodged in her throat. If only it were.

The drumming sound he heard when he came in recommences as her feet begin to piston up and down. It's as if she's marching in place. Her back arches. Her arms fly straight up. Now she's simultaneously marching and signaling that the field goal is good. One foot shoots out and kicks the coffee table. Her screwdriver glass falls over.

"Mom!"

She throws herself back against the sofa cushions, then forward. Her agonized eyes stare at him. She gurgles a muffled something that might or might not be his name.

What do you do for poisoning victims? Was it raw eggs? Or Coca-Cola? No, Coke's for upset stomachs, and she's gone far beyond that.

Have to stick my fingers down her throat, he thinks. Make her gag it up.

But then her teeth begin doing their own march and he pulls his tentatively extended hand back, pressing the palm over his mouth instead. He sees that she has already bitten her lower lip almost to tatters; that's where the blood on her shirt has come from. Some of it, anyway.

"Brayvie!" She draws in a hitching breath. What follows is guttural but understandable. "Caw . . . nie . . . wha . . . whan!"

Call 911.

He goes to the phone and picks it up before realizing he really can't do that. Think of the unanswerable questions that would ensue. He puts it back down and whirls to her.

"Why did you go snooping out there, Mom? *Why?"*

"Brayvie! Nie-wha-*whan!"*

"When did you eat it? How long has it been?"

Instead of answering, she begins to march

again. Her head snaps up and her bulging eyes regard the ceiling for a second or two before her head snaps forward again. Her back doesn't move at all; it's as if her head is mounted on bearings. The gurgling sounds return — the sound of water trying to go down a partially clogged drain. Her mouth yawns and she belches vomit. It lands in her lap with a wet splat, and oh God, it's half blood.

He thinks of all the times he's wished her dead. But I never wanted it to be like this, he thinks. Never like this.

An idea lights up his mind like a single bright flare over a stormy ocean. He can find out how to treat her online. *Everything's* online.

"I'm going to take care of it," he says, "but I have to go downstairs for a few minutes. You just . . . you hang in there, Mom. Try . . ."

He almost says *Try to relax.*

He runs into the kitchen, toward the door that leads to his control room. Down there he'll find out how to save her. And even if he can't, he won't have to watch her die.

28

The word to turn on the lights is *control,* but although he speaks it three times, the basement remains in darkness. Brady realizes the voice-recognition program isn't working because he doesn't sound like himself, and is it any wonder? Any fucking wonder at all?

He uses the switch instead and goes down, first shutting the door — and the beastly sounds coming from the living room — behind him.

He doesn't even try to voice-ac his bank of computers, just turns on his Number Three with the button behind the monitor. The countdown to Total Erasure appears and he stops it by typing in his password. But he doesn't seek out poison antidotes; it's far too late for that, and now that he's sitting here in his safe place, he allows himself to know it.

He also knows how this happened. She was good yesterday, staying sober long enough to make a nice supper for them, so she rewarded herself today. Got schnockered, then decided she'd better eat a little something to soak up the booze before her honeyboy got home. Didn't find anything in the pantry or the refrigerator that tickled her fancy. Oh but say, what about the mini-fridge in the garage? Soft drinks wouldn't interest her, but perhaps there were snacks. Only what she found was even better, a Baggie filled with nice fresh hamburger.

It makes Brady think of an old saying — whatever *can* go wrong, *will* go wrong. Is that the Peter Principle? He goes online to find out. After some investigation he discovers it's not the Peter Principle but Murphy's Law.

Named after a man named Edward Murphy. The guy made aircraft parts. Who knew?

He surfs a few other sites — actually quite a few — and plays a few hands of solitaire. When there's a particularly loud thump from upstairs, he decides to listen to a few tunes on his iPod. Something cheery. The Staple Singers, maybe.

And as "Respect Yourself" plays in the middle of his head, he goes on Debbie's Blue Umbrella to see if there's a message from the fat ex-cop.

29

When he can put it off no longer, Brady creeps upstairs. Twilight has come. The smell of seared hamburger is almost gone, but the smell of puke is still strong. He goes into the living room. His mother is on the floor next to the coffee table, which is now overturned. Her eyes glare up at the ceiling. Her lips are pulled back in a great big grin. Her hands are claws. She's dead.

Brady thinks, Why did you have to go out in the garage when you got hungry? Oh Mom, Mommy, what in God's name possessed you?

Whatever *can* go wrong *will* go wrong, he thinks, and then, looking at the mess she's made, he wonders if they have any carpet cleaner.

This is Hodges's fault. It all leads back to him.

He'll deal with the old Det-Ret, and soon. Right now, though, he has a more pressing problem. He sits down to consider it, taking the chair he uses on the occasions when he watches TV with her. He realizes she'll never watch another reality show. It's sad . . . but it does have its funny side. He imagines Jeff Probst sending flowers with a card reading *From all your* Survivor *pals,* and he just has to chuckle.

What is he to do with her? The neighbors won't miss her because she never ever had anything to do with them, called them stuck-up. She has no friends, either, not even of the barfly type, because she did all her drinking at home. Once, in a rare moment of self-appraisal, she told him she didn't go out to the bars because they were full of drunks just like her.

"That's why you didn't taste that shit and stop, isn't it?" he asks the corpse. "You were too fucking loaded."

He wishes they had a freezer case. If they did, he'd cram her body into it. He saw that in a movie once. He doesn't dare put her in the garage; that seems a little too public, somehow. He supposes he could wrap her in a rug and take her down to the basement, she'd certainly fit under the stairs, but how would he get any work done, knowing she was there? Knowing that, even inside a roll of rug, her eyes were glaring?

Besides, the basement's *his* place. His control room.

In the end he realizes there's only one thing to do. He grabs her under the arms and drags her toward the stairs. By the time he gets her there, her pajama pants have slid down, revealing what she sometimes calls (*called,* he reminds himself) her winky. Once, when he was in bed with her and she was giving him relief for a particularly bad headache, he tried to touch her winky and she slapped his hand away. Hard. Don't you *ever,* she had said. That's where you *came* from.

Brady pulls her up the stairs, a riser at a time. The pajama pants work down to her ankles and puddle there. He remembers how she did a sit-down march on the couch in her last extremity. How awful. But, like the thing about Jeff Probst sending flowers, it had its funny side, although it wasn't the kind of joke you could explain to people. It was kind of Zen.

Down the hall. Into her bedroom. He straightens up, wincing at the pain in his lower back. God, she's so *heavy.* It's as if death has stuffed her with some dense mystery meat.

Never mind. Get it done.

He yanks up her pants, making her decent again — as decent as a corpse in vomit-soaked pj's can be — and lifts her onto her bed, groaning as fresh pain settles into his back. When he straightens up this time, he can feel his spine crackling. He thinks about taking off her nightclothes and replacing them with something clean — one of the XL tee-shirts she sometimes wears to bed, maybe — but that would mean more lifting and manipulation of what is now just pounds of silent flesh hanging from bone coathangers. What if he threw his back out?

He could at least take off her top, that caught most of the mess, but then he'd have to look at her boobs. Those she did let him touch, but only once in awhile. My handsome boy, she'd say on these occasions. Running her fingers through his hair or massaging his neck where the headaches settled, crouched and snarling. My handsome honeyboy.

In the end he just pulls the bedspread up, covering her entirely. Especially those staring, glaring eyes.

"Sorry, Mom," he says, looking down at the white shape. "Not your fault."

No. It's the fat ex-cop's fault. Brady bought the Gopher-Go to poison the dog, true, but only as a way of getting to Hodges and messing with his head. Now it's Brady's head that's a mess. Not to mention the living room. He's got a lot of work to do down there, but he has something else to do first.

30

He's got control of himself again and this time his voice commands work. He doesn't waste time, just sits down in front of his Number Three and logs on to Debbie's Blue Umbrella. His message to Hodges is brief and to the point.

I'm going to kill you.
You won't see me coming.

Call for the Dead

1

On Monday, two days after Elizabeth Wharton's death, Hodges is once more seated in DeMasio's Italian Ristorante. The last time he was here, it was for lunch with his old partner. This time it's dinner. His companions are Jerome Robinson and Janelle Patterson.

Janey compliments him on his suit, which already fits better even though he's only lost a few pounds (and the Glock he's wearing on his hip hardly shows at all). It's the new hat Jerome likes, a brown fedora Janey bought Hodges on impulse that very day, and presented to him with some ceremony. Because he's a private detective now, she said, and every private dick should have a fedora he can pull down to one eyebrow.

Jerome tries it on and gives it that exact tilt. "What do you think? Do I look like Bogie?"

"I hate to disappoint you," Hodges says, "but Bogie was Caucasian."

"So Caucasian he practically shimmered," Janey adds.

"Forgot that." Jerome tosses the hat back to Hodges, who places it under his chair, reminding himself not to forget it when he leaves. Or step on it.

He's pleased when his two dinner guests take to each other at once. Jerome — an old head on top of a young body, Hodges often thinks — does the right thing as soon as the ice-breaking foolishness of the hat is finished, taking one of Janey's hands in both of his and telling her he's sorry for her loss.

"Both of them," he says. "I know you lost your sister, too. If I lost mine, I'd be the saddest guy on earth. Barb's a pain, but I love her to death."

She thanks him with a smile. Because Jerome's still too young for a legal glass of wine, they all order iced tea. Janey asks him about his college plans, and when Jerome mentions the possibility of Harvard, she rolls her eyes and says, "A *Hah*-vad man. Oh my *Gawd.*"

"Massa Hodges goan have to find hisself a new lawnboy!" Jerome exclaims, and Janey laughs so hard she has to spit a bite of shrimp into her napkin. It makes her blush, but Hodges is glad to hear that laugh. Her carefully applied makeup can't completely hide the pallor of her cheeks, or the dark circles under her eyes.

When he asks her how Aunt Charlotte, Uncle Henry, and Holly the Mumbler are enjoying the big house in Sugar Heights, Janey grabs the sides of her head as if afflicted with a monster headache.

"Aunt Charlotte called six times today. I'm not exaggerating. *Six.* The first time was to tell me that Holly woke up in the middle of the night, didn't know where she was, and had a panic attack. Auntie C said she was on the verge of calling an ambulance when Uncle Henry finally got her settled down by talking to her about NASCAR. She's crazy about stock car racing. Never misses it on TV, I understand. Jeff Gordon is her idol." Janey shrugs. "Go figure."

"How old is this Holly?" Jerome asks.

"About my age, but she suffers from a certain amount of . . . emotional retardation, I guess you'd say."

Jerome considers this silently, then says: "She probably needs to reconsider Kyle Busch."

"Who?"

"Never mind."

Janey says Aunt Charlotte has also called to marvel over the monthly electrical bill, which must be huge; to confide that the neighbors seem very standoffish; to announce there is an *awfully* large number of pictures and all that modern art is not to her taste; to point out (although it sounds like another announcement) that if Olivia thought all those lamps were carnival glass, she had almost certainly been taken to the cleaners. The last call, received just before Janey left for the restaurant, had been the most aggravating. Uncle Henry wanted Janey to know, her aunt said, that he had looked into the matter and it still wasn't too late to change her mind about the cremation. She said the idea made her brother very upset — he called it "a Viking funeral" — and Holly wouldn't even discuss it, because it gave her the horrors.

"Their Thursday departure is confirmed," Janey says, "and I'm already counting the minutes." She squeezes Hodges's hand, and says, "There's one bit of good news, though. Auntie C says that Holly was *very* taken with you."

Hodges smiles. "Must be my resemblance to Jeff Gordon."

Janey and Jerome order dessert. Hodges, feeling virtuous, does not. Then, over coffee, he gets down to business. He has brought two folders with him, and hands one to each of his dinner companions.

"All my notes. I've organized them as well as I can. I want you to have them in case anything happens to me."

Janey looks alarmed. "What else has he said to you on that site?"

"Nothing at all," Hodges says. The lie comes out smoothly and convincingly. "It's just a precaution."

"You sure of that?" Jerome asks.

"Absolutely. There's nothing definitive in the notes, but that doesn't mean we haven't made progress. I see a path of investigation that might — I repeat *might* — take us to this guy. In the meantime, it's important that you both remain very aware of what's going on around you at all times."

"BOLO our asses off," Janey says.

"Right." He turns to Jerome. "And what, specifically, are you going to be on the lookout for?"

The reply is quick and sure. "Repeat vehicles, especially those driven by males on the younger side, say between the ages of twenty-five and forty. Although I think forty's pretty old. Which makes you practically ancient, Bill."

"Nobody loves a smartass," Hodges says. "Experience will teach you that in time, young man."

Elaine, the hostess, drifts over to ask how everything was. They tell her everything was fine, and Hodges asks for more coffee all around.

"Right away," she says. "You're looking much better than the last time you were here, Mr. Hodges. If you don't mind me saying so."

Hodges doesn't mind. He *feels* better than the last time he was here. Lighter than the loss of seven or eight pounds can account for.

When Elaine's gone and the waiter has poured more coffee, Janey leans over the table with her eyes fixed on his. "What path? Tell us."

He finds himself thinking of Donald Davis, who has confessed to killing not only his wife but five other women at rest stops along the highways of the Midwest. Soon the handsome Mr. Davis will be in State, where he will no doubt spend the rest of his life.

Hodges has seen it all before.

He's not so naïve as to believe that every homicide is solved, but more often than not, murder *does* out. Something (a certain wifely body in a certain abandoned gravel pit, for instance) comes to light. It's as if there's a fumble-fingered but powerful universal force at work, always trying to put wrong things right. The detectives assigned to a murder case read reports, interview witnesses, work the phones, study forensic evidence . . . and wait for that force to do its job. When it does (*if* it does), a path appears. It often leads straight to the doer, the sort of person Mr. Mercedes refers to in his letters as a *perk.*

Hodges asks his dinner companions, "What if Olivia Trelawney actually *did* hear ghosts?"

2

In the parking lot, standing next to the used but serviceable Jeep Wrangler his parents gave him as a seventeenth birthday present, Jerome tells Janey how good it was to meet her, and kisses her cheek. She looks surprised but pleased.

Jerome turns to Hodges. "You all set, Bill? Need anything tomorrow?"

"Just for you to look into that stuff we talked about so you'll be ready when we check out Olivia's computer."

"I'm all over it."

"Good. And don't forget to give my best to your dad and mom."

Jerome grins. "Tell you what, I'll pass your best on to Dad. As for Mom . . ." Tyrone Feelgood Delight makes a brief cameo appearance. "I be steppin round *dat* lady fo' de nex' week or so."

Hodges raises his eyebrows. "Are you in dutch with your mother? That doesn't sound like you."

"Nah, she's just grouchy. And I can relate." Jerome snickers.

"What are you talking about?"

"Oh, man. There's a concert at the MAC Thursday night. This dopey boy band called 'Round Here. Barb and her friend Hilda and a couple of their other friends are insane to see them, although they're as vanilla pudding as can be."

"How old's your sister?" Janey asks.

"Nine. Going on ten."

"Vanilla pudding's what girls that age like. Take it from a former eleven-year-old who was crazy about the Bay City Rollers." Jerome looks puzzled, and she laughs. "If you knew who they were, I'd lose all respect for you."

"Anyway, none of them have ever been to a live show, right? I mean, other than *Barney* or *Sesame Street on Ice* or something. So they pestered and pestered — they even pestered *me* — and finally the moms got together and decided that since it was an early show, the girls could go even if it was a school night, as long as one of *them* did the chaperone thing. They literally drew straws, and my mom lost."

He shakes his head. His face is solemn but his eyes are sparkling. "My mom at the MAC with three or four thousand screaming girls between the ages of eight and fourteen. Do I have to explain any more about why I'm keeping out of her way?"

"I bet she has a great time," Janey says. "She probably screamed for Marvin Gaye or Al Green not so long ago."

Jerome hops into his Wrangler, gives them a final wave, and pulls out onto Lowbriar. That leaves Hodges and Janey standing beside Hodges's car, in an almost-summer night. A quarter moon has risen above the underpass that separates the more affluent part of the city from Lowtown.

"He's a good guy," Janey says. "You're lucky to have him."

"Yeah," Hodges says. "I am."

She takes the fedora off his head and puts it on her own, giving it a small but provocative tilt. "What's next, Detective? Your place?"

"Do you mean what I hope you mean?"

"I don't want to sleep alone." She stands on tiptoe to return his hat. "If I must surrender my body to make sure that doesn't happen, I suppose I must."

Hodges pushes the button that unlocks his car and says, "Never let it be said I failed to take advantage of a lady in distress."

"You are no gentleman, sir," she says, then adds, "Thank God. Let's go."

3

It's better this time because they know each other a little. Anxiety has been replaced by eagerness. When the lovemaking is done, she slips into one of his shirts (it's so big her breasts disappear completely and the tails hang down to the backs of her knees) and explores his small house. He trails her a bit anxiously.

She renders her verdict after they've returned to the bedroom. "Not bad for a bachelor pad. No dirty dishes in the sink, no hair in the bathtub, no porn videos on top of the TV. I even spied a green vegetable or two in the crisper, which earns you bonus points."

She's filched two cans of beer from the fridge and touches hers to his.

"I never expected to be here with another woman," Hodges says. "Except maybe for my daughter. We talk on the phone and email, but Allie hasn't actually visited in a couple of years."

"Did she take your ex's side in the divorce?"

"I suppose she did." Hodges has never thought about it in exactly those terms. "If so, she was probably right to."

"You might be too hard on yourself."

Hodges sips his beer. It tastes pretty good. As he sips again, a thought occurs to him.

"Does Aunt Charlotte have this number, Janey?"

"No way. That's not the reason I wanted to come here instead of going back to the condo, but I'd be a liar if I said it never crossed my mind." She looks at him gravely. "Will you come to the memorial service on Wednesday? Say you will. Please. I need a friend."

"Of course. I'll be at the viewing on Tuesday as well."

She looks surprised, but happily so. "That seems above and beyond."

Not to Hodges, it doesn't. He's in full investigative mode now, and attending the funeral of someone involved in a murder case — even peripherally — is standard police procedure. He doesn't really believe Mr. Mercedes will turn up at either the viewing or the service on Wednesday, but it's not out of the question. Hodges hasn't seen today's paper, but some alert reporter might well have linked Mrs. Wharton and Olivia Trelawney, the daughter who committed suicide after her car was used as a murder weapon. Such a connection is hardly news, but you could say the same about Lindsay Lohan's adventures with drugs and alcohol. Hodges thinks there might at least have been a sidebar.

"I want to be there," he says. "What's the deal with the ashes?"

"The mortician called them the *cremains,*" she says, and wrinkles her nose the way she does when she mocks his *yeah.* "Is that gross or what? It sounds like something you'd pour in your coffee. On the upside, I'm pretty sure I won't have to fight Aunt Charlotte or Uncle Henry for them."

"No, you won't have to do that. Is there going to be a reception?"

Janey sighs. "Auntie C insists. So the service at ten, followed by a luncheon at the house in Sugar Heights. While we're eating catered sandwiches and telling our favorite Elizabeth Wharton stories, the funeral home people will take care of the cremation. I'll decide what to do with the ashes after the three of them leave on Thursday. They'll never even have to look at the urn."

"That's a good idea."

"Thanks, but I dread the luncheon. Not Mrs. Greene and the rest of Mom's few old friends, but *them.* If Aunt Charlotte freaks, Holly's apt to have a meltdown. You'll come to lunch, too, won't you?"

"If you let me reach inside that shirt you're wearing, I'll do anything you want."

"In that case, let me help you with the buttons."

4

Not many miles from where Kermit William Hodges and Janelle Patterson are lying together in the house on Harper Road, Brady Hartsfield is sitting in his control room. Tonight he's at his worktable instead of his bank of computers. And doing nothing.

Nearby, lying amid the litter of small tools, bits of wire, and computer components, is the Monday paper, still rolled up inside its thin plastic condom. He brought it in when he got back from Discount Electronix, but only from force of habit. He has no interest in the news. He has other things to think about. How he's going to get the cop. How he's going to get into the 'Round Here concert at the MAC wearing his carefully constructed suicide vest. If he really intends to do it, that is. Right now it all seems like an awful lot of work. A long row to hoe. A high mountain to climb. A . . . a . . .

But he can't think of any other similes. Or are those metaphors?

Maybe, he thinks drearily, I just ought to kill myself now and be done with it. Get rid of these awful thoughts. These snapshots from hell.

Snapshots like the one of his mother, for instance, convulsing on the sofa after eating the poisoned meat meant for the Robinson family's dog. Mom with her eyes bugging out and her pajama shirt covered with puke — how would that picture look in the old family album?

He needs to think, but there's a hurricane going on in his head, a big bad Category Five Katrina, and everything is flying.

His old Boy Scout sleeping bag is spread out on the basement floor, on top of an air mattress he scrounged from the garage. The air mattress has a slow leak. Brady supposes he ought to replace it if he means to continue sleeping down here for whatever short stretch of life remains to him. And where else *can* he sleep? He can't bring himself to use his bed on the second floor, not with his mother lying dead in her own bed just down the hall, maybe already rotting her way into the sheets. He's turned on her air conditioner and cranked it up to HI COOL, but he's under no illusions about how well that will work. Or for how long. Nor is sleeping on the living room couch an option. He cleaned it as well as he could, and turned the cushions, but it still smells of her vomit.

No, it has to be down here, in his special place. His control room. Of course the basement has its own unpleasant history; it's where his little brother died. Only *died* is a bit of a euphemism, and it's a bit late for those.

Brady thinks about how he used Frankie's name when he posted to Olivia Trelawney under Debbie's Blue Umbrella. It was as if Frankie was alive again for a little while. Only when the Trelawney bitch died, Frankie died with her.

Died again.

"I never liked you anyway," he says, looking toward the foot of the stairs. It is a strangely childish voice, high and treble, but Brady doesn't notice. "And I had to." He pauses. "*We* had to."

He thinks of his mother, and how beautiful she was in those days.

Those old days.

5

Deborah Ann Hartsfield was one of those rare ex-cheerleaders who, even after bearing children, managed to hang on to the body that had danced and pranced its way along the sidelines under the Friday-night lights: tall, full-figured, honey-haired. During the early years of her marriage, she took no more than a glass of wine with dinner. Why drink to excess when life was good sober? She had her husband, she had her house on the North Side of the city — not exactly a palace, but what starter-home was? — and she had her two boys.

At the time his mother became a widow, Brady was eight and Frankie was three. Frankie was a plain child, and a bit on the slow side. Brady, on the other hand, had good looks and quick wits. Also, what a charmer! She doted on him, and Brady felt the same about her. They spent long Saturday afternoons cuddled together on the couch under a blanket, watching old movies and drinking hot chocolate while Norm puttered in the garage and Frankie crawled around on the carpet, playing with blocks or a little fire truck that he liked so well he had given it a name: Sammy.

Norm Hartsfield was a lineman for Central States Power. He made a good salary pole-climbing, but had his sights trained on bigger things. Perhaps it was those things he was eyeing instead of watching what he was doing that day beside Route 51, or maybe he just lost his balance a little and reached the wrong way in an effort to steady himself. No matter what the reason, the result was lethal. His partner was just reporting that they'd found the outage and repair was almost complete when he heard a crackling sound. That was twenty thousand volts of coal-fired CSP electricity pouring into Norm Hartsfield's body. The partner looked up just in time to see Norm tumble out of the cherry-picker basket and plunge forty feet to the ground with his left hand melted and the sleeve of his uniform shirt on fire.

Addicted to credit cards, like most middle Americans as the end of the century approached, the Hartsfields had savings of less than two thousand dollars. That was pretty thin, but there was a good insurance policy, and CSP kicked in an additional seventy thousand, trading it for Deborah Ann's signature on a paper absolving the company of all blame in the matter of Norman Hartsfield's death. To Deborah Ann, that seemed like a huge bucketful of cash. She paid off the mortgage on the house and bought a new car. Never did it occur to her that some buckets fill but once.

She had been working as a hairdresser when she met Norm, and went back to that trade after his death. Six months or so into her widowhood, she began seeing a man she had met one day at the bank — only a junior executive, she told Brady, but he had what she called *prospects.* She brought him home.

He ruffled Brady's hair and called him *champ.* He ruffled Frankie's hair and called him *little champ.* Brady didn't like him (he had big teeth, like a vampire in a scary movie), but he didn't show his dislike. He had already learned to wear a happy face and keep his feelings to himself.

One night, before taking Deborah Ann out to dinner, the boyfriend told Brady, Your mother's a charmer and so are you. Brady smiled and said thank you and hoped the boyfriend would get in a car accident and die. As long as his mother wasn't with him, that was. The boyfriend with the scary teeth had no right to take his father's place.

That was Brady's job.

Frankie choked on the apple during *The Blues Brothers.* It was supposed to be a funny movie. Brady didn't see what was so funny about it, but his mother and Frankie laughed fit to split. His mother was happy and all dressed up because she was going out with her boyfriend. In a little while the sitter would come in. The sitter was a stupid greedyguts who always looked in the refrigerator to see what was good to eat as soon as Deborah Ann left, bending over so her fat ass stuck out.

There were two snack-bowls on the coffee table; one contained popcorn, the other apple slices dusted with cinnamon. In one part of the movie people sang in church and one of the Blues Brothers did flips all the way up the center aisle. Frankie was sitting on the floor and laughed hard when the fat Blues Brother did his flips. When he drew in breath to laugh some more, he sucked a piece of cinnamon-dusted apple slice down his throat. That made him stop laughing. He began to jerk around and claw at his neck instead.

Brady's mother screamed and grabbed him in her arms. She squeezed him, trying to make the piece of apple come out. It didn't. Frankie's face went red. She reached into his mouth and down his throat, trying to get at the piece of apple. She couldn't. Frankie started to lose the red color.

"Oh-my-dear-Jesus," Deborah Ann cried, and ran for the phone. As she picked it up she shouted at Brady, "Don't just sit there like an asshole! Pound him on the back!"

Brady didn't like to be shouted at, and his mother had never called him an asshole before, but he pounded Frankie on the back. He pounded *hard.* The piece of apple slice did not come out. Now Frankie's face was turning blue. Brady had an idea. He picked Frankie up by his ankles so Frankie's head hung down and his hair brushed the rug. The apple slice did not come out.

"Stop being a brat, Frankie," Brady said.

Frankie continued to breathe — sort of, he was making little breezy whistling noises, anyway — almost until the ambulance got there. Then he stopped. The ambulance men came in. They were wearing black clothes with yellow patches on the jackets. They made Brady go into the kitchen, so Brady didn't see what they did, but his mother screamed and later he saw drops of blood on the carpet.

No apple slice, though.

Then everyone except Brady went away in the ambulance. He sat on the couch and ate popcorn and watched TV. Not *The Blues Brothers; The Blues Brothers* was stupid, just a bunch of singing and running around. He found a movie about a crazy guy who kidnapped a bunch of kids who were on their schoolbus. That was pretty exciting.

When the fat sitter showed up, Brady said, "Frankie choked on an apple slice. There's ice cream in the refrigerator. Vanilla Crunch. Have as much as you want." Maybe, he thought, if she ate enough ice cream, she'd have a heart attack and he could call 911.

Or just let the stupid bitch lay there. That would probably be better. He could watch her.

Deborah Ann finally came home at eleven o'clock. The fat sitter had made Brady go to bed, but he wasn't asleep, and when he came downstairs in his pj's, his mother hugged him to her. The fat babysitter asked how Frankie was. The fat babysitter was full of fake concern. The reason Brady knew it was fake was because *he* wasn't concerned, so why would the fat babysitter care?

"He's going to be fine," Deborah Ann said, with a big smile. Then, when the fat babysitter was gone, she started crying like crazy. She got her wine out of the refrigerator, but instead of pouring it into a glass, she drank straight from the neck of the bottle.

"He might not be," she told Brady, wiping wine from her chin. "He's in a coma. Do you know what that is?"

"Sure. Like in a doctor show."

"That's right." She got down on one knee, so they were face-to-face. Having her so close — smelling the perfume she'd put on for the date that never happened — gave him a feeling in his stomach. It was funny but good. He kept looking at the blue stuff on her eyelids. It was weird but good.

"He stopped breathing for a long time before the EMTs could make some room for the air to go down. The doctor at the hospital said that even if he comes out of his coma, there might be brain damage."

Brady thought Frankie was already brain-damaged — he was awful stupid, carrying around that fire truck all the time — but said nothing. His mother was wearing a blouse that showed the tops of her titties. That gave him a funny feeling in his stomach, too.

"If I tell you something, do you promise never to tell anyone? Not another living soul?"

Brady promised. He was good at keeping secrets.

"It might be better if he *does* die. Because if he wakes up and he's brain-damaged, I don't know what we'll do."

Then she clasped him to her and her hair tickled the side of his face and the smell of her perfume was very strong. She said: "Thank God it wasn't you, honeyboy. Thank God for that."

Brady hugged her back, pressing his chest against her titties. He had a boner.

Frankie *did* wake up, and sure enough, he was brain-damaged. He had never been smart ("Takes after his father," Deborah Ann said once), but compared to the way he was now, he had been a genius in those pre–apple slice days. He had toilet-trained late, not until he was almost three and a half, and now he was back in diapers. His vocabulary had been reduced to no more than a dozen words. Instead of walking he made his way around the house in a limping shuffle. Sometimes he fell abruptly and profoundly asleep, but that was only in the daytime. At night, he had a tendency to wander, and before he started out on these nocturnal safaris, he usually stripped off his Pampers. Sometimes he got into bed with his mother. More often he got in with Brady, who would awake to find the bed soaked and Frankie staring at him with goofy, creepy love.

Frankie had to keep going to the doctor. His breathing was never right. At its best it was a wet wheeze, at its worst, when he had one of his frequent colds, a rattling bark. He could no longer eat solid food; his meals had to be pureed in the blender and he ate them in a highchair. Drinking from a glass was out of the question, so it was back to sippy cups.

The boyfriend from the bank was long gone, and the fat babysitter didn't last, either. She said she was sorry, but she just couldn't cope with Frankie the way he was now. For awhile Deborah Ann got a full-time home care lady to come in, but the home care lady ended up getting more money than Deborah Ann made at the beauty shop, so she let the home care lady go and quit her job. Now they were living off savings. She began to drink more, switching from wine to vodka, which she called *a more efficient delivery system.* Brady would sit with her on the couch, drinking Pepsi. They would watch Frankie crawl around on the carpet with his fire truck in one hand and his blue sippy cup, also filled with Pepsi, in the other.

"It's shrinking like the icecaps," Deborah Ann would say, and Brady no longer had to ask her what *it* was. "And when it's gone, we'll be out on the street."

She went to see a lawyer (in the same strip mall where Brady would years later flick an annoying goofy-boy in the throat) and paid a hundred dollars for a consultation. She took Brady with her. The lawyer's name was Greensmith. He wore a cheap suit and kept sneaking glances at Deborah Ann's titties.

"I can tell you what happened," he said. "Seen it before. That piece of apple left just enough space around his windpipe to let him keep breathing. It's too bad you reached down his throat, that's all."

"I was trying to get it out!" Deborah Ann said indignantly.

"I know, any good mother would do the same, but you pushed it deeper instead, and blocked his windpipe entirely. If one of the EMTs had done that, you'd have a case. Worth a few hundred thousand at least. Maybe a million-five. Seen it before. But it was you. And you told them what you did. Didn't you?"

Deborah Ann admitted she had.

"Did they intubate him?"

Deborah Ann said they did.

"Okay, *that's* your case. They got an airway into him, but in doing so, they pushed that bad apple in even deeper." He sat back, spread his fingers on his slightly yellowed white shirt, and peeped at Deborah Ann's titties again, maybe just to make sure they hadn't slipped out of her bra and run away. "Hence, brain damage."

"So you'll take the case?"

"Happy to, if you can pay for the five years

it'll drag through the courts. Because the hospital and their insurance providers will fight you every step of the way. Seen it before."

"How much?"

Greensmith named a figure, and Deborah Ann left the office, holding Brady's hand. They sat in her Honda (then new) and she cried. When that part was over, she told him to play the radio while she ran another errand. Brady knew what the other errand entailed: a bottle of efficient delivery system.

She relived her meeting with Greensmith many times over the years, always ending with the same bitter pronouncement: "I paid a hundred dollars I couldn't afford to a lawyer in a suit from Men's Wearhouse, and all I found out was I couldn't afford to fight the big insurance companies and get what was coming to me."

The year that followed was five years long. There was a life-sucking monster in the house, and the monster's name was Frankie. Sometimes when he knocked something over or woke Deborah Ann up from a nap, she spanked him. Once she lost it completely and punched him in the side of the head, sending him to the floor in a twitching, eye-rolling daze. She picked him up and hugged him and cried and said she was sorry, but there was only so much a woman could take.

She went into Hair Today as a sub whenever

she could. On these occasions she called Brady in sick at school so he could babysit his little brother. Sometimes Brady would catch Frankie reaching for stuff he wasn't supposed to have (or stuff that belonged to Brady, like his Atari Arcade handheld), and then he would slap Frankie's hands until Frankie cried. When the wails started, Brady would remind himself that it wasn't Frankie's fault, he had brain damage from that damn, no, that *fucking* apple slice, and he would be overcome by a mixture of guilt, rage, and sorrow. He would take Frankie on his lap and rock him and tell him he was sorry, but there was only so much a man could take. And he *was* a man, Mom said so: the man of the house. He got good at changing Frankie's diapers, but when there was poo (no, it was *shit,* not poo but *shit*), he would sometimes pinch Frankie's legs and shout at him to lay still, damn you, lay still. Even if Frankie *was* laying still. Laying there with Sammy the Fire Truck clutched to his chest and looking up at the ceiling with his big stupid brain-damaged eyes.

That year was full of sometimes.

Sometimes he loved Frankie up and kissed him.

Sometimes he'd shake him and say This is your fault, we're going to have to live in the street and it's your fault.

Sometimes, putting Frankie to bed after a

day at the beauty parlor, Deborah Ann would see bruises on the boy's arms and legs. Once on his throat, which was scarred from the tracheotomy the EMTs had performed. She never commented on these.

Sometimes Brady loved Frankie. Sometimes he hated him. Usually he felt both things at the same time, and it gave him headaches.

Sometimes (mostly when she was drunk), Deborah Ann would rail at the train-wreck of her life. "I can't get assistance from the city, the state, or the goddam federal government, and why? Because we still have too much from the insurance and the settlement, that's why. Does anyone care that everything's going out and nothing's coming in? No. When the money's gone and we're living in a homeless shelter on Lowbriar Avenue, *then* I'll be eligible for assistance, and isn't that just *ducky.*"

Sometimes Brady would look at Frankie and think, You're in the *way.* You're in the *way,* Frankie, you're in the fucking goddam shitass *waaay.*

Sometimes — often — Brady hated the whole fucking goddam shitass world. If there was a God, like the Sunday guys said on TV, wouldn't He take Frankie up to heaven, so his mother could go back to work fulltime and they wouldn't have to be out on the street? Or living on Lowbriar Avenue, where his mother said there was nothing but nigger drug addicts with guns? If there was a God, why had He let Frankie choke on that fucking apple slice in the first place? And then letting him wake up brain-damaged afterward, that was going from bad to fucking goddam shit-ass *worse.* There was no God. You only had to watch Frankie crawling around the floor with goddam Sammy in one hand, then getting up and limping for awhile before giving that up and crawling again, to know that the idea of God was fucking ridiculous.

Finally Frankie died. It happened fast. In a way it was like running down those people at City Center. There was no forethought, only the looming reality that something had to be done. You could almost call it an accident. Or fate. Brady didn't believe in God, but he did believe in fate, and sometimes the man of the house had to be fate's right hand.

His mother was making pancakes for supper. Frankie was playing with Sammy. The basement door was standing open because Deborah Ann had bought two cartons of cheap off-brand toilet paper at Chapter 11 and they kept it down there. The bathrooms needed re-stocking, so she sent Brady down to get some. His hands had been full when he came back up, so he left the basement door open. He thought Mom would shut it, but when he came down from putting the toilet paper in the two upstairs bathrooms, it was still open. Frankie was on the floor, pushing Sammy across the linoleum and making *rrr-rrr* sounds. He was wearing red pants that bulged with his triple-thick diapers. He was working ever closer to the open door and the steep stairs beyond, but Deborah Ann still made no move to close the door. Nor did she ask Brady, now setting the table, to do it.

"Rrr-rrr," said Frankie. *"Rrr-rrr."*

He pushed the fire truck. Sammy rolled to the edge of the basement doorway, bumped against the jamb, and there he stopped.

Deborah Ann left the stove. She walked over to the basement door. Brady thought she would bend down and hand Frankie's fire truck back to him, but she didn't. She kicked it instead. There was a small clacking sound as it tumbled down the steps, all the way to the bottom.

"Oops," she said. "Sammy faw down go boom." Her voice was very flat.

Brady walked over. This was interesting.

"Why'd you do that, Mom?"

Deborah Ann put her hands on her hips, the spatula jutting from one of them. She said, "Because I'm just so sick of listening to him make that sound."

Frankie opened his mouth and began to blat.

"Quit it, Frankie," Brady said, but Frankie didn't. What Frankie did was crawl onto the top step and peer down into the darkness.

In that same flat voice Deborah Ann said,

"Turn on the light, Brady. So he can see Sammy."

Brady turned on the light and peered over his blatting brother.

"Yup," he said. "There he is. Right down at the bottom. See him, Frankie?"

Frankie crawled a little farther, still blatting. He looked down. Brady looked at his mother. Deborah Ann Hartsfield gave the smallest, most imperceptible nod. Brady didn't think. He simply kicked Frankie's triple-diapered butt and down Frankie went in a series of clumsy somersaults that made Brady think of the fat Blues Brother flipping his way along the church aisle. On the first somersault Frankie kept on blatting, but the second time around, his head connected with one of the stair risers and the blatting stopped all at once, as if Frankie were a radio and someone had turned him off. That was horrible, but had its funny side. He went over again, legs flying out limply to either side in a **Y** shape. Then he slammed headfirst into the basement floor.

"Oh my God, Frankie fell!" Deborah Ann cried. She dropped the spatula and ran down the stairs. Brady followed her.

Frankie's neck was broken, even Brady could tell that, because it was all croggled in the back, but he was still alive. He was breathing in little snorts. Blood was coming out of his nose. More was coming from the side of his head. His eyes moved back and forth, but nothing else did. Poor Frankie. Brady started to cry. His mother was crying, too.

"What should we do?" Brady asked. "What should we do, Mom?"

"Go upstairs and get me a pillow off the sofa."

He did as she said. When he came back down, Sammy the Fire Truck was lying on Frankie's chest. "I tried to get him to hold it, but he can't," Deborah Ann said.

"Yeah," Brady said. "He's prob'ly paralyzed. Poor Frankie."

Frankie looked up, first at his mother and then his brother. "Brady," he said.

"It'll be okay, Frankie," Brady said, and held out the pillow.

Deborah Ann took it and put it over Frankie's face. It didn't take long. Then she sent Brady upstairs again to put the sofa pillow back and get a wet washcloth. "Turn off the stove while you're up there," she said. "The pancakes are burning. I can smell them."

She washed Frankie's face to get rid of the blood. Brady thought that was very sweet and motherly. Years later he realized she'd also been making sure there would be no threads or fibers from the pillow on Frankie's face.

When Frankie was clean (although there was still blood in his hair), Brady and his mother sat on the basement steps, looking at him. Deborah Ann had her arm around Brady's shoulders. "I better call nine-one-one," she said.

"Okay."

"He pushed Sammy too hard and Sammy fell downstairs. Then he tried to go after him and lost his balance. I was making the pancakes and you were putting toilet paper in the bathrooms upstairs. You didn't see anything. When you got down to the basement, he was already dead."

"Okay."

"Say it back to me."

Brady did. He was an A student in school, and good at remembering things.

"No matter what anybody asks you, never say more than that. Don't add anything, and don't change anything."

"Okay, but can I say you were crying?"

She smiled. She kissed his forehead and cheek. Then she kissed him full on the lips. "Yes, honeyboy, you can say that."

"Will we be all right now?"

"Yes." There was no doubt in her voice. "We'll be fine."

She was right. There were only a few questions about the accident and no hard ones. They had a funeral. It was pretty nice. Frankie was in a Frankie-size coffin, wearing a suit. He didn't look brain-damaged, just fast asleep. Before they closed the coffin,

Brady kissed his brother's cheek and tucked Sammy the Fire Truck in beside him. There was just enough room.

That night Brady had the first of his really bad headaches. He started thinking Frankie was under his bed, and that made the headache worse. He went down to his mom's room and got in with her. He didn't tell her he was scared of Frankie being under his bed, just that his head ached so bad he thought it was going to explode. She hugged him and kissed him and he wriggled against her tight-tight-tight. It felt good to wriggle. It made the headache less. They fell asleep together and the next day it was just the two of them and life was better. Deborah Ann got her old job back, but there were no more boyfriends. She said Brady was the only boyfriend she wanted now. They never talked about Frankie's accident, but sometimes Brady dreamed about it. He didn't know if his mother did or not, but she drank plenty of vodka, so much she eventually lost her job again. That was all right, though, because by then he was old enough to go to work. He didn't miss going to college, either.

College was for people who didn't know they were smart.

6

Brady comes out of these memories — a reverie so deep it's like hypnosis — to discover he's got a lapful of shredded plastic. At first he doesn't know where it came from. Then he looks at the newspaper lying on his worktable and understands he tore apart the bag it was in with his fingernails while he was thinking about Frankie.

He deposits the shreds in the wastebasket, then picks up the paper and stares vacantly at the headlines. Oil is still gushing into the Gulf of Mexico and British Petroleum executives are squalling that they're doing the best they can and people are being mean to them. Nidal Hasan, the asshole shrink who shot up the Fort Hood Army base in Texas, is going to be arraigned in the next day or two. (You should have had a Mercedes, Nidal-baby, Brady thinks.) Paul McCartney, the ex-Beatle Brady's mom used to call Old Spaniel Eyes, is getting a medal at the White House. Why is it, Brady sometimes wonders, that people with only a little talent get so much of everything? It's just another proof that the world is crazy.

Brady decides to take the paper up to the kitchen and read the political columns. Those and a melatonin capsule might be enough to send him off to sleep. Halfway up the stairs he turns the paper over to see what's below the fold, and freezes. There are photos of two women, side by side. One is Olivia Trelawney. The other one is much older, but the resemblance is unmistakable. Especially those thin bitch-lips.

MOTHER OF OLIVIA TRELAWNEY DIES, the headline reads. Below it: *Protested Daughter's "Unfair Treatment," Claimed Press Coverage "Destroyed Her Life."*

What follows is a two-paragraph squib, really just an excuse to get last year's tragedy (If you want to use that word, Brady thinks — rather snidely) back on the front page of a newspaper that's slowly being strangled to death by the Internet. Readers are referred to the obituary on page twenty-six, and Brady, now sitting at the kitchen table, turns there double-quick. The cloud of dazed gloom that has surrounded him ever since his mother's death has been swept away in an instant. His mind is ticking over rapidly, ideas coming together, flying apart, then coming together again like pieces in a jigsaw puzzle. He's familiar with this process and knows it will continue until they connect with a click of finality and a clear picture appears.

ELIZABETH SIROIS WHARTON, 87, passed away peacefully on May 29, 2010, at Warsaw County Memorial Hospital. She was born on January 19, 1923, the son of Marcel and Catherine Sirois. She is survived by her brother, Henry Sirois, her sister, Charlotte Gibney, her niece, Holly Gibney, and her daughter, Janelle Patterson. Elizabeth was predeceased by her husband, Alvin Wharton, and her beloved daughter, Olivia. Private visitation will be held from 10 AM to 1 PM at Soames Funeral Home on Tuesday, June 1, followed by a 10 AM memorial service at Soames Funeral Home on Wednesday, June 2. After the service, a reception for close friends and family members will take place at 729 Lilac Drive, in Sugar Heights. The family requests no flowers, but suggests contributions to either the American Red Cross or the Salvation Army, Mrs. Wharton's favorite charities.

Brady reads all this carefully, with several related questions in mind. Will the fat ex-cop be at the visitation? At the Wednesday memorial service? At the reception? Brady's betting on all three. Looking for the perk. Looking for *him.* Because that's what cops do.

He remembers the last message he sent to Hodges, the good old Det-Ret. Now he smiles and says it out loud: "You won't see me coming."

"Make sure he doesn't," Deborah Ann Hartsfield says.

He knows she's not really there, but he can almost see her sitting across the table from him, wearing a black pencil-skirt and the blue blouse he especially likes, the one that's so filmy you can see the ghost of her underwear through it.

"Because he'll be looking for you."

"I know," Brady says. "Don't worry."

"Of course I'll worry," she says. "I have to. You're my honeyboy."

He goes back downstairs and gets into his sleeping bag. The leaky air mattress wheezes. The last thing he does before killing the lights via voice-command is to set his iPhone alarm for six-thirty. Tomorrow is going to be a busy day.

Except for the tiny red lights marking his sleeping computer equipment, the basement control room is completely dark. From beneath the stairs, his mother speaks.

"I'm waiting for you, honeyboy, but don't make me wait too long."

"I'll be there soon, Mom." Smiling, Brady closes his eyes. Two minutes later, he's snoring.

7

Janey doesn't come out of the bedroom until just after eight the following morning. She's wearing her pantsuit from the night before. Hodges, still in his boxers, is on the phone. He waves one finger to her, a gesture that says both *good morning* and *give me a minute.*

"It's not a big deal," he's saying, "just one

of those things that nibble at you. If you could check, I'd really appreciate it." He listens. "Nah, I don't want to bother Pete with it, and don't you, either. He's got all he can handle with the Donald Davis case."

He listens some more. Janey perches on the arm of the sofa, points at her watch, and mouths, *The viewing!* Hodges nods.

"That's right," he says into the phone. "Let's say between the summer of 2007 and the spring of 2009. In the Lake Avenue area downtown, where all those new ritzy condos are." He winks at Janey. "Thanks, Marlo, you're a doll. And I promise I'm not going to turn into an uncle, okay?" Listens, nodding. "Okay. Yeah. I have to run, but give my best to Phil and the kids. We'll get together soon. Lunch. Of *course* on me. Right. Bye."

He hangs up.

"You need to get dressed in a hurry," she says, "then take me back to the apartment so I can put on my damn makeup before we go over to the funeral home. It might also be fun to change my underwear. How fast can you hop into your suit?"

"Fast. And you don't really need the makeup."

She rolls her eyes. "Tell that to Aunt Charlotte. She's totally on crow's-feet patrol. Now get going, and bring a razor. You can shave at my place." She re-checks her watch. "I haven't slept this late in five years."

He heads for the bedroom to get dressed. She catches him at the door, turns him toward her, puts her palms on his cheeks, and kisses his mouth. "Good sex is the best sleeping pill. I guess I forgot that."

He lifts her high off her feet in a hug. He doesn't know how long this will last, but while it does, he means to ride it like a pony.

"And wear your hat," she says, looking down into his face and smiling. "I did right when I bought it. That hat is *you.*"

8

They're too happy with each other and too intent on getting to the funeral parlor ahead of the relatives from hell to BOLO, but even on red alert they almost certainly wouldn't have seen anything that rang warning bells. There are already more than two dozen cars parked in the little strip mall at the intersection of Harper Road and Hanover Street, and Brady Hartsfield's mud-colored Subaru is the most unobtrusive of the lot. He has picked his spot carefully so that the fat ex-cop's street is squarely in the middle of his rearview. If Hodges is going to the old lady's viewing, he'll come down the hill and make a left on Hanover.

And here he comes, at just past eight-thirty — quite a bit earlier than Brady expected, since the viewing's not until ten and the funeral parlor's only twenty minutes or so away. As the car makes its left turn, Brady is further surprised to see the fat ex-cop is not alone. His passenger is a woman, and although Brady only gets a quick glimpse, it's enough for him to ID Olivia Trelawney's sister. She's got the visor down so she can look into the mirror as she brushes her hair. The obvious deduction is that she spent the night in the fat ex-cop's bachelor bungalow.

Brady is thunderstruck. Why in God's name would she do that? Hodges is *old,* he's *fat,* he's *ugly.* She can't really be having sex with him, can she? The idea is beyond belief. Then he thinks of how his mother relieved his worst headaches, and realizes — reluctantly — that when it comes to sex, no pairing is beyond belief. But the idea of Hodges doing it with Olivia Trelawney's sister is infuriating (not in the least because you could say it was Brady himself who brought them together). Hodges is supposed to be sitting in front of his television and contemplating suicide. He has no right to enjoy a jar of Vaseline and his own right hand, let alone a good-looking blonde.

Brady thinks, She probably took the bed while he slept on the sofa.

This idea at least approaches logic, and makes him feel better. He supposes Hodges could have sex with a good-looking blonde if he really wanted to . . . but he'd have to pay for it. The whore would probably want a weight surcharge, too, he thinks, and laughs as he starts his car.

Before pulling out, he opens the glove compartment, takes out Thing Two, and places it on the passenger seat. He hasn't used it since last year, but he's going to use it today. Probably not at the funeral parlor, though, because he doubts they will be going there right away. It's too early. Brady thinks they'll be stopping at the Lake Avenue condo first, and it's not necessary that he beat them there, only that he be there when they come back out. He knows just how he's going to do it.

It will be like old times.

At a stoplight downtown, he calls Tones Frobisher at Discount Electronix and tells him he won't be in today. Probably not all week. Pinching his nostrils shut with his knuckles to give his voice a nasal honk, he informs Tones that he has the flu. He thinks of the 'Round Here concert at the MAC on Thursday night, and the suicide vest, and imagines adding *Next week I won't have the flu, I'll just be dead.* He breaks the connection, drops his phone onto the seat next to Thing Two, and begins laughing. He sees a woman in the next lane, all gussied up for work, staring at him. Brady, now laughing so hard tears are streaming down his cheeks and snot is running out of his nose, gives her the finger.

9

"You were talking to your friend in the Records Department?" Janey asks.

"Marlo Everett, yeah. She's always in early. Pete Huntley, my old partner, used to swear that was because she never left."

"What fairy tale did you feed her, pray tell?"

"That some of my neighbors have mentioned a guy trying cars to see if they were unlocked. I said I seemed to recall a spate of car burglaries downtown a couple of years back, the doer never apprehended."

"Uh-huh, and that thing you said about not turning into an uncle, what was that about?"

"Uncles are retired cops who can't let go of the job. They call in wanting Marlo to run the plate numbers of cars that strike them as hinky for one reason or another. Or maybe they brace some guy who looks wrong, go all cop-faced on his ass and ask for ID. Then they call in and have Marlo run the name for wants and warrants."

"Does she mind?"

"Oh, she bitches about it for form's sake, but I don't really think so. An old geezer named Kenny Shays called in a six-five a few years ago — that's suspicious behavior, a new code since 9/11. The guy he pegged wasn't a terrorist, just a fugitive who killed his whole family in Kansas back in 1987."

"Wow. Did he get a medal?"

"Nothing but an attaboy, which was all he wanted. He died six months or so later." Ate his gun is what Kenny Shays did, pulling the trigger before the lung cancer could get traction.

Hodges's cell phone rings. It's muffled, because he's once more left it in the glove compartment. Janey fishes it out and hands it over with a slightly ironic smile.

"Hey, Marlo, that was quick. What did you find out? Anything?" He listens, nodding along with whatever he's hearing and saying uh-huh and never missing a beat in the heavy flow of morning traffic. He thanks her and hangs up, but when he attempts to hand the Nokia back to Janey, she shakes her head.

"Put it in your pocket. Someone else might call you. I know it's a strange concept, but try to get your head around it. What did you find out?"

"Starting in September of 2007, there were over a dozen car break-ins downtown. Marlo says there could have been even more, because people who don't lose anything of value have a tendency not to report car burglaries. Some don't even realize it happened. The last report was logged in March of 2009, less than three weeks before the City Center Massacre. It was our guy, Janey. I'm sure of it. We're crossing his backtrail now, and that means we're getting closer."

"Good."

"I think we're going to find him. If we do, your lawyer — Schron — goes downtown to fill in Pete Huntley. He does the rest. We still see eye to eye on that, don't we?"

"Yes. But until then, he's *ours.* We still see eye to eye on *that,* right?"

"Absolutely."

He's cruising down Lake Avenue now, and there's a spot right in front of the late Mrs. Wharton's building. When your luck is running, it's running. Hodges backs in, wondering how many times Olivia Trelawney used this same spot.

Janey looks anxiously at her watch as Hodges feeds the meter.

"Relax," he says. "We've got plenty of time."

As she heads for the door, Hodges pushes the LOCK button on his key-fob. He doesn't think about it, Mr. Mercedes is what he's thinking about, but habit is habit. He pockets his keys and hurries to catch up with Janey so he can hold the door for her.

He thinks, I'm turning into a sap.

Then he thinks, So what?

10

Five minutes later, a mud-colored Subaru cruises down Lake Avenue. It slows almost to a stop when it comes abreast of Hodges's Toyota, then Brady puts on his left-turn blinker and pulls into the parking garage across the street.

There are plenty of vacant spots on the first and second levels, but they're all on the inside and no use to him. He finds what he wants on the nearly deserted third level: a spot on the east side of the garage, directly overlooking Lake Avenue. He parks, walks to the concrete bumper, and peers across the street and down at Hodges's Toyota. He puts the distance at about sixty yards. With nothing in the way to block the signal, that's a piece of cake for Thing Two.

With time to kill, Brady gets back into his car, fires up his iPad, and investigates the Midwest Culture and Arts Complex website. Mingo Auditorium is the biggest part of the facility. That figures, Brady thinks, because it's probably the only part of the MAC that makes money. The city's symphony orchestra plays there in the winter, plus there are ballets and lectures and arty-farty shit like that, but from June to August the Mingo is almost exclusively dedicated to pop music. According to the website, 'Round Here will be followed by an all-star Summer Cavalcade of Song including the Eagles, Sting, John Mellencamp, Alan Jackson, Paul Simon, and Bruce Springsteen. Sounds good, but Brady thinks the people who bought All-Concert Passes are going to be disappointed. There's only going to be one show in the Mingo this summer, a short one ending with a punk ditty called "Die, You Useless Motherfuckers."

The website says the auditorium's capacity is forty-five hundred.

It also says that the 'Round Here concert is sold out.

Brady calls Shirley Orton at the ice cream factory. Once more pinching his nose shut, he tells her she better put Rudy Stanhope on alert for later in the week. He says he'll try to get in Thursday or Friday, but she better not count on it; he has the flu.

As he expected, the f-word alarms Shirley. "Don't you come near this place until you can show me a note from your doctor saying you're not contagious. You can't be selling ice cream to kids if you've got the flu."

"I dno," Brady says through his pinched nostrils. "I'be sorry, Shirley. I thing I got id fromb by mother. I had to put her to bed." That hits his funnybone and his lips begin to twitch.

"Well, you take care of yourse—"

"I hab to go," he says, and breaks the connection just before another gust of hysterical laughter sweeps through him. Yes, he had to put his mother to bed. And yes, it was the flu. Not the Swine Flu or the Bird Flu, but a new strain called Gopher Flu. Brady howls and pounds the dashboard of his Subaru. He pounds so hard he hurts his hand, and that makes him laugh harder still.

This fit goes on until his stomach aches and

he feels a little like puking. It has just begun to ease off when he sees the lobby door of the condo across the street open.

Brady snatches up Thing Two and slides the on switch. The ready-lamp glows yellow. He raises the short stub of the antenna. He gets out of his car, not laughing now, and creeps to the concrete bumper again, being careful to stay in the shadow of the nearest support pillar. He puts his thumb on the toggle-switch and angles Thing Two down — but not at the Toyota. He's aiming at Hodges, who is rummaging in his pants pocket. The blonde is next to him, wearing the same pant-suit she had on earlier, but with different shoes and purse.

Hodges brings out his keys.

Brady pushes Thing Two's toggle-switch, and the yellow ready-lamp turns operational green. The lights of Hodges's car flash. At the same instant, the green light on Thing Two gives a single quick blink. It has caught the Toyota's PKE code and stored it, just as it caught the code of Mrs. Trelawney's Mercedes.

Brady used Thing Two for almost two years, stealing PKEs and unlocking cars so he could toss them for valuables and cash. The income from these ventures was uneven, but the thrill never faded. His first thought on finding the spare key in the glove compartment of Mrs. Trelawney's Mercedes (it was in a plastic bag along with her owner's manual and registration) was to steal the car and joyride it all the way across the city. Bang it up a little just for the hell of it. Maybe slice the upholstery. But some instinct had told him to leave everything just as it was. That the Mercedes might have a larger role to play. And so it had proved.

Brady hops into his car and puts Thing Two back in his own glove compartment. He's very satisfied with his morning's work, but the morning isn't over. Hodges and Olivia's sister will be going to a visitation. Brady has his own visitation to make. The MAC will be open by now, and he wants a look around. See what they have for security. Check out where the cameras are mounted.

Brady thinks, I'll find a way in. I'm on a roll.

Also, he'll need to go online and score a ticket to the concert Thursday night. Busy, busy, busy.

He begins to whistle.

11

Hodges and Janey Patterson step into the Eternal Rest parlor of the Soames Funeral Home at quarter to ten, and thanks to her insistence on hurrying, they're the first arrivals. The top half of the coffin is open. The bottom half is swaddled in a blue silk swag. Elizabeth Wharton is wearing a white dress sprigged with blue florets that match the swag. Her eyes are closed. Her cheeks are rosy.

Janey hurries down an aisle between two ranks of folding chairs, looks briefly at her mother, then hurries back. Her lips are trembling.

"Uncle Henry can call cremation pagan if he wants to, but this open-coffin shit is the real pagan rite. She doesn't look like my mother, she looks like a stuffed exhibit."

"Then why —"

"It was the trade-off I made to shut Uncle Henry up about the cremation. God help us if he looks under the swag and sees the coffin's pressed cardboard painted gray to look like metal. So it'll . . . you know . . ."

"I know," Hodges says, and gives her a one-armed hug.

The deceased woman's friends trickle in, led by Althea Greene, Wharton's nurse, and Mrs. Harris, who was her housekeeper. At twenty past ten or so (fashionably late, Hodges thinks), Aunt Charlotte arrives on her brother's arm. Uncle Henry leads her down the aisle, looks briefly at the corpse, then stands back. Aunt Charlotte stares fixedly into the upturned face, then bends and kisses the dead lips. In a barely audible voice she says, "Oh, sis, oh, sis." For the first time since he met her, Hodges feels something for her other than irritation.

There is some milling, some quiet talk, a few low outbursts of laughter. Janey makes the rounds, speaking to everyone (there aren't more than a dozen, all of the sort Hodges's daughter calls "goldie-oldies"), doing her due diligence. Uncle Henry joins her, and on the one occasion when Janey falters — she's trying to comfort Mrs. Greene — he puts an arm around her shoulders. Hodges is glad to see it. Blood tells, he thinks. At times like this, it almost always does.

He's the odd man out here, so he decides to get some air. He stands on the front step for a few moments, scanning the cars parked across the street, looking for a man sitting by himself in one of them. He sees no one, and realizes he hasn't seen Holly the Mumbler, either.

He ambles around to the visitors' parking lot and there she is, perched on the back step. She's dressed in a singularly unbecoming shin-length brown dress. Her hair is put up in unbecoming clumps at the sides of her head. To Hodges she looks like Princess Leia after a year on the Karen Carpenter diet.

She sees his shadow on the pavement, gives a jerk, and hides something behind her hand. He comes closer, and the hidden object turns out to be a half-smoked cigarette. She gives him a narrow, worried look. Hodges thinks it's the look of a dog that's been beaten too many times with a newspaper for piddling under the kitchen table.

"Don't tell my mother. She thinks I quit."

"Your secret's safe with me," Hodges says, thinking that Holly is surely too old to worry about Mommy's disapproval of what is probably her only bad habit. "Can I share your step?"

"Shouldn't you be inside with Janey?" But she moves over to make room.

"Just taking a breather. With the exception of Janey herself, I don't know any of those people."

She looks him over with the bald curiosity of a child. "Are you and my cousin lovers?"

He's embarrassed, not by the question but by the perverse fact that it makes him feel like laughing. He sort of wishes he'd just left her to smoke her illicit cigarette. "Well," he says, "we're good friends. Maybe we should leave it at that."

She shrugs and shoots smoke from her nostrils. "It's all right with me. I think a woman should have lovers if she wants them. I don't, myself. Men don't interest me. Not that I'm a lesbian. Don't get that idea. I write poetry."

"Yeah? Do you?"

"Yes." And with no pause, as if it's all the same thing: "My mother doesn't like Janey."

"Really?"

"She doesn't think Janey should have gotten all that money from Olivia. She says it isn't fair. It probably isn't, but I don't care, myself."

She's biting her lips in a way that gives Hodges an unsettling sense of déjà vu, and it takes only a second to realize why: Olivia Trelawney did the same thing during her police interviews. Blood tells. It almost always does.

"You haven't been inside," he says.

"No, and I'm not going, and *she* can't make me. I've never seen a dead person, and I'm not going to start now. It would give me nightmares."

She kills her cigarette on the side of the step, not rubbing it but *plunging* it out, stabbing it until the sparks fly and the filter splits. Her face is as pale as milk glass, she's started to quiver (her knees are almost literally knocking), and if she doesn't stop chewing her lower lip, it's going to split open.

"This is the worst part," she says, and she's not mumbling now. In fact, if her voice doesn't stop rising it will soon be a scream. "This is the worst part, this is the worst part, *this is the worst part*!"

He puts an arm around her vibrating shoulders. For a moment the vibration grows to a whole-body shake. He fully expects her to flee (perhaps lingering just long enough to call him a masher and slap his face). Then the shaking subsides and she actually puts her head on his shoulder. She's breathing rapidly.

"You're right," he says. "This is the worst part. Tomorrow will be better."

"Will the coffin be closed?"

"Yeah." He'll tell Janey it will have to be, unless she wants her cuz sitting out here with the hearses again.

Holly looks at him out of her naked face. She doesn't have a damn thing going for her, Hodges thinks, not a single scrap of wit, not a single wile. He will come to regret this misperception, but for now he finds himself once more musing on Olivia Trelawney. How the press treated her and how the cops treated her. Including him.

"Do you promise it'll be closed?"

"Yes."

"*Double* promise?"

"Pinky swear, if you want." Then, still thinking of Olivia and the computer-poison Mr. Mercedes fed her: "Are you taking your medication, Holly?"

Her eyes widen. "How do you know I take Lexapro? Did *she* tell you?"

"Nobody told me. Nobody had to. I used to be a detective." He tightens the arm around her shoulders a little and gives her a small, friendly shake. "Now answer my question."

"It's in my purse. I haven't taken it today, because . . ." She gives a small, shrill giggle.

"Because it makes me have to *pee.*"

"If I get a glass of water, will you take it now?"

"Yes. For you." Again that naked stare, the look of a small child sizing up an adult. "I like you. You're a good guy. Janey's lucky. I've never been lucky in my life. I've never even had a boyfriend."

"I'll get you some water," Hodges says, and stands up. At the corner of the building, he looks back. She's trying to light another cigarette, but it's hard going because the shakes are back. She's holding her disposable Bic in both hands, like a shooter on the police gun range.

Inside, Janey asks where he's been. He tells her, and asks if the coffin can be closed at the memorial service the following day. "I think it's the only way you'll get her inside," he says.

Janey looks at her aunt, now at the center of a group of elderly women, all of them talking animatedly. "That bitch hasn't even noticed Holly's not in here," she says. "You know what, I just decided the coffin's not even going to *be* here tomorrow. I'll have the funeral director stash it in the back, and if Auntie C doesn't like it, she can go spit. Tell Holly that, okay?"

The discreetly hovering funeral director shows Hodges into the next room, where drinks and snacks have been arranged. He gets a bottle of Dasani water and takes it out to the parking lot. He passes on Janey's message and sits with Holly until she takes one of her little white happy-caps. When it's down, she smiles at him. "I really do like you."

And, using that splendid, police-trained capacity for telling the convincing lie, Hodges replies warmly, "I like you too, Holly."

12

The Midwest Culture and Arts Complex, aka the MAC, is called "the Louvre of the Midwest" by the newspaper and the local Chamber of Commerce (the residents of this midwestern city call it "the Loovah"). The facility covers six acres of prime downtown real estate and is dominated by a circular building that looks to Brady like the giant UFO that shows up at the end of *Close Encounters of the Third Kind.* This is Mingo Auditorium.

He wanders around back to the loading area, which is as busy as an anthill on a summer day. Trucks bustle to and fro, and workers are unloading all sorts of stuff, including — weird but true — what looks like sections of a Ferris wheel. There are also flats (he thinks that's what they're called) showing a starry night sky and a white sand beach with couples walking hand-in-hand at the edge of the water. The workers, he notes, are all wearing ID badges around their necks or clipped to their shirts. Not good.

There's a security booth guarding the entrance to the loading area, and that's not good, either, but Brady wanders over anyway, thinking No risk, no reward. There are two guards. One is inside, noshing a bagel as he monitors half a dozen video screens. The other steps out to intercept Brady. He's wearing sunglasses. Brady can see himself reflected in the lenses, with a big old gosh-this-is-interesting smile on his face.

"Help you, sir?"

"I was just wondering what's going on," Brady says. He points. "That looks like a Ferris wheel!"

"Big concert here Thursday night," the guard says. "The band's flogging their new album. *Kisses on the Midway,* I think it's called."

"Boy, they really go all out, don't they?" Brady marvels.

The guard snorts. "The less they can sing, the bigger the set. You know what? When we had Tony Bennett here last September, it was just him. Didn't even have a band. The City Symphony backed him up. *That* was a show. No screaming kids. Actual music. What a concept, huh?"

"I don't suppose I could go over for a peek. Maybe snap a picture with my cell phone?"

"Nope." The guard is looking him over too

closely. Brady doesn't like that. "In fact, you're not supposed to be here at all. So . . ."

"Gotcha, gotcha," Brady says, widening his smile. Time to go. There's nothing here for him, anyway; if they have two guys on duty now, there's apt to be half a dozen on Thursday night. "Thanks for taking the time to talk to me."

"No problem."

Brady gives him a thumbs-up. The security goon returns it, but stands in the doorway of the security booth, watching him walk away.

He strolls along the edge of a vast and nearly empty parking lot that will be filled to capacity on the night of the 'Round Here show. His smile is gone. He's musing on the numbfuck ragheads who ran a pair of jetliners into the World Trade Center nine years before. He thinks (without the slightest trace of irony), They spoiled it for the rest of us.

A five-minute trudge takes him to the bank of doors where concertgoers will enter on Thursday night. He has to pay a five-dollar "suggested donation fee" to get in. The lobby is an echoing vault currently filled with art-lovers and student groups. Straight ahead is the gift shop. To the left is the corridor leading to the Mingo Auditorium. It's as wide as a two-lane highway. In the middle of it is a chrome stand with a sign reading NO BAGS NO BOXES NO BACKPACKS.

Also no metal detectors. It's possible they

haven't been set up yet, but Brady's pretty sure they won't be used at all. There are going to be over four thousand concertgoers pushing to get in, and metal detectors booping and beeping all over the place would create a nightmarish traffic jam. There will be *mucho* security guards, though, all of them just as suspicious and officious as the sunglasses-wearing ass-munch out back. A man in a quilted vest on a warm June evening would attract their attention at once. In fact, *any* man without a pigtailed teenybop daughter in tow would be apt to attract attention.

Would you step over here for a minute, sir?

Of course he could blow the vest right then and there and scrag a hundred or more, but that isn't what he wants. What he wants is to go home, search the Web, find out the name of 'Round Here's biggest song, and flick the switch halfway through it, when the little chickie-boos are screaming their very loudest and going out of their little chickie-boo minds.

But the obstacles are formidable.

Standing there in the lobby amid the guidebook-toting retirees and junior high school mouth-breathers, Brady thinks, I wish Frankie was alive. If he was, I'd take him to the show. He'd be just stupid enough to like it. I'd even let him bring Sammy the Fire Truck. The thought fills him with the deep and completely authentic sadness that often comes to him when he thinks about Frankie.

Maybe I ought to just kill the fat ex-cop, and myself, and then call it a career.

Rubbing at his temples, where one of his headaches has begun to gather (and now there's no Mom to ease it), Brady wanders across the lobby and into the Harlow Floyd Art Gallery, where a large hanging banner announces that JUNE IS MANET MONTH!

He doesn't know exactly who Manet was, probably another old frog painter like van Gogh, but some of the pictures are great. He doesn't care much for the still-lifes (why in God's name would you want to spend time painting a melon?), but some of the other ones are possessed of an almost feral violence. One shows a dead matador. Brady looks at it for nearly five minutes with his hands clasped behind him, ignoring the people who jostle by or peer over his shoulder for a look. The matador isn't mangled or anything, but the blood oozing from beneath his left shoulder looks more real than the blood in all the violent movies Brady has ever seen, and he's seen plenty. It calms him and clears him and when he finally walks on, he thinks: There has to be a way to do this.

On the spur of the moment he hooks into the gift shop and buys a bunch of 'Round Here shit. When he comes out ten minutes later, carrying a bag with I HAD A MAC ATTACK printed on the side, he again glances down the hallway leading to the Mingo. Just two nights from now, that hallway will become a cattle-chute filled with laughing, pushing, crazily excited girls, most accompanied by longsuffering parents. From this angle he can see that the far righthand side of the corridor has been sectioned off from the rest by velvet ropes. At the head of this sequestered mini-corridor is another sign on another chrome stand.

Brady reads it and thinks, Oh my God.

Oh . . . my . . . *God*!

13

In the apartment that used to belong to Elizabeth Wharton, Janey kicks off her heels and plunks down on the couch. "Thank God that's over. Did it last a thousand years, or two?"

"Two," Hodges says. "You look like a woman who could use a nap."

"I slept until eight," she protests, but to Hodges it sounds feeble.

"Still might be a good idea."

"Considering the fact that I'm having dinner with my relatives tonight in Sugar Heights, you could have something there, shamus. You're off the hook on dinner, by the way. I think they want to talk about everyone's favorite musical comedy, *Janey's Millions.*"

"Wouldn't surprise me."

"I'm going to split Ollie's loot with them. Straight down the middle."

Hodges starts to laugh. He stops when he realizes she's serious.

Janey hoists her eyebrows. "Got a problem with that? Maybe think a paltry three and a half mil won't be enough to see me through to my old age?"

"I guess it would, but . . . it's *yours.* Olivia willed it to you."

"Yes, and the will's unbreakable, Lawyer Schron assures me of that, but that still doesn't mean Ollie was in her right mind when she made it. You know that. You saw her, talked to her." She's massaging her feet through her stockings. "Besides, if I give them half, I get to watch how they divvy it up. Think of the amusement value."

"Sure you don't want me to come with you tonight?"

"Not tonight but definitely tomorrow. That I can't do alone."

"I'll pick you up at quarter past nine. Unless you want to spend another night at my place, that is."

"Tempting, but no. Tonight is strictly earmarked for family fun. There's one other thing before you take off. Very important." She rummages in her purse for a notepad and a pen. She writes, then tears off a page and holds it out to him. Hodges sees two groups of numbers.

Janey says, "The first one opens the gates to the house in Sugar Hill. The second kills the burglar alarm. When you and your friend Jerome are working on Ollie's computer Thursday morning, I'll be taking Aunt Charlotte, Holly, and Uncle Henry to the airport. If the guy rigged her computer the way you think he did . . . and the program's still there . . . I don't think I could stand it." She's looking at him pleadingly. "Do you get that? Say you do."

"I get it," Hodges says. He kneels beside her like a man getting ready to propose in one of the romantic novels his ex-wife used to like. Part of him feels absurd. Mostly he doesn't.

"Janey," he says.

She looks at him, trying to smile, not quite making it.

"I'm sorry. For everything. So, so sorry." It isn't just her he's thinking of, or her late sister, who was so troubled and troublesome. He's thinking of the ones who were lost at City Center, especially the woman and her baby.

When he was promoted to detective, his mentor was a guy named Frank Sledge. Hodges thought of him as an old guy, but back then Sledge was fifteen years younger than Hodges is now. *Don't you ever let me hear you call them the vics,* Sledge told him.

That shit's strictly for assholes and burnouts. Remember their names. Call them by their names.

The Crays, he thinks. They were the Crays. Janice and Patricia.

Janey hugs him. Her breath tickles his ear when she speaks, giving him goosebumps and half a hardon. "I'm going back to California when this is finished. I can't stay here. I think the world of you, Bill, and if I stayed here I could probably fall in love with you, but I'm not going to do that. I need to make a fresh start."

"I know." Hodges pulls away and holds her by the shoulders so he can look her in the face again. It's a beautiful face, but today she's looking her age. "It's all right."

She dives into her purse again, this time for Kleenex. After she's dried her eyes, she says, "You made a conquest today."

"A . . . ?" Then he gets it. "Holly."

"She thinks you're wonderful. She told me so."

"She reminds me of Olivia. Talking to her feels like a second chance."

"To do the right thing?"

"Yeah."

Janey wrinkles her nose at him and grins. *"Yeah."*

14

Brady goes shopping that afternoon. He takes the late Deborah Ann Hartsfield's Honda, because it's a hatchback. Still, one of the items barely fits in the rear. He thinks of stopping at Speedy Postal on his way home and checking for the Gopher-Go he ordered under his Ralph Jones alias, but all that seems like a thousand years ago now, and really, what would be the point? That part of his life is over. Soon the rest will be, too, and what a relief.

He leans the largest of his purchases against the garage wall. Then he goes into the house, and after a brief pause in the kitchen to sniff at the air (no whiff of decay, at least not yet), he goes down to his control room. He speaks the magic word that powers up his row of computers, but only out of habit. He has no urge to slip beneath Debbie's Blue Umbrella, because he has nothing more to say to the fat ex-cop. That part of his life is also over. He looks at his watch, sees that it's three-thirty in the afternoon, and calculates that the fat ex-cop now has roughly twenty hours to live.

If you really are fucking her, Detective Hodges, Brady thinks, you better get your end wet while you've still *got* an end.

He unlocks the padlock on the closet door and steps into the dry and faintly oily odor of homemade plastique. He regards the shoeboxes full of explosive and chooses the one that held the Mephisto walking shoes he's now wearing — a Christmas present from his mother just last year. From the next shelf up he grabs the shoebox filled with cell phones. He takes one of them and the box of boom-clay over to the table in the middle of the room and goes to work, putting the phone in the box and rigging it to a simple detonator powered by double-A batteries. He turns the phone on to make sure it works, then turns it off again. The chance of someone dialing this disposable's number by mistake and blowing his control room sky-high is small, but why risk it? The chances of his mother finding that poisoned meat and cooking it for her lunch were also small, and look how *that* turned out.

No, this baby is going to stay off until ten-twenty tomorrow morning. That's when Brady will stroll into the parking lot behind the Soames Funeral Home. If there's anyone back there, Brady will say he thought he could cut through the lot to the next street over, where there's a bus stop (which happens to be true; he checked it on MapQuest). But he doesn't expect anyone. They'll all be inside at the memorial service, bawling up a storm.

He'll use Thing Two to unlock the fat ex-cop's car and put the shoebox on the floor behind the driver's seat. He'll lock the Toyota again and return to his own car. To wait. To watch him go past. To let him reach the next intersection, where Brady can be sure that he, Brady, will be relatively safe from flying debris. Then . . .

"Ka-pow," Brady says. "They'll need another shoebox to bury him in."

That's pretty funny, and he's laughing as he goes back to the closet to get his suicide vest. He'll spend the rest of the afternoon disassembling it. Brady doesn't need the vest anymore.

He has a better idea.

15

Wednesday, June 2, 2010, is warm and cloudless. It may still be spring according to the calendar, and the local schools may still be in session, but those things don't change the fact that this is a perfect summer day in the heartland of America.

Bill Hodges, suited up but as yet blessedly tieless, is in his study, going over a list of car burglaries Marlo Everett sent him by fax. He has printed out a map of the city, and puts a red dot at each burglary location. He sees shoeleather in his future, maybe a lot of it if Olivia's computer doesn't pan out, but it's just possible that some of the burglary victims will mention seeing a similar vehicle. Because Mr. Mercedes *had* to watch the owners of his target vehicles. Hodges is sure of it. He had to make sure they were gone before he used his gadget to unlock their cars.

He watched them the way he was watching me, Hodges thinks.

This kicks something over in his mind — a brief spark of association that's bright but gone before he can see what it's illuminating. That's okay; if there's really something there, it will come back. In the meantime, he keeps on checking addresses and making red dots. He has twenty minutes before he has to noose on his tie and go after Janey.

Brady Hartsfield is in his control room. No headache today, and his thoughts, so often muddled, are as clear as the various *Wild Bunch* screensavers on his computers. He has removed the blocks of plastic explosive from his suicide vest, disconnecting them carefully from the detonator wires. Some of the blocks have gone into a bright red seat cushion printed with the saucy slogan ASS PARKING. He has slipped two more, re-molded into cylinders with detonator wires attached, down the throat of a bright blue Urinesta peebag. With that accomplished, he carefully attaches a stick-on decal to the peebag. He bought it, along with a souvenir tee-shirt, in the MAC gift shop yesterday. The sticker says 'ROUND HERE FANBOY #1. He checks his watch. Almost nine. The fat ex-cop now has an hour and a half to live. Maybe a little less.

Hodges's old partner Pete Huntley is in one of the interrogation rooms, not because he has anyone to question but because it's away from the morning hustle and flow of the squadroom. He has notes to go over. He's holding a press conference at ten, to talk about the latest dark revelations Donald Davis has made, and he doesn't want to screw anything up. The City Center killer — Mr. Mercedes — is the furthest thing from his mind.

In Lowtown, behind a certain pawnshop, guns are being bought and sold by people who believe they are not being watched.

Jerome Robinson is at his computer, listening to audio clips available at a website called Sounds Good to Me. He listens to a woman laughing hysterically. He listens to a man whistling "Danny Boy." He listens to a man gargling and a woman apparently in the throes of an orgasm. Eventually he finds the clip he wants. The title is simple: CRYING BABY.

On the floor below, Jerome's sister Barbara comes bursting into the kitchen, closely followed by Odell. Barbara is wearing a spangly skirt, clunky blue clogs, and a tee-shirt that shows a foxy teenage boy. Below his brilliant smile and careful coif is the legend I LUV CAM 4EVER! She asks her mother if this outfit looks too babyish to wear to the concert. Her mother (perhaps remembering what she wore to her own first concert) smiles and says it's perfect. Barbara asks if she can wear her mother's dangly peace-sign earrings. Yes, of course. Lipstick? Well . . . okay. Eye shadow? No, sorry. Barbara gives a no-harm-in-trying laugh and hugs her mother extravagantly. "I can't wait until tomorrow night," she says.

Holly Gibney is in the bathroom of the house in Sugar Heights, wishing she could skip the memorial service, knowing her mother will never let her. If she protests that she doesn't feel well, her mother's return serve will be one that goes all the way back to Holly's childhood: *What will people think.* And if Holly should protest that it doesn't *matter* what people think, they are never going to see any of these people (with the exception of Janey) again in their lives? Her mother would look at her as if Holly were speaking a foreign language. She takes her Lexapro, but her insides knot while she's brushing her teeth and she vomits it back up. Charlotte calls to ask if she's almost ready. Holly calls back that she almost is. She flushes the toilet and thinks, At least Janey's boyfriend will be there. Bill. He's nice.

Janey Patterson is dressing carefully in her late mother's condominium apartment: dark hose, black skirt, black jacket over a blouse of deepest midnight blue. She's thinking of how she told Bill she'd probably fall in love with him if she stayed here. That was a bodacious shading of the truth, because she's already in love with him. She's sure a shrink would smile and say it was a daddy thing. If so, Janey would smile right back and tell him that was a load of Freudian bullshit. Her father was a bald accountant who was barely there even when he was there. And one thing you can say about Bill Hodges is that he's *there.* It's what she likes about him. She also likes the hat she bought him. That Philip Marlowe fedora. She checks her watch and sees it's quarter past nine. He'd better be here soon.

If he's late, she'll kill him.

16

He's not late, and he's wearing the hat. Janey tells him he looks nice. He tells her she looks better than that. She smiles and kisses him.

"Let's get this done," he says.

Janey wrinkles her nose and says, *"Yeah."*

They drive to the funeral parlor, where they are once more the first to arrive. Hodges escorts her into the Eternal Rest parlor. She looks around and nods her approval. Programs for the service have been laid out on the seats of the folding chairs. The coffin is gone, replaced by a vaguely altarish table with sprays of spring flowers on it. Brahms, turned down almost too low to hear, is playing through the parlor's sound system.

"Okay?" Hodges asks.

"It'll do." She takes a deep breath and repeats what he said twenty minutes before: "Let's get this done."

It's basically the same bunch as yesterday. Janey meets them at the door. While she shakes hands and gives hugs and says all the right things, Hodges stands nearby, scanning the passing traffic. He sees nothing that raises a red flag, including a certain mud-colored Subaru that trundles by without slowing.

A rental Chevy with a Hertz sticker on the side of the windshield swings around back to the parking lot. Soon Uncle Henry appears, preceded by his gently swinging executive belly. Aunt Charlotte and Holly follow him, Charlotte with one white-gloved hand clamped just above her daughter's elbow. To Hodges, Auntie C looks like a matron escorting a prisoner — probably a drug addict — into county lockup. Holly is even paler than she was yesterday, if that is possible. She's wearing the same shapeless brown gunnysack, and has already bitten off most of her lipstick.

She gives Hodges a tremulous smile. Hodges offers his hand, and she seizes it with panicky tightness until Charlotte pulls her into the Hall of the Dead.

A young clergyman, from the church Mrs.

Wharton attended until she was too unwell to go out on Sundays, serves as master of ceremonies. He reads the predictable passage from Proverbs, the one about the virtuous woman. Hodges is willing to stipulate that the deceased may have been worth more than rubies, but has his doubts about whether she spent any time working with wool and flax. Still, it's poetical, and tears are flowing by the time the clergyman is finished. The guy may be young, but he's smart enough not to try eulogizing someone he hardly knew. Instead of that, he invites those with "precious memories" of the late Elizabeth to come forward. Several do, beginning with Althea Greene, the nurse, and ending with the surviving daughter. Janey is calm and brief and simple.

"I wish we'd had more time," she finishes.

17

Brady parks around the corner at five past ten and is careful to feed the meter until the green flag with MAX on it pops up. After all, it just took a parking ticket to catch Son of Sam in the end. From the back seat he takes a cloth carry-bag. Printed on the side is KROGER and REUSE ME! SAVE A TREE! Inside is Thing Two, resting on top of the Mephisto shoebox.

He turns the corner and strides briskly past

the Soames Funeral Home, just some citizen on a morning errand. His face is calm, but his heart is hammering like a steam-drill. He sees no one outside the funeral parlor, and the doors are shut, but there's still a possibility the fat ex-cop isn't with the other mourners. He could be in a back room, watching for suspicious characters. Watching for *him,* in other words. Brady knows this.

No risk, no reward, honeyboy, his mother murmurs. It's true. Also, he judges that the risk is minimal. If Hodges is pronging the blond bitch (or hoping to), he won't leave her side.

Brady does an about-face at the far corner, strolls back, and turns in to the funeral home drive without hesitation. He can hear faint music, some kind of classical shit. He spots Hodges's Toyota parked against the rear fence, nose-out for a quick getaway once the festivities are over. The old Det-Ret's last ride, Brady thinks. It's going to be a short one, pal.

He walks behind the larger of the two hearses, and once it blocks him from the view of anyone looking out the rear windows of the funeral parlor, he takes Thing Two out of the shopping bag and pulls up the antenna. His heart is driving harder than ever. There were times — only a few — when his gadget didn't work. The green light would flash, but the car's locks wouldn't pop. Some random glitch in the program or the microchip.

If it doesn't work, just slide the shoebox under the car, his mother advises him.

Of course. That would work just as well, or *almost* as well, but it wouldn't be so elegant.

He pushes the toggle. The green light flashes. So do the Toyota's headlights. Success!

He goes to the fat ex-cop's car as if he has every right to be there. He opens the rear door, takes the shoebox out of the carry-bag, turns on the phone, and puts the box on the floor behind the driver's seat. He closes the door and starts for the street, forcing himself to walk slowly and steadily.

As he's rounding the corner of the building, Deborah Ann Hartsfield speaks again. Didn't you forget something, honeyboy?

He stops. Thinks it over. Then goes back to the corner of the building and points Thing Two's stub of an antenna at Hodges's car.

The lights flash as the locks re-engage.

18

After the remembrances and a moment of silent reflection ("to use as you wish"), the clergyman asks the Lord to bless them and keep them and give them peace. Clothes rustle; programs are stowed in purses and jacket pockets. Holly seems fine until she's halfway up the aisle, but then her knees buckle. Hodges darts forward with surprising speed for a big man and catches her beneath her arms before she can go down. Her eyes roll up and for a moment she's on the verge of a full-fledged swoon. Then they come back into place and into focus. She sees Hodges and smiles weakly.

"Holly, stop that!" her mother says sternly, as if her daughter has uttered some jocose and inappropriate profanity instead of almost fainting. Hodges thinks what a pleasure it would be to backhand Auntie C right across her thickly powdered chops. Might wake her up, he thinks.

"I'm okay, Mother," Holly says. Then, to Hodges: "Thank you."

He says, "Did you eat any breakfast, Holly?"

"She had oatmeal," Aunt Charlotte announces. "With butter and brown sugar. I made it myself. You're quite the attention-getter sometimes, aren't you, Holly?" She turns to Janey. "Please don't linger, dear. Henry's useless at things like this, and I can't hostess all these people on my own."

Janey takes Hodges's arm. "I'd never expect you to."

Aunt Charlotte gives her a pinched smile. Janey's smile in return is brilliant, and Hodges decides that her decision to turn over half of her inherited loot is equally brilliant. Once that happens, she will never have to see this unpleasant woman again. She won't even have to take her calls.

The mourners emerge into the sunshine. On the front walk there's chatter of the wasn't-it-a-lovely-service sort, and then people begin walking around to the parking lot in back. Uncle Henry and Aunt Charlotte do so with Holly between them. Hodges and Janey follow along. As they reach the back of the mortuary, Holly suddenly slips free of her minders and wheels around to Hodges and Janey.

"Let me ride with you. I want to ride with you."

Aunt Charlotte, lips thinned almost to nothing, looms up behind her daughter. "I've had just about enough of your gasps and vapors for one day, miss."

Holly ignores her. She seizes one of Hodges's hands in a grip that's icy. "Please. *Please.*"

"It's fine with me," Hodges says, "if Janey doesn't m—"

Aunt Charlotte begins to sob. The sound is unlovely, the hoarse cries of a crow in a cornfield. Hodges remembers her bending over Mrs. Wharton, kissing her cold lips, and a sudden unpleasant possibility comes to him. He misjudged Olivia; he may have misjudged Charlotte Gibney as well. There's more to people than their surfaces, after all.

"Holly, you don't even *know* this man!"

Janey puts a much warmer hand on

Hodges's wrist. "Why don't you go with Charlotte and Henry, Bill? There's plenty of room. You can ride in back with Holly." She shifts her attention to her cousin. "Would that be all right?"

"Yes!" Holly is still gripping Hodges's hand. "That would be good!"

Janey turns to her uncle. "Okay with you?"

"Sure." He gives Holly a jovial pat on the shoulder. "The more the merrier."

"That's right, give her plenty of attention," Aunt Charlotte says. "It's what she likes. Isn't it, Holly?" She starts for the parking lot without waiting for a reply, heels clacking a Morse code message of outrage.

Hodges looks at Janey. "What about my car?"

"I'll drive it. Hand over the keys." And when he does: "There's just one other thing I need."

"Yeah?"

She plucks the fedora from his head, puts it on her own, and gives it the correct insouciant dip over her left eyebrow. She wrinkles her nose at him and says, *"Yeah."*

19

Brady has parked up the street from the funeral parlor, his heart beating harder than ever. He's holding a cell phone. The number of the burner attached to the bomb in the

Toyota's back seat is inked on his wrist.

He watches the mourners stand around on the walk. The fat ex-cop is impossible to miss; in his black suit he looks as big as a house. Or a hearse. On his head is a ridiculously old-fashioned hat, the kind you saw cops wearing in black-and-white detective movies from the nineteen-fifties.

People are starting around to the back, and after awhile, Hodges and the blond bitch head that way. Brady supposes the blond bitch will be with him when the car blows. Which will make it a clean sweep — the mother and both daughters. It has the elegance of an equation where all the variables have been solved.

Cars start pulling out, all moving in his direction because that's the way you go if you're heading to Sugar Heights. The sun glares on the windshields, which isn't helpful, but there's no mistaking the fat ex-cop's Toyota when it appears at the head of the funeral home driveway, pauses briefly, then turns toward him.

Brady doesn't even glance at Uncle Henry's rental Chevy when it passes him. All his attention is focused on the fat ex-cop's ride. When it goes by, he feels a moment's disappointment. The blond bitch must have gone with her relatives, because there's no one in the Toyota but the driver. Brady only gets a glimpse, but even with the sunglare, the fat ex-cop's stupid hat is unmistakable.

Brady keys in a number. "I said you wouldn't see me coming. Didn't I say that, asshole?"

He pushes SEND.

20

As Janey reaches to turn on the radio, a cell phone begins to ring. The last sound she makes on earth — everyone should be so lucky — is a laugh. Idiot, she thinks affectionately, you went and left it again. She reaches for the glove compartment. There's a second ring.

That's not coming from the glove compartment, that's coming from behi—

There's no sound, at least not that she hears, only the momentary sensation of a strong hand pushing the driver's seat. Then the world turns white.

21

Holly Gibney, also known as Holly the Mumbler, may have mental problems, but neither the psychotropic drugs she takes nor the cigarettes she smokes on the sneak have slowed her down physically. Uncle Henry slams on the brakes and she bolts from the rental Chevy while the explosion is still reverberating.

Hodges is right behind her, running hard. There's a stab of pain in his chest and he thinks he might be having a heart attack. Part of him actually hopes for this, but the pain goes away. The pedestrians are behaving as they always do when an act of violence punches a hole in the world they have previously taken for granted. Some drop to the sidewalk and cover their heads. Others are frozen in place, like statues. A few cars stop; most speed up and exit the vicinity immediately. One of these is a mud-colored Subaru.

As Hodges pounds after Janey's mentally unstable cousin, the last message from Mr. Mercedes beats in his head like a ceremonial drum: *I'm going to kill you. You won't see me coming. I'm going to kill you. You won't see me coming. I'm going to kill you. You won't see me coming.*

He rounds the corner, skidding on the slick soles of his seldom-worn dress shoes, and almost runs into Holly, who has stopped dead with her shoulders slumped and her purse dangling from one hand. She's staring at what remains of Hodges's Toyota. Its body has been blown clean off the axles and is burning furiously in a litter of glass. The back seat lies on its side twenty feet away, its torn upholstery on fire. A man staggers drunkenly across the street, holding his bleeding head. A woman is sitting on the curb outside a card-and-gift shop with a smashed-in show window, and for one wild moment he thinks it's Janey, but this woman is wearing a green dress and she has gray hair and of course it isn't Janey, it can't be Janey.

He thinks, This is my fault. If I'd used my father's gun two weeks ago, she'd be alive.

There's still enough cop inside him to push the idea aside (although it doesn't go easily). A cold shocked clarity flows in to replace it. This is *not* his fault. It's the fault of the son of a bitch who planted the bomb. The same son of a bitch who drove a stolen car into a crowd of job-seekers at City Center.

Hodges sees a single black high-heeled shoe lying in a pool of blood, he sees a severed arm in a smoldering sleeve lying in the gutter like someone's cast-off garbage, and his mind clicks into gear. Uncle Henry and Aunt Charlotte will be here shortly, and that means there isn't much time.

He seizes Holly by the shoulders and turns her around. Her hair has come loose from its Princess Leia rolls and hangs against her cheeks. Her wide eyes look right through him. His mind — colder than ever — knows she's no good to him as she is now. He slaps first one cheek, then the other. Not hard slaps, but enough to make her eyelids flutter.

People are screaming. Horns are honking,

and a couple of car alarms are blatting. He can smell gasoline, burning rubber, melting plastic.

"Holly. Holly. Listen to me."

She's looking, but is she listening? He doesn't know, and there's no time.

"I loved her, but you can't tell anyone. *You can't tell anyone I loved her.* Maybe later, but not now. Do you understand?"

She nods.

"I need your cell number. And I may need *you.*" His cold mind hopes he won't, that the house in Sugar Heights will be empty this afternoon, but he doesn't think it will be. Holly's mother and uncle will have to leave, at least for awhile, but Charlotte won't want her daughter to go with them. Because Holly has mental problems. Holly is delicate. Hodges wonders just how many breakdowns she's had, and if there have been suicide attempts. These thoughts zip across his mind like shooting stars, there at one moment, gone the next. He has no time for Holly's delicate mental condition.

"When your mother and uncle go to the police station, tell them you don't need anyone to stay with you. Tell them you're okay by yourself. Can you do that?"

She nods, although she almost certainly has no idea what he's talking about.

"Someone will call you. It might be me, or it might be a young man named Jerome.

Jerome. Can you remember that name?"

She nods, then opens her purse and takes out a glasses case.

This is not working, Hodges thinks. The lights are on but nobody's home. Still, he has to try. He grasps her shoulders.

"Holly, I want to catch the guy who did this. I want to make him pay. Will you help me?"

She nods. There's no expression on her face.

"Say it, then. Say you'll help me."

She doesn't. She slips a pair of sunglasses from the case instead, and pops them on as if there weren't a car burning in the street and Janey's arm in the gutter. As if there weren't people screaming and already the sound of an approaching siren. As if this were a day at the beach.

He shakes her lightly. *"I need your cell phone number."*

She nods agreeably but says nothing. She snaps her purse closed and turns back to the burning car. The greatest despair he has ever known sweeps through Hodges, sickening his belly and scattering the thoughts that were, for the space of thirty or forty seconds, perfectly clear.

Aunt Charlotte comes sidewheeling around the corner with her hair — mostly black but white at the roots — flying out behind her. Uncle Henry follows. His jowly face is pasty except for the clownish spots of red high on his cheeks.

"Sharlie, stop!" Uncle Henry cries. "I think I'm having a heart attack!"

His sister pays no attention. She grabs Holly's elbow, jerks her around, and hugs her fiercely, mashing Holly's not inconsiderable nose between her breasts. *"DON'T LOOK!"* Charlotte bellows, looking. *"DON'T LOOK, SWEETHEART, DON'T LOOK AT IT!"*

"I can hardly breathe," Uncle Henry announces. He sits on the curb and hangs his head down. "God, I hope I'm not dying."

More sirens have joined the first. People have begun to creep forward so they can get a closer look at the burning wreck in the street. A couple snap photos with their phones.

Hodges thinks, Enough explosive to blow up a car. How much more does he have?

Aunt Charlotte still has Holly in a death-grip, bawling at her not to look. Holly isn't struggling to get away, but she's got one hand behind her. There's something in it. Although he knows it's probably just wishful thinking, Hodges hopes it might be for him. He takes what she's holding out. It's the case her sunglasses were in. Her name and address are embossed on it in gold.

There's also a phone number.

22

Hodges takes his Nokia from his inside suit coat pocket, aware as he flips it open that it would probably be so much melted plastic and fizzing wire in the glove compartment of his baked Toyota, if not for Janey's gentle chaffing.

He hits Jerome on speed-dial, praying the kid will pick up, and he does.

"Mr. Hodges? Bill? I think we just heard a big explo—"

"Shut up, Jerome. Just listen." He's walking down the glass-littered sidewalk. The sirens are closer now, soon they'll be here, and all he has to go on is pure intuition. Unless, that is, his subconscious mind is already making the connections. It's happened before; he didn't get all those department commendations on Craigslist.

"Listening," Jerome says.

"You know nothing about the City Center case. You know nothing about Olivia Trelawney or Janey Patterson." Of course the three of them had dinner together at DeMasio's, but he doesn't think the cops will get that far for awhile, if ever.

"I know squat," Jerome says. There's no distrust or hesitance in his voice. "Who'll be asking? The police?"

"Maybe later. First it'll be your parents. Because that explosion you heard was my car.

Janey was driving. We swapped at the last minute. She's . . . gone."

"Christ, Bill, you have to tell five-oh! Your old partner!"

Hodges thinks of her saying He's *ours.* We still see eye to eye on *that,* right?

Right, he thinks. Still eye to eye on that, Janey.

"Not yet. Right now I'm going to roll on this, and I need you to help me. The scum-bucket killed her, I want his ass, and I mean to have it. Will you help?"

"Yes." Not *How much trouble could I get in.* Not *This could totally screw me up for Harvard.* Not *Leave me out of it.* Just *Yes.* God bless Jerome Robinson.

"You have to go on Debbie's Blue Umbrella as me and send the guy who did this a message. Do you remember my username?"

"Yeah. Kermitfrog19. Let me get some pa—"

"No time. Just remember the gist of it. And don't post for at least an hour. He has to know I didn't send it *before* the explosion. He has to know I'm still alive."

Jerome says, "Give it."

Hodges gives it and breaks the connection without saying goodbye. He slips the phone into his pants pocket, along with Holly's sunglasses case.

A fire truck comes swaying around the corner, followed by two police cars. They speed past the Soames Funeral Home, where the mortician and the minister from Elizabeth Wharton's service are now standing on the sidewalk, shading their eyes against the glare of the sun and the burning car.

Hodges has a lot of talking to do, but there's something more important to do first. He strips off his suit coat, kneels down, and covers the arm in the gutter. He feels tears pricking at his eyes and forces them back. He can cry later. Right now tears don't fit the story he has to tell.

The cops, two young guys riding solo, are getting out of their cars. Hodges doesn't know them. "Officers," he says.

"Got to ask you to clear the area, sir," one of them says, "but if you witnessed that —" He points to the burning remains of the Toyota. "— I need you to stay close so someone can interview you."

"I not only saw it, I should have been in it." Hodges takes out his wallet and flips it open to show the police ID card with RETIRED stamped across it in red. "Until last fall, my partner was Pete Huntley. You should call him ASAP."

One of the other cops says, "It was your car, sir?"

"Yeah."

The first cop says, "Then who was driving it?"

23

Brady arrives home well before noon with all his problems solved. Old Mr. Beeson from across the street is standing on his lawn. "Didja hear it?"

"Hear what?"

"Big explosion somewheres downtown. There was a lot of smoke, but it's gone now."

"I was playing the radio pretty loud," Brady says.

"I think that old paint fact'ry exploded, that's what I think. I knocked on your mother's door, but I guess she must be sleepun." His eyes twinkle with what's unsaid: *Sleepun it off.*

"I guess she must be," Brady says. He doesn't like the idea that the nosy old cock-knocker did that. Brady Hartsfield's idea of great neighbors would be no neighbors. "Got to go, Mr. Beeson."

"Tell your mum I said hello."

He unlocks the door, steps in, and locks it behind him. Scents the air. Nothing. Or . . . maybe not *quite* nothing. Maybe the tiniest whiff of unpleasantness, like the smell of a chicken carcass that got left a few days too long in the trash under the sink.

Brady goes up to her room. He turns down the coverlet, exposing her pale face and glaring eyes. He doesn't mind them so much now, and so what if Mr. Beeson's a neb-nose?

Brady only needs to keep things together for another few days, so *fuck* Mr. Beeson. Fuck her glaring eyes, too. He didn't kill her; she killed herself. The way the fat ex-cop was supposed to kill himself, and so what if he didn't? He's gone now, so *fuck* the fat ex-cop. The Det is definitely Ret. Ret in peace, Detective Hodges.

"I did it, Mom," he says. "I pulled it off. And you helped. Only in my head, but . . ." Only he's not completely sure of that. Maybe it really was Mom who reminded him to lock the fat ex-cop's car doors again. He wasn't thinking about that at all.

"Anyway, thanks," he finishes lamely. "Thanks for whatever. And I'm sorry you're dead."

The eyes glare up at him.

He reaches for her — tentatively — and uses the tips of his fingers to close her eyes the way people sometimes do in movies. It works for a few seconds, then they roll up like tired old windowshades and the glare resumes. The you-killed-me-honeyboy glare.

It's a major buzzkill and Brady pulls the coverlet back over her face. He goes downstairs and turns on the TV, thinking at least one of the local stations will be broadcasting from the scene, but none of them are. It's very annoying. Don't they know a car-bomb when one explodes in their faces? Apparently not. Apparently Rachael Ray making her favorite fucking meatloaf is more important.

He turns off the idiot box and hurries to the control room, saying *chaos* to light up his computers and *darkness* to kill the suicide program. He does a shuffling little dance, shaking his fists over his head and singing what he remembers of "Ding Dong the Witch Is Dead," only changing *witch* to *cop.* He thinks it will make him feel better, but it doesn't. Between Mr. Beeson's long nose and his mother's glaring eyes, his good feeling — the feeling he *worked for,* the feeling he *deserved* — is slipping away.

Never mind. There's a concert coming up, and he has to be ready for it. He sits at the long worktable. The ball bearings that used to be in his suicide vest are now in three mayonnaise jars. Next to them is a box of Glad food-storage bags, the gallon size. He begins filling them (but not overfilling them) with the steel bearings. The work soothes him, and his good feelings start to come back. Then, just as he's finishing up, a steamboat whistle toots.

Brady looks up, frowning. That's a special cue he programmed into his Number Three. It sounds when he's got a message on the Blue Umbrella site, but that's impossible. The only person he's been communicating with via the Blue Umbrella is Kermit William Hodges, aka the fat ex-cop, aka the permanently Ret Det.

He rolls over in his office chair, paddling his feet, and stares at Number Three. The Blue Umbrella icon is now sporting a **1** in a little red circle. He clicks on it. He stares, wide-eyed and open-mouthed, at the message on his screen.

kermitfrog19 wants to chat with you!
Do you want to chat with kermitfrog19?
Y N

Brady would like to believe this message was sent last night or this morning before Hodges and the blond bimbo left his house, but he can't. He just heard it come in.

Summoning his courage — because this is much scarier than looking into his dead mother's eyes — he clicks **Y** and reads.

Missed me.
☺

And here's something to remember, asshole: I'm like your side mirror. You know, OBJECTS ARE CLOSER THAN THEY APPEAR.

I know how you got into her Mercedes, and it wasn't the valet key. But you believed me about that, didn't you? Sure you did. Because you're an asshole.

I've got a list of all the other cars you burglarized between 2007 and 2009.

I've got other info I don't want to share

right now, but here's something I WILL share: it's PERP, not PERK.

Why am I telling you this? Because I'm no longer going to catch you and turn you in to the cops. Why should I? I'm not a cop anymore.

I'm going to kill you.

See you soon, mama's boy.

Even in his shock and disbelief, it's that last line that Brady's eyes keep returning to.

He walks to his closet on legs that feel like stilts. Once inside with the door closed, he screams and beats his fists on the shelves. Instead of the nigger family's dog, he managed to kill his own mother. That was bad. Now he's managed to kill someone else instead of the cop, and that's worse. Probably it was the blond bitch. The blond bitch wearing the Det-Ret's hat for some weirdo reason only another blonde could understand.

One thing he *is* sure of: this house is no longer safe. Hodges is probably gaming him about being close, but he might not be. He knows about Thing Two. He knows about the car burglaries. He says he knows other stuff, too. And —

See you soon, mama's boy.

He has to get out of here. Soon. Something to do first, though.

Brady goes back upstairs and into his

mother's bedroom, barely glancing at the shape under the coverlet. He goes into her bathroom and rummages in the drawers of her vanity until he finds her Lady Schick. Then he goes to work.

24

Hodges is in Interrogation Room 4 again — IR4, his lucky room — but this time he's on the wrong side of the table, facing Pete Huntley and Pete's new partner, a stunner with long red hair and eyes of misty gray. The interrogation is collegial, but that doesn't change the basic facts: his car has been blown up and a woman has been killed. Another fact is that an interrogation is an interrogation.

"Did it have anything to do with the Mercedes Killer?" Pete asks. "What do you think, Billy? I mean, that's the most likely, wouldn't you say? Given the vic was Olivia Trelawney's sister?"

There it is: the vic. The woman he slept with after he'd come to a point in his life where he thought he'd never sleep with any woman again. The woman who made him laugh and gave him comfort, the woman who was his partner in this last investigation as much as Pete Huntley ever was. The woman who wrinkled her nose at him and mocked his *yeah.*

Don't you ever let me hear you call them the vics, Frank Sledge told him, back in the old days . . . but right now he has to take it.

"I don't see how it can," he says mildly. "I know how it looks, but sometimes a cigar is just a smoke and a coincidence is just a coincidence."

"How did you —" Isabelle Jaynes begins, then shakes her head. "That's the wrong question. *Why* did you meet her? Were you investigating the City Center thing on your own?" Playing the uncle on a grand scale is what she doesn't say, perhaps in deference to Pete. After all, it's Pete's old running buddy they're questioning, this chunky man in rumpled suit pants and a blood-spotted white shirt, the tie he put on this morning now pulled halfway down his big chest.

"Could I have a drink of water before we get started? I'm still shook up. She was a nice lady."

Janey was a hell of a lot more than that, but the cold part of his mind, which is — for the time being — keeping the hot part in a cage, tells him this is the right way to go, the route that will lead into the rest of his story the way a narrow entrance ramp leads to a four-lane highway. Pete gets up and goes out. Isabelle says nothing until he gets back, just regards Hodges with those misty gray eyes.

Hodges drinks half the paper cup in a swallow, then says, "Okay. It goes back to that lunch we had at DeMasio's, Pete. Remember?"

"Sure."

"I asked you about all the cases we were working — the big ones, I mean — when I retired, but the one I was really interested in was the City Center Massacre. I think you knew that."

Pete says nothing, but smiles slightly.

"Do you remember me asking if you ever wondered about Mrs. Trelawney? Specifically if she was telling the truth about not having an extra key?"

"Uh-huh."

"What I was really wondering was if we gave her a fair shake. If we were wearing blinders because of how she was."

"What do you mean, how she was?" Isabelle asks.

"A pain in the ass. Twitchy and haughty and quick to take offense. To get a little perspective, turn it around a minute and think of all the people who believed Donald Davis when he claimed he was innocent. Why? Because he *wasn't* twitchy and haughty and quick to take offense. He could really put that grief-stricken haunted-husband thing across, and he was good-looking. I saw him on Channel Six once, and that pretty blond anchor's thighs were practically squeezing together."

"That's disgusting," Isabelle says, but she

says it with a smile.

"Yeah, but true. He was a charmer. Olivia Trelawney, on the other hand, was an *anti*-charmer. So I started to wonder if we ever gave her story a fair shot."

"We did." Pete says it flatly.

"*Maybe* we did. Anyway, there I am, retired, with time on my hands. Too much time. And one day — just before I asked you to lunch, Pete — I say to myself, Assume she *was* telling the truth. If so, where was that second key? And then — this was right *after* our lunch — I went on the Internet and started to do some research. And do you know what I came across? A techno-fiddle called 'stealing the peek.' "

"What's that?" Isabelle asks.

"Oh, man," Pete says. "You really think some computer genius stole her key-signal? Then just happened to find her spare key stowed in the glove compartment or under the seat? Her spare key that she *forgot*? That's pretty far-fetched, Bill. Especially when you add in that the woman's picture could have been next to Type A in the dictionary."

Calmly, as if he had not used his jacket to cover the severed arm of a woman he loved not three hours before, Hodges summarizes what Jerome found out about stealing the peek, representing it as his own research. He tells them that he went to the Lake Avenue condo to interview Olivia Trelawney's mother

("If she was still alive — I didn't know for sure") and found Olivia's sister, Janelle, living there. He leaves out his visit to the mansion in Sugar Heights and his conversation with Radney Peeples, the Vigilant security guard, because that might lead to questions he'd be hard-pressed to answer. They'll find out in time, but he's close to Mr. Mercedes now, he knows he is. A little time is all he needs.

He hopes.

"Ms. Patterson told me her mother was in a nursing home about thirty miles from here — Sunny Acres. She offered to go up there with me and make the introduction. So I could ask a few questions."

"Why would she do that?" Isabelle asks.

"Because she thought we might have jammed her sister up, and that caused her suicide."

"Bullshit," Pete says.

"I'm not going to argue with you about it, but you can understand the thinking, right? And the hope of clearing her sister of negligence?"

Pete gestures for him to go on. Hodges does, after finishing his water. He wants to get out of here. Mr. Mercedes could have read Jerome's message by now. If so, he may run. That would be fine with Hodges. A running man is easier to spot than a hiding man.

"I questioned the old lady and got nothing.

All I managed to do was upset her. She had a stroke and died soon after." He sighs. "Ms. Patterson — Janelle — was heartbroken."

"Was she also pissed at you?" Isabelle asks.

"No. Because she was for the idea, too. Then, when her mother died, she didn't know anyone in the city except her mother's nurse, who's pretty long in the tooth herself. I'd given her my number, and she called me. She said she needed help, especially with a bunch of relatives flying in that she hardly knew, and I was willing to give it. Janelle wrote the obituary. I made the other arrangements."

"Why was she in your car when it blew?"

Hodges explains about Holly's meltdown. He doesn't mention Janey appropriating his new hat at the last moment, not because it will destabilize his story but because it hurts too much.

"Okay," Isabelle says. "You meet Olivia Trelawney's sister, who you like well enough to call by her first name. The sister facilitates a Q-and-A with the mom. Mom strokes out and dies, maybe because reliving it all again got her too excited. The sister is blown up after the funeral — in your car — and you still don't see a connection to the Mercedes Killer?"

Hodges spreads his hands. "How would this guy know I was asking questions? I didn't take out an ad in the paper." He turns to

Pete. "I didn't talk to anyone about it, not even you."

Pete, clearly still brooding over the idea that their personal feelings about Olivia Trelawney might have colored the investigation, is looking dour. Hodges doesn't much care, because that's exactly what happened. "No, you just sounded me out about it at lunch."

Hodges gives him a big grin. It makes his stomach fold in on itself like origami. "Hey," he says, "it was my treat, wasn't it?"

"Who else could have wanted to bomb you to kingdom come?" Isabelle asks. "You on Santa's naughty list?"

"If I had to guess, I'd put my money on the Abbascia Family. How many of those shitbags did we put away on that gun thing back in '04, Pete?"

"A dozen or more, but —"

"Yeah, and RICO'd twice as many a year later. We smashed them to pieces, and Fabby the Nose said they'd get us both."

"Billy, the Abbascias can't get anyone. Fabrizio is dead, his brother is in a mental asylum where he thinks he's Napoleon or someone, and the rest are in jail."

Hodges just gives him the look.

"Okay," Pete says, "so you never catch all the cockroaches, but it's still crazy. All due respect, pal, but you're just a retired flatfoot. Out to pasture."

"Right. Which means they could go after

me without creating a firestorm. You, on the other hand, still have a gold shield pinned to your wallet."

"The idea is ridiculous," Isabelle says, and folds her arms beneath her breasts as if to say That ends the matter.

Hodges shrugs. "*Somebody* tried to blow me up, and I can't believe the Mercedes Killer somehow got an ESP vibe that I was looking into the Case of the Missing Key. Even if he did, why would he come after me? How could that lead to him?"

"Well, he's crazy," Pete says. "How about that for a start?"

"Sure, but I repeat — *how would he know*?"

"No idea. Listen, Billy, are you holding anything back? Anything at all?"

"No."

"I think you are," Isabelle says. She cocks her head. "Hey, you weren't sleeping with her, were you?"

Hodges shifts his gaze to her. "What do you think, Izzy? Look at me."

She holds his eyes for a moment, then drops them. Hodges can't believe how close she just came. Women's intuition, he thinks, and then, Probably a good thing I haven't lost any more weight, or put that Just For Men shit in my hair.

"Look, Pete, I want to shake. Go home and have a beer and try to get my head around this."

"You swear you're not holding anything back? This is you and me, now."

Hodges passes up his last chance to come clean without a qualm. "Not a thing."

Pete tells him to stay in touch; they'll want him in tomorrow or Friday for a formal statement.

"Not a problem. And Pete? In the immediate future I'd give my car a once-over before driving it, if I were you."

At the door, Pete puts an arm over Hodges's shoulders and gives him a hug. "I'm sorry about this," he says. "Sorry about what happened and about all the questions."

"It's okay. You're doing the job."

Pete tightens his grip and whispers in Hodges's ear. "You *are* holding back. You think I've been taking stupid pills?"

For a moment Hodges rethinks his options. Then he remembers Janey saying He's *ours.*

He takes Pete by the arms, looks him full in the face, and says, "I'm just as mystified about this as you are. Trust me."

25

Hodges crosses the Detective Division bullpen, fielding the curious glances and leading questions with a stone face that only breaks once. Cassie Sheen, with whom he worked most often when Pete was on vacation, says, "Look at you. Still alive and uglier than ever."

He smiles. "If it isn't Cassie Sheen, the Botox Queen." He lifts an arm in mock defense when she picks a paperweight up off her desk and brandishes it. It all feels both fake and real at the same time. Like one of those girl-fights on afternoon TV.

In the hall, there's a line of chairs near the snack and soda machines. Sitting in two of the chairs are Aunt Charlotte and Uncle Henry. Holly isn't with them, and Hodges instinctively touches the glasses case in his pants pocket. He asks Uncle Henry if he's feeling better. Uncle Henry says he is, and thanks him. He turns to Aunt Charlotte and asks how she's doing.

"I'm fine. It's Holly I'm worried about. I think she blames herself, because she's the reason . . . you know."

Hodges knows. The reason Janey was driving his car. Of course Janey would have been in it anyway, but he doubts if that changes the way Holly feels.

"I wish you'd talk to her. You *bonded* with her, somehow." Her eyes take on an unpleasant gleam. "The way you bonded with Janelle. You must have a way about you."

"I'll do that," Hodges says, and he will, but Jerome is going to talk to her first. Assuming the number on the glasses case works, that is. For all he knows, that number rings a landline in . . . where was it? Cincinnati? Cleveland?

"I hope we're not supposed to identify her," Uncle Henry says. In one hand he holds a Styrofoam cup of coffee. He's hardly touched it, and Hodges isn't surprised. The police department coffee is notorious. "How can we? She was blown to bits."

"Don't be an idiot," Aunt Charlotte says. "They don't want us to do that. They *can't.*"

Hodges says, "If she's ever been fingerprinted — most people have — they'll do it that way. They may show you photographs of her clothes, or personal pieces of jewelry."

"How would we know about her jewelry?" Aunt Charlotte cries. A cop getting a soda turns to look at her. "And I hardly noticed what she was wearing!"

Hodges guesses she priced out every stitch, but doesn't comment. "They may have other questions." Some about him. "It shouldn't take long."

There's an elevator, but Hodges chooses the stairs. On the landing one flight down, he leans against the wall, eyes closed, and takes half a dozen big, shuddering breaths. The tears come now. He swipes them away with his sleeve. Aunt Charlotte expressed concern about Holly — a concern Hodges shares — but no sorrow about her blown-to-bits niece. He guesses that Aunt Charlotte's biggest interest in Janey right now is what happens to all the lovely dosh Janey inherited from her sister.

I hope she left it to a fucking dog hospital, he thinks.

Hodges sits down with an out-of-breath grunt. Using one of the stairs as a makeshift desk, he lays out the sunglasses case and, from his wallet, a creased sheet of notepaper with two sets of numbers on it.

26

"Hello?" The voice is soft, tentative. "Hello, who is this?"

"My name's Jerome Robinson, ma'am. I believe Bill Hodges said I might call you."

Silence.

"Ma'am?" Jerome is sitting by his computer, holding his Android almost tightly enough to crack the casing. "Ms. Gibney?"

"I'm here." It's almost a sigh. "He said he wants to catch the person who killed my cousin. There was a terrible explosion."

"I know," Jerome says. Down the hall, Barb starts playing her new 'Round Here record for the thousandth time. *Kisses on the Midway,* it's called. It hasn't driven him crazy yet, but crazy gets closer with every play.

Meanwhile, the woman on the other end of the line has started to cry.

"Ma'am? Ms. Gibney? I'm very sorry for your loss."

"I hardly knew her, but she was my cousin, and she was nice to me. So was Mr. Hodges.

Do you know what he asked me?"

"No, uh-uh."

"If I'd eaten breakfast. Wasn't that considerate?"

"It sure was," Jerome says. He still can't believe the lively, vital lady he had dinner with is dead. He remembers how her eyes sparkled when she laughed and how she mocked Bill's way of saying *yeah.* Now he's on the phone with a woman he's never met, a very odd woman, from the sound of her. Talking to her feels like defusing a bomb. "Ma'am, Bill asked me to come out there."

"Will he come with you?"

"He can't right now. He's got other things he has to do."

There's more silence, and then, in a voice so low and timid he can barely hear it, Holly asks, "Are you safe? Because I worry about people, you know. I worry very much."

"Yes, ma'am, I'm safe."

"I want to help Mr. Hodges. I want to help catch the man who did it. He must be crazy, don't you think?"

"Yes," Jerome says. Down the hall another song starts and two little girls — Barbara and her friend Hilda — emit joyous shrieks almost high enough to shatter glass. He thinks of three or four thousand Barbs and Hildas all shrieking in unison tomorrow night, and thanks God his mother is pulling *that* duty.

"You could come, but I don't know how to let you in," she says. "My uncle Henry set the burglar alarm when he went out, and I don't know the code. I think he shut the gate, too."

"I've got all that covered," Jerome says.

"When will you come?"

"I can be there in half an hour."

"If you talk to Mr. Hodges, will you tell him something for me?"

"Sure."

"Tell him I'm sad, too." She pauses. "And that I'm taking my Lexapro."

27

Late that Wednesday afternoon, Brady checks in to a gigantic Motel 6 near the airport, using one of his Ralph Jones credit cards. He has a suitcase and a knapsack. In the knapsack is a single change of clothes, which is all he'll need for the few dozen hours of life that still remain to him. In the suitcase is the ASS PARKING cushion, the Urinesta peebag, a framed picture, several homemade detonator switches (he only expects to need one, but you can never have enough backup), Thing Two, several Glad storage bags filled with ball bearings, and enough homemade explosive to blow both the motel and the adjacent parking lot sky-high. He goes back to his Subaru, pulls out a larger item (with some effort; it barely fits), carries it into his room, and leans it against the wall.

He lies down on his bed. His head feels strange against the pillow. Naked. And sort of sexy, somehow.

He thinks, I've had a run of bad luck, but I've ridden it out and I'm still standing.

He closes his eyes. Soon he's snoring.

28

Jerome parks his Wrangler with the nose almost touching the closed gate at 729 Lilac Drive, gets out, and pushes the call button. He has a reason to be here if someone from the Sugar Heights security patrol should stop and query him, but it will only work if the woman inside confirms him, and he's not sure he can count on that. His earlier conversation with the lady has suggested that she's got one wheel on the road at most. In any case, he's not challenged, and after a moment or two of standing there and trying to look as if he belongs — this is one of those occasions when he feels especially black — Holly answers.

"Yes? Who is it?"

"Jerome, Ms. Gibney. Bill Hodges's friend?"

A pause so long he's about to push the button again when she says, "You have the gate code?"

"Yes."

"All right. And if you're a friend of Mr. Hodges, I guess you can call me Holly."

He pushes the code and the gate opens. He drives through and watches it close behind him. So far, so good.

Holly is at the front door, peering at him through one of the side windows like a prisoner in a high-security visitation area. She's wearing a housecoat over pajamas, and her hair is a mess. A brief nightmare scenario crosses Jerome's mind: she pushes the panic button on the burglar alarm panel (almost certainly right next to where she's standing), and when the security guys arrive, she accuses him of being a burglar. Or a would-be rapist with a flannel-pajama fetish.

The door is locked. He points to it. For a moment Holly just stands there like a robot with a dead battery. Then she turns the deadbolt. A shrill peeping sound commences when Jerome opens the door and she takes several steps backward, covering her mouth with both hands.

"Don't let me get in trouble! I don't want to get in trouble!"

She's twice as nervous as he is, and this eases Jerome's mind. He punches the code into the burglar alarm and hits ALL SECURE. The peeping stops.

Holly collapses into an ornately carved chair that looks like it might have cost enough to pay for a year at a good college (although maybe not Harvard), her hair hanging around her face in dank wings. "Oh, this has been the worst day of my life," she says. "Poor Janey. Poor poor Janey."

"I'm sorry."

"But at least it's not *my* fault." She looks up at him with thin and pitiable defiance. "No one can say it was. *I* didn't do anything."

"Of course you didn't," Jerome says.

It comes out sounding stilted, but she smiles a little, so maybe it's okay. "Is Mr. Hodges all right? He's a very, very, *very* nice man. Even though my mother doesn't like him." She shrugs. "But who *does* she like?"

"He's fine," Jerome says, although he doubts if that's true.

"You're *black,*" she says, looking at him, wide-eyed.

Jerome looks down at his hands. "I am, aren't I?"

She bursts into peals of shrill laughter. "I'm sorry. That was rude. It's *fine* that you're black."

"Black is whack," Jerome says.

"Of course it is. Totally whack." She stands up, gnaws at her lower lip, then pistons out her hand with an obvious effort of will. "Put it there, Jerome."

He shakes. Her hand is clammy. It's like shaking the paw of a small and timid animal.

"We have to hurry. If my mother and Uncle Henry come back and catch you in here, I'm in trouble."

You? Jerome thinks. What about the black kid?

"The woman who used to live here was also your cousin, right?"

"Yes. Olivia Trelawney. I haven't seen her since I was in college. She and my mother never got along." She looks at him solemnly. "I had to drop out of college. I had issues."

Jerome bets she did. And does. Still, there's something about her he likes. God knows what. It's surely not that fingernails-on-a-blackboard laugh.

"Do you know where her computer is?"

"Yes. I'll show you. Can you be quick?"

I better be, Jerome thinks.

29

The late Olivia Trelawney's computer is password-protected, which is silly, because when he turns over the keyboard, he finds OTRELAW written there with a Sharpie.

Holly, standing in the doorway and flipping the collar of her housecoat nervously up and down, mutters something he doesn't catch.

"Huh?"

"I asked what you're looking for."

"You'll know it if I find it." He opens the finder and types CRYING BABY into the search field. No result. He tries WEEPING INFANT. Nothing. He tries SCREAMING

WOMAN. Nothing.

"It could be hidden." This time he hears her clearly because her voice is right next to his ear. He jumps a little, but Holly doesn't notice. She's bent over with her hands on her housecoated knees, staring at Olivia's monitor. "Try AUDIO FILE."

That's a pretty good idea, so he does. But there's nothing.

"Okay," she says, "go to SYSTEM PREFERENCES and look at SOUND."

"Holly, all that does is control the input and output. Stuff like that."

"Well *duh.* Try it anyway." She's stopped biting her lips.

Jerome does. Under output, the menu lists SOUND STICKS, HEADPHONES, and LOG ME IN SOUND DRIVER. Under input, there's INTERNAL MICROPHONE and LINE IN. Nothing he didn't expect.

"Any other ideas?" he asks her.

"Open SOUND EFFECTS. Over there on the left."

He turns to her. "Hey, you know this stuff, don't you?"

"I took a computer course. From home. On Skype. It was interesting. Go on, look at SOUND EFFECTS."

Jerome does, and blinks at what he sees. In addition to FROG, GLASS, PING, POP, and PURR — the usual suspects — there's an item listed as SPOOKS.

"Never seen that one before."

"Me, either." She still won't look directly at his face, but her affect has changed remarkably otherwise. She pulls up a chair and sits beside him, tucking her lank hair behind her ears. "And I know Mac programs inside and out."

"Go with your bad self," Jerome says, and holds up a hand.

Still looking at the screen, Holly slaps him five. "Play it, Sam."

He grins. *"Casablanca."*

"Yes. I've seen that movie seventy-three times. I have a Movie Book. I write down everything I see. My mother says that's OCD."

"*Life* is OCD," Jerome says.

Unsmiling, Holly replies, "Go with your bad self."

Jerome highlights SPOOKS and bangs the return key. From the stereo sound sticks on either side of Olivia's computer, a baby begins to wail. Holly is okay with that; she doesn't clutch Jerome's shoulder until the woman shrieks, *"Why did you let him murder my baby?"*

"Fuck!" Jerome cries, and grabs Holly's hand. He doesn't even think about it, and she doesn't draw away. They stare at the computer as if it has grown teeth and bitten them.

There's a moment of silence, then the baby

starts crying again. The woman screams again. The program cycles a third time, then stops.

Holly finally looks directly at him, her eyes so wide they seem in danger of falling out of her head. "Did you know that was going to happen?"

"Jesus, *no.*" Maybe something, or Bill wouldn't have sent him here, but *that*? "Can you find out anything about the program, Holly? Like when it was installed? If you can't, that's all ri—"

"Push over."

Jerome is good with computers, but Holly plays the keyboard like a Steinway. After a few minutes of hunting around, she says, "Looks like it was installed on July first of last year. A whole bunch of stuff was installed that day."

"It could have been programmed to play at certain times, right? Cycle three times and then quit?"

She gives him an impatient glance. "Of course."

"Then how come it's not *still* playing? I mean, you guys have been staying here. You would have heard it."

She clicks the mouse like crazy and shows him something else. "I saw this already. It's a slave program, hidden in her Mail Contacts. I bet Olivia didn't know it was here. It's called Looking Glass. You can't use it to turn on a computer — at least I don't think so — but if it *is* on, you can run everything from your own computer. Open files, read emails, look at search histories . . . or deactivate programs."

"Like after she was dead," Jerome says.

"Oough." Holly grimaces.

"Why would the guy who installed this leave it? Why not erase it completely?"

"I don't know. Maybe he just forgot. I forget stuff all the time. My mother says I'd forget my own head if it wasn't attached to my neck."

"Yeah, mine says that, too. But who's *he*? Who are we talking about?"

She thinks it over. They both do. And after perhaps five seconds, they speak at the same time.

"Her I-T guy," Jerome says, just as Holly says, "Her geek freak."

Jerome starts going through the drawers of Olivia's computer station, looking for a computer-service invoice, a bill stamped PAID, or a business card. There ought to be at least one of those, but there's nothing. He gets on his knees and crawls into the kneehole under the desk. Nothing there, either.

"Look on the fridge," he says. "Sometimes people put shit there, under little magnets."

"There are plenty of magnets," Holly says, "but nothing on the fridge except for a real estate agent's card and one from the Vigilant security company. I think Janey must have taken down everything else. Probably threw it away."

"Is there a safe?"

"Probably, but why would my cousin put her I-T guy's business card in her safe? It's not like it's worth *money,* or anything."

"True-dat," Jerome says.

"If it was here, it would be by her computer. She wouldn't *hide* it. I mean, she wrote her password right under her goshdarn *keyboard.*"

"Pretty dumb," Jerome says.

"Totally." Holly suddenly seems to realize how close they are. She gets up and goes back to the doorway. She starts flipping the collar of her housecoat again. "What are you going to do now?"

"I guess I better call Bill."

He takes out his cell phone, but before he can make the call, she says his name. Jerome looks at her, standing there in the doorway, looking lost in her flappy comfort-clothes.

"There must be, like, a zillion I-T guys in this city," she says.

Nowhere near that many, but a lot. He knows it and Hodges knows it, too, because it was Jerome who told him.

30

Hodges listens carefully to everything Jerome has to say. He's pleased by Jerome's praise of Holly (and hopes Holly will be pleased, too, if she's listening), but bitterly disappointed that there's no link to the Computer Jack who worked on Olivia's machine. Jerome thinks it must be because Janey threw Computer Jack's business card away. Hodges, who has a mind trained to be suspicious, thinks Mr. Mercedes might have made damned sure Olivia didn't *have* a card. Only that doesn't track. Wouldn't you *ask* for one, if the guy did good work? And keep it handy? Unless, that is . . .

He asks Jerome to put Holly on.

"Hello?" So faint he has to strain to hear her.

"Holly, is there an address book on Olivia's computer?"

"Just a minute." He hears faint clicking. When she comes back, her voice is puzzled. "No."

"Does that strike you as weird?"

"Kinda, yeah."

"Could the guy who planted the spook sounds have deleted her address book?"

"Oh, sure. Easy. I'm taking my Lexapro, Mr. Hodges."

"That's great, Holly. Can you tell how much Olivia used her computer?"

"Sure."

"Let me talk to Jerome while you look."

Jerome comes on and says he's sorry they haven't been able to find more.

"No, no, you've done great. When you tossed her desk, you didn't find a *physical* address book?"

"Uh-uh, but lots of people don't bother with them anymore — they keep all their contacts on their computers and phones. You know that, right?"

Hodges supposes he *should* know it, but the world is moving too fast for him these days. He doesn't even know how to program his DVR.

"Hang on, Holly wants to talk to you again."

"You and Holly are getting along pretty well, huh?"

"We're cool. Here she is."

"Olivia had all kinds of programs and website faves," Holly says. "She was big on Hulu and Huffpo. And her search history . . . it looks to me like she spent even more time browsing than I do, and I'm online a *lot.*"

"Holly, why would a person who really depends on her computer not have a service card handy?"

"Because the guy snuck in and took it after she was dead," Holly says promptly.

"Maybe, but think of the risk — especially with the neighborhood security service keeping an eye on things. He'd have to know the gate code, the burglar alarm code . . . and even then he'd need a housekey . . ." He trails off.

"Mr. Hodges? Are you still there?"

"Yes. And go ahead and call me Bill."

But she won't. Maybe she can't. "Mr. Hodges, is he a master criminal? Like in James Bond?"

"I think just crazy." And *because* he's crazy, the risk might not matter to him. Look at the risk he took at City Center, plowing into that crowd of people.

It still doesn't ring right.

"Give me Jerome again, will you?"

She does, and Hodges tells him it's time to get out before Aunt Charlotte and Uncle Henry come back and catch him computer-canoodling with Holly.

"What are you going to do, Bill?"

He looks out at the street, where twilight has started to deepen the colors of the day. It's close to seven o'clock. "Sleep on it," he says.

31

Before going to bed, Hodges spends four hours in front of the TV, watching shows that go in his eyes just fine but disintegrate before reaching his brain. He tries to think about nothing, because that's how you open the door so the right idea can come in. The right idea always arrives as a result of the right connection, and there *is* a connection waiting to be made; he feels it. Maybe more than one. He will not let Janey into his thoughts. Later, yes, but for now all she can do is jam his gears.

Olivia Trelawney's computer is the crux of the matter. It was rigged with spook sounds, and the most likely suspect is her I-T guy. So why didn't she have his card? He could delete her computer address book at long distance — and Hodges is betting he did — but did he break into her house to steal a fucking *business card* after she was dead?

He gets a call from a newspaper reporter. Then from a Channel Six guy. After the third call from someone in the media, Hodges shuts his phone down. He doesn't know who spilled his cell number, but he hopes the person was well paid for the info.

Something else keeps coming into his mind, something that has nothing to do with anything: *She thinks they walk among us.*

A refresher glance through his notes allows him to put his finger on who said that to him: Mr. Bowfinger, the greeting-card writer. He and Bowfinger were sitting in lawn chairs, and Hodges remembers being grateful for the shade. This was while he was doing his canvass, looking for anyone who might have seen a suspicious vehicle cruising the street.

She thinks they walk among us.

Bowfinger was talking about Mrs. Melbourne across the street. Mrs. Melbourne who belongs to an organization of UFO nuts called NICAP, the National Investigations Committee on Aerial Phenomena.

Hodges decides it's just one of those echoes, like a snatch of pop music, that can start resounding in an overstressed brain. He gets undressed and goes to bed and Janey comes, Janey wrinkling her nose and saying *yeah,* and for the first time since childhood, he actually cries himself to sleep.

He wakes up in the small hours of Thursday morning, takes a leak, starts back to bed, and stops, eyes widening. What he's been looking for — the connection — is suddenly there, big as life.

You didn't bother keeping a business card if you didn't *need* one.

Say the guy wasn't an independent, running a little business out of his house, but someone who worked for a *company.* If that was the case, you could call the company number any time you needed him, because it would be something easy to remember, like 555-9999, or whatever the numbers were that spelled out COMPUTE.

If he worked for a company, he'd make his repair calls in a company car.

Hodges goes back to bed, sure that sleep will elude him this time, but it doesn't.

He thinks, *If he had enough explosive to blow up my car, he must have more.*

Then he's under again.

He dreams about Janey.

KISSES ON THE MIDWAY

1

Hodges is up at six A.M. on Thursday morning and makes himself a big breakfast: two eggs, four slices of bacon, four slices of toast. He doesn't want it, but he forces himself to eat every bite, telling himself it's body gasoline. He might get a chance to eat again today, but he might not. Both in the shower and as he chews his way resolutely through his big breakfast (no one to watch his weight for now), a thought keeps recurring to him, the same one he went to sleep with the night before. It's like a haunting.

Just how much explosive?

This leads to other unpleasant considerations. Like how the guy — the *perk* — means to use it. And when.

He comes to a decision: today is the last day. He wants to track Mr. Mercedes down himself, and confront him. Kill him? No, not that (*probably* not that), but beating the shit out of him would be *excellent.* For Olivia. For Janey. For Janice and Patricia Cray. For all the other people Mr. Mercedes killed and maimed at City Center the year before. People so desperate for jobs they got up in the middle of the night and stood waiting in a dank fog for the doors to open. Lost lives. Lost hopes. Lost *souls.*

So yes, he wants the sonofabitch. But if he can't nail him today, he'll turn the whole thing over to Pete Huntley and Izzy Jaynes and take the consequences . . . which, he knows, may well lead to some jail time. It doesn't matter. He's got plenty on his conscience already, but he guesses it can bear a little more weight. Not another mass killing, though. That would destroy what little of him there is left.

He decides to give himself until eight o'clock tonight; that's the line in the sand. He can do as much in those thirteen hours as Pete and Izzy. Probably more, because he's not constrained by routine or procedure. Today he will carry his father's M&P .38. And the Happy Slapper — that, too.

The Slapper goes in the right front pocket of his sportcoat, the revolver under his left arm. In his study, he grabs his Mr. Mercedes file — it's quite fat now — and takes it back to the kitchen. While he reads through it again, he uses the remote to fire up the TV on the counter and tunes in *Morning at Seven* on Channel Six. He's almost relieved to see that a crane has toppled over down by the lakeshore, half-sinking a barge filled with chemicals. He doesn't want the lake any more polluted than it already is (assuming that's possible), but the spill has pushed the car-bomb story back to second place. That's the good news. The bad is that he's identified as the detective, now retired, who was the lead investigator of the City Center Massacre task force, and the woman killed in the car-bombing is identified as Olivia Trelawney's sister. There's a still photo of him and Janey standing outside the Soames Funeral Home, taken by God knows who.

"Police are not saying if there's a connection to last year's mass killing at City Center," the newscaster says gravely, "but it's worth noting that the perpetrator of that crime has as yet not been caught. In other crime news, Donald Davis is expected to be arraigned . . ."

Hodges no longer gives Shit One about Donald Davis. He kills the TV and returns to the notes on his yellow legal pad. He's still going through them when his phone rings — not the cell (although today he's carrying it), but the one on the wall. It's Pete Huntley.

"You're up with the birdies," Pete says.

"Good detective work. How can I help you?"

"We had an interesting interview yesterday with Henry Sirois and Charlotte Gibney. You know, Janelle Patterson's aunt and uncle?"

Hodges waits for it.

"The aunt was especially fascinating. She thinks Izzy was right, and you and Patterson were a lot more than just acquaintances. She thinks you were very good friends."

"Say what you mean, Pete."

"Making the beast with two backs. Laying some pipe. Slicing the cake. Hiding the salami. Doing the horizontal b—"

"I think I get it. Let me tell you something about Aunt Charlotte, okay? If she saw a photo of Justin Bieber talking to Queen Elizabeth, she'd tell you the Beeb was tapping her. 'Just look at their eyes,' she'd say."

"So you weren't."

"No."

"I'll take that on a try-out basis — mostly for old times' sake — but I still want to know what you're hiding. Because this stinks."

"Read my lips: not . . . hiding . . . *anything.*"

Silence from the other end. Pete is waiting for Hodges to grow uncomfortable and break it, for the moment forgetting who taught him that trick.

At last he gives up. "I think you're digging yourself a hole, Billy. My advice is to drop the shovel before you're in too deep to climb out."

"Thanks, partner. Always good to get life-lessons at quarter past seven in the morning."

"I want to interview you again this afternoon. And this time I may have to read you the words."

The Miranda warning is what he means.

"Happy to make that work. Call me on my cell."

"Really? Since you retired, you never carry it."

"I'm carrying it today." Yes indeed. Because for the next twelve or fourteen hours, he's totally unretired.

He ends the call and goes back to his notes, wetting the tip of his index finger each time he turns a page. He circles a name: Radney Peeples. The Vigilant Guard Service guy he talked to out in Sugar Heights. If Peeples is even halfway doing his job, he may hold the key to Mr. Mercedes. But there's no chance he won't remember Hodges, not after Hodges first braced him for his company ID and then questioned him. And he'll know that today Hodges is big news. There's time to think about how to solve the problem; Hodges doesn't want to call Vigilant until regular business hours. Because the call has to look like ordinary routine.

The next call he receives — on his cell this time — is from Aunt Charlotte. Hodges isn't surprised to hear from her, but that doesn't mean he's pleased.

"I don't know what to do!" she cries. "You have to help me, Mr. Hodges!"

"Don't know what to do about what?"

"The *body*! Janelle's *body*! I don't even

know where it *is*!"

Hodges gets a beep and checks the incoming number.

"Mrs. Gibney, I have another call and I have to take it."

"I don't see why you can't —"

"Janey's not going anywhere, so just stand by. I'll call you back."

He cuts her off in the middle of a protesting squawk and goes to Jerome.

"I thought you might need a chauffeur today," Jerome says. "Considering your current situation."

For a moment Hodges doesn't know what the kid is talking about, then remembers that his Toyota has been reduced to charred fragments. What remains of it is now in the custody of the PD's Forensics Department, where later today men in white coats will be going over it to determine what kind of explosive was used to blow it up. He got home last night in a taxi. He *will* need a ride. And, he realizes, Jerome may be useful in another way.

"That would be good," he says, "but what about school?"

"I'm carrying a 3.9 average," Jerome says patiently. "I'm also working for Citizens United and team-teaching a computer class for disadvantaged kids. I can afford to skip a day. And I already cleared it with my mom and dad. They just asked me to ask you if anyone else was going to try to blow you up."

"Actually, that's not out of the question."

"Hang on a second." Faintly, Hodges hears Jerome calling: "He says no one will."

In spite of everything, Hodges has to smile.

"I'll be there double-quick," Jerome says.

"Don't break any speed laws. Nine o'clock will be fine. Use the time to practice your thespian skills."

"Really? What role am I thesping?"

"Law office paralegal," Hodges says. "And thanks, Jerome."

He breaks the connection, goes into his study, boots up his computer, and searches for a local lawyer named Schron. It's an unusual name and he finds it with no trouble. He notes down the firm and Schron's first name, which happens to be George. Then he returns to the kitchen and calls Aunt Charlotte.

"Hodges," he says. "Back atcha."

"I don't appreciate being hung up on, Mr. Hodges."

"No more than I appreciate you telling my old partner that I was fucking your niece."

He hears a shocked gasp, followed by silence. He almost hopes she'll hang up. When she doesn't, he tells her what she needs to know.

"Janey's remains will be at the Huron County Morgue. You won't be able to take possession today. Probably not tomorrow, either. There'll have to be an autopsy, which is absurd given the cause of death, but it's protocol."

"You don't understand! I have *plane* reservations!"

Hodges looks out his kitchen window and counts slowly to five.

"Mr. Hodges? Are you still there?"

"As I see it, you have two choices, Mrs. Gibney. One is to stay here and do the right thing. The other is to use your reservation, fly home, and let the city do it."

Aunt Charlotte begins to snivel. "I saw the way you were looking at her, and the way she was looking at you. All I did was answer the woman cop's questions."

"And with great alacrity, I have no doubt."

"With *what*?"

He sighs. "Let's drop it. I suggest you and your brother visit the County Morgue in person. Don't call ahead, let them see your faces. Talk to Dr. Galworthy. If Galworthy's not there, talk to Dr. Patel. If you ask them in person to expedite matters — and if you can manage to be nice about it — they'll give you as much help as they can. Use my name. I go back to the early nineties with both of them."

"We'd have to leave Holly again," Aunt Charlotte says. "She's locked herself in her room. She's clicking away on her laptop and won't come out."

Hodges discovers he's pulling his hair and makes himself stop. "How old is your daughter?"

A long pause. "Forty-five."

"Then you can probably get away with not hiring a sitter." He tries to suppress what comes next, and can't quite manage it. "Think of the money you'll save."

"I can hardly expect you to understand Holly's situation, Mr. Hodges. As well as being mentally unstable, my daughter is very sensitive."

Hodges thinks: That must make you especially difficult for her. This time he manages not to say it.

"Mr. Hodges?"

"Still here."

"You don't happen to know if Janelle left a will, do you?"

He hangs up.

2

Brady spends a long time in the motel shower with the lights off. He likes the womblike warmth and the steady drumming sound. He also likes the darkness, and it's good that he does because soon he'll have all he ever wanted. He'd like to believe there's going to be a tender mother-and-child reunion — perhaps even one of the mother-and-lover type — but in his heart he doesn't. He can pretend, but . . . no.

Just darkness.

He's not worried about God, or about spending eternity being slow-roasted for his crimes. There's no heaven and no hell. Anyone with half a brain knows those things don't exist. How cruel would a supreme being have to be to make a world as fucked-up as this one? Even if the vengeful God of the televangelists and child-molesting blackrobes *did* exist, how could that thunderbolt-thrower possibly blame Brady for the things he's done? Did Brady Hartsfield grab his father's hand and wrap it around the live power line that electrocuted him? No. Did he shove that apple slice down Frankie's throat? No. Was he the one who talked on and on about how the money was going to run out and they'd end up living in a homeless shelter? No. Did he cook up a poisoned hamburger and say, *Eat this, Ma, it's delicious?*

Can he be blamed for striking out at the world that has made him what he is?

Brady thinks not.

He muses on the terrorists who brought down the World Trade Center (he muses on them often). Those clowns actually thought they were going to paradise, where they'd live in a kind of eternal luxury hotel being serviced by gorgeous young virgins. Pretty funny, and the best part? The joke was on them . . . not that they knew it. What they got was a momentary view of all those windows and a final flash of light. After that, they and their thousands of victims were just gone. Poof. Seeya later, alligator. Off you go, killers and killed alike, off you go into the universal null set that surrounds one lonely blue planet and all its mindlessly bustling denizens. Every religion lies. Every moral precept is a delusion. Even the stars are a mirage. The truth is darkness, and the only thing that matters is making a statement before one enters it. Cutting the skin of the world and leaving a scar. That's all history is, after all: scar tissue.

3

Brady dresses and drives to a twenty-four-hour drugstore near the airport. He's seen in the bathroom mirror that his mother's electric razor left a lot to be desired; his skull needs more maintenance. He gets disposable razors and shaving cream. He grabs more batteries, because you can never have enough. He also picks up a pair of clear glass spectacles from a spinner rack. He chooses hornrims because they give him a studently look. Or so it seems to him.

On his way to the checkout, he stops at a cardboard stand-up display featuring the four clean-cut boys in 'Round Here. The copy reads GET YOUR GEAR ON FOR THE BIG SHOW JUNE 3RD! Only someone has crossed out JUNE 3RD and written 2NITE below it.

Although Brady usually takes an M tee-shirt — he's always been slim — he picks out an XL and adds it to the rest of his swag. No need to stand in line; this early he's the only customer.

"Going to the show tonight?" the checkout girl asks.

Brady gives her a big grin. "I sure am."

On his way back to the motel, Brady starts to think about his car. To *worry* about his car. The Ralph Jones alias is all very fine, but the Subaru is registered to Brady Hartsfield. If the Det-Ret discovers his name and tells five-oh, that could be a problem. The motel is safe enough — they no longer ask for plate numbers, just a driver's license — but the car is not.

The Det-Ret's not close, Brady tells himself. He was just trying to freak you out.

Except maybe not. This particular Det solved a lot of cases before he was Ret, and some of those skills still seem to be there.

Instead of going directly back to the Motel 6, Brady swings into the airport, takes a ticket, and leaves the Subaru in long-term parking. He'll need it tonight, but for now it's fine where it is.

He glances at his watch. Ten to nine. Eleven hours until the showtime, he thinks. Maybe twelve hours until the darkness. Could be less; could be more. But not *much* more.

He puts on his new glasses and carries his purchases the half-mile back to the motel, whistling.

4

When Hodges opens his front door, the first thing Jerome keys on is the .38 in the shoulder rig. “You’re not going to shoot anyone with that, are you?”

“I doubt it. Think of it as a good luck charm. It was my father’s. And I have a permit to carry concealed, if that was on your mind.”

“What’s on my mind,” Jerome says, “is whether or not it’s loaded.”

“Of course it is. What did you think I was going to do if I did have to use it? Throw it?”

Jerome sighs and ruffles his cap of dark hair. “This is getting heavy.”

“Want out? If you do, you’re taillights. Right this minute. I can still rent a car.”

“No, I’m good. It’s you I’m wondering about. Those aren’t bags under your eyes, they’re suitcases.”

“I’ll be okay. Today is it for me, anyway. If I can’t track this guy down by nightfall, I’m going to see my old partner and tell him everything.”

“How much trouble will you be in?”

“Don’t know and don’t much care.”

"How much trouble will *I* be in?"

"None. If I couldn't guarantee that, you'd be in period one algebra right now."

Jerome gives him a pitying look. "Algebra was four years ago. Tell me what I can do."

Hodges does so. Jerome is willing but doubtful.

"Last month — you can't ever tell my folks this — a bunch of us tried to get into Punch and Judy, that new dance club downtown? The guy at the door didn't even look at my beautiful fake ID, just waved me out of the line and told me to go get a milkshake."

Hodges says, "I'm not surprised. Your face is seventeen, but fortunately for me, your voice is at least twenty-five." He slides Jerome a piece of paper with a phone number written on it. "Make the call."

Jerome tells the Vigilant Guard Service receptionist who answers that he is Martin Lounsbury, a paralegal at the firm of Canton, Silver, Makepeace, and Jackson. He says he's currently working with George Schron, a junior partner assigned to tie up a few loose ends concerning the estate of the late Olivia Trelawney. One of those loose ends has to do with Mrs. Trelawney's computer. His job for the day is to locate the I-T specialist who worked on the machine, and it seems possible that one of the Vigilant employees in the Sugar Heights area may be able to help him locate the gentleman.

Hodges makes a thumb-and-forefinger circle to indicate Jerome is doing well, and passes him a note.

Jerome reads it and says, "One of Mrs. Trelawney's neighbors, Mrs. Helen Wilcox, mentioned a Rodney Peeples?" He listens, then nods. "*Radney,* I see. What an interesting name. Perhaps he could call me, if it's not too much trouble? My boss is a bit of a tyrant, and I'm really under the gun here." He listens. "Yes? Oh, that's great. Thanks so much." He gives the receptionist the numbers of his cell and Hodges's landline, then hangs up and wipes make-believe sweat from his forehead. "I'm glad that's over. Whoo!"

"You did fine," Hodges assures him.

"What if she calls Canton, Silver, and Whoozis to check? And finds out they never heard of Martin Lounsbury?"

"Her job is to pass messages on, not investigate them."

"What if the Peeples guy checks?"

Hodges doesn't think he will. He thinks the name Helen Wilcox will stop him. When he talked to Peeples that day outside the Sugar Heights mansion, Hodges caught a strong vibe that Peeples's relationship with Helen Wilcox was more than just platonic. Maybe a little more, maybe a lot. He thinks Peeples will give Martin Lounsbury what he wants so he'll go away.

"What do we do now?" Jerome asks.

What they do is something Hodges spent at least half his career doing. "Wait."

"How long?"

"Until Peeples or some other security grunt calls." Because right now Vigilant Guard Service is looking like his best lead. If it doesn't pan out, they'll have to go out to Sugar Heights and start interviewing neighbors. Not a prospect he relishes, given his current news-cycle celebrity.

In the meantime, he finds himself thinking again of Mr. Bowfinger, and Mrs. Melbourne, the slightly crackers woman who lives across the street from him. With her talk about mysterious black SUVs and her interest in flying saucers, Mrs. Melbourne could have been a quirky supporting character in an old Alfred Hitchcock movie.

She thinks they walk among us, Bowfinger had said, giving his eyebrows a satirical wiggle, and why in God's name should that keep bouncing around in Hodges's head?

It's ten of ten when Jerome's cell rings. The little snatch of AC/DC's "Hells Bells" makes them both jump. Jerome grabs it.

"It says CALL BLOCKED. What should I do, Bill?"

"Take it. It's him. And remember who you are."

Jerome opens the line and says, "Hello, this is Martin Lounsbury." Listens. "Oh, hello,

Mr. Peeples. Thanks so much for getting back to me."

Hodges scribbles a fresh note and pushes it across the table. Jerome scans it quickly.

"Uh-huh . . . yes . . . . Mrs. Wilcox speaks very highly of you. Very highly, indeed. But my job has to do with the late Mrs. Trelawney. We can't finish clearing her estate until we can inventory her computer, and . . . yes, I know it's been over six months. Terrible how slowly these things move, isn't it? We had a client last year who actually had to apply for food stamps, even though he had a seventy-thousand-dollar bequest pending."

Don't over-butter the muffin, Jerome, Hodges thinks. His heart is hammering in his chest.

"No, it's nothing like that. I just need the name of the fellow who worked on it for her. The rest is up to my boss." Jerome listens, eyebrows pulling together. "You can't? Oh, that's a sha—"

But Peeples is talking again. The sweat on Jerome's brow is no longer imaginary. He reaches across the table, grabs Hodges's pen, and begins to scribble. While he writes, he keeps up a steady stream of *uh-huh*s and *okay*s and *I see*s. Finally:

"Hey, that's great. Totally great. I'm sure Mr. Schron can roll with this. You've been a big help, Mr. Peeples. So I'll just . . ." He listens some more. "Yes, it's a terrible thing. I believe Mr. Schron is dealing with some . . . uh . . . some aspects of that even as we speak, but I really don't know anythi . . . you did? Wow! Mr. Peeples, you've been great. Yes, I'll mention that. I certainly will. Thanks, Mr. Peeples."

He breaks the connection and puts the heels of his hands to his temples, as if to quell a headache.

"Man, that was *intense.* He wanted to talk about what happened yesterday. And to say that I should tell Janey's relatives that Vigilant stands ready to help in any way they can."

"That's great, I'm sure he'll get an attaboy in his file, but —"

"He also said he talked to the guy whose car got blown up. He saw your picture on the news this morning."

Hodges isn't surprised and at this minute doesn't care. "Did you get a name? Tell me you got a name."

"Not of the I-T guy, but I did get the name of the company he works for. It's called Cyber Patrol. Peeples says they drive around in green VW Beetles. He says they're in Sugar Heights all the time, and you can't miss them. He's seen a woman and a man driving them, both probably in their twenties. He called the woman 'kinda dykey.' "

Hodges has never even considered the idea that Mr. Mercedes might actually be Ms. Mercedes. He supposes it's technically possible, and it would make a neat solution for an Agatha Christie novel, but this is real life.

"Did he say what the guy looked like?"

Jerome shakes his head.

"Come on in my study. You can drive the computer while I co-pilot."

In less than a minute they are looking at a rank of three green VW Beetles with CYBER PATROL printed on the sides. It's not an independent company, but part of a chain called Discount Electronix with one big-box store in the city. It's located in the Birch Hill Mall.

"Man, I've shopped there," Jerome says. "I've shopped there *lots* of times. Bought video games, computer components, a bunch of chop-sockey DVDs on sale."

Below the photo of the Beetles is a line reading MEET THE EXPERTS. Hodges reaches over Jerome's shoulder and clicks on it. Three photos appear. One is of a narrow-faced girl with dirty-blond hair. Number two is a chubby guy wearing John Lennon specs and looking serious. Number three is a generically handsome fellow with neatly combed brown hair and a bland say-cheese smile. The names beneath are FREDDI LINKLATTER, ANTHONY FROBISHER, and BRADY HARTSFIELD.

"What now?" Jerome asks.

"Now we take a ride. I just have to grab something first."

Hodges goes into his bedroom and punches the combo of the small safe in the closet. Inside, along with a couple of insurance policies and a few other financial papers, is a rubber-banded stack of laminated cards like the one he currently carries in his wallet. City cops are issued new IDs every two years, and each time he got a new one, he stored the old one in here. The crucial difference is that none of the old ones have RETIRED stamped across them in red. He takes out the one that expired in December of 2008, removes his final ID from his wallet, and replaces it with the one from his safe. Of course flashing it is another crime — State Law 190.25, impersonating a police officer, a Class E felony punishable by a $25,000 fine, five years in jail, or both — but he's far beyond worrying about such things.

He tucks his wallet away in his back pocket, starts to close the safe, then re-thinks. There's something else in there he might want: a small flat leather case that looks like the sort of thing a frequent flier might keep his passport in. This was also his father's.

Hodges slips it into his pocket with the Happy Slapper.

5

After cleansing the stubble on his skull and donning his new plain glass specs, Brady strolls down to the Motel 6 office and pays for another night. Then he returns to his room and unfolds the wheelchair he bought on Wednesday. It was pricey, but what the hell. Money is no longer an issue for him.

He puts the explosives-laden ASS PARKING cushion on the seat of the chair, then slits the lining of the pocket on the back and inserts several more blocks of his homemade plastic explosive. Each block has been fitted with a lead azide blasting plug. He gathers the connecting wires together with a metal clip. Their ends are stripped down to the bare copper, and this afternoon he'll braid them into a single master wire.

The actual detonator will be Thing Two.

One by one, he tapes Baggies filled with ball bearings beneath the wheelchair's seat, using crisscrossings of filament tape to hold them in place. When he's done, he sits on the end of the bed, looking solemnly at his handiwork. He really has no idea if he'll be able to get this rolling bomb into the Mingo Auditorium . . . but he had no idea if he'd be able to escape from City Center after the deed was done, either. That worked out; maybe this will, too. After all, this time he won't have to escape, and that's half the battle. Even if they get wise and try to grab him, the hallway will be crammed with concertgoers, and his score will be a lot higher than eight.

Out with a bang, Brady thinks. Out with a bang, and fuck you, Detective Hodges. Fuck you very much.

He lies down on the bed and thinks about masturbating. Probably he should while he's still got a prick to masturbate with. But before he can even unsnap his Levi's, he's fallen asleep.

On the night table beside him stands a framed picture. Frankie smiles from it, holding Sammy the Fire Truck in his lap.

6

It's nearly eleven A.M. when Hodges and Jerome arrive at Birch Hill Mall. There's plenty of parking, and Jerome pulls his Wrangler into a spot directly in front of Discount Electronix, where all the windows are sporting big SALE signs. A teenage girl is sitting on the curb in front of the store, knees together and feet apart, bent studiously over an iPad. A cigarette smolders between the fingers of her left hand. It's only as they approach that Hodges sees there's gray in the teenager's hair. His heart sinks.

"Holly?" Jerome says, at the same time Hodges says, "What in the hell are you doing here?"

"I was pretty sure you'd figure it out," she says, butting her butt and standing up, "but I was starting to worry. I was going to call you if you weren't here by eleven-thirty. I'm taking my Lexapro, Mr. Hodges."

"So you said, and I'm glad to hear it. Now answer my question and tell me what you're doing here."

Her lips tremble, and although she managed eye contact to begin with, her gaze now sinks to her loafers. Hodges isn't surprised he took her for a teenager at first, because in many ways she still is one, her growth stunted by insecurities and by the strain of keeping her balance on the emotional highwire she's been walking all her life.

"Are you mad at me? *Please* don't be mad at me."

"We're not mad," Jerome says. "Just surprised."

Shocked is more like it, Hodges thinks.

"I spent the morning in my room, browsing the local I-T community, but it's like we thought, there are hundreds of them. Mom and Uncle Henry went out to talk to people. About Janey, I think. I guess there'll have to be another funeral, but I hate to think about what will be in the coffin. It just makes me cry and cry."

And yes, big tears are rolling down her cheeks. Jerome puts an arm around her. She gives him a shy grateful glance.

"Sometimes it's hard for me to think when my mother is around. It's like she puts interference in my head. I guess that makes me sound crazy."

"Not to me," Jerome says. "I feel the same way about my sister. Especially when she plays her damn boy-band CDs."

"When they were gone and the house was quiet, I got an idea. I went back down to Olivia's computer and looked at her email."

Jerome slaps his forehead. "Shit! I never even thought of checking her mail."

"Don't worry, there wasn't any. She had three accounts — Mac Mail, Gmail, and AO-Hell — but all three folders were empty. Maybe she deleted them herself, but I don't think so because —"

"Because her desktop and hard drive were full of stuff," Jerome says.

"That's right. She has *The Bridge on the River Kwai* in her iTunes. I've never seen that. I might check it out if I get a chance."

Hodges glances toward Discount Electronix. With the sun glaring on the windows it's impossible to tell if anyone's watching them. He feels exposed out here, like a bug on a rock. "Let's take a little stroll," he says, and leads them toward Savoy Shoes, Barnes & Noble, and Whitey's Happy Frogurt Shoppe.

Jerome says, "Come on, Holly, give. You're drivin me crazy here."

That makes her smile, which makes her look older. More her age. And once they're away from the big Discount Electronix show windows, Hodges feels better. It's obvious to him that Jerome is delighted with her, and he feels the same (more or less in spite of himself), but it's humbling to find he's been scooped by a Lexapro-dependent neurotic.

"He forgot to take off his SPOOK program, so I thought maybe he forgot to empty her junk mail as well, and I was right. She had like four dozen emails from Discount Electronix. Some of them were sales notices — like the one they're having now, although I bet the only DVDs they have left aren't much good, they're probably Korean or something — and some of them were coupons for twenty percent off. She also had coupons for thirty percent off. The thirty percent coupons were for her next Cyber Patrol out-call." She shrugs. "And here I am."

Jerome stares at her. "That's all it took? Just a peek into her junk mail folder?"

"Don't be so surprised," Hodges says. "All it took to catch the Son of Sam was a parking ticket."

"I walked around back while I was waiting for you," Holly says. "Their Web page says there are only three I-Ts in the Cyber Patrol, and there are three of those green Beetles back there. So I guess the guy is working today. Are you going to arrest him, Mr. Hodges?" She's biting her lips again. "What if he fights? I don't want you to get hurt."

Hodges is thinking hard. Three computer

techs in the Cyber Patrol: Frobisher, Hartsfield, and Linklatter, the skinny blond woman. He's almost positive it will turn out to be Frobisher or Hartsfield, and whichever one it is won't be prepared to see **kermitfrog19** walking through the door. Even if Mr. Mercedes doesn't run, he won't be able to hide the initial shock of recognition.

"I'm going in. You two are staying here."

"Going in with no backup?" Jerome asks. "Gee, Bill, I don't think that's very sma—"

"I'll be all right, I've got the element of surprise going for me, but if I'm not back out in ten minutes, call nine-one-one. Got it?"

"Yes."

Hodges points at Holly. "You stay close to Jerome. No more lone-wolf investigations." I should talk, he thinks.

She nods humbly, and Hodges walks away before they can engage him in further discussion. As he approaches the doors of Discount Electronix, he unbuttons his sportcoat. The weight of his father's gun against his ribcage is comforting.

7

As they watch Hodges enter the electronics store, a question occurs to Jerome. "Holly, how did you get here? Taxi?"

She shakes her head and points into the parking lot. There, parked three rows back from Jerome's Wrangler, is a gray Mercedes sedan. "It was in the garage." She notes Jerome's slack-jawed amazement and immediately becomes defensive. "I *can* drive, you know. I have a valid driver's license. I've never had an accident, and I have Safe Driver's Insurance. From Allstate. Do you know that the man who does the Allstate ads on TV used to be the president on *24*?"

"That's the car . . ."

She frowns, puzzled. "What's the big deal, Jerome? It was in the garage and the keys were in a basket in the front hall. So what's the big fat deal?"

The dents are gone, he notes. The headlights and windshield have been replaced. It looks as good as new. You'd never know it was used to kill people.

"Jerome? Do you think Olivia would mind?"

"No," he says. "Probably not." He is imagining that grille covered with blood. Pieces of shredded cloth dangling from it.

"It wouldn't start at first, the battery was dead, but she had one of those portable jump-stations, and I knew how to use it because my father had one. Jerome, if Mr. Hodges doesn't make an arrest, could we walk down to the frogurt place?"

He barely hears her. He's still staring at the Mercedes. They returned it to her, he thinks. Well, of course they did. It was her property, after all. She even got the damage repaired.

But he'd be willing to bet she never drove it again. If there were spooks — real ones — they'd be in there. Probably screaming.

"Jerome? Earth to Jerome."

"Huh?"

"If everything turns out okay, let's get frogurt. I was sitting in the sun and waiting for you guys and I'm awfully hot. I'll treat. I'd really like ice cream, but . . ."

He doesn't hear the rest. He's thinking Ice cream.

The click in his head is so loud he actually winces, and all at once he knows why one of the Cyber Patrol faces on Hodges's computer looked familiar to him. The strength goes out of his legs and he leans against one of the walkway support posts to keep from falling.

"Oh my God," he says.

"What's wrong?" She shakes his arm, chewing her lips frantically. "What's *wrong*? Are you sick, Jerome?"

But at first he can only say it again: "Oh my God."

8

Hodges thinks that the Birch Hill Mall Discount Electronix looks like an enterprise with about three months to live. Many of the shelves are empty, and the stock that's left has a disconsolate, neglected look. Almost all of the browsers are in the Home Entertainment department, where fluorescent pink signs proclaim WOW! DVD BLOWOUT! ALL DISCS 50% OFF! EVEN BLURAY! Although there are ten checkout lines, only three are open, staffed by women in blue dusters with the yellow DE logo on them. Two of these women are looking out the window; the third is reading *Twilight.* A couple of other employees are wandering the aisles, doing a lot of nothing much.

Hodges doesn't want any of them, but he sees two of the three he *does* want. Anthony Frobisher, he of the John Lennon specs, is talking to a customer who has a shopping basket full of discounted DVDs in one hand and a clutch of coupons in the other. Frobisher's tie suggests that he might be the store manager as well as a Cyber Patrolman. The narrow-faced girl with the dirty-blond hair is at the back of the store, seated at a computer. There's a cigarette parked behind one ear.

Hodges strolls up the center aisle of the DVD BLOWOUT. Frobisher looks at him and raises a finger to say *Be with you soon.* Hodges smiles and gives him a little *I'm okay* wave. Frobisher returns to the customer with the coupons. No recognition there. Hodges walks on to the back of the store.

The dirty blond looks up at him, then back at the screen of the computer she's using. No recognition from her, either. She's not wearing a Discount Electronix shirt; hers says

WHEN I WANT MY OPINION, I'LL GIVE IT TO YOU. He sees she's playing an updated version of Pitfall!, a cruder version of which fascinated his daughter Alison a quarter of a century before. Everything that goes around comes around, Hodges thinks. A Zen concept for sure.

"Unless you've got a computer question, talk to Tones," she says. "I only do crunchers."

"Tones would be Anthony Frobisher?"

"Yeah. Mr. Spiffy in the tie."

"You'd be Freddi Linklatter. Of the Cyber Patrol."

"Yeah." She pauses Pitfall Harry in mid-jump over a coiled snake in order to give him a closer inspection. What she sees is Hodges's police ID, with his thumb strategically placed to hide its year of expiration.

"Oooh," she says, and holds out her hands with the twig-thin wrists together. "I'm a bad, bad girl and handcuffs are what I deserve. Whip me, beat me, make me write bad checks."

Hodges gives a brief smile and tucks his ID away. "Isn't Brady Hartsfield the third member of your happy band? I don't see him."

"Out with the flu. *He* says. Want my best guess?"

"Hit me."

"I think maybe he finally had to put dear old Mom in rehab. He says she drinks and he has to take care of her most of the time. Which is probably why he's never had a gee-eff. You know what that is, right?"

"I'm pretty sure, yeah."

She examines him with bright and mordant interest. "Is Brady in trouble? I wouldn't be surprised. He's a little on the, you know, peekee-*yoolier* side."

"I just need to speak to him."

Anthony Frobisher — Tones — joins them. "May I help you, sir?"

"It's five-oh," Freddi says. She gives Frobisher a wide smile that exposes small teeth badly in need of cleaning. "He found out about the meth lab in the back."

"Can it, Freddi."

She makes an extravagant lip-zipping gesture, finishing with the twist of an invisible key, but doesn't go back to her game.

In Hodges's pocket, his cell phone rings. He silences it with his thumb.

"I'm Detective Bill Hodges, Mr. Frobisher. I have a few questions for Brady Hartsfield."

"He's out with the flu. What did he do?"

"Tones is a poet and don't know it," Freddi Linklatter observes. "Although his feet show it, because they're Longfel—"

"Shut up, Freddi. For the last time."

"Can I have his address, please?"

"Of course. I'll get it for you."

"Can I un-shut for a minute?" Freddi asks.

Hodges nods. She punches a key on her

computer. Pitfall Harry is replaced by a spread-sheet headed STORE PERSONNEL.

"Presto," she says. "Forty-nine Elm Street. That's on the —"

"North Side, yeah," Hodges says. "Thank you both. You've been very helpful."

As he leaves, Freddi Linklatter calls after him, "It's something with his mom, betcha anything. He's freaky about her."

9

Hodges has no more than stepped out into the bright sunshine when Jerome almost tackles him. Holly lurks just behind. She's stopped biting her lips and gone to her fingernails, which look badly abused. "I called you," Jerome says. "Why didn't you pick up?"

"I was asking questions. What's got you all white-eyed?"

"Is Hartsfield in there?"

Hodges is too surprised to reply.

"Oh, it's him," Jerome says. "Got to be. You were right about him watching you, and I know how. It's like that Hawthorne story about the purloined letter. Hide in plain sight."

Holly stops munching her fingernails long enough to say, "Poe wrote that story. Don't they teach you kids anything?"

Hodges says, "Slow down, Jerome."

Jerome takes a deep breath. "He's got two

jobs, Bill. *Two.* He must only work here until mid-afternoon or something. After that he works for Loeb's."

"Loeb's? Is that the —"

"Yeah, the ice cream company. He drives the Mr. Tastey truck. The one with the bells. I've bought stuff from him, my sister has, too. All the kids do. He's on our side of town a lot. *Brady Hartsfield is the ice cream man!*"

Hodges realizes he's heard those cheerful, tinkling bells more than a lot lately. In the spring of his depression, crashed out in his La-Z-Boy, watching afternoon TV (and sometimes playing with the gun now riding against his ribs), it seems he heard them every day. Heard them and ignored them, because only kids pay actual attention to the ice cream man. Except some deeper part of his mind didn't *completely* ignore them. It was the deep part that kept coming back to Bowfinger, and his satiric comment about Mrs. Melbourne.

She thinks they walk among us, Mr. Bowfinger said, but it hadn't been space aliens Mrs. Melbourne had been concerned about on the day Hodges had done his canvass; it had been black SUVs, and chiropractors, and the people on Hanover Street who played loud music late at night.

Also, the Mr. Tastey man.

That one looks suspicious, she had said.

This spring it seems like he's always *around,*

she had said.

A terrible question surfaces in his mind, like one of the snakes always lying in wait for Pitfall Harry: if he had paid attention to Mrs. Melbourne instead of dismissing her as a harmless crank (the way he and Pete dismissed Olivia Trelawney), would Janey still be alive? He doesn't think so, but he's never going to know for sure, and he has an idea that the question will haunt a great many sleepless nights in the weeks and months to come.

Maybe the years.

He looks out at the parking lot . . . and there he sees a ghost. A *gray* one.

He turns back to Jerome and Holly, now standing side by side, and doesn't even have to ask.

"Yeah," Jerome says. "Holly drove it here."

"The registration and the sticker decal on the license plate are both a tiny bit expired," Holly says. "Please don't be mad at me, okay? I had to come. I wanted to help, but I knew if I just called you, you'd say no."

"I'm not mad," Hodges says. In fact, he doesn't know *what* he is. He feels like he's entered a dreamworld where all the clocks run backward.

"What do we do now?" Jerome asks. "Call the cops?"

But Hodges is still not ready to let go. The young man in the picture may have a cauldron of crazy boiling away behind his bland face, but Hodges has met his share of psychopaths and knows that when they're taken by surprise, most collapse like puffballs. They're only dangerous to the unarmed and unsuspecting, like the broke folks waiting to apply for jobs on that April morning in 2009.

"Let's you and I take a ride to Mr. Hartsfield's place of residence," Hodges says. "And let's go in that." He points to the gray Mercedes.

"But . . . if he sees us pull up, won't he recognize it?"

Hodges smiles a sharklike smile Jerome Robinson has never seen before. "I certainly hope so." He holds out his hand. "May I have the key, Holly?"

Her abused lips tighten. "Yes, but I'm going."

"No way," Hodges says. "Too dangerous."

"If it's too dangerous for me, it's too dangerous for you." She won't look directly at him and her eyes keep skipping past his face, but her voice is firm. "You can make me stay, but if you do, I'll call the police and give them Brady Hartsfield's address just as soon as you're gone."

"You don't have it," Hodges says. This sounds feeble even to him.

Holly doesn't reply, which is a form of courtesy. She won't even need to go inside Discount Electronix and ask the dirty blonde;

now that they have the name, she can probably suss out the Hartsfield address from her devilish iPad.

Fuck.

"All right, you can come. But I drive, and when we get there, you and Jerome are going to stay in the car. Do you have a problem with that?"

"No, Mr. Hodges."

This time her eyes go to his face and stay there for three whole seconds. It might be a step forward. With Holly, he thinks, who knows.

10

Because of drastic budget cuts that kicked in the previous year, most city patrol cars are solo rides. This isn't the case in Lowtown. In Lowtown every shop holds a deuce, the ideal deuce containing at least one person of color, because in Lowtown the minorities are the majority. At just past noon on June third, Officers Laverty and Rosario are cruising Lowbriar Avenue about half a mile beyond the overpass where Bill Hodges once stopped a couple of trolls from robbing a shorty. Laverty is white. Rosario is Latina. Because their shop is CPC 54, they are known in the department as Toody and Muldoon, after the cops in an ancient sitcom called *Car 54, Where Are You?* Amarilis Rosario sometimes amuses her fellow blue knights at roll call by saying, "Ooh, ooh, Toody, I got an idea!" It sounds extremely cute in her Dominican accent, and always gets a laugh.

On patrol, however, she's Ms. Taking Care of Business. They both are. In Lowtown you have to be.

"The cornerboys remind me of the Blue Angels in this air show I saw once," she says now.

"Yeah?"

"They see us coming, they peel off like they're in formation. Look, there goes another one."

As they approach the intersection of Lowbriar and Strike, a kid in a Cleveland Cavaliers warmup jacket (oversized and totally superfluous on this day) suddenly decamps from the corner where he's been jiving around and heads down Strike at a trot. He looks about thirteen.

"Maybe he just remembered it's a schoolday," Laverty says.

Rosario laughs. "As if, esse."

Now they are approaching the corner of Lowbriar and Martin Luther King Avenue. MLK is the ghetto's other large thoroughfare, and this time half a dozen cornerboys decide they have business elsewhere.

"That's formation flying, all right," Laverty says. He laughs, although it's not really funny. "Listen, where do you want to eat?"

"Let's see if that wagon's on Randolph," she says. "I'm in a taco state of mind."

"Señor Taco it is," he says, "but lay off the beans, okay? We've got another four hours in this . . . huh. Check it, Rosie. That's weird."

Up ahead, a man is coming out of a storefront with a long flower box. It's weird because the storefront isn't a florist's; it's King Virtue Pawn & Loan. It's also weird because the man looks Caucasian and they are now in the blackest part of Lowtown. He's approaching a dirty white Econoline van that's standing on a yellow curb: a twenty-dollar fine. Laverty and Rosario are hungry, though, they've got their faces fixed for tacos with that nice hot picante sauce Señor Taco keeps on the counter, and they might have let it go. Probably would have.

But.

With David Berkowitz, it was a parking ticket. With Ted Bundy, it was a busted taillight. Today a florist's box with badly folded flaps is all it takes to change the world. As the guy fumbles for the keys to his old van (not even Emperor Ming of Mongo would leave his vehicle unlocked in Lowtown), the box tilts downward. The end comes open and something slides partway out.

The guy catches it and shoves it back in before it can fall into the street, but Jason Laverty spent two tours in Iraq and he knows an RPG launcher when he sees it. He flips on the blues and hooks in behind the guy, who looks around with a startled expression.

"Sidearm!" he snaps at his partner. "Get it out!"

They fly out the doors, double-fisted Glocks pointing at the sky.

"Drop the box, sir!" Laverty shouts. "Drop the box and put your hands on the van! Lean forward. Do it now!"

For a moment the guy — he's about forty, olive-skinned, round-shouldered — hugs the florist's box tighter against his chest, like a baby. But when Rosie Rosario lowers her gun and points it at his chest, he drops the box. It splits wide open and reveals what Laverty tentatively identifies as a Russian-made Hashim antitank grenade launcher.

"Holy shit!" Rosario says, and then: "Toody, Toody, I got an id—"

"Officers, lower your weapons."

Laverty keeps his focus on Grenade Launcher Guy, but Rosario turns and sees a gray-haired Cauc in a blue jacket. He's wearing an earpiece and has his own Glock. Before she can ask him anything, the street is full of men in blue jackets, all running for King Virtue Pawn & Loan. One is carrying a Stinger battering ram, the kind cops call a baby doorbuster. She sees ATF on the backs of the jackets, and all at once she has that unmistakable I-stepped-in-shit feeling.

"*Officers, lower your weapons.* Agent James

Kosinsky, ATF."

Laverty says, "Maybe you'd like one of us to cuff him first? Just asking."

ATF agents are piling into the pawnshop like Christmas shoppers into Walmart on Black Friday. A crowd is gathering across the street, as yet too stunned by the size of the strike force to start casting aspersions. Or stones, for that matter.

Kosinsky sighs. "You may as well," he says. "The horse has left the barn."

"We didn't know you had anything going," Laverty says. Meanwhile, Grenade Launcher Guy already has his hands off the van and behind him with the wrists pressed together. It's pretty clear this isn't his first rodeo. "He was unlocking his van and I saw *that* poking out of the end of the box. What was I supposed to do?"

"What you did, of course." From inside the pawnshop there comes the sound of breaking glass, shouts, and then the boom of the doorbuster being put to work. "Tell you what, now that you're here, why don't you throw Mr. Cavelli there in the back of your car and come on inside. See what we've got."

While Laverty and Rosario are escorting their prisoner to the cruiser, Kosinsky notes the number.

"So," he says. "Which one of you is Toody and which one is Muldoon?"

11

As the ATF strike force, led by Agent Kosinsky, begins its inventory of the cavernous storage area behind King Virtue Pawn & Loan's humble façade, a gray Mercedes sedan is pulling to the curb in front of 49 Elm Street. Hodges is behind the wheel. Today Holly is riding shotgun — because, she claims (with at least some logic), the car is more hers than theirs.

"Someone is home," she points out. "There's a very badly maintained Honda Civic in the driveway."

Hodges notes the shuffling approach of an old man from the house directly across the street. "I will now speak with Mr. Concerned Citizen. You two will keep your mouths shut."

He rolls down his window. "Help you, sir?"

"I thought maybe I could help *you,*" the old guy says. His bright eyes are busy inventorying Hodges and his passengers. Also the car, which doesn't surprise Hodges. It's a mighty fine car. "If you're looking for Brady, you're out of luck. That in the driveway is Missus Hartsfield's car. Haven't seen it move in weeks. Not sure it even runs anymore. Maybe Missus Hartsfield went off with him, because I haven't seen her today. Usually I do, when she toddles out to get her post." He points to the mailbox beside the door of 49. "She likes the catalogs. Most women do." He extends a knuckly hand. "Hank Beeson."

Hodges shakes it briefly, then flashes his ID, careful to keep his thumb over the expiration date. "Good to meet you, Mr. Beeson. I'm Detective Bill Hodges. Can you tell me what kind of car Mr. Hartsfield drives? Make and model?"

"It's a brown Subaru. Can't help you with the model or the year. All those rice-burners look the same to me."

"Uh-huh. Have to ask you to go back to your house now, sir. We may come by to ask you a few questions later."

"Did Brady do something wrong?"

"Just a routine call," Hodges says. "Go on back to your house, please."

Instead of doing that, Beeson bends lower for a look at Jerome. "Aren't you kinda young to be on the cops?"

"I'm a trainee," Jerome says. "Better do as Detective Hodges says, sir."

"I'm goin, I'm goin." But he gives the trio another stem-to-stern onceover first. "Since when do city cops drive around in Mercedes-Benzes?"

Hodges has no answer for that, but Holly does. "It's a RICO car. RICO stands for Racketeer Influenced and Corrupt Organizations. We take their stuff. We can use it any way we want because we're the police."

"Well, yeah. Sure. Stands to reason." Beeson looks partly satisfied and partly mystified. But he goes back to his house, where he soon appears to them again, this time looking out a front window.

"RICO is the feds," Hodges says mildly.

Holly tips her head fractionally toward their observer, and there's a faint smile on her hard-used lips. "Do you think *he* knows that?" When neither of them answers, she becomes businesslike. "What do we do now?"

"If Hartsfield's in there, I'm going to make a citizen's arrest. If he's not but his mother is, I'm going to interview her. You two are going to stay in the car."

"I don't know if that's a good idea," Jerome says, but by the expression on his face — Hodges can see it in the rearview mirror — he knows this objection will be overruled.

"It's the only one I have," Hodges says.

He gets out of the car. Before he can close the door, Holly leans toward him and says: "There's no one home." He doesn't say anything, but she nods as if he had. "Can't you feel it?"

Actually, he can.

12

Hodges walks up the driveway, noting the drawn drapes in the big front window. He looks briefly in the Honda and sees nothing worth noting. He tries the passenger door. It opens. The air inside is hot and stale, with a faintly boozy smell. He shuts the door, climbs the porch steps, and rings the doorbell. He hears it *cling-clong* inside the house. Nobody comes. He tries it again, then knocks. Nobody comes. He hammers with the side of his fist, very aware that Mr. Beeson from across the street is taking all this in. Nobody comes.

He strolls to the garage and peers through one of the windows in the overhead door. A few tools, a mini-fridge, not much else.

He takes out his cell phone and calls Jerome. This block of Elm Street is very still, and he can hear — faintly — the AC/DC ringtone as the call goes through. He sees Jerome answer.

"Have Holly jump on her iPad and check the city tax records for the owner's name at 49 Elm. Can she do that?"

He hears Jerome asking Holly.

"She says she'll see what she can do."

"Good. I'm going around back. Stay on the line. I'll check in with you at roughly thirty-second intervals. If more than a minute goes by without hearing from me, call nine-one-one."

"You positive you want to do this, Bill?"

"Yes. Be sure Holly knows that getting the name isn't a big deal. I don't want her getting squirrelly."

"She's chill," Jerome says. "Already tapping away. Just make sure you stay in touch."

"Count on it."

He walks between the garage and the house. The backyard is small but neatly kept. There's a circular bed of flowers in the middle. Hodges wonders who planted them, Mom or Sonny Boy. He mounts three wooden steps to the back stoop. There's an aluminum screen door with another door inside. The screen door is unlocked. The house door isn't.

"Jerome? Checking in. All quiet."

He peers through the glass and sees a kitchen. It's squared away. There are a few plates and glasses in the drainer by the sink. A neatly folded dishwiper hangs over the oven handle. There are two placemats on the table. No placemat for Poppa Bear, which fits the profile he has fleshed out on his yellow legal pad. He knocks, then hammers. Nobody comes.

"Jerome? Checking in. All quiet."

He puts his phone down on the back stoop and takes out the flat leather case, glad he thought of it. Inside are his father's lockpicks — three silver rods with hooks of varying sizes at the ends. He selects the medium pick. A good choice; it slides in easily. He fiddles around, turning the pick first one way, then the other, feeling for the mechanism. He's just about to pause and check in with Jerome again when the pick catches. He twists, quick and hard, just as his father taught him, and there's a click as the locking button pops up on the kitchen side of the door. Meanwhile, his phone is squawking his name. He picks it up.

"Jerome? All quiet."

"You had me worried," Jerome says. "What are you doing?"

"Breaking and entering."

13

Hodges steps into the Hartsfield kitchen. The smell hits him at once. It's faint, but it's there. Holding his cell phone in his left hand and his father's .38 in the right, Hodges follows his nose first into the living room — empty, although the TV remote and scattering of catalogs on the coffee table makes him think that the couch is Mrs. Hartsfield's downstairs nest — and then up the stairs. The smell gets stronger as he goes. It's not a stench yet, but it's headed in that direction.

There's a short upstairs hall with one door on the right and two on the left. He clears the righthand room first. It's guest quarters where no guests have stayed for a long time. It's as sterile as an operating theater.

He checks in with Jerome again before opening the first door on the left. This is where the smell is coming from. He takes a deep breath and enters fast, crouching until he's assured himself there's no one behind the door. He opens the closet — this door is the kind that folds on a center hinge — and shoves back the clothes. No one.

"Jerome? Checking in."

"Is anyone there?"

Well . . . sort of. The coverlet of the double bed has been pulled up over an unmistakable shape.

"Wait one."

He looks under the bed and sees nothing but a pair of slippers, a pair of pink sneakers, a single white ankle sock, and a few dust kitties. He pulls the coverlet back and there's Brady Hartsfield's mother. Her skin is waxy-pale, with a faint green undertint. Her mouth hangs ajar. Her eyes, dusty and glazed, have settled in their sockets. He lifts an arm, flexes it slightly, lets it drop. Rigor has come and gone.

"Listen, Jerome. I've found Mrs. Hartsfield. She's dead."

"Oh my God." Jerome's usually adult voice cracks on the last word. "What are you —"

"Wait one."

"You already said that."

Hodges puts his phone on the night table and draws the coverlet down to Mrs. Hartsfield's feet. She's wearing blue silk pajamas. The shirt is stained with what appears to be vomit and some blood, but there's no visible bullet hole or stab wound. Her face is swollen, yet there are no ligature marks or bruises on her neck. The swelling is just the slow death-march of decomposition. He pulls up her pajama top enough so he can see her belly. Like her face, it's slightly swollen, but he's betting that's gas. He leans close to her mouth, looks inside, and sees what he expected: clotted goop on her tongue and in the gutters between her gums and her cheeks. He's guessing she got drunk, sicked up her last meal, and went out like a rock star. The blood could be from her throat. Or an aggravated stomach ulcer.

He picks up the phone and says, "He might have poisoned her, but it's more likely she did it to herself."

"Booze?"

"Probably. Without a postmortem, there's no way to tell."

"What do you want us to do?"

"Sit tight."

"We still don't call the police?"

"Not yet."

"Holly wants to talk to you."

There's a moment of dead air, then she's on the line, and clear as a bell. She sounds calm. Calmer than Jerome, actually.

"Her name is Deborah Hartsfield. The kind of Deborah that ends in an H."

"Good job. Give the phone back to Jerome."

A second later Jerome says, "I hope you know what you're doing."

I don't, he thinks as he checks the bathroom. I've lost my mind and the only way to get it back is to let go of this. You *know* that.

But he thinks of Janey giving him his new hat — his snappy private eye fedora — and knows he can't. Won't.

The bathroom is clean . . . or almost. There's some hair in the sink. Hodges sees it but doesn't take note of it. He's thinking of the crucial difference between accidental death and murder. Murder would be bad, because killing close family members is all too often how a serious nutcase starts his final run. If it was an accident or suicide, there might still be time. Brady could be hunkered down somewhere, trying to decide what to do next.

Which is too close to what I'm doing, Hodges thinks.

The last upstairs room is Brady's. The bed is unmade. The desk is piled helter-skelter with books, most of them science fiction. There's a *Terminator* poster on the wall, with Schwarzenegger wearing dark glasses and toting a futuristic elephant gun.

I'll be back, Hodges thinks, looking at it.

"Jerome? Checking in."

"The guy from across the street is still scoping us. Holly thinks we should come inside."

"Not yet."

"When?"

"When I'm sure this place is clear."

Brady has his own bathroom. It's as neat as a GI's footlocker on inspection day. Hodges gives it a cursory glance, then goes back downstairs. There's a small alcove off the living room, with just enough space for a small desk. On it is a laptop. A purse hangs by its strap from the back of the chair. On the wall is a large framed photograph of the woman upstairs and a teenage version of Brady Hartsfield. They're standing on a beach somewhere with their arms around each other and their cheeks pressed together. They're wearing identical million-dollar smiles. It's more girlfriend-boyfriend than mother-son.

Hodges looks with fascination upon Mr. Mercedes in his salad days. There's nothing in his face that suggests homicidal tendencies, but of course there almost never is. The resemblance between the two of them is faint, mostly in the shape of the noses and the color of the hair. She was a pretty woman, really just short of beautiful, but Hodges is willing to guess that Brady's father didn't have similar good looks. The boy in the photo seems . . . ordinary. A kid you'd pass on the street without a second glance.

That's probably the way he likes it, Hodges thinks. The Invisible Man.

He goes back into the kitchen and this time sees a door beside the stove. He opens it and looks at steep stairs descending into darkness. Aware that he makes a perfect silhouette for anyone who might be down there, Hodges moves to one side while he feels for the light switch. He finds it and steps into the doorway again with the gun leveled. He sees a worktable. Beyond it, a waist-high shelf runs the length of the room. On it is a line of computers. It makes him think of Mission Control at Cape Canaveral.

"Jerome? Checking in."

Without waiting for an answer, he goes down with the gun in one hand and his phone in the other, perfectly aware of what a grotesque perversion of all established police procedure this is. What if Brady is under the stairs with his own gun, ready to shoot Hodges's feet off at the ankles? Or suppose he's set up a boobytrap? He can do it; this Hodges now knows all too well.

He strikes no tripwire, and the basement is empty. There's a storage closet, the door standing open, but nothing is stored there. He sees only empty shelves. In one corner is a litter of shoeboxes. They also appear to be empty.

The message, Hodges thinks, is Brady either killed his mother or came home and found her dead. Either way, he then decamped. If he *did* have explosives, they were on those closet shelves (possibly in the shoeboxes) and he took them along.

Hodges goes upstairs. It's time to bring in his new partners. He doesn't want to drag them in deeper than they already are, but there are those computers downstairs. He knows jack shit about computers. "Come around to the back," he says. "The kitchen door is open."

14

Holly steps in, sniffs, and says, "Oough. Is that Deborah Hartsfield?"

"Yes. Try not to think about it. Come downstairs, you guys. I want you to look at something."

In the basement, Jerome runs a hand over the worktable. "Whatever else he is, he's Mr. Awesomely Neat."

"Are you going to call the police, Mr. Hodges?" Holly is biting her lips again. "You probably are and I can't stop you, but my mother is going to be *so* mad at me. Also, it doesn't seem fair, since we're the ones who found out who he is."

"I haven't decided *what* I'm going to do," Hodges says, although she's right; it doesn't seem fair at all. "But I'd sure like to know what's on those computers. That might help me make up my mind."

"He won't be like Olivia," Holly says. "He'll have a *good* password."

Jerome picks one of the computers at random (it happens to be Brady's Number Six; not much on that one) and pushes the recessed button on the back of the monitor.

It's a Mac, but there's no chime. Brady hates that cheery chime, and has turned it off on all his computers.

Number Six flashes gray, and the boot-up worry-circle starts going round and round. After five seconds or so, gray turns to blue. This should be the password screen, even Hodges knows that, but instead a large 20 appears on the screen. Then 19, 18, and 17.

He and Jerome stare at it in perplexity.

"No, no!" Holly nearly screams it. "Turn it *off*!"

When neither of them moves immediately, she darts forward and pushes the power button behind the monitor again, holding it down until the screen goes dark. Then she lets out a breath and actually smiles.

"Jeepers! That was a close one!"

"What are you thinking?" Hodges asks. "That they're wired up to explode, or something?"

"Maybe they only lock up," Holly says, "but I bet it's a suicide program. If the countdown gets to zero, that kind of program scrubs the data. *All* the data. Maybe just in the one that's on, but in all of them if they're wired together. Which they probably are."

"So how do you stop it?" Jerome asks. "Keyboard command?"

"Maybe that. Maybe voice-ac."

"Voice-what?" Hodges asks.

"Voice-activated command," Jerome tells

him. "Brady says *Milk Duds* or *underwear* and the countdown stops."

Holly giggles through her fingers, then gives Jerome a timid push on the shoulder. "You're silly," she says.

15

They sit at the kitchen table with the back door open to let in fresh air. Hodges has an elbow on one of the placemats and his brow cupped in his palm. Jerome and Holly keep quiet, letting him think it through. At last he raises his head.

"I'm going to call it in. I don't want to, and if it was just between Hartsfield and me, I probably wouldn't. But I've got you two to consider —"

"Don't do it on my account," Jerome says. "If you see a way to go on, I'll stick with you."

Of course you will, Hodges thinks. You might think you know what you're risking, but you don't. When you're seventeen, the future is strictly theoretical.

As for Holly . . . previously he would have said she was a kind of human movie screen, with every thought in her head projected large on her face, but at this moment she's inscrutable.

"Thanks, Jerome, only . . ." Only this is hard. Letting go is hard, and this will be the second time he has to relinquish Mr. Mercedes.

But.

"It's not just us, see? He could have more explosive, and if he uses it on a crowd . . ." He looks directly at Holly. ". . . the way he used your cousin Olivia's Mercedes on a crowd, it would be on me. I won't take that chance."

Speaking carefully, enunciating each word as if to make up for what has probably been a lifetime of mumbling, Holly says, "No one can catch him but you."

"Thanks, but no," he says gently. "The police have resources. They'll start by putting a BOLO out on his car, complete with license plate number. I can't do that."

It sounds good but he doesn't believe it *is* good. When he's not taking insane risks like the one he took at City Center, Brady's one of the smart ones. He will have stashed the car somewhere — maybe in a downtown parking lot, maybe in one of the airport parking lots, maybe in one of those endless mall parking lots. His ride is no Mercedes-Benz; it's an unobtrusive shit-colored Subaru, and it won't be found today or tomorrow. They might still be looking for it next week. And if they *do* find it, Brady won't be anywhere near it.

"No one but you," she insists. "And only with us to help you."

"Holly —"

"How can you give up?" she cries at him. She balls one hand into a fist and strikes herself in the middle of the forehead with it, leaving a red mark. "How can you? Janey *liked* you! She was even sort of your girlfriend! Now she's *dead*! Like the woman upstairs! Both of them, *dead*!"

She goes to hit herself again and Jerome takes her hand. "Don't," he says. "Please don't hit yourself. It makes me feel terrible."

Holly starts to cry. Jerome hugs her clumsily. He's black and she's white, he's seventeen and she's in her forties, but to Hodges Jerome looks like a father comforting his daughter after she came home from school and said no one invited her to the Spring Dance.

Hodges looks out at the small but neatly kept Hartsfield backyard. He also feels terrible, and not just on Janey's account, although that is bad enough. He feels terrible for the people at City Center. He feels terrible for Janey's sister, whom they refused to believe, who was reviled in the press, and who was then driven to suicide by the man who lived in this house. He even feels terrible about his failure to pay heed to Mrs. Melbourne. He knows that Pete Huntley would let him off the hook on that one, and that makes it worse. Why? Because Pete isn't as good at this job as he, Hodges, still is. Pete never will be, not even on his best day. A good enough guy, and a hard worker, but . . .

But.

But but *but.*

All that changes nothing. He needs to call it in, even if it feels like dying. When you shove everything else aside, there's just one thing left: Kermit William Hodges is at a dead end. Brady Hartsfield is in the wind. There might be a lead in the computers — something to indicate where he is now, what his plans might be, or both — but Hodges can't access them. Nor can he justify continuing to withhold the name and description of the man who perpetrated the City Center Massacre. Maybe Holly's right, maybe Brady Hartsfield will elude capture and commit some new atrocity, but kermitfrog19 is out of options. The only thing left for him to do is to protect Jerome and Holly if he can. At this point, he may not even be able to manage that. The nosyparker across the street has seen them, after all.

He steps out on the stoop and opens his Nokia, which he has used more today than in all the time since he retired.

He thinks Doesn't this just suck, and speed-dials Pete Huntley.

16

Pete picks up on the second ring. *"Partner!"* he shouts exuberantly. There's a babble of voices in the background, and Hodges's first thought is that Pete's in a bar somewhere, half-shot and on his way to totally smashed.

"Pete, I need to talk to you about —"

"Yeah, yeah, I'll eat all the crow you want, just not right now. Who called you? Izzy?"

"Huntley!" someone shouts. "Chief's here in five! With press! Where's the goddam PIO?"

PIO, Public Information Officer. Pete's not in a bar and not drunk, Hodges thinks. He's just over-the-moon fucking happy.

"No one called me, Pete. What's going on?"

"You don't know?" Pete laughs. "Just the biggest armaments bust in this city's history. Maybe the biggest in the history of the USA. Hundreds of M2 and HK91 machine guns, rocket launchers, fucking *laser cannons,* crates of Lahti L-35s in mint condition, Russian AN-9s still in grease . . . there's enough stuff here to stock two dozen East European militias. And the ammo! Christ! It's stacked two stories high! If the fucking pawnshop had caught on fire, all of Lowtown would have gone up!"

Sirens. He hears sirens. More shouts. Someone is bawling for someone else to get those sawhorses up.

"What pawnshop?"

"King Virtue Pawn & Loan, south of MLK. You know the place?"

"Yeah . . ."

"And guess who owns it?" But Pete is far too excited to give him a chance to guess. "Alonzo Moretti! Get it?"

Hodges doesn't.

"Moretti is Fabrizio Abbascia's grandson, Bill! Fabby the Nose! Is it starting to come into focus now?"

At first it still doesn't, because when Pete and Isabelle questioned him, Hodges simply plucked Abbascia's name out of his mental file of old cases where someone might bear him animus . . . and there have been several hundred of those over the years.

"Pete, King Virtue's black-owned. All the businesses down there are."

"The fuck it is. Bertonne Lawrence's name is on the sign, but the shop's a lease, Lawrence is a front, and he's spilling his guts. You know the best part? We own part of the bust, because a couple of patrol cops kicked it off a week or so before the ATF was gonna roll these guys up. Every detective in the department is down here. The Chief's on his way, and he's got a press caravan bigger than the Macy's Thanksgiving Day Parade with him. No way are the feds gonna hog this one! No *way*!" This time his laugh is positively loonlike.

Every detective in the department, Hodges thinks. Which leaves what for Mr. Mercedes? Bupkes is what.

"Bill, I gotta go. This . . . man, this is *amazing.*"

"Sure, but first tell me what it has to do with me."

"What you said. The car-bomb was revenge. Moretti trying to pay off his grandfather's blood debt. In addition to the rifles, machine guns, grenades, pistols, and other assorted hardware, there's at least four dozen crates of Hendricks Chemicals Detasheet. Do you know what that is?"

"Rubberized explosive." *Now* it's coming into focus.

"Yeah. You set it off with lead azide detonators, and we know already that was the kind that was used to blow the stuff in your car. We haven't got a chem analysis on the explosive itself, but when we do, it'll turn out to be Detasheet. You can count on it. You're one lucky old sonofabitch, Bill."

"That's right," Hodges says. "I am."

He can picture the scene outside King Virtue: cops and ATF agents everywhere (probably arguing over jurisdiction already), and more coming all the time. Lowbriar closed off, probably MLK Avenue, too. Crowds of lookie-loos gathering. The Chief of Police and other assorted big boys on their way. The mayor won't miss the chance to make a speech. Plus all those reporters, TV crews, and live broadcast vans. Pete is bullshit with excitement, and is Hodges going to launch into a long and complicated story about the City Center Massacre, and a computer chat-room called Debbie's Blue Umbrella, and a dead mommy who probably drank herself to death, and a fugitive computer repairman?

No, he decides, I am not.

What he does is wish Pete good luck and push END.

17

When he comes back into the kitchen, Holly is no longer there, but he can hear her. Holly the Mumbler has turned into Holly the Revival Preacher, it seems. Certainly her voice has that special good-God-a'mighty cadence, at least for the moment.

"I'm with Mr. *Hodges* and his friend *Jerome,*" she's saying. "They're my *friends,* Momma. We had a nice *lunch* together. Now we're seeing some of the *sights,* and this *evening* we're going to have a nice *supper* together. We're talking about *Janey.* I can do that if I *want.*"

Even in his confusion over their current situation and his continuing sadness about Janey, Hodges is cheered by the sound of Holly standing up to Aunt Charlotte. He can't be sure it's for the first time, but by the living God, it might be.

"Who called who?" he asks Jerome, nodding toward her voice.

"Holly made the call, but it was my idea. She had her phone turned off so her mother couldn't call her. She wouldn't do it until I said her mother might call the cops."

"So what if I *did,*" Holly is saying now. "It was *Olivia's* car and it's not like I *stole* it. I'll be back tonight, Momma. Until then, *leave me alone*!"

She comes back into the room looking flushed, defiant, years younger, and actually pretty.

"You rock, Holly," Jerome says, and holds his hand up for a high-five.

She ignores this. Her eyes — still snapping — are fixed on Hodges. "If you call the police and I get in trouble, I don't care. But unless you already did, you *shouldn't. They* can't find him. *We* can. I *know* we can."

Hodges realizes that if catching Mr. Mercedes is more important to anyone on earth than it is to him, that person is Holly Gibney. Maybe for the first time in her life she's doing something that matters. And doing it with others who like and respect her.

"I'm going to hold on to it a little longer. Mostly because the cops are otherwise occupied this afternoon. The funny part — or maybe I mean the ironic part — is that they think it has to do with me."

"What are you talking about?" Jerome asks.

Hodges glances at his watch and sees it's twenty past two. They have been here long enough. "Let's go back to my place. I can tell you on the way, and then we can kick this around one more time. If we don't come up with anything, I'll have to call my partner back. I'm not risking another horror show."

Although the risk is already there, and he can see by their faces that Jerome and Holly know it as well as he does.

"I went in that little study beside the living room to call my mother," Holly says. "Mrs. Hartsfield's got a laptop. If we're going to your house, I want to bring it."

"Why?"

"I may be able to find out how to get into his computers. She might have written down the keyboard prompts or voice-ac password."

"Holly, that doesn't seem likely. Mentally ill guys like Brady go to great lengths to hide what they are from everyone."

"I know that," Holly says. "Of course I do. Because *I'm* mentally ill, and *I* try to hide it."

"Hey, Hol, come on." Jerome tries to take her hand. She won't let him. She takes her cigarettes from her pocket instead.

"I am and I know I am. My mother knows, too, and she keeps an *eye* on me. She *snoops* on me. Because she wants to *protect* me. Mrs. Hartsfield will have been the same. He was her *son,* after all."

"If the Linklatter woman at Discount Electronix was right," Hodges says, "Mrs. Hartsfield would have been drunk on her ass a good deal of the time."

Holly replies, "She could have been a *high-functioning* drunk. Have you got a better idea?"

Hodges gives up. "Okay, take the laptop. What the hell."

"Not yet," she says. "In five minutes. I want to smoke a cigarette. I'll go out on the stoop."

She goes out. She sits down. She lights up.

Through the screen door, Hodges calls: "When did you become so assertive, Holly?"

She doesn't turn around to answer. "I guess when I saw pieces of my cousin burning in the street."

18

At quarter to three that afternoon, Brady leaves his Motel 6 room for a breath of fresh air and spies a Chicken Coop on the other side of the highway. He crosses and orders his last meal: a Clucker Delight with extra gravy and coleslaw. The restaurant section is almost deserted, and he takes his tray to a table by the windows so he can sit in the sunshine. Soon there will be no more of that for him, so he might as well enjoy a little while he still can.

He eats slowly, thinking of all the times he brought home takeout from the Chicken Coop, and how his mother always asked for a Clucker with double slaw. He has ordered her meal without even thinking about it. This brings tears, and he wipes them away with a paper napkin. Poor Mom!

Sunshine is nice, but its benefits are ephemeral. Brady considers the more lasting benefits darkness will provide. No more listening to Freddi Linklatter's lesbo-feminist rants. No more listening to Tones Frobisher explain why he can't go out on service calls because of his RESPONSIBILITY TO THE STORE, when it's really because he wouldn't know a hard drive crash if it bit him on the dick. No more feeling his kidneys turning to ice as he drives around in the Mr. Tastey truck in August with the freezers on high. No more whapping the Subaru's dashboard when the radio cuts out. No more thinking about his mother's lacy panties and long, long thighs. No more fury at being ignored and taken for granted. No more headaches. And no more sleepless nights, because after today it will be all sleep, all the time.

With no dreams.

When he's finished his meal (he eats every bite), Brady buses his table, wipes up a splatter of gravy with another napkin, and dumps his trash. The girl at the counter asks him if everything was all right. Brady says it was, wondering how much of the chicken and gravy and biscuits and coleslaw will have a chance to digest before the explosion rips his stomach open and sprays what's left everywhere.

They'll remember me, he thinks as he stands at the edge of the highway, waiting for a break in traffic so he can go back to the motel. Highest score ever. I'll go down in history. He's glad now that he didn't kill the fat ex-cop. Hodges should be alive for what's coming tonight. He should have to remember. He should have to live with it.

Back in the room, he looks at the wheelchair and the explosives-stuffed urine bag lying on the explosives-stuffed ASS PARKING cushion. He wants to get to the MAC early (but not *too* early; the last thing he wants is to stand out more than he will just by being male and older than thirteen), but there's still a little time. He's brought his laptop, not for any particular reason but just out of habit, and now he's glad. He opens it, connects to the motel's WiFi, and goes to Debbie's Blue Umbrella. There he leaves one final message — a kind of insurance policy.

With that attended to, he walks back to the airport's long-term parking lot and retrieves his Subaru.

19

Hodges and his two apprentice detectives arrive on Harper Road shortly before three-thirty. Holly shoots a cursory glance around, then totes the late Mrs. Hartsfield's laptop into the kitchen and powers it up. Jerome and Hodges stand by, both hoping there will be no password screen . . . but there is.

"Try her name," Jerome says.

Holly does. The Mac shakes its screen: *no.*

"Okay, try Debbie," Jerome says. "Both the *–ie* one and the one that ends with an *i.*"

Holly brushes a clump of mouse-brown hair out of her eyes so he can see her annoyance clearly. "Find something to do, Jerome, okay? I don't want you looking over my shoulder. I hate that." She shifts her attention to Hodges. "Can I smoke in here? I hope I can. It helps me think. Cigarettes help me think."

Hodges gets her a saucer. "Smoking lamp's lit. Jerome and I will be in my study. Give a holler if you find something."

Small chance of that, he thinks. Small chance of *anything,* really.

Holly pays no attention. She's lighting up. She's left the revival-preacher voice behind and returned to mumbling. "Hope she left a hint. I have hint-hope. Hint-hope is what Holly has."

Oh boy, Hodges thinks.

In the study, he asks Jerome if he has any idea what kind of hint she's talking about.

"After three tries, some computers will give you a password hint. To jog your memory in case you forget. But only if one has been programmed."

From the kitchen there comes a hearty, non-mumbled cry: *"Shit! Double shit! Triple shit!"*

Hodges and Jerome look at each other.

"Guess not," Jerome says.

20

Hodges turns his own computer on and tells Jerome what he wants: a list of all public gatherings for the next seven days.

"I can do that," Jerome says, "but you might want to check this out first."

"What?"

"It's a message. Under the Blue Umbrella."

"Click it." Hodges's hands are clenched into fists, but as he reads **merckill**'s latest communiqué, they slowly open. The message is short, and although it's of no immediate help, it contains a ray of hope.

So long, SUCKER.
PS: Enjoy your Weekend, I know I will.

Jerome says, "I think you just got a Dear John, Bill."

Hodges thinks so, too, but he doesn't care. He's focused on the PS. He knows it might be a red herring, but if it's not, they have some time.

From the kitchen comes a waft of cigarette smoke and another hearty cry of *shit.*

"Bill? I just had a bad thought."

"What's that?"

"The concert tonight. That boy band, 'Round Here. At the Mingo. My sister and my mother are going to be there."

Hodges considers this. Mingo Auditorium seats four thousand, but tonight's attendees will be eighty percent female — mommies and their preteen daughters. There will be men in attendance, but almost every one of them will be chaperoning their daughters and their daughters' friends. Brady Hartsfield is a good-looking guy of about thirty, and if he tries going to that concert by himself, he'll stick out like a sore thumb. In twenty-first-century America, any single man at an event primarily aimed at little girls attracts notice and suspicion.

Also: **Enjoy your Weekend, I know I will**.

"Do you think I should call Mom and tell her to keep the girls home?" Jerome looks dismayed at the prospect. "Barb'll probably never speak to me again. Plus there's her friend Hilda and a couple of others . . ."

From the kitchen: "Oh, you damn thing! *Give it up!*"

Before Hodges can reply, Jerome says, "On the other hand, it sure sounds like he has something planned for the weekend, and this is only Thursday. Or is that just what he wants us to think?"

Hodges tends to think the taunt is real. "Find that Cyber Patrol picture of Hartsfield again, would you? The one you get when you click on MEET THE EXPERTS."

While Jerome does that, Hodges calls Marlo Everett in Police Records.

"Hey, Marlo, Bill Hodges again. I . . . yeah, lot of excitement in Lowtown, I heard about it from Pete. Half the force is down there, right? . . . uh-huh . . . well, I won't keep you long. Do you know if Larry Windom is still head of security at the MAC? Yeah, that's right, Romper-Stomper. Sure, I'll hold."

While he does, he tells Jerome that Larry Windom took early retirement because the MAC offered him the job at twice the salary he was making as a detective. He doesn't say that wasn't the only reason Windom pulled the pin after twenty. Then Marlo is back. Yes, Larry's still at the MAC. She even has the number of the MAC's security office. Before he can say goodbye, she asks him if there's a problem. "Because there's a big concert there tonight. My niece is going. She's crazy about those twerps."

"It's fine, Marls. Just some old business."

"Tell Larry we could use him today," Marlo

says. "The squadroom is dead empty. Nary a detective in sight."

"I'll do that."

Hodges calls MAC Security, identifies himself as Detective Bill Hodges, and asks for Windom. While he waits, he stares at Brady Hartsfield. Jerome has enlarged the photo so it fills the whole screen. Hodges is fascinated by the eyes. In the smaller version, and in a line with the two I-T colleagues, those eyes seemed pleasant enough. With the picture filling the screen, however, that changes. The mouth is smiling; the eyes aren't. The eyes are flat and distant. Almost dead.

Bullshit, Hodges tells himself (*scolds* himself). This is a classic case of seeing something that's not there based on recently acquired knowledge — like a bank-robbery witness saying *I thought he looked shifty even before he pulled out that gun.*

Sounds good, sounds *professional,* but Hodges doesn't believe it. He thinks the eyes looking out of the screen are the eyes of a toad hiding under a rock. Or under a cast-off blue umbrella.

Then Windom's on the line. He has the kind of booming voice that makes you want to hold the phone two inches from your ear while you talk to him, and he's the same old yapper. He wants to know all about the big bust that afternoon. Hodges tells him it's a mega-bust, all right, but beyond that he knows from nothing. He reminds Larry that he's retired.

But.

"With all that going on," he says, "Pete Huntley kind of drafted me to call you. Hope you don't mind."

"Jesus, no. I'd like to have a drink with you, Billy. Talk over old times now that we're both out. You know, hash and trash."

"That would be good." Pure hell is what it would be.

"How can I help?"

"You've got a concert there tonight, Pete says. Some hot boy band. The kind all the little girls love."

"Iy-yi-yi, do they ever. They're already lining up. And *tuning* up. Someone'll shout out one of those kids' names, and they all scream. Even if they're still coming in from the parking lot they scream. It's like Beatlemania back in the day, only from what I hear, this crew ain't the Beatles. You got a bomb threat or something? Tell me you don't. The chicks'll tear me apart and the mommies will eat the leftovers."

"What I've got is a tip that you may have a child molester on your hands tonight. This is a bad, bad boy, Larry."

"Name and description?" Hard and fast, no bullshit. The guy who left the force because he was a bit too quick with his fists.

Anger issues, in the language of the department shrink. Romper-Stomper, in the language of his colleagues.

"His name is Brady Hartsfield. I'll email you his picture." Hodges glances at Jerome, who nods and makes a circle with his thumb and forefinger. "He's approximately thirty years old. If you see him, call me first, then grab him. Use caution. If he tries to resist, subdue the motherfucker."

"With pleasure, Billy. I'll pass this along to my guys. Any chance he'll be with a . . . I don't know . . . a beard? A teenage girl or someone even younger?"

"Unlikely but not impossible. If you spot him in a crowd, Lar, you gotta take him by surprise. He could be armed."

"How good are the chances he's going to be at the show?" He actually sounds hopeful, which is typical Larry Windom.

"Not very." Hodges absolutely believes this, and it's not just the Blue Umbrella hint Hartsfield dropped about the weekend. He *has* to know that in a girls-night-out audience, he'd have no way of being unobtrusive. "In any case, you understand why the department can't send cops, right? With all that's going on in Lowtown?"

"Don't need them," Windom says. "I've got thirty-five guys tonight, most of the regulars retired po-po. We know what we're doing."

"I know you do," Hodges says. "Remember,

call me first. Us retired guys don't get much action, and we have to protect what we do get."

Windom laughs. "I hear you on that. Email me the picture." He recites an e-address which Hodges jots down and hands to Jerome. "If we see him, we grab him. After that, it's your bust . . . *Uncle* Bill."

"Fuck you, *Uncle* Larry," Hodges says. He hangs up, turns to Jerome.

"The pic just went out to him," Jerome says.

"Good." Then Hodges says something that will haunt him for the rest of his life. "If Hartsfield's as clever as I think he is, he won't be anywhere near the Mingo tonight. I think your mom and sis are good to go. If he does try crashing the concert, Larry's guys will have him before he gets in the door."

Jerome smiles. "Great."

"See what else you can find. Concentrate on Saturday and Sunday, but don't neglect next week. Don't neglect tomorrow, either, because —"

"Because the weekend starts on Friday. Gotcha."

Jerome gets busy. Hodges walks out to the kitchen to check on how Holly's doing. What he sees stops him cold. Lying next to the borrowed laptop is a red wallet. Deborah Hartsfield's ID, credit cards, and receipts are scattered across the table. Holly, already on her third cigarette, is holding up a MasterCard and studying it through a haze of blue smoke. She gives him a look that's both frightened and defiant.

"I'm just trying to find her diddly-dang password! Her purse was hanging over the back of her office chair, and her billfold was right there on top, so I put it in my pocket. Because sometimes people keep their passwords in their billfolds. Women especially. I didn't want her *money,* Mr. Hodges. I have my own *money.* I get an *allowance.*"

An allowance, Hodges thinks. Oh, Holly.

Her eyes are brimming with tears and she's biting her lips again. "I'd never *steal.*"

"Okay," he says. He thinks of patting her hand and decides it might be a bad idea just now. "I understand."

And Jesus-God, what's the BFD? On top of all the shit he's pulled since that goddam letter dropped through his mail slot, lifting a dead woman's wallet is chump-change. When all this comes out — as it surely will — Hodges will say he took it himself.

Holly, meanwhile, is not finished.

"I have my own credit card, and I have money. I even have a checking account. I buy video games and apps for my iPad. I buy clothes. Also earrings, which I like. I have fifty-six pairs. And I buy my own cigarettes, although they're very expensive now. It might interest you to know that in New York City, a pack of cigarettes now costs *eleven dollars.* I try not to be a burden because I can't work and she says I'm not but I know I *am* —"

"Holly, stop. You need to save that stuff for your shrink, if you have one."

"Of *course* I have one." She flashes a grim grin at the stubborn password screen of Mrs. Hartsfield's laptop. "I'm fucked up, didn't you notice?"

Hodges chooses to ignore this.

"I was looking for a slip of paper with the password on it," she says, "but there wasn't one. So I tried her Social Security number, first forwards and then backwards. Same deal with her credit cards. I even tried the credit card security codes."

"Any other ideas?"

"A couple. Leave me alone." As he leaves the room, she calls: "I'm sorry about the smoke, but it really does help me think."

21

With Holly crunching in the kitchen and Jerome doing likewise in his study, Hodges settles into the living room La-Z-Boy, staring at the blank TV. It's a bad place to be, maybe the worst place. The logical part of his mind understands that everything which has happened is Brady Hartsfield's fault, but sitting in the La-Z-Boy where he spent so many vapid, TV-soaked afternoons, feeling useless and out of touch with the essential self he took for granted during his working life, logic loses its power. What creeps in to take its place is a terrifying idea: he, Kermit William Hodges, has committed the crime of shoddy police work, and has aided and abetted Mr. Mercedes by so doing. They are the stars of a reality TV show called *Bill and Brady Kill Some Ladies.* Because when Hodges looks back, so many of the victims seem to be women: Janey, Olivia Trelawney, Janice Cray and her daughter Patricia . . . plus Deborah Hartsfield, who might have been poisoned instead of poisoning herself. And, he thinks, I haven't even added Holly, who'll likely come out of this even more grandly fucked up than she was going in, if she can't find that password . . . or if she *does* find it and there's nothing on Mom's computer that can help us to find Sonny Boy. And really, how likely is that?

Sitting here in this chair — knowing he should get up but as yet unable to move — Hodges thinks his own destructive record with women stretches back even further. His ex-wife is his ex for a reason. Years of near-alcoholic drinking were part of it, but for Corinne (who liked a drink or three herself and probably still does), not the major part. It was the coldness that first stole through the cracks in the marriage and finally froze it solid. It was how he shut her out, telling himself it was for her own good, because so much of what he did was nasty and depressing. How he made it clear in a dozen ways — some large, some small — that in a race between her and the job, Corinne Hodges always came in second. As for his daughter . . . well. Jeez. Allie never misses sending him birthday and Christmas cards (although the Valentine's Day cards stopped about ten years ago), and she hardly ever misses the Saturday-evening duty-call, but she hasn't been to see him in a couple of years. Which really says all that needs saying about how he bitched up *that* relationship.

His mind drifts to how beautiful she was as a kid, with those freckles and that mop of red hair — his little carrot-top. She'd pelt down the hall to him when he came home and jump fearlessly, knowing he'd drop whatever he was holding and catch her. Janey mentioned being crazy about the Bay City Rollers, and Allie'd had her own faves, her own bubble-gum boy-toys. She bought their records with her own allowance, little ones with the big hole in the center. Who was on them? He can't remember, only that one of the songs went on and on about every move you make and every step you take. Was that Bananarama or the Thompson Twins? He doesn't know, but he does know he never took her to a concert, although Corrie might have taken her to see Cyndi Lauper.

Thinking about Allie and her love of pop

music rings in a new thought, one that makes him sit up straight, eyes wide, hands clutching the La-Z-Boy's padded arms.

Would he have let *Allie* go to that concert tonight?

The answer is absolutely not. No way.

Hodges checks his watch and sees it's closing in on four o'clock. He gets up, meaning to go into the study and tell Jerome to call his moms and tell her to keep those girls away from the MAC no matter how much they piss and moan. He's called Larry Windom and taken precautions, but precautions be damned. He would never have put Allie's life in Romper-Stomper's hands. *Never.*

Before he can get two steps toward the study, Jerome calls out: "Bill! Holly! Come here! I think I found something!"

22

They stand behind Jerome, Hodges looking over his left shoulder and Holly over his right. On the screen of Hodges's computer is a press release.

Synergy Corp., Citibank, 3 Restaurant Chains to Put on Midwest's Biggest Summer Careers Day at Embassy Suites

FOR IMMEDIATE RELEASE. Career businesspeople and military veterans are encouraged to attend the biggest Ca-

reers Day of the year on Saturday, June 5th, 2010. This recession-busting event will be held at the downtown Embassy Suites, 1 Synergy Square. Prior registration is encouraged but not necessary. You will discover hundreds of exciting and high-paying jobs at the Citibank website, at your local McDonald's, Burger King, and Chicken Coop, or at www.synergy.com. Jobs available include customer service, retail, security, plumbing, electrical, accounting, financial analysts, telemarketing, cashiers. You will find trained and helpful Job Guides and useful seminars in all conference rooms. There is no charge. Doors open at 8 AM. Bring your resume and dress for success. Remember that prior registration will speed the process and improve your chances of finding that job you've been looking for.

TOGETHER WE WILL BEAT THIS RECESSION!

"What do you think?" Jerome asks.

"I think you nailed it." An enormous wave of relief sweeps through Hodges. Not the concert tonight, or a crowded downtown dance club, or the Groundhogs-Mudhens minor league baseball game tomorrow night. It's this thing at Embassy Suites. Got to be, it's too perfectly rounded to be anything else. There's method in Brady Hartsfield's madness; to him, alpha equals omega. Hartsfield means to finish his career as a mass murderer the same way he started it, by killing the city's jobless.

Hodges turns to see how Holly is taking this, but Holly has left the room. She's back in the kitchen, sitting in front of Deborah Hartsfield's laptop and staring at the password screen. Her shoulders are slumped. In the saucer beside her, a cigarette has smoldered down to the filter, leaving a neat roll of ash.

This time he risks touching her. "It's okay, Holly. The password doesn't matter because now we've got the location. I'm going to get with my old partner in a couple of hours, when this Lowtown thing's had a chance to settle a bit, and tell him everything. They'll put out a BOLO on Hartsfield and his car. If they don't get him before Saturday morning, they'll get him as he approaches the job fair."

"Isn't there anything we can do tonight?"

"I'm thinking about that." There *is* one thing, although it's such a long shot it's practically a no-shot.

Holly says, "What if you're wrong about it being the career-day? What if he plans to blow up a movie theater *tonight*?"

Jerome comes into the room. "It's Thursday, Hol, and still too early for the big summer pictures. Most screens won't be playing to even a dozen people."

"The concert, then," she says. "Maybe he doesn't *know* it'll be all girls."

"He'll know," Hodges says. "He's a creature of improvisation, but that doesn't make him stupid. He'll have done at least some advance planning."

"Can I have just a little more time to try and crack her password? Please?"

Hodges glances at his watch. Ten after four. "Sure. Until four-thirty, how's that?"

A bargaining glint comes into her eyes. "Quarter to five?"

Hodges shakes his head.

Holly sighs. "I'm out of cigarettes, too."

"Those things will kill you," Jerome says.

She gives him a flat look. "Yes! That's part of their charm."

23

Hodges and Jerome drive down to the little shopping center at the intersection of Harper and Hanover to buy Holly a pack of cigarettes and give her the privacy she clearly wants.

Back in the gray Mercedes, Jerome tosses the Winstons from hand to hand and says, "This car gives me the creeps."

"Me too," Hodges admits. "But it didn't seem to bother Holly, did it? Sensitive as she is."

"Do you think she'll be all right? After this is over, I mean."

A week ago, maybe even two days, Hodges would have said something vague and politically correct, but he and Jerome have been through a lot since then. "For awhile," he says. "Then . . . no."

Jerome sighs the way people do when their own dim view of things has been confirmed. "Fuck."

"Yeah."

"So what now?"

"Now we go back, give Holly her coffin nails, and let her smoke one. Then we pack up the stuff she filched from the Hartsfield house. I drive you two back to the Birch Hill Mall. You return Holly to Sugar Heights in your Wrangler, then go home yourself."

"And just let Mom and Barb and her friends go to that show."

Hodges blows out a breath. "If it'll make you feel easier, tell your mother to pull the plug."

"If I do that, it all comes out." Still tossing the cigarettes back and forth. "Everything we've been doing today."

Jerome is a bright boy and Hodges doesn't need to confirm this. Or remind him that eventually it's all going to come out anyway.

"What will you do, Bill?"

"Go back to the North Side. Park the Mercedes a block or two away from the Hartsfield place, just to be safe. I'll return Mrs. Hartsfield's laptop and billfold, then stake out the house. In case he decides to come back."

Jerome looks doubtful. "That basement room looked like he made a pretty clean sweep. What are the chances?"

"Slim and none, but it's all I've got. Until I turn this thing over to Pete."

"You really wanted to make the collar, didn't you?"

"Yes," Hodges says, and sighs. "Yes I did."

24

When they come back, Holly's head is down on the table and hidden in her arms. The deconstructed contents of Deborah Hartsfield's wallet are an asteroid belt around her. The laptop is still on and still showing the stubborn password screen. According to the clock on the wall, it's twenty to five.

Hodges is afraid she'll protest his plan to return her home, but Holly only sits up, opens the fresh pack of cigarettes, and slowly removes one. She's not crying, but she looks tired and dispirited.

"You did your best," Jerome says.

"I always do my best, Jerome. And it's never good enough."

Hodges picks up the red wallet and starts returning the credit cards to the slots. They're probably not in the same order Mrs. Hartsfield had them in, but who's going to notice?

Not her.

There are photos in an accordion of transparent envelopes, and he flips through them idly. Here's Mrs. Hartsfield standing arm-in-arm with a broad-shouldered, burly guy in a blue work coverall — the absent Mr. Hartsfield, perhaps. Here's Mrs. Hartsfield standing with a bunch of laughing ladies in what appears to be a beauty salon. Here's one of a chubby little boy holding a fire truck — Brady at age three or four, probably. And one more, a wallet-sized version of the picture in Mrs. Hartsfield's alcove office: Brady and his mom with their cheeks pressed together.

Jerome taps it and says, "You know what that reminds me of a little? Demi Moore and what's-his-name, Ashton Kutcher."

"Demi Moore has black hair," Holly says matter-of-factly. "Except in *G.I. Jane,* where she hardly had any at all, because she was learning to be a SEAL. I saw that movie three times, once in the theater, once on videotape, and once on my iTunes. Very enjoyable. Mrs. Hartsfield is blond-headed." She considers, then adds: "Was."

Hodges slides the photo out of the pocket for a better look, then turns it over. Carefully printed on the back is *Mom and Her Honeyboy, Sand Point Beach, Aug 2007.* He flicks the picture against the side of his palm a time or two, almost puts it back, then slides it across to Holly, photo-side down.

"Try that."

She frowns at him. "Try what?"

"Honeyboy."

Holly types it in, hits RETURN . . . and utters a very un-Hollylike scream of joy. Because they're in. Just like that.

There's nothing of note on the desktop — an address book, a folder marked FAVORITE RECIPES and another marked SAVED EMAILS; a folder of online receipts (she seemed to have paid most of her bills that way); and an album of photos (most of Brady at various ages). There are a lot of TV shows in her iTunes, but only one album of music: *Alvin and the Chipmunks Celebrate Christmas.*

"Christ," Jerome says. "I don't want to say she deserved to die, but . . ."

Holly gives him a forbidding look. "Not funny, Jerome. Do not go there."

He holds up his hands. "Sorry, sorry."

Hodges scrolls rapidly through the saved emails and sees nothing of interest. Most appear to be from Mrs. Hartsfield's old high school buddies, who refer to her as Debs.

"There's nothing here about Brady," he says, and glances at the clock. "We should go."

"Not so fast," Holly says, and opens the finder. She types BRADY. There are several results (many in the recipe file, some tagged as *Brady Favorites*), but nothing of note.

"Try HONEYBOY," Jerome suggests.

She does and gets one result — a document buried deep in the hard drive. Holly clicks it. Here are Brady's clothing sizes, also a list of all the Christmas and birthday presents she's bought him for the last ten years, presumably so she won't repeat herself. She's noted his Social Security number. There's a scanned copy of his car registration, his car insurance card, and his birth certificate. She's listed his co-workers at both Discount Electronix and Loeb's Ice Cream Factory. Next to the name Shirley Orton is a notation that would have made Brady laugh hysterically: *Wonder is she his gf?*

"What's up with this crap?" Jerome asks. "He's a grown *man,* for God's sake."

Holly smiles darkly. "What I said. She knew he wasn't right."

At the very bottom of the HONEYBOY file, there's a folder marked BASEMENT.

"That's it," Holly says. "Gotta be. Open it, open it, open it!"

Jerome clicks BASEMENT. The document inside is less than a dozen words long.

Control = lights

Chaos?? Darkness??

Why don't they work for me????

They stare at the screen for some time

without speaking. At last Hodges says, "I don't get it. Jerome?"

Jerome shakes his head.

Holly, seemingly hypnotized by this message from the dead woman, speaks a single word, almost too low to hear: "Maybe . . ." She hesitates, chewing her lips, and says it again. "Maybe."

25

Brady arrives at the Midwest Culture and Arts Complex just before six P.M. Although the show isn't scheduled to start for over an hour, the vast parking lot is already three-quarters full. Long lines have formed outside the doors that open on to the lobby, and they're getting longer all the time. Little girls are screeching at the top of their lungs. Probably that means they're happy, but to Brady they sound like ghosts in a deserted mansion. It's impossible to look at the growing crowd and not recall that April morning at City Center. Brady thinks, If I had a Humvee instead of this Jap shitbox, I could drive into them at forty miles an hour, kill fifty or more that way, then hit the switch and blow the rest into the stratosphere.

But he doesn't have a Humvee, and for a moment he's not even sure what to do next — he can't be seen while he makes his final preparations. Then, at the far end of the lot, he sees a tractor-trailer box. The cab is gone and it's up on jacks. On the side is a Ferris wheel and a sign reading 'ROUND HERE SUPPORT TEAM. It's one of the trucks he saw in the loading area during his reconnaissance. Later, after the show, the cab would be reconnected and driven around back for the load-out, but now it looks deserted.

He pulls in on the far side of the box, which is at least fifty feet long and hides the Subaru completely from the bustling parking lot. He takes his fake glasses from the glove compartment and puts them on. He gets out and does a quick walk-around to assure himself the trailer box is as deserted as it looks. When he's satisfied on that score, he returns to the Subaru and works the wheelchair out of the back. It's not easy. The Honda would have been better, but he doesn't trust its unmaintained engine. He places the ASS PARKING cushion on the wheelchair's seat, and connects the wire protruding from the center of the A in PARKING to the wires hanging from the side pockets, where there are more blocks of plastic explosive. Another wire, connected to a block of plastic in the rear pocket, dangles from a hole he has punched in the seatback.

Sweating profusely, Brady begins the final unification, braiding copper cores and wrapping exposed connection-points with precut strips of masking tape he has stuck to the front of the oversized 'Round Here tee-shirt he bought that morning in the drugstore. The shirt features the same Ferris wheel logo as the one on the truck. Above it are the words KISSES ON THE MIDWAY. Below, it says I LUV CAM, BOYD, STEVE, AND PETE!

After ten minutes of work (with occasional breaks to peek around the edge of the box and make sure he still has this far edge of the parking lot to himself), a spiderweb of connected wires lies on the seat of the wheelchair. There's no way to wire in the explosives-stuffed Urinesta peebag, at least not that he could figure out on short notice, but that's okay; Brady has no doubt the other stuff will set it off.

Not that he'll know for sure, one way or the other.

He returns to the Subaru one more time and takes out the eight-by-ten framed version of a picture Hodges has already seen: Frankie holding Sammy the Fire Truck and smiling his dopey where-the-fuck-am-I smile. Brady kisses the glass and says, "I love you, Frankie. Do you love me?"

He pretends Frankie says yes.

"Do you want to help me?"

He pretends Frankie says yes.

Brady goes back to the wheelchair and sits down on ASS PARKING. Now the only wire showing is the master wire, dangling over the front of the wheelchair seat between his spread thighs. He connects it to Thing Two and takes a deep breath before flicking the power switch. If the electricity from the double-A batteries leaks through . . . even a little . . .

But it doesn't. The yellow ready-lamp goes on, and that's all. Somewhere, not far away but in a different world, little girls are screaming happily. Soon many of them will be vaporized; many more will be missing arms and legs and screaming for real. Oh well, at least they'll get to listen to some music by their favorite band before the big bang.

Or maybe not. He's aware of what a crude and makeshift plan this is; the stupidest no-talent screenwriter in Hollywood could do better. Brady remembers the sign in the corridor leading to the auditorium: NO BAGS NO BOXES NO BACKPACKS. He has none of those things, but all it will take to blow the deal is one sharp-eyed security guard observing a single unconcealed wire. Even if that doesn't happen, a cursory glance into the wheelchair's storage pockets will reveal the fact that it's a rolling bomb. Brady has stuck a 'Round Here pennant in one of those pockets, but otherwise made no effort at concealment.

It doesn't faze him. He doesn't know if that makes him confident or just fatalistic, and doesn't think it matters. In the end, confidence and fatalism are pretty much the same, aren't they? He got away with running those people over at City Center, and there was almost no planning involved with that, either — just a mask, a hairnet, and some DNA-killing bleach. In his heart, he never really expected to escape, and in this case his expectations are zero. In a don't-give-a-fuck world, he is about to become the ultimate don't-give-a-fucker.

He slips Thing Two beneath the oversized tee-shirt. There's a slight bulge, and he can see a dim yellow glimmer from the ready-lamp through the thin cotton, but both the bulge and the glimmer disappear when he places Frankie's picture in his lap. He's pretty much ready to go.

His fake glasses slide down the bridge of his sweat-slippery nose. Brady pushes them back up. By craning his neck slightly, he can see himself in the Subaru's passenger-side rearview mirror. Bald and bespectacled, he looks nothing like his former self. He looks sick, for one thing — pale and sweaty with dark circles under his eyes.

Brady runs his hand over the top of his head, feeling smooth skin where no stubble will ever have the chance to grow out. Then he backs the wheelchair out of the slot where he has parked his car and begins to roll himself slowly across the expanse of parking lot toward the growing crowd.

26

Hodges gets snared in rush-hour traffic and doesn't arrive back on the North Side until shortly after six P.M. Jerome and Holly are still with him; they both want to see this through, regardless of the consequences, and since they seem to understand what those consequences may be, Hodges has decided he can't refuse them. Not that he has much of a choice; Holly won't divulge what she knows. Or thinks she knows.

Hank Beeson is out of his house and crossing the street before Hodges can bring Olivia Trelawney's Mercedes to a stop in the Hartsfield driveway. Hodges sighs and powers down the driver's-side window.

"I sure would like to know what's going on," Mr. Beeson says. "Does it have anything to do with all that mess down in Lowtown?"

"Mr. Beeson," Hodges says, "I appreciate your concern, but you need to go back to your house and —"

"No, wait," Holly says. She's leaning across the center console of Olivia Trelawney's Mercedes so she can look up at Beeson's face. "Tell me how Mr. Hartsfield sounds. I need to know how his voice sounds."

Beeson looks perplexed. "Like anyone, I guess. Why?"

"Is it low? You know, baritone?"

"You mean like one of those fat opera singers?" Beeson laughs. "Hell, no. What kind of question is that?"

"Not high and squeaky, either?"

To Hodges, Beeson says, "Is your partner crazy?"

Only a little, Hodges thinks. "Just answer the question, sir."

"Not low, not high and squeaky. Regular! What's going on?"

"No accent?" Holly persists. "Like . . . um . . . Southern? Or New England? Or Brooklyn, maybe?"

"No, I said. He sounds like anybody."

Holly sits back, apparently satisfied.

Hodges says, "Go back inside, Mr. Beeson. Please."

Beeson snorts but backs off. He pauses at the foot of his steps to cast a glare over his shoulder. It's one Hodges has seen many times before, the *I pay your salary, asshole* glare. Then he goes inside, slamming the door behind him to make sure they get the point. Soon he appears once more at the window with his arms folded over his chest.

"What if he calls the cop shop to ask what we're doing here?" Jerome asks from the back seat.

Hodges smiles. It's wintry but genuine. "Good luck with that tonight. Come on."

As he leads them single-file along the narrow path between the house and the garage, he checks his watch. Quarter past six. He thinks, How the time flies when you're having fun.

They enter the kitchen. Hodges opens the basement door and reaches for the light switch.

"No," Holly says. "Leave it off."

He looks at her questioningly, but Holly has turned to Jerome.

"You have to do it. Mr. Hodges is too old and I'm a woman."

For a moment Jerome doesn't get it, then he does. "Control equals lights?"

She nods. Her face is tense and drawn. "It should work if your voice is anywhere close to his."

Jerome steps into the doorway, clears his throat self-consciously, and says, "Control."

The basement remains dark.

Hodges says, "You've got a naturally low voice. Not baritone, but low. It's why you sound older than you really are when you're on the phone. See if you can raise it up a little."

Jerome repeats the word, and the lights in the basement come on. Holly Gibney, whose life has not exactly been a sitcom, laughs and claps her hands.

27

It's six-twenty when Tanya Robinson arrives at the MAC, and as she joins the line of incoming vehicles, she wishes she'd listened to the girls' importuning and left for the concert an hour earlier. The lot is already three-quarters full. Guys in orange vests are flagging traffic. One of them waves her to the left. She turns that way, driving with slow care because she's borrowed Ginny Carver's Tahoe for tonight's safari, and the last thing she wants is to get into a fender-bender. In the seats behind her, the girls — Hilda Carver, Betsy DeWitt, Dinah Scott, and her own Barbara — are literally bouncing with excitement. They have loaded the Tahoe's CD changer with their 'Round Here CDs (among them they have all six), and they squeal "Oh, I *love* this one!" every time a new tune comes on. It's noisy and it's stressful and Tanya is surprised to find she's enjoying herself quite a lot.

"Watch out for the crippled guy, Mrs. Robinson," Betsy says, pointing.

The crippled guy is skinny, pale, and bald, all but floating inside his baggy tee-shirt. He's holding what looks like a framed picture in his lap, and she can also see one of those urine bags. A sadly jaunty 'Round Here pennant juts from a pocket on the side of his wheelchair. Poor man, Tanya thinks.

"Maybe we should help him," Barbara says. "He's going awful slow."

"Bless your kind heart," Tanya says. "Let me get us parked, and if he hasn't made it to the building when we walk back, we'll do just that."

She slides the borrowed Tahoe into an empty space and turns it off with a sigh of relief.

"Boy, look at the *lines,*" Dinah says. "There must be a zillion people here."

"Nowhere near that many," Tanya says, "but it *is* a lot. They'll open the doors soon, though. And we've got good seats, so don't worry about that."

"You've still got the tickets, right, Mom?"

Tanya ostentatiously checks her purse. "Got them right here, hon."

"And we can have souvenirs?"

"One each, and nothing that costs over ten dollars."

"I've got my own money, Mrs. Robinson," Betsy says as they climb out of the Tahoe. The girls are a little nervous at the sight of the crowd growing outside the MAC. They cluster together, their four shadows becoming a single dark puddle in the strong early-evening sunlight.

"I'm sure you do, Bets, but this is on me," Tanya says. "Now listen up, girls. I want you to give me your money and phones for safekeeping. Sometimes there are pickpockets at these big public gatherings. I'll give everything back when we're safe in our seats, but no texting or calling once the show starts — are we clear on that?"

"Can we each take a picture first, Mrs. Robinson?" Hilda asks.

"Yes. One each."

"Two!" Barbara begs.

"All right, two. But hurry up."

They each take two pictures, promising to email them later, so everyone has a complete set. Tanya takes a couple of her own, with the four girls grouped together and their arms around each other's shoulders. She thinks they look lovely.

"Okay, ladies, hand over the cash and the cackleboxes."

The girls give up thirty dollars or so among them and their candy-colored phones. Tanya puts everything in her purse and locks Ginny Carver's van with the button on the key-fob. She hears the satisfying thump of the locks engaging — a sound that means safety and security.

"Now listen, you crazy females. We're all going to hold hands until we're in our seats, okay? Let me hear your okay."

"Okaay!" the girls shout, and grab hands. They're tricked out in their best skinny jeans and their best sneakers. All are wearing 'Round Here tees, and Hilda's ponytail has been tied with a white silk ribbon that says I LUV CAM in red letters.

"And we're going to have fun, right? Best time ever, right? Let me hear your okay."

"OKAAAYYYY!"

Satisfied, Tanya leads them toward the MAC. It's a long walk across hot macadam, but none of them seems to mind. Tanya looks for the bald man in the wheelchair and spies him making his way toward the back of the handicapped line. That one is much shorter, but it still makes her sad to see all those broken folks. Then the wheelchairs start to move. They're letting the handicapped people in first, and she thinks that's a good idea. Let all or at least most of them get settled in their own section before the stampede begins.

As Tanya's party reaches the end of the shortest line of abled people (which is still very long), she watches the skinny bald guy propel himself up the handicap ramp and thinks how much easier it would be for him if he had one of those motorized chairs. She wonders about the picture in his lap. Some loved relative who's gone on? That seems the most likely.

Poor man, she thinks again, and sends up a brief prayer to God, thanking Him that her own two kids are all right.

"Mom?" Barbara says.

"Yes, honey?"

"Best time ever, right?"

Tanya Robinson squeezes her daughter's hand. "You bet."

A girl starts singing "Kisses on the Midway" in a clear, sweet voice. *"The sun, baby, the sun shines when you look at me . . . The moon, baby, the moon glows when you're next to me . . ."*

More girls join in. *"Your love, your touch, just a little is never enough . . . I want to love you my way . . ."*

Soon the song is floating up into the warm evening air a thousand voices strong. Tanya is happy to add her voice, and after the CD-a-thon coming from Barbara's room these last two weeks, she knows all the words.

Impulsively, she bends down and kisses the top of her daughter's head.

Best time ever, she thinks.

28

Hodges and his junior Watsons stand in Brady's basement control room, looking at the row of silent computers.

"Chaos first," Jerome says. "Then darkness. Right?"

Hodges thinks, It sounds like something out of the Book of Revelation.

"I think so," Holly says. "At least that's the order she had them in." To Hodges, she says, "She was listening, see? I bet she was listening a lot more than he knew she was listening." She turns back to Jerome. "One thing. Very important. Don't waste time if you get *chaos* to turn them on."

"Right. The suicide program. Only what if I get nervous and my voice goes all high and squeaky like Mickey Mouse?"

She starts to reply, then sees the look in his eye. "Hardy-har-har." But she smiles in spite of herself. "Go on, Jerome. Be Brady Hartsfield."

He only has to say *chaos* once. The computers flash on, and the numbers start descending.

"Darkness!"

The numbers continue to count down.

"Don't *shout,*" Holly says. "Jeez."

16. 15. 14.

"Darkness."

"I think you're too low again," Hodges says, trying not to sound as nervous as he feels.

12. 11.

Jerome wipes his mouth. "D-darkness."

"Mushmouth," Holly observes. Perhaps not helpfully.

8. 7. 6.

"Darkness."

5.

The countdown disappears. Jerome lets out a gusty sigh of relief. What replaces the numbers is a series of color photographs of men in old-timey Western clothes, shooting and being shot. One has been frozen as he and his horse crash through a plate glass window.

"What kind of screensavers are those?" Jerome asks.

Hodges points at Brady's Number Five.

"That's William Holden, so I guess they must be scenes from a movie."

"The Wild Bunch," Holly says. "Directed by Sam Peckinpah. I only watched it once. It gave me nightmares."

Scenes from a movie, Hodges thinks, looking at the grimaces and gunfire. Also scenes from inside Brady Hartsfield's head. "Now what?"

Jerome says, "Holly, you start at the first one. I'll start at the last one. We'll meet in the middle."

"Sounds like a plan," Holly says. "Mr. Hodges, can I smoke in here?"

"Why the hell not?" he says, and goes over to the cellar stairs to sit and watch them work. As he does, he rubs absently at the hollow just below his left collarbone. That annoying pain is back. He must have pulled a muscle running down the street after his car exploded.

29

The air conditioning in the MAC's lobby strikes Brady like a slap, causing his sweaty neck and arms to break out in gooseflesh. The main part of the corridor is empty, because they haven't let in the regular concertgoers yet, but the right side, where there are velvet ropes and a sign reading HANDICAPPED ACCESS, is lined with wheelchairs that are moving slowly toward the checkpoint and the auditorium beyond.

Brady doesn't like how this is playing out.

He had assumed that everyone would smoosh in at the same time, as they had at the Cleveland Indians game he'd gone to when he was eighteen, and the security guys would be overwhelmed, just giving everyone a cursory look and then passing them on. The concert staff letting in the crips and gooniebirds first is something he should have forseen, but didn't.

There are at least a dozen men and women in blue uniforms with brown patches on their shoulders reading MAC SECURITY, and for the time being they have nothing to do but check out the handicapped folks rolling slowly past them. Brady notes with growing coldness that although they're not checking the storage pockets on *all* the wheelchairs, they are indeed checking the pockets on some of them — every third or fourth, and sometimes two in a row. When the crips clear security, ushers dressed in 'Round Here tee-shirts are directing them toward the auditorium's handicapped section.

He always knew he might be stopped at the security checkpoint, but had believed he could still take plenty of 'Round Here's young fans with him if that happened. Another bad assumption. Flying glass might kill a few of those closest to the doors, but their bodies would also serve as a blast-shield.

Shit, he thinks. Still — I only got eight at City Center. I'm bound to do better than that.

He rolls forward, the picture of Frankie in his lap. The edge of the frame rests against the toggle-switch. The minute one of those security goons bends to look into the pockets on the sides of the wheelchair, Brady will press a hand down on the picture, the yellow lamp will turn green, and electricity will flow to the lead azide detonators nestled in the homemade explosive.

There are only a dozen wheelchairs ahead of him. Chilled air blows down on his hot skin. He thinks of City Center, and how the Trelawney bitch's heavy car jounced and rocked as it ran over the people after he hit them and knocked them down. As if it were having an orgasm. He remembers the rubbery air inside the mask, and how he screamed with delight and triumph. Screamed until he was so hoarse he could hardly speak at all and had to tell his mother and Tones Frobisher at DE that he had come down with laryngitis.

Now there's just ten wheelchairs between him and the checkpoint. One of the guards — probably the head honcho, since he's the oldest and the only one wearing a hat — takes a backpack from a young girl who's as bald as Brady himself. He explains something to her, and gives her a claim-check.

They're going to catch me, Brady thinks coldly. They are, so get ready to die.

He *is* ready. Has been for some time now.

Eight wheelchairs between him and the checkpoint. Seven. Six. It's like the countdown on his computers.

Then the singing starts outside, muffled at first.

"The sun, baby, the sun shines when you look at me . . . The moon, baby . . . ."

When they hit the chorus, the sound swells to that of a cathedral choir: girls singing at the top of their lungs.

"I WANT TO LOVE YOU MY WAY . . . WE'LL DRIVE THE BEACHSIDE HIGHWAY . . ."

At that moment, the main doors swing open. Some girls cheer; most continue singing, and louder than ever.

"IT'S GONNA BE A NEW DAY . . . I'LL GIVE YOU KISSES ON THE MIDWAY!"

Chicks wearing 'Round Here tops and their first makeup pour in, their parents (mostly mommies) struggling to keep up and stay connected to their brats. The velvet rope between the main part of the corridor and the handicapped zone is knocked over and trampled underfoot. A beefy twelve- or thirteen-year-old with an ass the size of Iowa is shoved into the wheelchair ahead of Brady's, and the girl inside it, who has a cheerfully pretty face and sticks for legs, is almost knocked over.

"Hey, watch it!" the wheelchair-girl's mother shouts, but the fat bitch in the double-wide jeans is already gone, waving a 'Round Here pennant in one hand and her ticket in the other. Someone thumps into Brady's chair, the picture shifts in his lap, and for one cold second he thinks they're all going to go up in a white flash and a hail of steel bearings. When they don't, he raises the picture enough to peer underneath, and sees the ready-lamp is still glowing yellow.

Close one, Brady thinks, and grins.

It's happy confusion in the hallway, and all but one of the security guards who were checking the handicapped concertgoers move to do what they can with this new influx of crazed singing teens and preteens. The one guard who remains on the handicapped side of the corridor is a young woman, and she's waving the wheelchairs through with barely a glance. As Brady approaches her he spots the guy in charge, Hat Honcho, standing on the far side of the corridor almost directly opposite. At six-three or so, he's easy to see, because he towers over the girls, and his eyes never stop moving. In one hand he holds a piece of paper, which he glances down at every now and again.

"Show me your tickets and go," the security woman says to the pretty wheelchair-girl and her mother. "Righthand door."

Brady sees something interesting. The tall security guy in the hat grabs a guy of twenty or so who looks to be on his own and pulls him out of the scrum.

"Next!" the security woman calls to him. "Don't hold up the line!"

Brady rolls forward, ready to push Frankie's picture against the toggle-switch on Thing Two if she shows even a passing interest in the pockets of his wheelchair. The corridor is now wall to wall with pushing, singing girls, and his score will be a lot higher than thirty. If the corridor has to do, that will be fine.

The security woman points at the picture. "Who's that, hon?"

"My little boy," Brady says with a game smile. "He was killed in an accident last year. The same one that left me . . ." He indicates the chair. "He loved 'Round Here, but he never got to hear their new album. Now he will."

She's harried, but not too harried for sympathy; her eyes soften. "I'm so sorry for your loss."

"Thank you, ma'am," Brady says, thinking: You stupid cunt.

"Go straight ahead, sir, then bear to the right. You'll find the two handicapped aisles halfway down the auditorium. Great views. If you need help getting down the ramp — it's pretty steep — look for one of the ushers wearing the yellow armbands."

"I'll be okay," Brady says, smiling at her. "Great brakes on this baby."

"Good for you. Enjoy the show."

"Thank you, ma'am, I sure will. Frankie will, too."

Brady rolls toward the main entrance. Back at the security checkpoint, Larry Windom — known to his police colleagues as Romper-Stomper — releases the young man who decided on the spur of the moment to use his kid sister's ticket when she came down with mono. He looks nothing like the creep in the photo Bill Hodges sent him.

The auditorium features stadium seating, which delights Brady. The bowl shape will concentrate the explosion. He can imagine the packets of ball bearings taped under his seat fanning out. If he's lucky, he thinks, he'll get the band as well as half the audience.

Pop music plays from the overhead speakers, but the girls who are filling the seats and choking the aisles drown it out with their own young and fervent voices. Spotlights swing back and forth over the crowd. Frisbees fly. A couple of oversized beachballs bounce around. The only thing that surprises Brady is that there's no sign of the Ferris wheel and all that midway shit onstage. Why did they haul it all in, if they weren't going to use it?

An usher with a yellow armband has just finished placing the pretty girl with the stick legs, and comes up to assist Brady, but Brady waves him off. The usher gives him a grin and a pat on the shoulder as he goes by to help someone else. Brady rolls down to the first of the two sections reserved for the handicapped. He parks next to the pretty girl with the stick legs.

She turns to him with a smile. "Isn't this exciting?"

Brady smiles back, thinking, You don't know the half of it, you crippled bitch.

30

Tanya Robinson is looking at the stage and thinking of the first concert she ever went to — it was the Temps — and how Bobby Wilson kissed her right in the middle of "My Girl." Very romantic.

She's roused from these thoughts by her daughter, who's shaking her arm. "Look, Mom, there's the crippled man. Over there with the other wheelchair-people." Barbara points to the left and down a couple of rows. Here the seats have been removed to make room for two ranks of wheelchairs.

"I see him, Barb, but it's not polite to stare."

"I hope he has a good time, don't you?"

Tanya smiles at her daughter. "I sure do, honey."

"Can we have our phones back? We need them for the start of the show."

To take pictures with is what Tanya Robinson assumes . . . because it's been a long time since she's been to a rock show. She opens her purse and doles out the candy-colored phones. For a wonder, the girls just hold them. For the time being, they're too busy goggling around to call or text. Tanya puts a quick kiss on top of Barb's head and then sits back, lost in the past, thinking of Bobby Wilson's kiss. Not quite the first, but the first good one.

She hopes that when the time comes, Barb will be as lucky.

31

"Oh my happy clapping Jesus," Holly says, and hits her forehead with the heel of her hand. She's finished with Brady's Number One — nothing much there — and has moved on to Number Two.

Jerome looks up from Number Five, which seems to have been exclusively dedicated to video games, most of the *Grand Theft Auto* and *Call of Duty* sort. "What?"

"It's just that every now and then I run across someone even more screwed in the head than me," she says. "It cheers me up. That's terrible, I know it is, but I can't help it."

Hodges gets up from the stairs with a grunt and comes over to look. The screen is filled with small photos. They appear to be harmless cheesecake, not much different from the kind he and his friends used to moon over in *Adam* and *Spicy Leg Art* back in the late fifties. Holly enlarges three of them and arranges them in a row. Here is Deborah Hartsfield wearing a filmy robe. And Deborah Hartsfield wearing babydoll pajamas. And Deborah Hartsfield in a frilly pink bra-and-panty set.

"My God, it's his *mother,*" Jerome says. His face is a study in revulsion, amazement, and fascination. "And it looks like she *posed.*"

It looks that way to Hodges, too.

"Yup," Holly says. "Paging Dr. Freud. Why do you keep rubbing your shoulder, Mr. Hodges?"

"Pulled a muscle," he says. But he's starting to wonder about that.

Jerome glances at the desktop screen of Number Three, starts to check out the photos of Brady Hartsfield's mother again, then does a double-take. "Whoa," he says. "Look at this, Bill."

Sitting in the lower lefthand corner of Number Three's desktop is a Blue Umbrella icon.

"Open it," Hodges says.

He does, but the file is empty. There's nothing unsent, and as they now know, all old correspondence on Debbie's Blue Umbrella goes straight to data heaven.

Jerome sits down at Number Three. "This

must be his go-to glowbox, Hols. Almost got to be."

She joins him. "I think the other ones are mostly for show — so he can pretend he's on the bridge of the Starship *Enterprise* or something."

Hodges points to a file marked **2009**. "Let's look at that one."

A mouse-click discloses a subfile titled CITY CENTER. Jerome opens it and they stare at a long list of stories about what happened there in April of 2009.

"The asshole's press clippings," Hodges says.

"Go through everything on this one," Holly tells Jerome. "Start with the hard drive."

Jerome opens it. "Oh man, look at this shit." He points to a file titled EXPLOSIVES.

"Open it!" Holly says, shaking his shoulder. "Open it, open it, open it!"

Jerome does, and reveals another loaded subfile. Drawers within drawers, Hodges thinks. A computer's really nothing but a Victorian rolltop desk, complete with secret compartments.

Holly says, "Hey guys, look at this." She points. "He downloaded the whole *Anarchist Cookbook* from BitTorrent. That's illegal!"

"Duh," Jerome says, and she punches him in the arm.

The pain in Hodges's shoulder is worse. He walks back to the stairs and sits heavily.

Jerome and Holly, huddled over Number Three, don't notice him go. He puts his hands on his thighs (My overweight thighs, he thinks, my *badly* overweight thighs) and begins taking long slow breaths. The only thing that can make this evening worse would be having a heart attack in a house he's illegally entered with a minor and a woman who is at least a mile from right in the head. A house where a bullshit-crazy killer's pinup girl is lying dead upstairs.

Please God, no heart attack. *Please.*

He takes more long breaths. He stifles a belch and the pain begins to ease.

With his head lowered, he finds himself looking between the stairs. Something glints there in the light of the overhead fluorescents. Hodges drops to his knees and crawls underneath to see what it is. It turns out to be a stainless steel ball bearing, bigger than the ones in the Happy Slapper, heavy in his palm. He looks at the distorted reflection of his face in its curved side, and an idea starts to grow. Only it doesn't exactly grow; it *surfaces,* like the bloated body of something drowned.

Farther beneath the stairs is a green garbage bag. Hodges crawls to it with the ball bearing clutched in one hand, feeling the cobwebs that dangle from the undersides of the steps caress his receding hair and growing forehead. Jerome and Holly are chattering excitedly, but he pays no attention.

He grabs the garbage bag with his free hand and begins to back out from beneath the stairs. A drop of sweat runs into his left eye, stinging, and he blinks it away. He sits down on the steps again.

"Open his email," Holly says.

"God, you're bossy," Jerome says.

"Open it, open it, open it!"

Right you are, Hodges thinks, and opens the garbage bag. There are snippets of wire inside, and what appears to be a busted circuit board. They are lying on top of a khaki-colored garment that looks like a shirt. He brushes the bits of wire aside, pulls the garment out, holds it up. Not a shirt but a hiker's vest, the kind with lots of pockets. The lining has been slashed in half a dozen places. He reaches into one of these cuts, feels around, and pulls out two more ball bearings. It's *not* a hiker's vest, at least not anymore. It's been customized.

Now it's a suicide vest.

Or was. Brady unloaded it for some reason. Because his plans changed to the Careers Day thing on Saturday? That has to be it. The explosives are probably in his car, unless he's stolen another one already. He —

"No!" Jerome cries. Then he screams it. *"No! No, no, OH GOD NO!"*

"Please don't let it be," Holly whimpers. "Don't let it be that."

Hodges drops the vest and hurries across

to the bank of computers to see what they're looking at. It's an email from a site called FanTastic, thanking Mr. Brady Hartsfield for his order.

You may download your printable ticket at once. No bags or backpacks will be allowed at this event. Thank you for ordering from FanTastic, where all the best seats to all the biggest shows are only a click away.

Below this: **'ROUND HERE MINGO AUDITORIUM MID-WEST CULTURE AND ARTS COMPLEX JUNE 3, 2010 7 PM.**

Hodges closes his eyes. It's the fucking concert after all. We made an understandable mistake . . . but not a forgivable one. Please God, don't let him get inside. Please God, let Romper-Stomper's guys catch him at the door.

But even that could be a nightmare, because Larry Windom is under the impression that he's looking for a child molester, not a mad bomber. If he spots Brady and tries to collar him with his usual heavy-handed lack of grace —

"It's quarter of seven," Holly says, pointing to the digital readout on Brady's Number Three. "He might still be waiting in line, but he's probably inside already."

Hodges knows she's right. With that many kids going, seating will have started no later than six-thirty.

"Jerome," he says.

The boy doesn't reply. He's staring at the ticket receipt on the computer screen, and when Hodges puts his hand on Jerome's shoulder, it's like touching a stone.

"Jerome."

Slowly, Jerome turns around. His eyes are huge. "We been so stupid," he whispers.

"Call your moms." Hodges's voice remains calm, and it's not even that much of an effort, because he's in deep shock. He keeps seeing the ball bearing. And the slashed vest. "Do it now. Tell her to grab Barbara and the other kids she brought and beat feet out of there."

Jerome pulls his phone from the clip on his belt and speed-dials his mother. Holly stares at him with her arms crossed tightly over her breasts and her chewed lips pulled down in a grimace.

Jerome waits, mutters a curse, then says: "You have to get out of there, Mom. Just take the girls and go. Don't call me back and ask questions, just *go.* Don't run. But get out!"

He ends the call and tells them what they already know. "Voicemail. It rang plenty of times, so she's not talking on it and it's not shut off. I don't get it."

"What about your sister?" Hodges says. "She must have a phone."

Jerome is hitting speed-dial again before he

can finish. He listens for what seems to Hodges like an age, although he knows it can only be ten or fifteen seconds. Then he says, "Barb! Why in hell aren't you picking up? You and Mom and the other girls have to get out of there!" He ends the call. "I don't get this. She *always* carries it, that thing is practically grafted to her, and she should at least feel it vibra—"

Holly says, "Oh shit and piss." But that's not enough for her. "Oh, *fuck*!"

They turn to her.

"How big is the concert place? How many people can fit inside?"

Hodges tries to retrieve what he knows about the Mingo Auditorium. "Seats four thousand. I don't know if they allow standees or not, I can't remember that part of the fire code."

"And for this show, almost all of them are girls," she says. "Girls with cell phones practically grafted to them. Most of them gabbing away while they wait for the show to start. Or texting." Her eyes are huge with dismay. "It's the circuits. They're overloaded. You have to keep trying, Jerome. You have to keep trying until you get through."

He nods numbly, but he's looking at Hodges. "You should call your friend. The one in the security department."

"Yeah, but not from here. In the car." Hodges looks at his watch again. Ten of seven. "We're going to the MAC."

Holly clenches a fist on either side of her face. *"Yes,"* she says, and Hodges finds himself remembering what she said earlier: *They* can't find him. *We* can.

In spite of his desire to confront Hartsfield — to wrap his hands around Hartsfield's neck and see the bastard's eyes bulge as his breath stops — Hodges hopes she's wrong about that. Because if it's up to them, it may already be too late.

32

This time it's Jerome behind the wheel and Hodges in back. Olivia Trelawney's Mercedes gathers itself slowly, but once the twelve-cylinder engine gets cranking, it goes like a rocket . . . and with the lives of his mother and sister on the line, Jerome drives it like one, weaving from lane to lane and ignoring the protesting honks of the cars around him. Hodges estimates they can be at the MAC in twenty minutes. If the kid doesn't pile them up, that is.

"Call the security man!" Holly says from the passenger seat. "Call him, call him, call him!"

As Hodges takes his Nokia out of his jacket pocket, he instructs Jerome to take the City Bypass.

"Don't backseat-drive me," Jerome says.

"Just make the call. And hurry."

But when he tries to access his phone's memory, the fucking Nokia gives a single weak tweet and then dies. When was the last time he charged it? Hodges can't remember. He can't remember the number of the security office, either. He should have written it down in his notebook instead of depending on the phone.

Goddam technology, he thinks . . . but whose fault is it, really?

"Holly. Dial 555-1900 and then give me your phone. Mine's dead." Nineteen hundred is the department. He can get Windom's number from Marlo again.

"Okay, what's the area code here? My phone's on —"

She breaks off as Jerome swerves around a panel truck and drives straight at an SUV in the other lane, flashing his lights and yelling, *"Get out of the way!"* The SUV swerves and Jerome skates the Mercedes past with a coat of paint to spare.

"— on Cincinnati," Holly finishes. She sounds as cool as a Popsicle.

Hodges, thinking he could use some of the drugs she's on, recites the area code. She dials and hands her phone to him over the seat.

"Police Department, how may I direct your call?"

"I need to talk to Marlo Everett in Records, and right away."

"I'm sorry, sir, but I saw Ms. Everett leave half an hour ago."

"Have you got her cell number?"

"Sir, I'm not allowed to give that information ou—"

He has no inclination to engage in a time-consuming argument that will surely prove fruitless, and clicks off just as Jerome swings onto the City Bypass, doing sixty. "What's the holdup, Bill? Why aren't you —"

"Shut up and drive, Jerome," Holly says. "Mr. Hodges is doing the best he can."

The truth is, she really doesn't want me to reach anyone, Hodges thinks. Because it's supposed to be us and only us. A crazy idea comes to him, that Holly is using some weird psychic vibe to make sure it *stays* them and only them. And it might. Based on the way Jerome's driving, they'll be at the MAC before Hodges is able to get hold of *anyone* in authority.

A cold part of his mind is thinking that might be best. Because no matter who Hodges reaches, Larry Windom is the man in charge at the Mingo, and Hodges doesn't trust him. Romper-Stomper was always a bludgeoner, a go-right-at-em kind of guy, and Hodges doubts he has changed.

Still, he has to try.

He hands Holly's phone back to her and says, "I can't figure this fucking thing out. Call Directory Assistance and —"

"Try my sister again first," Jerome says, and raps off the number.

Holly dials Barbara's phone, her thumb moving so fast it's a blur. Listens. "Voicemail."

Jerome curses and drives faster. Hodges can only hope there's an angel riding on his shoulder.

"Barbara!" Holly hollers. No mumbling now. *"You and whoever's with you get your asses out of there right away! ASAP! Pronto!"* She clicks off. "Now what? Directory Assistance, you said?"

"Yeah. Get the MAC Security Department number, dial it, and give the phone back to me. Jerome, take Exit 4A."

"3B's the MAC."

"It is if you're going in front. We're going to the back."

"Bill, if my mom and sis get hurt —"

"They won't. Take 4A." Holly's discussion with Directory Assistance has lasted too long. "Holly, what's the holdup?"

"No direct line into their Security Department." She dials a new number, listens, and hands him the phone. "You have to go through the main number."

He presses Holly's iPhone to his ear hard enough to hurt. It rings. And rings. And rings some more.

As they pass Exits 2A and 2B, Hodges can see the MAC. It's lit up like a jukebox, the parking lot a sea of cars. His call is finally answered, but before he can say a word, a fembot begins to lecture him. She does it slowly and carefully, as if addressing a person who speaks English as a second language, and not well.

"Hello, and thank you for calling the Midwest Culture and Arts Complex, where we make life better and all things are possible."

Hodges listens with Holly's phone mashed against his ear and sweat rolling down his cheeks and neck. It's six past seven. The bastard won't do it until the show starts, he tells himself (he's actually praying), and rock acts always start late.

"Remember," the fembot says sweetly, "we depend on *you* for support, and season's passes to the City Symphony and this fall's Playhouse Series are available now. Not only will you save fifty percent —"

"What's happening?" Jerome shouts as they pass 3A and 3B. The next sign reads EXIT 4A SPICER BOULEVARD 1/2 MILE. Jerome has tossed Holly his own phone and Holly is trying first Tanya, then Barbara again, with no result.

"I'm listening to a fucking recorded ad," Hodges says. He's rubbing the hollow of his shoulder again. That ache is like an infected tooth. "Go left at the bottom of the ramp. You'll want a right turn I think about a block up. Maybe two. By the McDonald's, anyway."

Although the Mercedes is now doing eighty, the sound of the engine has yet to rise above a sleepy purr.

"If we hear an explosion, I'm going to lose my mind," Jerome says matter-of-factly.

"Just drive," Holly says. An unlit Winston jitters between her teeth. "If you don't wreck us, we'll be fine." She's gone back to Tanya's number. "We're going to get him. We're going to get him get him get him."

Jerome snatches a glance at her. "Holly, you're nuts."

"Just drive," she repeats.

"You can also use your MAC card to obtain a ten percent discount at selected fine restaurants and local retail businesses," the fembot informs Hodges.

Then, at long last, she gets down to business.

"There is no one in the main office to take your call now. If you know the number of the extension you wish to reach, you may dial it at any time. If not, please listen carefully, because our menu options have changed. To call the Avery Johns Drama Office, dial one-oh. To call the Belinda Dean Box Office, dial one-one. To reach City Symphony —"

Oh dear Jesus, Hodges thinks, it's the fucking Sears catalogue. And in alphabetical order.

The Mercedes dips and swerves as Jerome takes the 4A exit and shoots down the curved ramp. The light is red at the bottom. "Holly. How is it your way?"

She checks with the phone still at her ear. "You're okay if you hurry. If you want to get us all killed, take your time."

Jerome buries the accelerator. Olivia's Mercedes shoots across four lanes of traffic listing hard to port, the tires squalling. There's a thud as they bounce across the concrete divider. Horns blare a discordant flourish. From the corner of his eye, Hodges sees a panel truck climb the curb to avoid them.

"To reach Craft Service and Set Design, dial —"

Hodges punches the roof of the Mercedes. "What happened to *HUMAN FUCKING BEINGS*?"

Just as the Golden Arches of McDonald's appear ahead on the right, the fembot tells Hodges he can reach the MAC's Security Department by dialing three-two.

He does so. The phone rings four times, then is picked up. What he hears makes him wonder if he is losing his mind.

"Hello, and thank you for calling the Midwest Culture and Arts Complex," the fembot says cordially. "Where we make life better and all things are possible."

33

"Why isn't the show starting, Mrs. Robinson?" Dinah Scott asks. "It's already ten past seven."

Tanya thinks of telling them about the Stevie Wonder concert she went to when she was in high school, the one that was scheduled to start at eight and finally got underway at nine-thirty, but decides it might be counterproductive.

Hilda's frowning at her phone. "I still can't get Gail," she complains. "All the darn circuits are b—"

The lights begin to dim before she can finish. This provokes wild cheering and waves of applause.

"Oh God, Mommy, I'm so excited!" Barbara whispers, and Tanya is touched to see tears welling in her daughter's eyes. A guy in a BAM-100 Good Guys tee-shirt struts out. A spotlight tracks him to center stage.

"Hey, you guys!" he shouts. "Howya doin out there?"

A fresh wave of noise assures him that the sellout crowd is doing just fine. Tanya sees the two ranks of Wheelchair People are also applauding. Except for the bald man. He's just sitting there. Probably doesn't want to drop his picture, Tanya thinks.

"Are you ready for some Boyd, Steve, and Pete?" the DJ host inquires.

More cheers and screams.

"And are you ready for some CAM KNOWLES?"

The girls (most of whom would be struck utterly dumb in their idol's actual presence) shriek deliriously. They're ready, all right. *God,* are they ready. They could just die.

"In a few minutes you're going to see a set that'll knock your eyes out, but for now, ladies and gentlemen — and especially you girls — give it up for . . . *'ROUND . . . HEEER-RRRE!!!"*

The audience surges to its feet, and as the lights on the stage go completely dark, Tanya understands why the girls just had to have their phones. In her day, everyone held up matches or Bic lighters. These kids hold up their cell phones, the combined light of all those little screens casting a pallid moonglow across the bowl of the auditorium.

How do they know to do these things? she wonders. Who tells them? For that matter, who told *us*?

She cannot remember.

The stage lights come up to bright furnace red. At that moment, a call finally slips through the clogged network and Barbara Robinson's cell vibrates in her hand. She ignores it. Answering a phone call is the last thing in the world she wants to do right now (a first in her young life), and she couldn't hear the person on the other end — probably her brother — even if she did. The racket inside the Mingo is deafening . . . and Barb loves it. She waves her vibrating phone back and forth above her head in big slow swoops. Everyone is doing the same, even her mom.

The lead singer of 'Round Here, dressed in the tightest jeans Tanya Robinson has ever seen, strides onstage. Cam Knowles throws back a tidal wave of blond hair and launches into "You Don't Have to Be Lonely Again."

Most of the audience remains on its feet for the time being, holding up their phones. The concert has begun.

34

The Mercedes turns off Spicer Boulevard and onto a feeder road marked with signs reading MAC DELIVERIES and EMPLOYEES ONLY. A quarter of a mile up is a rolling gate. It's closed. Jerome pulls up next to a post with an intercom on it. The sign here reads CALL FOR ENTRY.

Hodges says, "Tell them you're the police."

Jerome rolls down his window and pushes the button. Nothing happens. He pushes it again and this time holds it. Hodges has a nightmarish thought: When Jerome's buzz is finally answered, it will be the fembot, offering several dozen new options.

But this time it's an actual human, albeit not a friendly one. "Back's closed."

"Police," Jerome says. "Open the gate."

"What do you want?"

"I just told you. Open the goddam gate. This is an emergency."

The gate begins to trundle open, but instead of rolling forward, Jerome pushes the button again. "Are you security?"

"Head custodian," the crackly voice returns. "If you want security, you gotta call the Security Department."

"Nobody there," Hodges tells Jerome. "They're in the auditorium, the whole bunch of them. Just *go.*"

Jerome does, even though the gate isn't fully open. He scrapes the side of the Mercedes's refurbished body. "Maybe they caught him," he says. "They had his description, so maybe they already caught him."

"They didn't," Hodges says. "He's in."

"How do you know?"

"Listen."

They can't pick up actual music yet, but with the driver's window still down, they can hear a thudding bass progression.

"The concert's on. If Windom's men had collared a guy with explosives, they would have shut it down right away and they'd be evacuating the building."

"How could he get in?" Jerome asks, and thumps the steering wheel. *"How?"* Hodges can hear the terror in the boy's voice. All because of him. Everything because of him.

"I have no idea. They had his photo."

Ahead is a wide concrete ramp leading down to the loading area. Half a dozen roadies are sitting on amp crates and smoking, their work over for the time being. There's an open door leading to the rear of the auditorium, and through it Hodges can hear music coalescing around the bass progression. There's another sound, as well: thousands of happily screaming girls, all of them sitting on ground zero.

How Hartsfield got in no longer matters unless it helps to find him, and just how in God's name are they supposed to do that in a dark auditorium filled with thousands of people?

As Jerome parks at the bottom of the ramp, Holly says: "De Niro gave himself a Mohawk. That could be it."

"What are you talking about?" Hodges asks as he heaves himself out of the back seat. A man in khaki Carhartts has come into the open door to meet them.

"In *Taxi Driver,* Robert De Niro played a crazy guy named Travis Bickle," Holly explains as the three of them hurry toward the custodian. "When he decided to assassinate the politician, he shaved his head so he could get close without being recognized. Except for the middle, that is, which is called a Mohawk. Brady Hartsfield probably didn't do that, it'd make him look too weird."

Hodges remembers the leftover hair in the bathroom sink. It was not the bright (and probably tinted) color of the dead woman's hair. Holly may be nuts, but he thinks she's right about this; Hartsfield has gone skinhead. Yet Hodges doesn't see how even that could have been enough, because —

The head custodian steps to meet them. "What's it about?"

Hodges takes out his ID and flashes it briefly, his thumb once more strategically placed. "Detective Bill Hodges. What's your name, sir?"

"Jamie Gallison." His eyes flick to Jerome and Holly.

"I'm his partner," Holly says.

"I'm his trainee," Jerome says.

The roadies are watching. Some have hurriedly snuffed smokes that may contain something a bit stronger than tobacco. Through the open door, Hodges can see work-lights illuminating a storage area loaded with props and swatches of canvas scenery.

"Mr. Gallison, we've got a serious problem," Hodges says. "I need you to get Larry Windom down here, right away."

"Don't do that, Bill." Even in his growing distress, he realizes it's the first time Holly has called him by his first name.

He ignores her. "Sir, I need you to call him on your cell."

Gallison shakes his head. "The security

guys don't carry cell phones when they're on duty, because every time we have one of these big shows — big *kid* shows, I mean, it's different with adults — the circuits jam up. The security guys carry —"

Holly is twitching Hodges's arm. "Don't do it. You'll spook him and he'll set it off. I know he will."

"She could be right," Jerome says, and then (perhaps recalling his trainee status) adds, "Sir."

Gallison is looking at them with alarm. "Spook who? Set off what?"

Hodges remains fixed on the custodian. "They carry what? Walkies? Radios?"

"Radios, yuh. They have . . ." He pulls his earlobe. "You know, things that look like hearie-aids. Like the FBI and Secret Service wear. What's going on here? Tell me it's not a bomb." And, not liking what he sees on Hodges's pale and sweating face: "Christ, is it?"

Hodges walks past him into the cavernous storage area. Beyond the attic-like profusion of props, flats, and music stands, there's a carpentry shop and a costume shop. The music is louder than ever, and he's started to have trouble breathing. The pain is creeping down his left arm, and his chest feels too heavy, but his head is clear.

Brady has either gone bald or mowed it short and dyed what's left. He may have

added makeup to darken his skin, or colored contacts, or glasses. But even with all that, he'd still be a single man at a concert filled with young girls. After the heads-up he gave Windom, Hartsfield still would have attracted notice and suspicion. And there's the explosive. Holly and Jerome know about that, but Hodges knows more. There were also steel ball bearings, probably a shitload. Even if he wasn't collared at the door, how could Hartsfield have gotten all that inside? Is the security here really that bad?

Gallison grabs his left arm, and when he shakes it, Hodges feels the pain all the way up to his temples. "I'll go myself. Grab the first security guy I see and have him radio for Windom to come down here and talk to you."

"No," Hodges says. "You will not do that, sir."

Holly Gibney is the only one of them seeing clearly. Mr. Mercedes is in. He's got a bomb, and it's only by the grace of God that he hasn't triggered it already. It's too late for the police and too late for MAC Security. It's also too late for him.

But.

Hodges sits down on an empty crate. "Jerome. Holly. Get with me."

They do. Jerome is white-eyed, barely holding back panic. Holly is pale but outwardly calm.

"Going bald wouldn't have been enough.

He had to make himself look harmless. I might know how he did that, and if I'm right, I know his location."

"Where?" Jerome asks. "Tell us. We'll get him. *We* will."

"It won't be easy. He's going to be on red alert right now, always checking his personal perimeter. And he knows you, Jerome. You've bought ice cream from that damn Mr. Tastey truck. You told me so."

"Bill, he's sold ice cream to thousands of people."

"Sure, but how many *black* people on the West Side?"

Jerome is silent, and now he's the one biting his lips.

"How big a bomb?" Gallison asks. "Maybe I should pull the fire alarm?"

"Only if you want to get a whole shitload of people killed," Hodges says. It's becoming progressively difficult to talk. "The minute he senses danger, he'll blow whatever he's got. Do you want that?"

Gallison doesn't reply, and Hodges turns back to the two unlikely associates God — or some whimsical fate — has ordained should be with him tonight.

"We can't take a chance on you, Jerome, and we *certainly* can't take a chance on me. He was stalking me long before I even knew he was alive."

"I'll come up from behind," Jerome says.

"Blindside him. In the dark, with nothing but the lights from the stage, he'll never see me."

"If he's where I think he is, your chances of doing that would be fifty-fifty at best. That's not good enough."

Hodges turns to the woman with the graying hair and the face of a neurotic teenager. "It's got to be you, Holly. By now he'll have his finger on the trigger, and you're the only one who can get close without being recognized."

She covers her abused mouth with one hand, but that isn't enough and she adds the other. Her eyes are huge and wet. God help us, Hodges thinks. It isn't the first time he has had this thought in relation to Holly Gibney.

"Only if you come with me," she says through her hands. "Maybe then —"

"I can't," Hodges says. "I'm having a heart attack."

"Oh *great,*" Gallison moans.

"Mr. Gallison, is there a handicapped area? There must be, right?"

"Sure. Halfway down the auditorium."

Not only did he get in with his explosives, Hodges thinks, he's perfectly located to inflict maximum casualties.

He says: "Listen, you two. Don't make me say this twice."

35

Thanks to the emcee's introduction, Brady has relaxed a bit. The carnival crap he saw being offloaded during his reconnaissance trip is either offstage or suspended overhead. The band's first four or five songs are just warm-ups. Pretty soon the set will roll in either from the sides or drop down from overhead, because the band's main job, the reason they're here, is to sell their latest helping of audio shit. When the kids — many of them attending their first pop concert — see those bright blinking lights and the Ferris wheel and the beachy backdrop, they're going to go out of their teeny-bop minds. It's then, right *then,* that he'll push the toggle-switch on Thing Two, and ride into the darkness on a golden bubble of all that happiness.

The lead singer, the one with all the hair, is finishing a syrupy ballad on his knees. He holds the last note, head bowed, emoting his faggy ass off. He's a lousy singer and probably already overdue for a fatal drug overdose, but when he raises his head and blares, *"How ya feelin out there?"* the audience goes predictably batshit.

Brady looks around, as he has every few seconds — checking his perimeter, just as Hodges said he would — and his eyes fix on a little black girl sitting a couple of rows up to his right.

Do I know her?

"Who are you looking for?" the pretty girl with the stick legs shouts over the intro to the next song. He can barely hear her. She's grinning at him, and Brady thinks how ridiculous it is for a girl with stick legs to grin at anything. The world has fucked her royally, up the ying-yang and out the wazoo, and how does that deserve even a small smile, let alone such a cheek-stretching moony grin? He thinks, She's probably stoned.

"Friend of mine!" Brady shouts back.

Thinking, As if I had any.

As if.

36

Gallison leads Holly and Jerome away to . . . well, to somewhere. Hodges sits on the crate with his head lowered and his hands planted on his thighs. One of the roadies approaches hesitantly and offers to call an ambulance for him. Hodges thanks him but refuses. He doesn't believe Brady could hear the warble of an approaching ambulance (or anything else) over the din 'Round Here is producing, but he won't take the chance. Taking chances is what brought them to this pass, with everyone in the Mingo Auditorium, including Jerome's mother and sister, at risk. He'd rather die than take another chance, and rather hopes he will before he has to explain this shit-coated clusterfuck.

Only . . . Janey. When he thinks of Janey, laughing and tipping his borrowed fedora at just the right insouciant angle, he knows that if he had it to do over again, he'd likely do it the same way.

Well . . . most of it. Given a do-over, he might have listened a little more closely to Mrs. Melbourne.

She thinks they walk among us, Bowfinger had said, and the two of them had had a manly chuckle over that, but the joke was on them, wasn't it? Because Mrs. Melbourne was right. Brady Hartsfield really *is* an alien, and he was among them all the time, fixing computers and selling ice cream.

Holly and Jerome are gone, Jerome carrying the .38 that belonged to Hodges's father. Hodges has grave doubts about sending the boy into a crowded auditorium with a loaded gun. Under ordinary circumstances he's a beautifully levelheaded kid, but he's not apt to be so levelheaded with his mom and sis in danger. Holly needs to be protected, though. *Remember you're just the backup,* Hodges told the boy before Gallison led them away, but Jerome made no acknowledgement. He's not sure Jerome even heard him.

In any case, Hodges has done all he can do. The only thing left is to sit here, fighting the pain and trying to get his breath and waiting for an explosion he prays will not come.

37

Holly Gibney has been institutionalized twice in her life, once in her teens and once in her twenties. The shrink she saw later on (in her so-called *maturity*) labeled these enforced vacations *breaks with reality,* which were not good but still better than *psychotic breaks,* from which many people never returned. Holly herself had a simpler name for said breaks. They were her *total freakouts,* as opposed to the state of low to moderate freakout in which she lived her day-to-day life.

The total freakout in her twenties had been caused by her boss at a Cincinnati real estate firm called Frank Mitchell Fine Homes and Estates. Her boss was Frank Mitchell, Jr., a sharp dresser with the face of an intelligent trout. He insisted her work was substandard, that her co-workers loathed her, and the only way she could be assured of remaining with the company would be if he continued to cover for her. Which he would do if she slept with him. Holly didn't want to sleep with Frank Mitchell, Jr., and she didn't want to lose her job. If she lost her job, she would lose her apartment, and have to go back home to live with her milquetoast father and overbearing mother. She finally resolved the conflict by coming in early one day and trashing Frank Mitchell, Jr.'s, office. She was found in her own cubicle, curled up in a corner. The tips of her fingers were bloody. She had chewed at them like an animal trying to escape a trap.

The cause of her first total freakout was Mike Sturdevant. He was the one who coined the pestiferous nickname Jibba-Jibba.

In those days, as a high school freshman, Holly had wanted nothing except to scurry from place to place with her books clutched to her newly arrived breasts and her hair screening her acne-spotted face. But even then she had problems that went far beyond acne. Anxiety problems. Depression problems. Insomnia problems.

Worst of all, stimming.

Stimming was short for self-stimulation, which sounded like masturbation but wasn't. It was compulsive movement, often accompanied by fragments of self-directed dialogue. Biting one's fingernails and chewing one's lips were mild forms of stimming. More extravagant stimmers waved their hands, slapped at their chests and cheeks, or did curling movements with their arms, as if lifting invisible weights.

Starting at roughly age eight, Holly began wrapping her arms around her shoulders and shivering all over, muttering to herself and making facial grimaces. This would go on for five or ten seconds, and then she would simply continue with whatever she had been doing — reading, sewing, shooting baskets in the driveway with her father. She was hardly aware that she was doing it unless her mother saw her and told her to stop shaking and making faces, people would think she was having a fit.

Mike Sturdevant was one of those behaviorally stunted males who look back on high school as the great lost golden age of their lives. He was a senior, and — very much like Cam Knowles — a boy of godlike good looks: broad shoulders, narrow hips, long legs, and hair so blond it was a kind of halo. He was on the football team (of course) and dated the head cheerleader (of course). He lived on an entirely different level of the high school hierarchy from Holly Gibney, and under ordinary circumstances, she never would have attracted his notice. But notice her he did, because one day, on her way to the caff, she had one of her stimming episodes.

Mike Sturdevant and several of his football-playing buddies happened to be passing. They stopped to stare at her — this girl who was clutching herself, shivering, and making a face that pulled her mouth down and turned her eyes into slits. A series of small, inarticulate sounds — perhaps words, perhaps not — came squeezing through her clenched teeth.

"What are you gibbering about?" Mike asked her.

Holly relaxed her grip on her shoulders, staring at him in wild surprise. She didn't know what he was saying; she only knew he was staring at her. All his friends were staring at her. And grinning.

She gaped at him. "What?"

"Gibbering!" Mike shouted. "Jibba-jibba-gibbering!"

The others took it up as she ran toward the cafeteria with her head lowered, bumping into people as she went. From then on, Holly Gibney was known to the student body at Walnut Hills High School as Jibba-Jibba, and so she remained until just after the Christmas break. That was when her mother found her curled up naked in the bathtub, saying that she would never go to Walnut Hills again. If her mother tried to make her, she said, she would kill herself.

Voilà! Total freakout!

When she got better (a little), she went to a different school where things were less stressful (a little less). She never had to see Mike Sturdevant again, but she still has dreams in which she's running down an endless high school corridor — sometimes dressed only in her underwear — while people laugh at her, and point at her, and call her Jibba-Jibba.

She's thinking of those dear old high school days as she and Jerome follow the head custodian through the warren of rooms below the Mingo Auditorium. That's what Brady Hartsfield will look like, she decides, like Mike Sturdevant, only bald. Which she hopes

Mike is, wherever he may now reside. Bald . . . fat . . . pre-diabetic . . . afflicted with a nagging wife and ungrateful children . . .

Jibba-Jibba, she thinks.

Pay you back, she thinks.

Gallison leads them through the carpentry shop and costume shop, past a cluster of dressing rooms, then down a corridor wide enough to transport flats and completed sets. The corridor ends at a freight elevator with the doors standing open. Happy pop music booms down the shaft. The current song is about love and dancing. Nothing Holly can relate to.

"You don't want the elevator," Gallison says, "it goes backstage and you can't get to the auditorium from there without walking right through the band. Listen, is that guy really having a heart attack? Are you guys really cops? You don't look like cops." He glances at Jerome. "You're too young." Then to Holly, his expression even more doubtful. "And you're . . ."

"Too freaky?" Holly supplies.

"I wasn't going to say that." Maybe not, but it's what he's thinking. Holly knows; a girl once nicknamed Jibba-Jibba always does.

"I'm calling the cops," Gallison says. "The *real* cops. And if this is some kind of joke —"

"Do what you need to do," Jerome says, thinking Why not? Let him call in the National Guard if he wants to. This is going to be over, one way or the other, in the next few minutes. Jerome knows it, and he can see that Holly does, too. The gun Hodges gave him is in his pocket. It feels heavy and weirdly warm. Other than the air rifle he had when he was nine or ten (a birthday present given to him despite his mother's reservations), he has never carried a gun in his life, and this one feels *alive.*

Holly points to the left of the elevator. "What about that door?" And when Gallison doesn't reply immediately: "Help us. Please. Maybe we're not real cops, maybe you're right about that, but there really is a man in the audience tonight who's very dangerous."

She takes a deep breath and says words she can hardly believe, even though she knows they are true. "Mister, we're all you've got."

Gallison thinks it over, then says, "The stairs'll take you to Auditorium Left. It's a long flight. At the top, there's two doors. The one on the left goes outside. The one on the right opens on the auditorium, way down by the stage. That close, the music's apt to bust your eardrums."

Touching the grip of the pistol in his pocket, Jerome asks, "And exactly where's the handicapped section?"

38

Brady *does* know her. He *does.*

At first he can't get it, it's like a word that's stuck on the tip of your tongue. Then, as the band starts some song about making love on the dancefloor, it comes to him. The house on Teaberry Lane, the one where Hodges's pet boy lives with his family, a nest of niggers with white names. Except for the dog, that is. He's named O'dell, a nigger name for sure, and Brady meant to kill him . . . only he ended up killing his mother instead.

Brady remembers the day the niggerboy came running to the Mr. Tastey truck, his ankles still green from cutting the fat ex-cop's lawn. And his sister shouting, *Get me a chocolate! Pleeeease?*

The sister's name is Barbara, and that's her, big as life and twice as ugly. She's sitting two rows up to the right with her friends and a woman who has to be her mother. Jerome isn't with them, and Brady is savagely glad. Let Jerome live, that's fine.

But without his sister.

Or his mother.

Let him see what *that* feels like.

Still looking at Barbara Robinson, his finger creeps beneath Frankie's picture and finds Thing Two's toggle-switch. He caresses it through the thin fabric of the tee-shirt the way he was allowed — on a few fortunate occasions only — to caress his mother's nipples. Onstage, the lead singer of 'Round Here does a split that must just about crush his balls (always supposing he has any) in those tight jeans he's wearing, then springs to his feet and approaches the edge of the stage. Chicks scream. Chicks reach out as if to touch him, their hands waving, their fingernails — painted in every girlish color of the rainbow — gleaming in the footlights.

"Hey, do you guys like an amusement park?" Cam hollers.

They scream that they do.

"Do you guys like a carnival?"

They scream that they *love* a carnival.

"Have you ever been kissed on the midway?"

The screams are utterly delirious now. The audience is on its feet again, the roving spotlights once more skimming over the crowd. Brady can no longer see the band, but it doesn't matter. He already knows what's coming, because he was there at the load-in.

Lowering his voice to an intimate, amplified murmur, Cam Knowles says, "Well, you're gonna get that kiss tonight."

Carnival music starts up — a Korg synthesizer set to play a calliope tune. The stage is suddenly bathed in a swirl of light: orange, blue, red, green, yellow. There's a gasp of amazement as the midway set starts to descend. Both the carousel and the Ferris wheel are already turning.

"THIS IS THE TITLE TRACK OF OUR NEW ALBUM, AND WE REALLY HOPE YOU ENJOY IT!" Cam bellows, and the other instruments fall in around the synth.

"The desert cries in all directions," Cam Knowles intones. *"Like eternity, you're my infection."* To Brady he sounds like Jim Morrison after a prefrontal lobotomy. Then he yells jubilantly: *"What'll cure me, guys?"*

The audience knows, and roars out the words as the band kicks in full-force.

"BABY, BABY, YOU'VE GOT THE LOVE THAT I NEED . . . YOU AND I, WE GOT IT BAD . . . LIKE NOTHIN' THAT I EVER HAD . . ."

Brady smiles. It is the beatific smile of a troubled man who at long last finds himself at peace. He glances down at the yellow glow of the ready-lamp, wondering if he will live long enough to see it turn green. Then he looks back at the niggergirl, who is on her feet, clapping and shaking her tail.

Look at me, he thinks. Look at me, Barbara. I want to be the last thing you ever see.

39

Barbara takes her eyes from the wonders onstage long enough to see if the bald man in the wheelchair is having as much fun as she is. He has become, for reasons she doesn't understand, *her* man in the wheelchair. Is it because he reminds her of someone? Surely that can't be, can it? The only crippled person she knows is Dustin Stevens at school, and he's just a little second-grader. Still, there's *something* familiar about the crippled bald man.

This whole evening has been like a dream, and what she sees now also seems dreamlike. At first she thinks the man in the wheelchair is waving to her, but that's not it. He's smiling . . . and he's giving her the finger. At first she can't believe it, but that's it, all right.

There's a woman approaching him, climbing the aisle stairs two by two, going so fast she's almost running. And behind her, almost on her heels . . . maybe all this really *is* a dream, because it looks like . . .

"Jerome?" Barbara tugs Tanya's sleeve to draw her attention away from the stage. "Mom, is that . . ."

Then everything happens.

40

Holly's initial thought is that Jerome could have gone first after all, because the bald and bespectacled man in the wheelchair isn't — for the moment, at least — even looking at the stage. He's turned away and staring at someone in the center section, and it appears to her that the vile son of a bitch is actually flipping that someone the bird. But it's too late to change places with Jerome, even though he's the one with the revolver. The man's got his hand beneath the framed picture in his lap and she's terribly afraid that means he's ready to do it. If so, there are only seconds left.

At least he's on the aisle, she thinks.

She has no plan, the extent of Holly's planning usually goes no further than what snack she might prepare to go with her evening movie, but for once her troubled mind is clear, and when she reaches the man they're looking for, the words that come out of her mouth seem exactly right. *Divinely* right. She has to bend down and shout to be heard over the driving, amplified beat of the band and the delirious shrieks of the girls in the audience.

"Mike? Mike Sturdevant, is that you?"

Brady turns from his contemplation of Barbara Robinson, startled, and as he does, Holly swings the knotted sock Bill Hodges has given her — his Happy Slapper — with adrenaline-loaded strength. It flies a short hard arc and connects with Brady's bald head just above the temple. She can't hear the sound it makes over the combined cacophony of the band and the fans, but she sees a section of skull the size of a small teacup cave in. His hands fly up, the one that was hidden knocking Frankie's picture to the floor, where the glass shatters. His eyes are sort of looking at her, except now they're rolled up in their sockets so that only the bottom halves of the irises show.

Next to Brady, the girl with the stick-thin legs is staring at Holly, shocked. So is Barbara Robinson. No one else is paying any attention. They're on their feet, clapping and swaying and singing along.

"I WANT TO LOVE YOU MY WAY . . . WE'LL DRIVE THE BEACHSIDE HIGHWAY . . ."

Brady's mouth is opening and closing like the mouth of a fish that has just been pulled from a river.

"IT'S GONNA BE A NEW DAY . . . I'LL GIVE YOU KISSES ON THE MIDWAY!"

Jerome lays a hand on Holly's shoulder and shouts to be heard. *"Holly! What's he got under his shirt?"*

She hears him — he's so close she can feel his breath puff against her cheek with each word — but it's like one of those radio transmissions that come wavering in late at night, some DJ or gospel-shouter halfway across the country.

"Here's a little present from Jibba-Jibba, Mike," she says, and hits him again in exactly the same place, only even harder, deepening the divot in his skull. The thin skin splits and the blood comes, first in beads and then in a freshet, pouring down his neck to color the top of his blue 'Round Here tee-shirt a muddy purple. This time Brady's head snaps all the way over onto his right shoulder and he begins to shiver and shuffle his feet. She thinks, Like a dog dreaming about chasing rabbits.

Before Holly can hit him again — and she really really wants to — Jerome grabs her and spins her around. "He's out, Holly! He's out! What are you doing?"

"Therapy," she says, and then all the strength runs out of her legs. She sits down in the aisle. Her fingers relax on the knotted end of the Happy Slapper, and it drops beside one sneaker.

Onstage, the band plays on.

41

A hand is tugging at his arm.

"Jerome? *Jerome!*"

He turns from Holly and the slumped form of Brady Hartsfield to see his little sister, her eyes wide with dismay. His mom is right behind her. In his current hyper state, Jerome isn't a bit surprised, but at the same time he knows the danger isn't over.

"What did you *do*?" a girl is shouting. "What did you *do* to him?"

Jerome wheels back the other way and sees the girl sitting one wheelchair in from the aisle reaching for Hartsfield. Jerome shouts, *"Holly! Don't let her do that!"*

Holly lurches to her feet, stumbles, and

almost falls on top of Brady. It surely would have been the last fall of her life, but she manages to keep her feet and grab the wheelchair girl's hands. There's hardly any strength in them, and she feels an instant of pity. She bends down close and shouts to be heard. *"Don't touch him! He's got a bomb, and I think it's hot!"*

The wheelchair girl shrinks away. Perhaps she understands; perhaps she's only afraid of Holly, who's looking even wilder than usual just now.

Brady's shivers and twitches are strengthening. Holly doesn't like that, because she can see something, a dim yellow light, under his shirt. Yellow is the color of trouble.

"Jerome?" Tanya says. "What are you doing here?"

An usher is approaching. "Clear the aisle!" the usher shouts over the music. "You have to clear the aisle, folks!"

Jerome grasps his mother's shoulders. He pulls her to him until their foreheads are touching. "You have to get out of here, Mom. Take the girls and go. Right now. Make the usher go with you. Tell her your daughter is sick. Please don't ask questions."

She looks in his eyes and doesn't ask questions.

"Mom?" Barbara begins. "What . . ." The rest is lost in the crash of the band and the choral accompaniment from the audience.

Tanya takes Barbara by the arm and approaches the usher. At the same time she's motioning for Hilda, Dinah, and Betsy to join her.

Jerome turns back to Holly. She's bent over Brady, who continues to shudder as cerebral storms rage inside his head. His feet tap-dance, as if even in unconsciousness he's really feeling that goodtime 'Round Here beat. His hands fly aimlessly around, and when one of them approaches the dim yellow light under his tee-shirt, Jerome bats it away like a basketball guard rejecting a shot in the paint.

"I want to get out of here," the wheelchair girl moans. "I'm scared."

Jerome can relate to that — he also wants to get out of here, and he's scared to death — but for now she has to stay where she is. Brady has her blocked in, and they don't dare move him. Not yet.

Holly is ahead of Jerome, as she so often is. "You have to stay still for now, honey," she tells the wheelchair girl. "Chill out and enjoy the concert." She's thinking how much simpler this would be if she'd managed to kill him instead of just bashing his sicko brains halfway to Peru. She wonders if Jerome would shoot Hartsfield if she asked him to. Probably not. Too bad. With all this noise, he could probably get away with it.

"Are you *crazy*?" the wheelchair girl asks

wonderingly.

"People keep asking me that," Holly says, and — very gingerly — she begins to pull up Brady's tee-shirt. "Hold his hands," she tells Jerome.

"What if I can't?"

"Then OJ the motherfucker."

The sell-out audience is on its feet, swaying and clapping. The beachballs are flying again. Jerome takes one quick glance behind him and sees his mother leading the girls up the aisle to the exit, the usher accompanying them. That's one for our side, at least, he thinks, then turns back to the business at hand. He grabs Brady's flying hands and pins them together. The wrists are slippery with sweat. It's like holding a couple of struggling fish.

"I don't know what you're doing, but do it fast!" he shouts at Holly.

The yellow light is coming from a plastic gadget that looks like a customized TV remote control. Instead of numbered channel buttons, there's a white toggle-switch, the kind you use to flip on a light in your living room. It's standing straight up. There's a wire leading from the gadget. It goes under the man's butt.

Brady makes a grunting sound and suddenly there's an acidic smell. His bladder has let go. Holly looks at the peebag on his lap, but it doesn't seem to be attached to anything. She grabs it and hands it to the wheelchair girl. "Hold this."

"Eeuw, it's *pee,*" the wheelchair girl says, and then: "It's *not* pee. There's something inside. It looks like clay."

"Put it down." Jerome has to shout to be heard over the music. "Put it on the floor. *Gently.*" Then, to Holly: "Hurry the hell up!"

Holly is studying the yellow ready-lamp. And the little white nub of the toggle-switch. She could push it forward or back and doesn't dare do either one, because she doesn't know which way is *off* and which way is *boom.*

She plucks Thing Two from where it was resting on Brady's stomach. It's like picking up a snake that's bloated with poison, and takes all her courage. "Hold his hands, Jerome, you just hold his hands."

"He's *slippery,*" Jerome grunts.

We already knew that, Holly thinks. One slippery son of a bitch. One slippery *motherfucker.*

She turns the gadget over, willing her hands not to shake and trying not to think of the four thousand people who don't even know their lives now depend on poor messed-up Holly Gibney. She looks at the battery cover. Then, holding her breath, she slides it down and lets it drop to the floor.

Inside are two double-A batteries. Holly hooks a fingernail onto the ridge of one and thinks, God, if You're there, please let this work. For a moment she can't make her finger move. Then one of Brady's hands slips free of Jerome's grip and slaps her upside the head.

Holly jerks and the battery she's been worrying pops out of the compartment. She waits for the world to explode, and when it doesn't, she turns the remote control over. The yellow light has gone out. Holly begins to cry. She grabs the master wire and yanks it free of Thing Two.

"You can let him go n—" she begins, but Jerome already has. He's hugging her so tight she can hardly breathe. Holly doesn't care. She hugs him back.

The audience is cheering wildly.

"They think they're cheering for the song, but they're really cheering for us," she manages to whisper in Jerome's ear. "They just don't know it yet. Now let me go, Jerome. You're hugging me too tight. Let me go before I pass out."

42

Hodges is still sitting on the crate in the storage area, and not alone. There's an elephant sitting on his chest. Something's happening. Either the world is going away from him or he's going away from the world. He thinks it's the latter. It's like he's inside a camera and the camera is going backwards on one of those dolly-track things. The world is as bright as ever, but getting smaller, and there's a growing circle of darkness around it.

He holds on with all the force of his will, waiting for either an explosion or no explosion.

One of the roadies is bending over him and asking if he's all right. "Your lips are turning blue," the roadie informs him. Hodges waves him away. He must listen.

Music and cheers and happy screams. Nothing else. At least not yet.

Hold on, he tells himself. Hold on.

"What?" the roadie asks, bending down again. "What?"

"I have to hold on," Hodges whispers, but now he can hardly breathe at all. The world has shrunk to the size of a fiercely gleaming silver dollar. Then even that is blotted out, not because he's lost consciousness but because someone is walking toward him. It's Janey, striding slow and hipshot. She's wearing his fedora tipped sexily over one eye. Hodges remembers what she said when he asked her how he had been so lucky as to end up in her bed: I have no regrets . . . Can we leave it at that?

Yeah, he thinks. *Yeah.* He closes his eyes, and tumbles off the crate like Humpty off his wall.

The roadie grabs him but can only soften

the fall, not stop it. The other roadies gather.

"Who knows CPR?" asks the one who grabbed Hodges.

A roadie with a long graying ponytail steps forward. He's wearing a faded Judas Coyne tee-shirt, and his eyes are bright red. "I do, but man, I'm so stoned."

"Try it anyway."

The roadie with the ponytail drops to his knees. "I think this guy is on the way out," he says, but goes to work.

Upstairs, 'Round Here starts a new song, to the squeals and cheers of their female admirers. These girls will remember this night for the rest of their lives. The music. The excitement. The beachballs flying above the swaying, dancing crowd. They will read about the explosion that didn't happen in the newspapers, but to the young, tragedies that don't happen are only dreams.

The memories: they're the reality.

43

Hodges awakens in a hospital room, surprised to find himself still alive but not at all surprised to see his old partner sitting at his bedside. His first thought is that Pete — hollow-eyed, needing a shave, the points of his collar turning up so they almost poke his throat — looks worse than Hodges feels. His second thought is for Jerome and Holly.

"Did they stop it?" he rasps. His throat is bone-dry. He tries to sit up. The machines surrounding him begin to beep and scold. He lies back down, but his eyes never leave Pete Huntley's face. *"Did they?"*

"They did," Pete says. "The woman says her name is Holly Gibney, but I think she's really Sheena, Queen of the Jungle. That guy, the perp —"

"The perk," Hodges says. "He thinks of himself as the perk."

"Right now he doesn't think of himself as anything, and the doctors say his thinking days are probably over for good. Gibney belted the living shit out of him. He's in a deep coma. Minimal brain function. When you get on your feet again, you can visit him, if you want. He's three doors down."

"Where am I? County?"

"Kiner. The ICU."

"Where are Jerome and Holly?"

"Downtown. Answering a shitload of questions. Meanwhile, Sheena's mother is running around and threatening her own murder-spree if we don't stop harassing her daughter."

A nurse comes in and tells Pete he'll have to leave. She says something about Mr. Hodges's vital signs and doctor's orders. Hodges holds up his hand to her, although it's an effort.

"Jerome's a minor and Holly's got . . . issues. This is all on me, Pete."

"Oh, we know that," Pete says. "Yes indeed. This gives a whole new meaning to going off the reservation. What in God's name did you think you were doing, Billy?"

"The best I could," he says, and closes his eyes.

He drifts. He thinks of all those young voices, singing along with the band. They got home. They're okay. He holds that thought until sleep takes him under.

The Proclamation

THE OFFICE OF THE MAYOR

THE OFFICE OF THE MAYOR

WHEREAS, Holly Rachel Gibney and Jerome Peter Robinson uncovered a plot to commit an act of Terrorism at the Mingo Auditorium adjacent to the Midwest Culture and Arts Complex; and

WHEREAS, in realizing that to inform MAC Security Personnel might cause said Terrorist to set off an explosive device of great power, said explosive device accompanied by several pounds of metal shrapnel, they raced to the Mingo Auditorium; and

WHEREAS, they did confront said Terrorist themselves, at great personal risk; and

WHEREAS, they did subdue said Terrorist and prevent great loss of life and injury; and

WHEREAS, they have done this City a great and heroic service,

NOW THEREFORE, I, Richard M. Tewky, Mayor, do hereby award Holly Rachel Gibney and Jerome Peter Robinson the Medal of Service, this city's highest honor, and proclaim that all City Services shall be rendered to them without charge for a period of ten (10) years; and

NOW THEREFORE, recognizing that some Acts are beyond repayment, we thank them with all our hearts.

In testimony thereof,
I set my signature and
The City Seal.

Richard M. Tewky

Richard M. Tewky
Mayor

▪ ▪ ▪ ▪

Blue Mercedes

▪ ▪ ▪ ▪

1

On a warm and sunny day in late October of 2010, a Mercedes sedan pulls into the nearly empty lot at McGinnis Park, where Brady Hartsfield not so long ago sold ice cream to Little Leaguers. It snuggles up to a tidy little Prius. The Mercedes, once gray, has now been painted baby blue, and a second round of bodywork has removed a long scrape from the driver's side, inflicted when Jerome drove into the loading area behind the Mingo Auditorium before the gate was fully opened.

Holly's behind the wheel today. She looks ten years younger. Her long hair — formerly graying and untidy — is now a glossy black cap, courtesy of a visit to a Class A beauty salon, recommended to her by Tanya Robinson. She waves to the owner of the Prius, who's sitting at a table in the picnic area not far from the Little League fields.

Jerome gets out of the Mercedes, opens the trunk, and hauls out a picnic basket. "Jesus Christ, Holly," he says. "What have you got in here? Thanksgiving dinner?"

"I wanted to make sure there was plenty for everybody."

"You know he's on a strict diet, right?"

"You're not," she says. "You're a growing boy. Also, there's a bottle of champagne, so don't drop it."

From her pocket, Holly takes a box of Nicorette and pops a piece into her mouth.

"How's that going?" Jerome asks as they walk down the slope.

"I'm getting there," she says. "The hypnosis helps more than the gum."

"What if the guy tells you you're a chicken and gets you to run around his office, clucking?"

"First of all, my therapist is a she. Second of all, she wouldn't do that."

"How would *you* know?" Jerome asks. "You'd be, like, hypnotized."

"You're an idiot, Jerome. Only an idiot would want to take the *bus* down here with all this *food.*"

"Thanks to the proclamation, we ride free. I like free."

Hodges, still wearing the suit he put on that morning (although the tie is now in his pocket), comes to meet them, moving slowly. He can't feel the pacemaker ticking away in his chest — he's been told they're very small now — but he senses it in there, doing its work. Sometimes he imagines it, and in his mind's eye it always looks like a smaller version of Hartsfield's gadget. Only his is supposed to stop an explosion instead of causing one.

"Kids," he says. Holly is no kid, but she's almost two decades younger than he is, and to Hodges that almost makes her one. He reaches for the picnic basket, but Jerome holds it away from him.

"Nuh-uh," he says. "I'll carry it. Your heart."

"My heart's fine," Hodges says, and according to his last checkup this is true, but he still can't quite believe it. He has an idea that anyone who's suffered a coronary feels the same way.

"And you look good," Jerome says.

"Yes," Holly agrees. "Thank God you got some new clothes. You looked like a scarecrow the last time I saw you. How much weight have you lost?"

"Thirty-five pounds," Hodges says, and the thought that follows, I wish Janey could see me now, sends a pang through his electronically regulated heart.

"Enough with the Weight Watchers," Jerome says. "Hols brought champagne. I want to know if we have a reason to drink it. How did it go this morning?"

"The DA isn't going to prosecute anything. All charges dropped. Billy Hodges is good to go."

Holly throws herself into his arms and gives

him a hug. Hodges hugs her back and kisses her cheek. With her short hair and her face fully revealed — for the first time since her childhood, although he doesn't know this — he can see her resemblance to Janey. This hurts and feels fine at the same time.

Jerome feels moved to call on Tyrone Feelgood Delight. "Massa Hodges, you free at last! Free at last! Great God A'mighty, you is free at last!"

"Stop talking like that, Jerome," Holly says. "It's juvenile." She takes the bottle of champagne from the picnic basket, along with a trio of plastic glasses.

"The district attorney escorted me into the chambers of Judge Daniel Silver, a guy who heard my testimony a great many times in my cop days," Hodges says. "He gave me a ten-minute tongue-lashing and told me that my reckless behavior had put four thousand lives at risk."

Jerome is indignant. "That's outrageous! You're the reason those people are still alive."

"No," Hodges says quietly. "You and Holly are the reason for that."

"If Hartsfield hadn't gotten in touch with you in the first place, the cops still wouldn't know him from Adam. And those people would be *dead.*"

This may or may not be true, but in his own mind, Hodges is okay with how things turned out at the Mingo. What he's not okay with — and will never be — is Janey. Silver accused him of playing "a pivotal role" in her death, and he thinks that might be so. But he has no doubt that Hartsfield would have gone on to kill more, if not at the concert or the Careers Day at Embassy Suites, then somewhere else. He'd gotten a taste for it. So there's a rough equation here: Janey's life in exchange for the lives of all those hypothetical others. And if it *had* been the concert in that alternate (but very possible) reality, two of the victims would have been Jerome's mother and sister.

"What did you say back?" Holly asks. "What did you say back to him?"

"Nothing. When you're taken to the woodshed, the best thing you can do is wait out the whipping and shut up."

"That's why you weren't with us to get a medal, isn't it?" she asks. "And why you weren't on the proclamation. Those poops were punishing you."

"I imagine," Hodges says, although if the powers that be thought that was a punishment, they were wrong. The last thing in the world he wanted was to have a medal hung over his neck and to be presented with a key to the city. He was a cop for forty years. *That's* his key to the city.

"A shame," Jerome says. "You'll never get to ride the bus free."

"How are things on Lake Avenue, Holly?

Settling down?"

"Better," Holly says. She's easing the cork out of the champagne bottle with all the delicacy of a surgeon. "I'm sleeping through the night again. Also seeing Dr. Leibowitz twice a week. She's helping a lot."

"And how are things with your mother?" This, he knows, is a touchy subject, but he feels he has to touch, just this once. "She still calling you five times a day, begging you to come back to Cincinnati?"

"She's down to twice a day," Holly says. "First thing in the morning, last thing at night. She's lonely. And I think more afraid for herself than she is for me. It's hard to change your life when you're old."

Tell me about it, Hodges thinks. "That's a very important insight, Holly."

"Dr. Leibowitz says habits are hard to break. It's hard for me to give up smoking, and it's hard for Mom to get used to living alone. Also to realize I don't have to be that fourteen-year-old-girl curled up in the bathtub for the rest of my life."

They're silent for awhile. A crow takes possession of the pitcher's rubber on Little League Field 3 and caws triumphantly.

Holly's partition from her mother was made possible by Janelle Patterson's will. The bulk of her estate — which came to Janey courtesy of another of Brady Hartsfield's victims — went to Uncle Henry Sirois and Aunt Charlotte Gibney, but Janey also left half a million dollars to Holly. It was in a trust fund to be administered by Mr. George Schron, the lawyer Janey had inherited from Olivia. Hodges has no idea when Janey did it. Or why she did it. He doesn't believe in premonitions, but . . .

But.

Charlotte had been dead set against Holly moving, claiming her daughter was not ready to live on her own. Given that Holly was closing in on fifty, that was tantamount to saying she would never be ready. Holly believed she was, and with Hodges's help, she had convinced Schron that she would be fine.

Being a heroine who had been interviewed on all the major networks no doubt helped with Schron. It didn't with her mother; in some ways it was Holly's status as heroine that dismayed that lady the most. Charlotte would never be entirely able to accept the idea that her precariously balanced daughter had played a crucial role (maybe *the* crucial role) in preventing a mass slaughter of the innocents.

By the terms of Janey's will, the condo apartment with its fabulous lake view is now owned jointly by Aunt Charlotte and Uncle Henry. When Holly asked if she could live there, at least to start with, Charlotte had refused instantly and adamantly. Her brother could not convince her to change her mind.

It was Holly herself who had done that, saying she intended to stay in the city, and if her mother would not give in on the apartment, she'd find one in Lowtown.

"In the very worst part of Lowtown," she said. "Where I'll buy everything with cash. Which I will flash around ostentatiously."

That did it.

Holly's time in the city — the first extended period she has ever spent away from her mother — hasn't been easy, but her shrink gives her plenty of support, and Hodges visits her frequently. Far more important, Jerome visits frequently, and Holly is an even more frequent guest at the Robinson home on Teaberry Lane. Hodges believes that's where the real healing is taking place, not on Dr. Leibowitz's couch. Barbara has taken to calling her Aunt Holly.

"What about you, Bill?" Jerome asks. "Any plans?"

"Well," he says, smiling, "I was offered a job with Vigilant Guard Service, how about that?"

Holly clasps her hands together and bounces up and down on the picnic bench like a child. "Are you going to take it?"

"Can't," Hodges says.

"Heart?" Jerome asks.

"Nope. You have to be bonded, and Judge Silver shared with me this morning that my chances of being bonded and the chances of the Jews and Palestinians uniting to build the first interfaith space station are roughly equal. My dreams of getting a private investigator's license are equally kaput. However, a bail bondsman I've known for years has offered me a part-time job as a skip-tracer, and for that I don't need to be bonded. I can do it mostly from home, on my computer."

"I could help you," Holly says. "With the computer part, that is. I don't want to actually chase anybody. Once was enough."

"What about Hartsfield?" Jerome asks. "Anything new, or just the same?"

"Just the same," Hodges says.

"I don't care," Holly says. She sounds defiant, but for the first time since arriving at McGinnis Park, she's biting her lips. "I'd do it again." She clenches her fists. "Again again again!"

Hodges takes one of those fists and soothes it open. Jerome does the same with the other.

"Of course you would," Hodges says. "That's why the mayor gave you a medal."

"Not to mention free bus rides and trips to the museum," Jerome adds.

She relaxes, a little at a time. "Why should I ride the bus, Jerome? I have lots of money in trust, and I have Cousin Olivia's Mercedes. It's a wonderful car. And such low mileage!"

"No ghosts?" Hodges asks. He's not joking about this; he's honestly curious.

For a long time she doesn't reply, just looks up at the big German sedan parked beside Hodges's tidy Japanese import. At least she's stopped biting her lips.

"There were at first," she says, "and I thought I might sell it. I had it painted instead. That was *my* idea, not Dr. Leibowitz's." She looks at them proudly. "I didn't even ask her."

"And now?" Jerome is still holding her hand. He has come to love Holly, difficult as she sometimes is. They have both come to love her.

"Blue is the color of forgetting," she says. "I read that in a poem once." She pauses. "Bill, why are you crying? Are you thinking about Janey?"

Yes. No. Both.

"I'm crying because we're here," he says. "On a beautiful fall day that feels like summer."

"Dr. Leibowitz says crying is good," Holly says matter-of-factly. "She says tears wash the emotions."

"She could be right about that." Hodges is thinking about how Janey wore his hat. How she gave it just the right tilt. "Now are we going to have some of that champagne or not?"

Jerome holds the bottle while Holly pours. They hold up their glasses.

"To us," Hodges says.

They echo it. And drink.

2

On a rain-soaked evening in November of 2011, a nurse hurries down the corridor of the Lakes Region Traumatic Brain Injury Clinic, an adjunct to John M. Kiner Memorial, the city's premier hospital. There are half a dozen charity cases at the TBI, including one who is infamous . . . although his infamy has already begun to fade with the passage of time.

The nurse is afraid the clinic's chief neurologist will have left, but he's still in the doctor's lounge, going through case files.

"You may want to come, Dr. Babineau," she says. "It's Mr. Hartsfield. He's awake." This only makes him look up, but what the nurse says next gets him to his feet. "He spoke to me."

"After seventeen months? Extraordinary. Are you sure?"

The nurse is flushed with excitement. "Yes, Doctor, absolutely."

"What did he say?"

"He says he has a headache. And he's asking for his mother."

September 14, 2013

AUTHOR'S NOTE

While there is indeed such a thing as "stealing the peek" (as in PKE), it would be impossible to do so with any of the cars identified in the book, including the Mercedes-Benz SL500s made during the passive keyless entry age. SL500s, like all Benzes, are high-performance cars with high-performance security features.

Thanks are due to Russ Dorr and Dave Higgins, who provided research assistance. Also to my wife, Tabitha, who knows more about cell phones than I do, and to my son, the novelist Joe Hill, who helped me solve the problems Tabby pointed out. If I got it right, thank my support crew. If I got it wrong, chalk it up to my failure to understand.

Nan Graham of Scribner did her usual sterling editorial job, and my son Owen followed up with a valuable second pass. My agent, Chuck Verrill, is a Yankees fan, but I love him anyway.

ABOUT THE AUTHOR

Stephen King is the author of more than fifty books, all of them worldwide bestsellers. His novel *11/22/63* was named a top ten book of 2011 by *The New York Times Book Review* and won the *Los Angeles Times* Book Prize for Mystery/Thriller as well as the Best Hardcover Book Award from the International Thriller Writers Association. He is the recipient of the 2003 National Book Foundation Medal for Distinguished Contribution to American Letters. He lives in Bangor, Maine, with his wife, novelist Tabitha King.

The employees of Thorndike Press hope you have enjoyed this Large Print book. All our Thorndike, Wheeler, and Kennebec Large Print titles are designed for easy reading, and all our books are made to last. Other Thorndike Press Large Print books are available at your library, through selected bookstores, or directly from us.

For information about titles, please call:
(800) 223-1244

or visit our Web site at:
http://gale.cengage.com/thorndike

To share your comments, please write:
Publisher
Thorndike Press
10 Water St., Suite 310
Waterville, ME 04901